NON SANS DROICT.

William Shakespeare
FOUR GREAT COMEDIES

The Taming of the Shrew
edited by Robert B. Heilman

A Midsummer Night's Dream
edited by Wolfgang Clemen

Twelfth Night
edited by Herschel Baker

The Tempest
edited by Robert Langbaum

WITH AN INTRODUCTION
BY SYLVAN BARNET

Introduction

If we turn to the Elizabethans for remarks about comedy to get an idea of what they thought a comedy was, we find some help—not a great deal, perhaps, but enough to give us our bearings. Thomas Heywood, a playwright contemporary with Shakespeare, tells us that "comedies begin in trouble and end in peace." And so they do. We will see that Shakespeare's comedies begin with people at each other's throats: in *The Taming of the Shrew* Kate flails out at everyone; in *A Midsummer Night's Dream* Lysander challenges Demetrius for Hermia's hand, and Hermia's crabby father demands that she obey him and wed Demetrius; in *Twelfth Night* Olivia rejects the love of Orsino, and Viola is shipwrecked in an alien country; in *The Tempest* a ship is wrecked and some survivors plot a murder. But all of these plays end with peace, symbolized by happy marriages. Of course, these capsule descriptions are a bit too pat, as we will see when we look at the plays in some detail later, but Heywood's formula is roughly true: Shakespeare's comedies move from disunity to unity. By the end of the plays, as Puck says in *A Midsummer Night's Dream,*

> Jack shall have Jill;
> Nought shall go ill;
> The man shall have his mare again, and all shall be well.
> (III.ii.461-63)

Now for a second Elizabethan comment, this one by Sir Philip Sidney. Sidney argues that comedy imitates or reproduces on the stage the foolish behavior we sometimes see in the real world, and it does this in order to cure us of such behavior. Comedy, he says, "is an imitation of the common errors of our life, which [the dramatist] representeth in the most ridiculous and scornful sort that may be, so as it is impossible that any beholder can be content to be such a one." The idea goes back to Greek and Roman comic theory, the gist of which is that "comedy chastens morals with ridicule." Essentially this classical view holds that comedy is satiric, showing mental deformity: the shrewishness of Kate in *The Taming of the Shrew,* and the love-sickness of the Athenian youths and the irascibility of Hermia's father in *A Midsummer Night's Dream,* for instance. The spectators of course cannot identify themselves with such figures, and thus (the theory holds) they purify their behavior of any comparable traits. Hamlet apparently held such a view. At least he sets it forth in his lecture to the players who visit Elsinore. The purpose of drama, Hamlet says, echoing a definition of comedy attributed to Cicero,

> was and is, to hold, as 'twere, the mirror up to nature; to show virtue her own feature, scorn her own image, and the very age and body of the time his form and pressure [i.e. impression, image].

But the fact that Hamlet has to lecture the players on the nature of their job is perhaps a clue that Elizabethan playwrights and actors did not always or even usually practice what classical theory preached. In *The Taming of the Shrew* a messenger informs the drunken Christopher Sly that a play will be performed, and advises Sly to

> frame your mind to mirth and merriment,
> Which bars a thousand harms and lengthens life.

There is only the tiniest hint here of any moral purpose (comedy prevents "a thousand harms"), though there is still something of an emphasis on the usefulness of comedy (it "lengthens life"). Yet Sly, low fellow that he is, is aware only of the sheer joy of comedy, which he vulgarly mispronounces "comontie": "Is not a comontie a Christmas gambold [i.e. a game, a frolic] or a tumbling trick?"

So there we have it: comedy as morally educative,

working by satirizing improper behavior, and comedy as sheer fun, innocent merriment providing release from the pressure of daily morality by offering immersion in a holiday spirit. The noble Hamlet wants moral drama, but the earthy Sly wants high jinks.

Let's say that most Elizabethan comedy can be divided into two sorts: satiric comedy showing a world of people whose unreasonable behavior is ludicrous and in need of reform, and romantic comedy showing a dreamlike or holiday never-never world, whose inhabitants for all of their folly are endearing. In the first of these, satiric comedy, we see a world beneath us, a world of fools who entertain us by their folly but whose folly we (in Sidney's word) "scorn." In the second of these, romantic comedy, we see a golden world, a world of fantasy, a world of heart's desire, a world above us which we would—at least in our daydreaming moods—like to enter. For the Elizabethan playwright familiar with the classical theory of comedy, the trouble seems to have been that the Elizabethan audience preferred fun to morality. (When in *Twelfth Night* the Clown, responding to a request to sing, asks Sir Toby and Sir Andrew "Would you have a love song, or a song of good life?" Sir Toby's ready response is "A love song, a love song," to which Sir Andrew adds, "Ay, ay, I care not for good life.") Ben Jonson, Shakespeare's slightly later contemporary, in *Every Man Out of His Humor* took the opportunity to satirize the popular interest in what he felt was the meaningless nonsense of romance. In the following passage, the first speaker, Mitis (i.e. Meek, Spineless), complains (foolishly, in Jonson's view) that a certain comedy was insufficiently romantic and was too close to an image of real life. The second speaker, Cordatus (i.e. Prudent), then offers what Jonson obviously thinks is the correct view of comedy:

Mitis: The argument of his comedy might have been of some other nature, as of a duke to be in love with a countess, and that countess to be in love with the duke's son, and the son to love the lady's waiting-maid: some such cross-wooing, with a clown to their serving man,

better than to be thus near and familiarly allied to the
time.
Cordatus: You say well, but I would fain hear one of
these autumn-judgments define once, Quid sit comoedia
[what is comedy]? If he cannot, let him content himself
with Cicero's definition (till he have strength to propose
to himself a better) who would have a comedy to be
Imitatio vitae, speculum consuetudinis, imago veritatis
[an imitation of life, a mirror of customs, an image of
truth]; a thing throughout pleasant and ridiculous, and
accommodated to the correction of manners.

Quite simply, Jonson assumes that comedy should teach.
Mitis's desire—a foolish one, from Jonson's point of
view—for a chain of lovers is almost a description of
Twelfth Night, in which Orsino loves Olivia, Olivia loves
Cesario (Cesario is Orsino's page—but really is Viola disguised as a boy), and Cesario-Viola loves Orsino. Here
indeed is the sort of "cross-wooing" Mitis describes, and
Twelfth Night even has the clown that Mitis hopes for.
Curiously, however, *Twelfth Night,* as we shall see, is—
for all of its nonsensical cross-wooing—rather Jonsonian
in some aspects. It is enough to say here that if Shakespeare's comedies do not have the obvious morality of
satiric drama—in *A Midsummer Night's Dream* Duke
Theseus, sounding rather like Hamlet or Jonson, finds the
reports of the lovers' cross-wooing "more strange than
true"—they nevertheless (to quote Theseus' bride) "grow
to something of great constancy."
   About half of Shakespeare's thirty-seven plays are
comedies, that is, they follow Heywood's formula of beginning with dissension and ending with union; specifically, they end with marriage or with the promise of
marriage. But each of the comedies is unique, and though
some of them share enough qualities with others to form
groups that have been called "the mature comedies," "the
problem comedies," and "the romances," even a reading
of only the four plays in this book will demonstrate
Shakespeare's range within the genre.
   The Taming of the Shrew, probably written in 1593 or

1594, is one of Shakespeare's earliest comedies. As poetry it cannot rank with his later plays, but even so, it is among the most stageworthy of all Elizabethan comedies. The play begins with some prose speeches, then turns to unrhymed verse. Any of these verse speeches can serve as an example of Shakespeare's early dramatic poetry, but perhaps the clearest begins at line 34, when the Lord sees the drunken tinker asleep, looking like a corpse.

> O monstrous beast, how like a swine he lies!
> Grim death, how foul and loathsome is thine image!
> Sirs, I will practice on this drunken man.
> What think you, if he were conveyed to bed,
> Wrapped in sweet clothes, rings put upon his fingers,
> A most delicious banquet by his bed,
> And brave attendants near him when he wakes—
> Would not the beggar then forget himself?

There is nothing very imaginative in calling a drunken man a "monstrous beast" or in comparing him to "a swine," or in speaking of death as "grim." The lines are blank verse, unrhymed iambic pentameter, i.e. ten syllables, every second syllable being accented. More exactly, this is the general pattern—mechanically perfect in the first line ("O mónstrous beast, how like a swine he lies") but, mercifully, somewhat varied in later lines. Thus, in the third line, "will practice on this drunken man" is iambic, but the line begins with a stress, "Sirs, I . . ." Other variants from the iambic pattern, such as "Grim death" and "Wrapped in" also give the passage something of the sound of speech rather than of mechanical utterance, but on the whole the speech remains fairly stiff, partly because each line ends with a pause. That is, the young Shakespeare is building up the speech out of single lines rather than out of longer units. Even when, in other speeches, punctuation does not call for a pause at the end of a line we still sense that the line is the unit of thought. Lines 45–51 illustrate the point:

> Then take him up and manage well the jest.

Carry him gently to my fairest chamber
And hang it round with all my wanton pictures;
Balm his foul head in warm distilled waters
And burn sweet wood to make the lodging sweet.
Procure me music ready when he wakes
To make a dulcet and a heavenly sound.

We have only to contrast such lines with Theseus' speech at the start of *A Midsummer Night's Dream,* written a year or so later, to see how far Shakespeare progressed in writing blank verse that (largely because the thought does not end with each line) catches the sound of human speech:

Now, fair Hippolyta, our nuptial hour
Draws on apace. Four happy days bring in
Another moon; but, O, methinks, how slow
This old moon wanes! She lingers my desires,
Like to a stepdame, or a dowager,
Long withering out a young man's revenue.

But if much of the verse of *The Taming of the Shrew,* when compared with Shakespeare's later verse, seems rather stiffly assembled, it is often redeemed by the energetic characters who speak it. Here is Petruchio announcing that he will woo the ferocious Katherine:

Why came I hither but to that intent?
Think you a little din can daunt mine ears?
Have I not in my time heard lions roar?
Have I not heard the sea, puffed up with winds,
Rage like an angry boar chafèd with sweat?
Have I not heard great ordnance in the field
And heaven's artillery thunder in the skies?
Have I not in a pitchèd battle heard
Loud 'larums, neighing steeds, and trumpets' clang?
And do you tell me of a woman's tongue,
That gives not half so great a blow to hear
As will a chestnut in a farmer's fire?

(I.ii.198-209)

The angry sea, the roar of lions, the angry boar, and most of the rest are stock stuff, and again the unit is for the most part the single line; but the speech is richly comic given the fact that it is spoken by one about to woo, and there is a touch of genius in the unexpectedly domestic assertion that Kate's voice is quieter than a chestnut roasting. Moreover, if we turn to the prose of this comedy, we find that Shakespeare has already mastered the art of setting forth a character in a few lines. The play begins with Sly brushing off the Hostess, who threatens to have him put in the stocks for failure to pay for his drinks.

> *Sly.*   I'll pheeze [i.e. get, fix] you, faith.
> *Hostess.* A pair of stocks, you rogue!
> *Sly.*   Y'are a baggage, the Slys are no rogues. Look in the chronicles: we came in with Richard Conqueror. Therefore, paucas pallabris; let the world slide. Sessa!

The vigor of Sly's "I'll pheeze you" and of the Hostess's angry response immediately hold our attention, and we are further captivated by Sly's pretentious claim that his family is mentioned in the old history books ("the chronicles"), a claim made the more ludicrous by his ignorant but thoroughly engaging confusion of Richard with William the Conqueror. Note, too, his garbled Spanish (presumably he wishes to show that he is a man of breeding), his Olympian calm in "let the world slide," and, finally, his unintelligible but decisive "Sessa," something apparently equivalent to "cease."

If we omit the Induction, *The Taming of the Shrew* consists of two plots, both concerned with courting: the plot of Petruchio and Kate, and the plot of Bianca and the three suitors. The Induction is related to both of these plots, for all three are based on pretenses. The pretenses of the Bianca plot—most evident in the disguise of the suitors—need scarcely be discussed, but we should note that Bianca too is pretending, for the "mild behavior and sobriety" that characterize her at the beginning disappear at the end, when she seems to have acquired something of

Kate's shrewishness. The chief pretense of the Kate-Petruchio plot is Petruchio's repeated assertion, in the face of all evidence, that Kate is mild-mannered; and this pretense turns out to work, for Kate is, finally, transformed into what Petruchio claims she already is. Similarly, because the Lord pretends that Sly is a gentleman, Sly—for a while—accepts his transformation from drunken tinker to wellbred lord. Notice that in Induction ii.68 he drops the prose that up to this point has been his medium of speech and he begins (like a lord) to speak verse:

> Am I a lord, and have I such a lady?
> Or do I dream? Or have I dreamed till now?
> I do not sleep: I see, I hear, I speak,
> I smell sweet savors, and I feel soft things.
> Upon my life, I am a lord indeed
> And not a tinker, nor Christopher Sly.
> Well, bring our lady hither to our sight,
> And once again a pot o' th' smallest ale.

Convinced that he is "a lord indeed," he shifts from "I" to "our" (the "royal we"), though of course his taste remains irremediably but delightfully vulgar: he requests not wine but a pot of cheap ale. While this speech is in front of us, it is appropriate to notice that Sly's "do I dream? Or have I dreamed till now?/I do not sleep" is very briefly paralleled with a servant's description of Kate later in the play. Under Petruchio's zany but effective tutelage the shrewish Kate is losing her shrewishness:

> she, poor soul,
> Knows not which way to stand, to look, to speak
> And sits as one new-risen from a dream.
> (IV.i.177-80)

This motif of a transformation that seems dreamlike will, of course, be given far greater emphasis in *A Midsummer Night's Dream*.

I have said that Petruchio's tutelage is zany but effective. Petruchio uses two strategies: first, he continuously praises Kate's mild behavior although she acts shrewishly, and (to simplify) she indeed becomes mild. We might say that by treating her lovingly, he transforms her into someone worthy of love. But, and this is Petruchio's second pedagogic device, by himself behaving violently, he shows her the unloveliness of her own behavior; he holds the mirror up to her, and thus he enables her to shed her crippling personality and to find within herself her true, loving (and lovely) nature. In short, in Sidney's and Hamlet's terms, he reforms her by showing her the absurdity of her behavior. Some readers have found Petruchio's "taming school" cruel, but few if any viewers will agree, for when the play is staged it is impossible to feel sympathy and pity for Kate—or for anyone else. The play is essentially farcical; we laugh with or at the broadly-drawn characters, but we cannot take their feelings much more seriously than those of, say, the Marx Brothers, Laurel and Hardy, or the figures in a comic strip or an animated cartoon. The outrageousness of the actions, the absurd behavior of the personages, and (again) the relatively unsubtle poetry all insure that we will not *feel* the pains that any of the characters are alleged to feel.

Finally, something must be said about Kate's last big speech (V.ii.136-79), in which she—now the submissive wife—lectures other women on their duty to submit to men. Can the speech mean what it says? And can we swallow it? Several answers have been proposed. 1) Kate has been reduced to slavishness. But the speech is too eloquent for this view to be convincing; and by virtue of its eloquence, its length, and its context (Kate dominates the other women), the scene is, from a theatrical point of view, Kate's, and so we cannot regard her as defeated. 2) Shakespeare couldn't have been so gross a male chauvinist; the speech must be ironic, and Kate is merely playing, humoring Petruchio as she humored him earlier, when, for example in IV.v.37-49 she showed that she could play his game as well as he and pretended that Old Vincentio was a young girl. According to this view, Kate has learned What Every Woman Knows: men are babes, and by seeming to submit to them a woman may rule them. But this interpretation is virtually impossible to enact upon the stage, without crude oglings that go ill with the eloquence of the lines. 3) Kate has come to her senses and is uttering sound Elizabethan doctrine (women should be ruled by men)—and in pretty good verse, too. We no longer believe this doctrine, but we can enjoy—or at least tolerate—hearing it uttered eloquently. Moreover, in lecturing the disobedient wives Kate now has some of her old energy, and we enjoy seeing this spirited woman in action. It seems best, then, to set aside our own views of the equality of men and women and to try to see the play as Shakespeare's audience saw it. One trait of mature readers of literature is that they can value the artistic expression of ideas that are not their own. Such readers do not insist that Shakespeare is our contemporary.

A Midsummer Night's Dream, written about 1595, shows a remarkable advance over *The Taming of the Shrew*. Let's look, again, briefly, at the opening line of *A Midsummer Night's Dream,* where we saw that the single line is no longer the unit of thought. Theseus is speaking to his betrothed:

> Now, fair Hippolyta, our nuptial hour
> Draws on apace. Four happy days bring in
> Another moon; but, O, methinks, how slow
> This old moon wanes! She lingers my desires,
> Like to a stepdame, or a dowager,
> Long withering out a young man's revenue.

The audience would immediately see (and a reader will soon learn) that Theseus is middle-aged, but his impatience for his wedding day is admirably conveyed in the simile of the last three lines: the slow waning of the moon is like the dwindling of a young man's estate as his stepmother or widowed mother continues to hold on to life and to his inheritance. Although middle-aged, Theseus, about to wed, feels young and he longs to possess what is coming to him. Note too (although it is risky to talk about Elizabethan pronunciation) that the long vowels in "but, *O*, methinks, how sl*o*w / This *o*ld moon w*a*nes" probably help to convey his sense that although only four days of bachelorhood remain, the period before the marriage-day is interminable. In short, the verse perfectly suits the character. How different, twenty-five lines later, is the verse of the irascible Egeus denouncing the man whom his daughter loves:

> Thou, thou, Lysander, thou hast given her rhymes.

Even if Egeus had not told us that he was "full of vexation," we would have heard vexation in those three spluttering "thou's." Egeus is still at it in the fourth act, when he and Theseus discover his daughter with Lysander rather than with Demetrius, the suitor of Egeus's choice:

> Enough, enough, my lord; you have enough.
> I beg the law, the law, upon his head.
> They would have stol'n away, they would, Demetrius,
> Thereby to have defeated you and me,
> You of your wife and me of my consent,
> Of my consent that she should be your wife.
>   (IV.i.157-62)

These speeches are given here not as passages notable in themselves, but as examples of Shakespeare's ability to write dramatic poetry—poetry that is fully appropriate to the situation and to the speakers. Thus, the four young lovers often fall into rather simple rhyming couplets; if their speeches seem rather jingling and sometimes interchangeable, that is quite all right, for these young lovers (this is part of the joke) are themselves almost interchangeable, although of course each feels that his or her passions are unique:

> Before the time I did Lysander see,
> Seemed Athens as a paradise to me.
> O, then, what graces in my love do dwell,
> That he hath turned a heaven unto a hell!
>   (I.i.204-07)

Substitute the name, and another lover might have said these lines.

By the way, about 14 percent of the lines in *A Midsummer Night's Dream* rhyme (like these), whereas only 6 percent of those in *The Shrew* rhyme. Or, to look at another relevant statistic, 37 percent of *A Midsummer Night's Dream* is in blank verse, compared to 71 percent of *The Shrew*. In both plays 23 percent of the lines are prose. Note, too, that in *A Midsummer Night's Dream* the fairies are often associated with short rhyming lines and with songs. In brief, *A Midsummer Night's Dream* is far more lyrical than *The Shrew*, and at the same time the language is far more varied and flexible—far more adapted to individual speakers, who range from royal classical lovers (Theseus and Hippolyta) to young lovers (Helena, Hermia, Demetrius, and Lysander) to fairy lovers (Oberon and Titania) to rough laborers (Bottom and his rustic crew), not to mention the crabby Egeus and Pyramus and Thisby, the absurd lovers in the play staged by the rustics.

There can be no doubt about the play's artistry (evident not only in the poetry and prose but in the miraculous blending of all of the plots), but what does *A Midsummer Night's Dream* add up to? For Samuel Pepys, writing in the later seventeenth century, this play was "the most insipid, ridiculous play that ever I saw in my life." For Elizabeth Griffin, writing in the later eighteenth century, the play was pointless: "I can see no general moral that can be deducted." We can sympathize with her (she was writing a book called *The Morality of Shakespeare's Dramas Illustrated*); like Bottom we can say that we have seen "a most rare vision," but (again quoting Bottom) it is "past the wit of man to say what dream it was." Perhaps we should be content with Puck, who delights in the absurdity of the lovers' antics:

Shall we their fond pageant see?
Lord, what fools these mortals be.

• • •

And those things do best please me
That befall prepost'rously.
(III.ii.114-21)

Surely we too delight in the confusions of the lovers, but
is there more? Hippolyta and Theseus, at the start of the
fifth act, discuss the story that the four young lovers have
told of their dreamlike adventures in the woods:

Hippolyta. 'Tis strange, my Theseus, that these lovers
    speak of.
Theseus. More strange than true. I never may believe
    These antique fables, nor these fairy toys.
    Lovers and madmen have such seething brains,
    Such shaping fantasies, that apprehend
    More than cool reason ever comprehends.
    The lunatic, the lover and the poet
    Are of imagination all compact.
    One sees more devils than vast hell can hold,
    That is the madman. The lover, all as frantic,
    Sees Helen's beauty in a brow of Egypt.
    The poet's eye, in a fine frenzy rolling,
    Doth glance from heaven to earth, from earth to heaven;
    And as imagination bodies forth
    The forms of things unknown, the poet's pen
    Turns them to shapes, and gives to airy nothing
    A local habitation and a name.
    Such tricks hath strong imagination,
    That, if it would but apprehend some joy,
    It comprehends some bringer of that joy;
    Or in the night, imagining some fear,
    How easy is a bush supposed a bear!
Hippolyta. But all the story of the night told over,
    And all their minds transfigured so together,
    More witnesseth than fancy's images,
    And grows to something of great constancy;
    But, howsoever, strange and admirable.

(V.i.1-27)

A brief discussion of these speeches cannot do justice to their complexity, but a few things must be said. 1) Theseus, who is so dismissive of "antique fables," is himself the creation of ancient mythology and he lives again in this "toy" of a play. 2) His dismissal of poetry as a sort of lunacy is spoken so eloquently—so poetically—that we can*not* dismiss poetry. 3) Although Theseus is sublimely confident of the rightness of his power of reason, he himself is a lover. 4) Theseus governs Athens, but the play has included a fairy world of which he is utterly unaware. 5) Hippolyta is quite right; however fanciful the stories of the four young lovers, they are not random accounts, for they are rooted in a reality that is no less real for being hard to believe. It is not strange, then, that they "grow to something of great constancy." And this gets us back to the construction of the play, with its depiction of mature love, youthful love, the quirky jealous love of the fairies, and even the unintentionally comic love of the tragic play-within-the-play performed by the well-meaning laborers. Take, for instance, this last part of the comedy: the story of Pyramus and Thisby is yet another reminder that love—which so entertainingly drives most of the other characters—is an irrepressible energy that can produce tragic results. Puck, in the epilogue, suggests that the "vision" (that is, the entire play) we have seen is of no more account than a "dream," but in fact the dreams in the play (both Hermia's and Bottom's) are well-founded. Puck's suggestions, then, that we take the play as a mere dream is not so innocent as it seems: phantasy may afford insight into reality.

Both of the plays that we have thus far looked at have dealt with love, and love is the central theme of most of Shakespeare's comedies; but perhaps it is the love of Viola for Orsino in *Twelfth Night* that most stirs the heart, or, to quote from the play, that gives "a very echo to the seat/Where love is throned." Yet the assertion that *Twelfth Night*, or at least part of it, echoes our own highest feelings seems to contradict the widespread—and largely true—view that the spectator at a comedy is notably detached from the action, much more detached, for instance, than the spectator at a tragedy. We observe comic characters at something of a distance (again one thinks of Puck's "Lord, what fools these mortals be"), whereas we intensely feel the passions of the tragic figures. William Butler Yeats went so far as to argue that in comedy "character" (e.g. the young lover, the benevolent duke, the angry father) is continuously present, whereas in the great moments of tragedy "it is always ourselves we see upon the stage." He amplified the point: "Tragedy must always be a drowning and breaking of the dykes that separate man from man, . . . it is upon these dykes comedy keeps house." Yet *Twelfth Night,* and particularly Viola, lets us have it both ways. Take, for example, her speech to Olivia, when, wooing on Orsino's behalf, Viola explains how she would speak if she shared Orsino's love for Olivia. (In fact, Viola is deeply in love with Orsino, but she must keep her love to herself while she loyally serves Orsino as his page.) To Olivia's question, "Why, what would you do?" Viola replies:

> Make me a willow cabin at your gate
> And call upon my soul within the house;
> Write loyal cantons of contemnèd love
> And sing them loud even in the dead of night;
> Hallo your name to the reverberate hills
> And make the babbling gossip of the air
> Cry out "Olivia!" O, you should not rest
> Between the elements of air and earth
> But you should pity me.

> (I.v.269-77)

The speech is extravagant and smacks of the conventions of faintly ridiculous or even faintly crazy love poetry—we can recall Theseus' identification of "the lunatic, the lover and the poet"—but it is nevertheless moving, an expression of a state of mind that we need not be ashamed to acknowledge in ourselves. Or, to look at it in its context, we can say that we are amused by Viola's rather theatrical performance of her role as stand-in for Orsino—and yet we are touched by the knowledge that

Viola is indeed moved by love, and that if here she speaks in a somewhat artificial way, it is because she cannot speak her feelings directly. The lines are thus simultaneously delightful, beautiful, and suffused with pathos.

Still, we should notice that in many scenes in this play we are indeed kept at a distance from the characters; we regard them, or, rather some of them, from a superior point of view, which enables us to laugh—almost scornfully—at their folly. Although Jonson's disapproval of romantic comedy with a chain of lovers suggests that Jonson would not much approve of *Twelfth Night,* the play in some ways is surprisingly Jonsonian—that is, surprisingly satiric. There is gentle satire of Orsino, whose first speeches show that he is more in love with himself as a lover than he is with Olivia ("my desires, like fell and cruel hounds . . . pursue me"), and there is somewhat sharper satire of Olivia, whose mourning for her brother has taken the absurd form of a vow to weep daily for seven years:

> The element itself, till seven years' heat,
> Shall not behold her face at ample view;
> But like a cloistress she will veilèd walk,
> And water once a day her chamber round
> With eye-offending brine; all this to season
> A brother's dead love, which she would keep fresh
> And lasting in her sad remembrance.
>
> (I.i.27-33)

She needs to be shaken into her senses, to be reminded that (even though a brother dies) life must go on. We can pause a moment to remark that at the start of *A Midsummer Night's Dream* we learn that if the beautiful young Hermia does not obey her father and marry Demetrius, Egeus can have her shut up in a cloister. That is, Egeus is the chief obstacle to the fullness or renewal of life that comedy celebrates with its emphasis on marriage; but in *Twelfth Night* the beautiful Olivia, by her excessive loyalty to her dead brother, provides her own obstacle to the fullness of her life. Viola aptly says to her,

Lady, you are the cruelest she alive
If you will lead these graces to the grave,
And leave the world no copy.

(I.v.241-43)

Olivia is soon freed from her obsession with her dead brother; by the end of the interview with Viola (who is disguised as the page Cesario) she has fallen hopelessly in love with "Cesario." Olivia will continue, almost to the end of the play, to be possessed by an obsession that we find comic—and we find it comic partly because we are in on the joke (*we* know that Cesario is a girl) and partly because we are confident that we could never behave so foolishly.

But it is in what can be called the subplot, the scenes concerned with the deception of Malvolio, that Shakespeare comes closest to Jonsonian comedy, which specializes in the unmasking of pretensions. Jonson's spokesman, we recall, said that proper comedy seeks "the correction of manners," i.e. the reformation of improper behavior. Early in *Twelfth Night* Olivia aptly tells Malvolio that he is "sick of self-love," and Malvolio throughout demonstrates the truth of the charge. (Olivia herself suffers, though in a lesser degree, from the same malady, as Viola notes when she says to Olivia, "I see you what you are; you are too proud," but this is only to say that the theme of the "correction of manners" is by no means confined to the plot against Malvolio.) We soon learn that the steward Malvolio cherishes the fantasy of rising above his proper rank by marrying Olivia, thus becoming Count Malvolio, from which position he can tyrannize over the household. But a summary cannot do justice to the fifth scene of the second act, where Malvolio utters his megalomaniacal phatansy to the outrage of his hearers concealed behind a tree onstage and to the delight of his hearers in the theater. This revelation of a rigid character, and the plotting that allows the character to express himself, is about as close to Jonsonian comedy as Shakespeare ever comes. Jonson, we have seen, claimed (like

most writers of satire) that the exposure of folly is correc-
tive; alas, in this play it is not so, for Malvolio seems at
the end more than ever the enemy of sociability. His last
words are, "I'll be revenged on the whole pack of you."
In *The Taming of the Shrew,* the drunken Christopher Sly
disappears, and in *A Midsummer Night's Dream* the angry father obligingly is absent from the fifth act, so nothing mars the happy ending, but in *Twelfth Night*
Shakespeare casts a faint shadow over the final joy,
showing us one character who refuses to forgive and to
join in the communal fun, who unregenerately goes his
own way while all others find fulfillment in giving themselves up to others.

In the last few decades there has been a tendency to
emphasize the melancholy, even the darkness, of this
comedy, by calling attention to Malvolio's isolation, to the
role that chance plays in resolving the complication (Viola's twin brother conveniently appears and takes Olivia
off Viola's hands; Olivia out of the way, Orsino can turn
his affection toward Viola), and to the clown's epilogue.
True, if we compare the play to the two earlier plays that
have been discussed, there is a greater sense of the fragil-
ity of happiness, but if no other comedy of Shakespeare's
is so bitter-sweet as *Twelfth Night,* neither is any other
comedy so full of the holiday foolery that is glanced at in
the title, for Twelfth Night—the twelfth day after Christmas, celebrating the Feast of the Epiphany, when the
Wise Men arrived at the manager—was the culmination of
the Christmas revels, a time of joyful release that allowed
for extravagant or carefree behavior before one settled
down again to the routine of orderly workaday behavior.

The Tempest (1611), Shakespeare's last play, is usually put in a group of comedies (the others are *Pericles,*
Cymbeline, and *The Winter's Tale*) that critics call "the
romances." A dominant motif of these plays is the restoration of losses (in *The Tempest,* Prospero regains his
dukedom and Alonso regains his son), a restoration that
is closely related to a sense of renewal consequent upon
suffering and repentance. Another characteristic may be
observed in the heroines. For the most part the heroines

of earlier comedies are witty and resourceful—Viola is a good example—but the heroines of the romances are notable for their innocence. Miranda, the heroine in *The Tempest,* has never seen a young man—or indeed anyone other than her father and his two slaves, neither of whom is human. Coupled with this emphasis on innocence and the restoration of losses is a strong sense of providence. In *The Tempest,* Prospero's magic enables him, godlike, to charm the seas and to bring his enemies to his remote island. Of course *A Midsummer Night's Dream* also had a magician, Oberon, but Oberon's plans miscarried for a while when Puck inadvertently enchanted the wrong Athenian youth. Moreover, we don't feel that *A Midsummer Night's Dream* is largely about Oberon's plan and power, but we do feel that *The Tempest* is largely about Prospero's—about, as we shall see, what he can do and what he cannot do.

Before he began to write *The Tempest,* Shakespeare had been reading, or had heard of, accounts of *The Sea-Venture,* a ship that sailed from Plymouth for Virginia in 1609, carrying the new governor of the Virginia colony. *The Sea-Venture* was caught in a storm off the Bermudas and was thought to have been destroyed, but it was (miraculously, so it seemed) preserved. Bermuda proved to be rich in fish and fowl ("The Almighty God wrought for us and sent us, miraculously delivered from the calamities of the sea, all blessings upon the shore"), but some of the sailors were mutinous, requiring all of the firmness that the governor could muster. Numerous connections can be made between Shakespeare's play and the pamphlets describing the voyage to Bermuda and thence to Virginia, but one connection, very much of its time, is especially interesting. After recording that the governor tried to deal peaceably with the Indians but came to learn, when the Indians killed one of his men, "how little a fair and noble entreaty works upon a barbarous disposition," the writer wonders, "Can a leopard change his spots? Can a savage remaining savage be civil?" Such a reflection as this, of course, is relevant to Caliban, the "savage" of *The Tempest,* and to Prospero, who first sought to educate Caliban with "kindness" but who came to find kindness less effective than "stripes," i.e., lashes. (The name Caliban probably is an anagram of "canibal," the Spanish name for the allegedly man-eating Caribs of Cuba and Haiti.)

The Tempest, then, though set on an island in the Mediterranean, owes much to English and European thinking about the nature of the inhabitants of the New World, that is, to thinking about the nature of the "natural" man. Was the Indian a sort of unfallen man, a noble savage in an unfallen Eden, or was he even lower than the sinful European, who had been brought to some degree of civility by Christ's teachings and by the stern discipline of governors? The pamphlet's comment about the leopard's spots is followed by the modest assertion that even the ancient British were beasts until disciplined by their Roman conquerors: "Were not we ourselves made and not born civil . . . ? And were not Caesar's Britons as brutish as Virginians? The Roman swords were best teachers of civility."

And so the play can be seen as an early document in the history of English colonialism. Prospero, having enslaved the brutish Caliban and having seized his island, is now dependent on the slave: "We cannot miss [i.e. do without] him. He does make our fire,/Fetch in our wood, and serves in offices/That profit us." Caliban has the qualities that the imperialistic white man customarily attributes to what Kipling almost three hundred years later called "the lesser breeds without the Law": he is lazy, smelly, and drunken (there is low comedy here), he worships devils, and he is lecherous and treacherous. The loyal courtier Gonzalo, unaware of Caliban, finds the air of the island sweet, the grass lush, a place fit for a utopian society in which there would be no crime and no need for hard labor, but Prospero finds that he must govern severely so long as Caliban and most of the shipwrecked people are on the island. All of this is to say, again, that *The Tempest*, is of its own age, for it toys with the idea of Utopia—a word (meaning "no place" in Greek) invented by Sir Thomas More early in the English Renaissance.

Much can be said about *The Tempest* as a work of its age, but space is short and we must turn to the play as a work for all time. If *The Tempest* can be seen as a document in the history of colonialism, or in the history of Renaissance utopian thought, it can—and should—also be seen as a play that has very little to do with colonialization and very little to do with utopian thought, if by utopian thought we mean naive proposals for systems of government that will bring happiness to all citizens. In this, paradoxically, *The Tempest* resembles More's *Utopia,* for despite More's description of the admirable government of his imaginary people, More is not, at bottom, setting forth a proposal for a new kind of government that will convert European savages into moral people. More is chiefly telling us not what government must do but what individuals must do if life is to be decent. Each person must try to make his own Utopia, by trying to behave as the Utopians behave. Moral behavior is not something that needs the new surroundings of a fertile or unfallen America; as Goethe told Europeans early in the nineteenth century, "Your America is *here* or nowhere." What is needed is not an ideal government, but wise or enlightened self-government of the individual. Let's look at one of Prospero's speeches. It is less exotic than many other passages in the play—for instance Caliban's description of the fertile isle or his touching speech about the solace offered in his dreams and the sorrow with which he wakes—but it brings us, if any single speech does, close to the heart of the play. By the start of the fifth act, Prospero has at his mercy his treacherous brother, who had usurped the throne and set Prospero and Prospero's infant daughter adrift in a flimsy boat without a sail. Also under Prospero's magic spell are several other "men of sin." Prospero says:

> Though with their high wrongs I am struck to th' quick,
> Yet with my nobler reason 'gainst my fury
> Do I take part. The rarer action is
> In virtue than in vengeance. They being penitent,
> The sole drift of my purpose doth extend

Not a frown further. Go, release them, Ariel.
My charms I'll break, their senses I'll restore,
And they shall be themselves.

(V.i.25-32)

"The rarer action is/In virtue than in vengeance." "Virtue," here contrasted with "vengeance," obviously includes mercy; earlier in the play Prospero spoke of "The
virtue of compassion." To put it a little differently, Prospero has conquered not only his wicked foes but his own
quite understandable desire for vengeance, substituting
forgiveness for it. This is an important part of the happy
ending of the comedy. His self-conquest, his greatest
achievement, can be contrasted to the explosive passion of
Caliban, who sought to rape Prospero's daughter, and to
the murderous assertiveness of Prospero's brother and his
allies. When, near the end of the play, Prospero says,
"This thing of darkness I acknowledge mine," he is expli-
citly speaking of Caliban, but we can sense that he is also
glancing at an enemy more dangerous than the savage islander; he is glancing at the dark impulse in himself, over
which, however, he has triumphed.

And so, if Shakespeare was "of an age," he is also, in
Ben Jonson's words "for all time." *The Tempest,* despite
Gonzalo's utopian speech in II.i.152-69, like Utopia and
like Plato's Republic, is not a treatise on government but
a dramatic comedy on self-government. The connection
with *The Republic* can be pursued for a moment. *The
Republic* is a myth whose subject is the mind, for Plato's
philosopher-kings are symbols of reason ruling over the
passions of the enlightened man. When, in *The Republic,*
Glaucon (who doesn't quite get the point) doubts that
Socrates' ideal state exists anywhere on earth, the reply is,
"In heaven there is laid up a pattern of it, which he who
desires may behold, and beholding, may set his own house
in order." *The Tempest,* like all good drama, gives us
heightened images of our life, not merely life as it was
lived at some remote historical period but life as we know
it and feel it. To take a simple example, we feel the truth
of even the loutish Trinculo's bitter observation that in

England men will not give a coin "to relieve a lame beggar, [but] will lay out ten to see a dead Indian." But *The Tempest* goes further than giving us a vivid image of life as we know it; like all other great drama, it gives us a memorable image of life to live up to, and thus perhaps it can, at least so far as any work of art can, help us to set our house in order. If Shakespeare was a colonialist, he was one in the sense that any great artist is: he explores the remote territory of the self, brings back his discoveries, and puts them at our service.

Sylvan Barnet
TUFTS UNIVERSITY

The Taming of the Shrew

EDITED BY
ROBERT B. HEILMAN

[*Dramatis Personae*

Induction (and ending of Act I, Scene i)
  Christopher Sly, a tinker
  Hostess of an alehouse
  A Lord
  Huntsmen and Servants of the Lord
  Players in a traveling company
  Bartholomew, a page
Acts I–V
  Baptista Minola, of Padua, father of Kate and Bianca
  Kate, the shrew
  Bianca
  Petruchio, of Verona, suitor of Kate
  Lucentio (Cambio) ⎫
  Gremio, a pantaloon ⎬ suitors of Bianca
  Hortensio (Litio) ⎭
  Vincentio, of Pisa, father of Lucentio
  A Pedant (impersonating Vincentio)
  Tranio (later impersonating ⎫
    Lucentio) ⎬ servants of Lucentio
  Biondello ⎭
  Grumio ⎫
  Curtis ⎪
  Nathaniel, Nicholas ⎬ servants of Petruchio
  Joseph, Philip, Peter ⎭
  A Tailor
  A Haberdasher
  A Widow
  Servants of Baptista and Lucentio

Scene: Warwick (Induction);
Padua; the country near Verona]

The Taming of the Shrew

[INDUCTION]

Scene I. [*Outside rural alehouse.*]

Enter Hostess and Beggar, Christophero Sly.

Sly. I'll pheeze°¹ you, in faith.

Hostess. A pair of stocks,° you rogue!

Sly. Y'are a baggage, the Slys are no rogues. Look in the chronicles: we came in with Richard° Conqueror. Therefore, *paucas pallabris;*° let the world   *5* slide.° Sessa!°

Hostess. You will not pay for the glasses you have burst?

Sly. No, not a denier.° Go, by St. Jeronimy,° go to thy cold bed and warm thee.   *10*

Hostess. I know my remedy: I must go fetch the thirdborough.°   [*Exit.*]

Sly. Third or fourth or fifth borough, I'll answer him by law. I'll not budge an inch, boy;° let him come and kindly.°   *Falls asleep.*   *15*

¹ The degree sign (°) indicates a footnote, which is keyed to the text by line number. Text references are printed in **boldface;** the annotation follows in roman type.
Ind.i.1 **pheeze** do for (cf. *faze*) 2 **stocks** (threatened punishment) 4 **Richard** (he means William) 5 **paucas pallabris** few words (Spanish *pocas palabras*) 6 **slide** go by (proverb; cf. Ind.ii.143) 6 **Sessa** scram (?) shut up (?) 9 **denier** very small coin (cf. "a copper") 9 **Jeronimy** (Sly's oath inaccurately reflects a line in Kyd's *Spanish Tragedy*) 12 **thirdborough** constable 14 **boy** wretch 15 **kindly** by all means

45

Wind° horns. Enter a Lord from hunting,
with his train.

Lord. Huntsman, I charge thee, tender° well my
   hounds.
   Broach° Merriman—the poor cur is embossed°—
   And couple Clowder with the deep-mouthed brach.'
   Saw'st thou not, boy, how Silver made it good
20   At the hedge-corner in the coldest fault?°
   I would not lose the dog for twenty pound.

First Huntsman. Why, Bellman is as good as he, my
   lord;
   He cried upon it at the merest loss°
   And twice today picked out the dullest scent.
25   Trust me, I take him for the better dog.

Lord. Thou art a fool. If Echo were as fleet,
   I would esteem him worth a dozen such.
   But sup them well and look unto them all.
   Tomorrow I intend to hunt again.

30 **First Huntsman.** I will, my lord.

Lord. What's here? One dead or drunk? See, doth
   he breathe?

Second Huntsman. He breathes, my lord. Were he not
   warmed with ale,
   This were a bed but cold to sleep so soundly.

Lord. O monstrous beast, how like a swine he lies!
35   Grim death, how foul and loathsome is thine image!
   Sirs, I will practice on° this drunken man.
   What think you, if he were conveyed to bed,
   Wrapped in sweet clothes, rings put upon his fin-
      gers,
   A most delicious banquet by his bed,

15.s.d. **Wind** blow 16 **tender** look after 17 **Broach** bleed, i.e.,
medicate (some editors emend to *Breathe*) 17 **embossed** foaming
at the mouth 18 **brach** hunting bitch 20 **fault** lost ("cold") scent
23 **cried . . . loss** gave cry despite complete loss (of scent) 36 **practice on** play a trick on

And brave° attendants near him when he wakes—   40
Would not the beggar then forget himself?

First Huntsman. Believe me, lord, I think he cannot
    choose.

Second Huntsman. It would seem strange unto him
    when he waked.

Lord. Even as a flatt'ring dream or worthless fancy.
    Then take him up and manage well the jest.   45
    Carry him gently to my fairest chamber
    And hang it round with all my wanton° pictures;
    Balm° his foul head in warm distillèd waters
    And burn sweet wood to make the lodging sweet.
    Procure me music ready when he wakes   50
    To make a dulcet° and a heavenly sound;
    And if he chance to speak, be ready straight°
    And with a low submissive reverence
    Say, "What is it your honor will command?"
    Let one attend him with a silver basin   55
    Full of rose water and bestrewed with flowers;
    Another bear the ewer, the third a diaper,°
    And say, "Will't please your lordship cool your
        hands?"
    Some one be ready with a costly suit
    And ask him what apparel he will wear,   60
    Another tell him of his hounds and horse
    And that his lady mourns at his disease.
    Persuade him that he hath been lunatic,
    And when he says he is,° say that he dreams,
    For he is nothing but a mighty lord.   65
    This do, and do it kindly,° gentle sirs.
    It will be pastime passing excellent
    If it be husbanded with modesty.°

First Huntsman. My lord, I warrant you we will play
    our part

40 **brave** well dressed   47 **wanton** gay   48 **Balm** bathe   51 **dulcet**
sweet   52 **straight** without delay   57 **diaper** towel   64 **is** i.e., is
"lunatic" now   66 **kindly** naturally   68 **husbanded with modesty**
carried out with moderation

70   As° he shall think by our true diligence
            He is no less than what we say he is.

      Lord. Take him up gently and to bed with him,
            And each one to his office° when he wakes.
                          [*Sly is carried out.*] *Sound trumpets.*
            Sirrah,° go see what trumpet 'tis that sounds.
                                          [*Exit Servingman.*]
75   Belike° some noble gentleman that means,
            Traveling some journey, to repose him here.

                          Enter Servingman.

            How now? Who is it?

      Servingman.   An't° please your honor, players
            That offer service to your lordship.

                          Enter Players.

      Lord. Bid them come near.
                          Now, fellows, you are welcome.

80   *Players.* We thank your honor.

      Lord. Do you intend to stay with me tonight?

      A Player. So please your lordship to accept our duty.°

      Lord. With all my heart. This fellow I remember
            Since once he played a farmer's eldest son;
85   'Twas where you wooed the gentlewoman so well.
            I have forgot your name, but sure that part
            Was aptly fitted° and naturally performed.

      Second Player. I think 'twas Soto° that your honor
            means.

      Lord. 'Tis very true; thou didst it excellent.
90   Well, you are come to me in happy° time,
            The rather for° I have some sport in hand

_____

70 **As** so that   73 **office** assignment   74 **Sirrah** (term of address
used to inferiors)   75 **Belike** likely   77 **An't** if it   82 **duty** respect-
ful greeting   87 **aptly fitted** well suited (to you)   88 **Soto** (in John
Fletcher's *Women Pleased,* 1620; reference possibly inserted here
later)   90 **in happy** at the right   91 **The rather for** especially because

Wherein your cunning° can assist me much.
There is a lord will hear you play tonight.
But I am doubtful of your modesties,°
Lest over-eyeing° of his odd behavior—   95
For yet his honor never heard a play—
You break into some merry passion°
And so offend him, for I tell you, sirs,
If you should smile he grows impatient.

A Player. Fear not, my lord, we can contain ourselves   100
Were he the veriest antic° in the world.

Lord. Go, sirrah, take them to the buttery°
And give them friendly welcome every one.
Let them want° nothing that my house affords.
                    Exit one with the Players.
Sirrah, go you to Barthol'mew my page   105
And see him dressed in all suits° like a lady.
That done, conduct him to the drunkard's chamber
And call him "madam"; do him obeisance.
Tell him from me—as he will° win my love—
He bear himself with honorable action   110
Such as he hath observed in noble ladies
Unto their lords, by them accomplishèd.°
Such duty to the drunkard let him do
With soft low tongue and lowly courtesy,
And say, "What is't your honor will command   115
Wherein your lady and your humble wife
May show her duty and make known her love?"
And then, with kind embracements, tempting kisses,
And with declining head into his bosom,
Bid him shed tears, as being overjoyed   120
To see her noble lord restored to health
Who for this seven years hath esteemèd him
No better than a poor and loathsome beggar.
And if the boy have not a woman's gift

---

92 **cunning** talent   94 **modesties** self-restraint   95 **over-eyeing** seeing   97 **merry passion** fit of merriment   101 **antic** odd person
102 **buttery** liquor pantry, bar   104 **want** lack   106 **suits** respects
(with pun)   109 **as he will** if he wishes to   112 **by them accomp-**
lishèd i.e., as carried out by the ladies

125 To rain a shower of commanded tears,
An onion will do well for such a shift,°
Which in a napkin° being close conveyed°
Shall in despite° enforce a watery eye.
See this dispatched with all the haste thou canst;
130 Anon° I'll give thee more instructions.

Exit a Servingman.

I know the boy will well usurp° the grace,
Voice, gait, and action of a gentlewoman.
I long to hear him call the drunkard husband,
And how my men will stay themselves from laughter
135 When they do homage to this simple peasant.
I'll in to counsel them; haply° my presence
May well abate the over-merry spleen°
Which otherwise would grow into extremes.

[Exeunt.]

[Scene II. *Bedroom in the Lord's house.*]

*Enter aloft° the Drunkard [Sly] with Attendants—
some with apparel, basin and ewer, and
other appurtenances—and Lord.*

Sly. For God's sake, a pot of small° ale!

First Servingman. Will't please your lordship drink a
cup of sack?°

Second Servingman. Will't please your honor taste of
these conserves?°

Third Servingman. What raiment will your honor
wear today?

126 **shift** purpose   127 **napkin** handkerchief   127 **close conveyed**
secretly carried   128 **Shall in despite** can't fail to   130 **Anon**
then   131 **usurp** take on   136 **haply** perhaps   137 **spleen** spirit
Ind.ii.s.d. **aloft** (on balcony above stage at back)   1 **small** thin,
diluted (inexpensive)   2 **sack** imported sherry (costly)   3 **conserves**
i.e., of fruit

Sly. I am Christophero Sly; call not me "honor" nor   5
"lordship." I ne'er drank sack in my life, and if you
give me any conserves, give me conserves of beef.°
Ne'er ask me what raiment I'll wear, for I have no
more doublets° than backs, no more stockings than
legs nor no more shoes than feet—nay, sometime   10
more feet than shoes or such shoes as my toes look
through the overleather.

Lord. Heaven cease this idle humor° in your honor!
O that a mighty man of such descent,
Of such possessions and so high esteem,   15
Should be infusèd with so foul a spirit!

Sly. What, would you make me mad? Am not I Christopher Sly, old Sly's son of Burton-heath,° by birth
a peddler, by education a cardmaker,° by transmu-
tation a bearherd,° and now by present profession   20
a tinker? Ask Marian Hacket, the fat ale-wife of
Wincot,° if she know me not. If she say I am not
fourteen pence on the score° for sheer ale,° score
me up for the lying'st knave in Christendom. What,
I am not bestraught!° Here's—   25

Third Servingman. O, this it is that makes your lady
mourn.

Second Servingman. O, this is it that makes your servants droop.

Lord. Hence comes it that your kindred shuns your
house
As beaten hence by your strange lunacy.
O noble lord, bethink thee of thy birth,
Call home thy ancient thoughts° from banishment   30

---

7 **conserves of beef** salt beef   9 **doublets** close-fitting jackets
13 **idle humor** unreasonable fantasy   18 **Burton-heath** (probably
Barton-on-the-Heath, south of Stratford)   19 **cardmaker** maker of
cards, or combs, for arranging wool fibers before spinning   20 **bearherd** leader of a tame bear   22 **Wincot** village near Stratford (some
Hackets lived there)   23 **score** charge account   23 **sheer ale** ale
alone (?) undiluted ale (?)   25 **bestraught** distraught, crazy   31
ancient thoughts original sanity

And banish hence these abject lowly dreams.
Look how thy servants do attend on thee,
Each in his office ready at thy beck.
35   Wilt thou have music? Hark, Apollo° plays, *Music.*
And twenty cagèd nightingales do sing.
Or wilt thou sleep? We'll have thee to a couch
Softer and sweeter than the lustful bed
On purpose trimmed up for Semiramis.°
40   Say thou wilt walk, we will bestrow° the ground.
Or wilt thou ride? Thy horses shall be trapped,°
Their harness studded all with gold and pearl.
Dost thou love hawking? Thou hast hawks will soar
Above the morning lark. Or wilt thou hunt?
45   Thy hounds shall make the welkin° answer them
And fetch shrill echoes from the hollow earth.

First Servingman. Say thou wilt course,° thy grey-
    hounds are as swift
    As breathèd° stags, ay, fleeter than the roe.°

Second Servingman. Dost thou love pictures? We will
    fetch thee straight
50   Adonis° painted by a running brook
    And Cytherea all in sedges° hid,
    Which seem to move and wanton° with her breath
    Even as the waving sedges play with wind.

Lord. We'll show thee Io° as she was a maid
55   And how she was beguilèd and surprised,
    As lively° painted as the deed was done.

Third Servingman. Or Daphne° roaming through a
    thorny wood,

---

35 **Apollo** here, god of music   39 **Semiramis** mythical Assyrian
queen, noted for beauty and sexuality (cf. *Titus Andronicus*, II.i.22,
II.iii.118)   40 **bestrow** cover   41 **trapped** decorated   45 **welkin** sky
47 **course** hunt hares   48 **breathèd** having good wind   48 **roe** small
deer   50 **Adonis** young hunter loved by Venus (Cytherea) and killed
by wild boar   51 **sedges** grasslike plant growing in marshy places
52 **wanton** sway sinuously   54 **Io** mortal loved by Zeus and changed
into a heifer   56 **lively** lifelike   57 **Daphne** nymph loved by Apollo
and changed into laurel to evade him

Scratching her legs that one shall swear she bleeds,
And at that sight shall sad Apollo weep,
So workmanly the blood and tears are drawn.   60

Lord. Thou art a lord and nothing but a lord.
  Thou hast a lady far more beautiful
  Than any woman in this waning° age.

First Servingman. And till the tears that she hath shed
    for thee
  Like envious floods o'errun her lovely face,   65
  She was the fairest creature in the world,
  And yet° she is inferior to none.

Sly. Am I a lord, and have I such a lady?
  Or do I dream? Or have I dreamed till now?
  I do not sleep: I see, I hear, I speak,   70
  I smell sweet savors and I feel soft things.
  Upon my life, I am a lord indeed
  And not a tinker nor Christopher Sly.
  Well, bring our lady hither to our sight,
  And once again a pot o' th' smallest° ale.   75

Second Servingman. Will't please your mightiness to
    wash your hands?
  O, how we joy to see your wit° restored!
  O, that once more you knew but what you are!
  These fifteen years you have been in a dream,
  Or when you waked so waked as if you slept.   80

Sly. These fifteen years! By my fay,° a goodly nap.
  But did I never speak of° all that time?

First Servingman. O yes, my lord, but very idle words,
  For though you lay here in this goodly chamber,
  Yet would you say ye were beaten out of door   85
  And rail upon the hostess of the house°
  And say you would present her at the leet°

63 **waning** decadent   67 **yet** now, still   75 **smallest** weakest   77 **wit** mind   81 **fay** faith   82 **of** in   86 **house** inn   87 **present her at the leet** accuse her at the court under lord of a manor

Because she brought stone jugs and no sealed°
   quarts.
Sometimes you would call out for Cicely Hacket.

90   *Sly.* Ay, the woman's maid of the house.

Third Servingman. Why, sir, you know no house nor
   no such maid
Nor no such men as you have reckoned up,
As Stephen Sly° and old John Naps of Greece,°
And Peter Turph and Henry Pimpernell,
95   And twenty more such names and men as these
Which never were nor no man ever saw.

Sly. Now, Lord be thankèd for my good amends!°

All. Amen.

   Enter [the Page, as a] Lady, with Attendants.

Sly. I thank thee; thou shalt not lose by it.

100   *Page.* How fares my noble lord?

Sly. Marry,° I fare well, for here is cheer enough.
   Where is my wife?

Page. Here, noble lord. What is thy will with her?

Sly. Are you my wife and will not call me husband?
   My men should call me "lord"; I am your good-
105   man.°

Page. My husband and my lord, my lord and husband,
   I am your wife in all obedience.

Sly. I know it well. What must I call her?

Lord. Madam.

110   *Sly.* Al'ce madam or Joan madam?

Lord. Madam and nothing else. So lords call ladies.

---

88 **sealed** marked by a seal guaranteeing quantity   93 **Stephen Sly**
Stratford man (Naps, etc., may also be names of real persons)   93
Greece the Green (?) Greet, hamlet not far from Stratford (?)   97
amends recovery   101 **Marry** in truth (originally, [by St.] Mary)
105 **goodman** husband

Sly. Madam wife, they say that I have dreamed
   And slept above some fifteen year or more.

Page. Ay, and the time seems thirty unto me,
   Being all this time abandoned° from your bed.   *115*

Sly. 'Tis much. Servants, leave me and her alone.
   Madam, undress you and come now to bed.

Page. Thrice noble lord, let me entreat of you
   To pardon me yet for a night or two
   Or, if not so, until the sun be set.   *120*
   For your physicians have expressly charged,
   In peril to incur° your former malady,
   That I should yet absent me from your bed.
   I hope this reason stands for my excuse.

Sly. Ay, it stands so° that I may hardly tarry so long, *125*
   but I would be loath to fall into my dreams again.
   I will therefore tarry in despite of the flesh and the
   blood.

Enter a Messenger.

Messenger. Your Honor's players, hearing your
   amendment,
   Are come to play a pleasant comedy.   *130*
   For so your doctors hold it very meet,
   Seeing too much sadness hath congealed your blood,
   And melancholy is the nurse of frenzy.°
   Therefore they thought it good you hear a play
   And frame your mind to mirth and merriment,   *135*
   Which bars a thousand harms and lengthens life.

Sly. Marry, I will let them play it. Is not a comontie°
   a Christmas gambold° or a tumbling trick?

Page. No, my good lord, it is more pleasing stuff.

---

115 **abandoned** excluded   122 **In peril to incur** because of the
danger of a return of   125 **stands so** will do (with phallic pun, playing on "reason," which was pronounced much like "raising")
133 **frenzy** mental illness   137 **comontie** comedy (as pronounced by
Sly   138 **gambold** gambol (game, dance, frolic)

140 *Sly.* What, household stuff?°

Page. It is a kind of history.

Sly. Well, we'll see't. Come, madam wife, sit by my side
And let the world slip.° We shall ne'er be younger.

[ACT I

Scene I. *Padua. A street.*]

Flourish.° Enter Lucentio and his man° Tranio.

Lucentio. Tranio, since for the great desire I had
To see fair Padua,° nursery of arts,
I am arrived for fruitful Lombardy,
The pleasant garden of great Italy,
And by my father's love and leave am armed   5
With his good will and thy good company,
My trusty servant well approved° in all,
Here let us breathe and haply institute
A course of learning and ingenious° studies.
Pisa, renownèd for grave citizens,   10
Gave me my being and my father first,°
A merchant of great traffic° through the world,
Vincentio, come of the Bentivolii.
Vincentio's son, brought up in Florence,
It shall become to serve° all hopes conceived,   15
To deck his fortune with his virtuous deeds;
And therefore, Tranio, for the time I study,
Virtue and that part of philosophy
Will I apply° that treats of happiness
By virtue specially to be achieved.   20
Tell me thy mind, for I have Pisa left
And am to Padua come, as he that leaves

I.i.s.d. **Flourish** fanfare of trumpets **s.d. man** servant 2 **Padua**
(noted for its university) 7 **approved** proved, found reliable 9
ingenious mind-training 11 **first** i.e., before that 12 **traffic** business 15 **serve** work for 19 **apply** apply myself to

57

A shallow plash° to plunge him in the deep
And with satiety seeks to quench his thirst.

25 *Tranio.* Mi perdonato,° gentle master mine,
I am in all affected° as yourself,
Glad that you thus continue your resolve
To suck the sweets of sweet philosophy.
Only, good master, while we do admire
30 This virtue and this moral discipline,
Let's be no stoics nor no stocks,° I pray,
Or so devote° to Aristotle's checks°
As° Ovid° be an outcast quite abjured.
Balk logic° with acquaintance that you have
35 And practice rhetoric in your common talk.
Music and poesy use to quicken° you.
The mathematics and the metaphysics,
Fall to them as you find your stomach° serves you.
No profit grows where is no pleasure ta'en.
40 In brief, sir, study what you most affect.°

Lucentio. Gramercies,° Tranio, well dost thou advise.
If, Biondello, thou wert come ashore,
We could at once put us in readiness
And take a lodging fit to entertain
45 Such friends as time in Padua shall beget.
But stay awhile, what company is this?

Tranio. Master, some show to welcome us to town.

*Enter Baptista with his two daughters, Kate and
Bianca; Gremio, a pantaloon;° [and] Hortensio,
suitor to Bianca. Lucentio [and]
Tranio stand by.°*

Baptista. Gentlemen, importune me no farther,
For how I firmly am resolved you know,

23 **plash** pool   25 **Mi perdonato** pardon me   26 **affected** inclined
31 **stocks** sticks (with pun on Stoics)   32 **devote** devoted   32
checks restraints   33 **As** so that   33 **Ovid** Roman love poet (cf.
III.i.28–29, IV.ii.8)   34 **Balk logic** engage in arguments   36 **quicken**
make alive   38 **stomach** taste, preference   40 **affect** like   41
Gramercies many thanks   47s.d. **pantaloon** laughable old man (a
stock character with baggy pants, in Italian Renaissance comedy)
47s.d. **by** nearby

That is, not to bestow my youngest daughter   *50*
Before I have a husband for the elder.
If either of you both love Katherina,
Because I know you well and love you well,
Leave shall you have to court her at your pleasure.

Gremio. To cart° her rather. She's too rough for me.   *55*
  There, there, Hortensio, will you any wife?

Kate. I pray you, sir, is it your will
  To make a stale° of me amongst these mates?°

Hortensio. Mates, maid? How mean you that? No
    mates for you
  Unless you were of gentler, milder mold.   *60*

Kate. I' faith, sir, you shall never need to fear:
  Iwis° it° is not halfway to her° heart.
  But if it were, doubt not her care should be
  To comb your noddle with a three-legged stool
  And paint° your face and use you like a fool.   *65*

Hortensio. From all such devils, good Lord deliver us!

Gremio. And me too, good Lord!

Tranio. [*Aside*] Husht, master, here's some good pas-
    time toward.°
  That wench is stark mad or wonderful froward.°

Lucentio. [*Aside*] But in the other's silence do I see   *70*
  Maid's mild behavior and sobriety.
  Peace, Tranio.

Tranio. [*Aside*] Well said, master. Mum, and gaze
  your fill.

Baptista. Gentlemen, that I may soon make good
  What I have said: Bianca, get you in,   *75*
  And let it not displease thee, good Bianca,

---

55 **cart** drive around in an open cart (a punishment for prostitutes)
58 **stale** (1) laughingstock (2) prostitute   58 **mates** low fellows (with
pun on *stalemate* and leading to pun on *mate* = husband)   62 **Iwis**
certainly   62 **it** i.e., getting a mate   62 **her** Kate's   65 **paint** i.e.,
red with blood   68 **toward** coming up   69 **froward** willful

For I will love thee ne'er the less, my girl.

Kate. A pretty peat!° It is best
Put finger in the eye,° and° she knew why.

80 *Bianca.* Sister, content you in my discontent.
Sir, to your pleasure humbly I subscribe.
My books and instruments shall be my company,
On them to look and practice by myself.

Lucentio. [*Aside*] Hark, Tranio, thou mayst hear
Minerva° speak.

85 *Hortensio.* Signior Baptista, will you be so strange?°
Sorry am I that our good will effects
Bianca's grief.

Gremio.   Why will you mew° her up,
Signior Baptista, for this fiend of hell
And make her bear the penance of her tongue?

90 *Baptista.* Gentlemen, content ye. I am resolved.
Go in, Bianca.   [*Exit Bianca.*]
And for° I know she taketh most delight
In music, instruments, and poetry,
Schoolmasters will I keep within my house,
95 Fit to instruct her youth. If you, Hortensio,
Or Signior Gremio, you, know any such,
Prefer° them hither; for to cunning° men
I will be very kind, and liberal
To mine own children in good bringing up.
100 And so, farewell. Katherina, you may stay,
For I have more to commune with° Bianca.   *Exit.*

Kate. Why, and I trust I may go too, may I not?
What, shall I be appointed hours, as though, belike,°
I knew not what to take and what to leave? Ha!
                                        Exit.

78 **peat** pet (cf. "teacher's pet")   79 **Put finger in the eye** cry   79
and if   84 **Minerva** goddess of wisdom   85 **strange** rigid   87 **mew**
cage (falconry term)   92 **for** because   97 **Prefer** recommend   97
cunning talented   101 **commune with** communicate to   103 **belike**
it seems likely

Gremio. You may go to the devil's dam;° your gifts   105
are so good, here's none will hold you. Their love is
not so great,° Hortensio, but we may blow our
nails together° and fast it fairly out. Our cake's
dough on both sides.° Farewell. Yet for the love I
bear my sweet Bianca, if I can by any means light   110
on a fit man to teach her that wherein she delights,
I will wish° him to her father.

Hortensio. So will I, Signior Gremio. But a word, I
pray. Though the nature of our quarrel yet never
brooked parle,° know now, upon advice,° it touch-   115
eth° us both—that we may yet again have access
to our fair mistress and be happy rivals in Bianca's
love—to labor and effect one thing specially.

Gremio. What's that, I pray?

Hortensio. Marry, sir, to get a husband for her sister.   120

Gremio. A husband! A devil.

Hortensio. I say, a husband.

Gremio. I say, a devil. Think'st thou, Hortensio,
though her father be very rich, any man is so very°
a fool to° be married to hell?   125

Hortensio. Tush, Gremio, though it pass your patience and mine to endure her loud alarums,° why,
man, there be good fellows in the world, and° a man
could light on them, would take her with all faults,
and money enough.   130

Gremio. I cannot tell, but I had as lief° take her
dowry with this condition, to be whipped at the
high cross° every morning.

---

105 **dam** mother (used of animals)   107 **great** important   107–08
blow our nails together i.e., wait patiently   108–09 **Our cake's dough
on both sides** we've both failed (proverbial)   112 **wish** commend
115 **brooked parle** allowed negotiation   115 **advice** consideration
115–16 **toucheth** concerns   124 **very** thorough   125 **to** as to   127
alarums outcries   128 **and** if   131 **had as lief** would as willingly
133 **high cross** market cross (prominent spot)

Hortensio. Faith, as you say, there's small choice in
135   rotten apples. But come, since this bar in law°
         makes us friends, it shall be so far forth° friendly
         maintained, till by helping Baptista's eldest daugh-
         ter to a husband, we set his youngest free for a hus-
         band, and then have to't° afresh. Sweet Bianca!
140   Happy man be his dole!° He that runs fastest gets
         the ring. How say you, Signior Gremio?

Gremio. I am agreed, and would I had given him the
         best horse in Padua to begin his wooing, that°
         would thoroughly woo her, wed her, and bed her
145   and rid the house of her. Come on.

       Exeunt ambo.° Manet° Tranio and Lucentio.

Tranio. I pray, sir, tell me, is it possible
         That love should of a sudden take such hold?

Lucentio. O Tranio, till I found it to be true
         I never thought it possible or likely.
150   But see, while idly I stood looking on,
         I found the effect of love-in-idleness°
         And now in plainness do confess to thee,
         That art to me as secret° and as dear
         As Anna° to the Queen of Carthage was,
155   Tranio, I burn, I pine, I perish, Tranio,
         If I achieve not this young modest girl.
         Counsel me, Tranio, for I know thou canst.
         Assist me, Tranio, for I know thou wilt.

Tranio. Master, it is no time to chide you now.
160   Affection is not rated° from the heart.

---

135 **bar in law** legal action of preventive sort   136 **so far forth** so
long   139 **have to't** renew our competition   140 **Happy man be his
dole** let being a happy man be his (the winner's) destiny   143 **that**
(antecedent is *his*)   145 s.d. **ambo** both   145 s.d. **Manet** remain
(though the Latin plural is properly *manent*, the singular with a
plural subject is common in Elizabethan texts)   151 **love-in-idleness**
popular name for pansy (believed to have mysterious power in love;
cf. *Midsummer Night's Dream*, II.i. 165 ff.)   153 **to me as secret** as
much in my confidence   154 **Anna** sister and confidante of Queen
Dido   160 **rated** scolded

If love have touched you, naught remains but so,°
"*Redime te captum, quam queas minimo.*"°

Lucentio. Gramercies,° lad, go forward. This contents.
The rest will comfort, for thy counsel's sound.

Tranio. Master, you looked so longly° on the maid,   165
Perhaps you marked not what's the pith of all.°

Lucentio. O yes, I saw sweet beauty in her face,
Such as the daughter of Agenor° had,
That made great Jove to humble him to her hand
When with his knees he kissed the Cretan strond.°   170

Tranio. Saw you no more? Marked you not how her
    sister
Began to scold and raise up such a storm
That mortal ears might hardly endure the din?

Lucentio. Tranio, I saw her coral lips to move
And with her breath she did perfume the air.   175
Sacred and sweet was all I saw in her.

Tranio. Nay, then, 'tis time to stir him from his trance.
I pray, awake, sir. If you love the maid,
Bend thoughts and wits to achieve her. Thus it
    stands:
Her elder sister is so curst and shrewd°   180
That till the father rid his hands of her,
Master, your love must live a maid at home;
And therefore has he closely mewed° her up,
Because° she will not be annoyed with suitors.

Lucentio. Ah, Tranio, what a cruel father's he!   185
But art thou not advised° he took some care
To get her cunning° schoolmasters to instruct her?

161 **so** to act thus   162 **Redime ... minimo** ransom yourself, a captive, at the smallest possible price (from Terence's play *The Eunuch*,
as quoted inaccurately in Lilly's *Latin Grammar*)   163 **Gramercies**
many thanks   165 **longly** (1) longingly (2) interminably   166 **pith
of all** heart of the matter   168 **daughter of Agenor** Europa, loved
by Jupiter, who, in the form of a bull, carried her to Crete   170
strond strand, shore   180 **curst and shrewd** sharp-tempered and
shrewish   183 **mewed** caged   184 **Because** so that   186 **advised**
informed   187 **cunning** knowing

Tranio. Ay, marry, am I, sir—and now 'tis plotted!°

Lucentio. I have it, Tranio!

Tranio.   Master, for° my hand,
190   Both our inventions° meet and jump in one.°

Lucentio. Tell me thine first.

Tranio.   You will be schoolmaster
    And undertake the teaching of the maid.
    That's your device.

Lucentio.   It is. May it be done?

Tranio. Not possible, for who shall bear° your part
195   And be in Padua here Vincentio's son?
    Keep house and ply his book, welcome his friends,
    Visit his countrymen and banquet them?

Lucentio. Basta,° content thee, for I have it full.°
    We have not yet been seen in any house,
200   Nor can we be distinguished by our faces
    For man or master. Then it follows thus:
    Thou shalt be master, Tranio, in my stead,
    Keep house and port° and servants as I should.
    I will some other be—some Florentine,
205   Some Neapolitan, or meaner° man of Pisa.
    'Tis hatched and shall be so. Tranio, at once
    Uncase° thee, take my colored° hat and cloak.
    When Biondello comes he waits on thee,
    But I will charm° him first to keep his tongue.

210 *Tranio.* So had you need.
    In brief, sir, sith° it your pleasure is
    And I am tied° to be obedient—
    For so your father charged me at our parting;

188 'tis plotted I've a scheme   189 for I bet   190 inventions
schemes   190 jump in one are identical   194 bear act   198 Basta
enough (Italian)   198 full fully (worked out)   203 port style   205
meaner of lower rank   207 Uncase undress   207 colored (masters
dressed colorfully; servants wore dark blue)   209 charm exercise
power over (he tells him a fanciful tale, lines 225–34)   211 sith
since   212 tied obligated

"Be serviceable to my son," quoth he,
Although I think 'twas in another sense—   213
I am content to be Lucentio
Because so well I love Lucentio.

Lucentio. Tranio, be so, because Lucentio loves,
And let me be a slave, t'achieve that maid
Whose sudden sight hath thralled° my wounded eye.   220

Enter Biondello

Here comes the rogue. Sirrah, where have you been?

Biondello. Where have I been? Nay, how now, where
    are you?
Master, has my fellow Tranio stol'n your clothes,
Or you stol'n his, or both? Pray, what's the news?

Lucentio. Sirrah, come hither. 'Tis no time to jest,   225
And therefore frame your manners to the time.°
Your fellow Tranio, here, to save my life,
Puts my apparel and my count'nance° on,
And I for my escape have put on his,
For in a quarrel since I came ashore   230
I killed a man and fear I was descried.°
Wait you on him, I charge you, as becomes,
While I make way from hence to save my life.
You understand me?

Biondello.   I, sir? Ne'er a whit.

Lucentio. And not a jot of Tranio in your mouth.   235
Tranio is changed into Lucentio.

Biondello. The better for him. Would I were so too.

Tranio. So could I, faith, boy, to have the next wish
    after,
That Lucentio indeed had Baptista's youngest
    daughter.

---

220 **thralled** enslaved   226 **frame your manners to the time** adjust
your conduct to the situation   228 **count'nance** demeanor   231
descried seen, recognized

But, sirrah, not for my sake but your master's, I
240   advise
You use your manners discreetly in all kind of com-
    panies.
When I am alone, why, then I am Tranio,
But in all places else your master, Lucentio.

Lucentio. Tranio, let's go.
245   One thing more rests,° that thyself execute°—
To make one among these wooers. If thou ask me
    why,
Sufficeth my reasons are both good and weighty.
                              Exeunt.

The Presenters° above speaks.

First Servingman. My lord, you nod; you do not mind°
    the play.

Sly. Yes, by Saint Anne, do I. A good matter, surely.
250   Comes there any more of it?

Page. My lord, 'tis but begun.

Sly. 'Tis a very excellent piece of work, madam lady.
    Would 'twere done!   *They sit and mark.°*

[Scene II. *Padua. The street in front of*
Hortensio's house.]

Enter Petruchio° and his man Grumio.

Petruchio. Verona, for a while I take my leave
To see my friends in Padua, but of all
My best belovèd and approvèd friend,

---

245 **rests** remains   245 **execute** are to perform   247s.d. **Presenters**
commentators, actors thought of collectively, hence the singular verb
248 **mind** pay attention to   253s.d. **mark** observe   I.ii.s.d. **Petruchio**
(correct form *Petrucio,* with *c* pronounced *tch*)

    Hortensio, and I trow° this is his house.
    Here, sirrah Grumio, knock, I say.   *5*

Grumio. Knock, sir? Whom should I knock? Is there
    any man has rebused° your worship?

Petruchio. Villain, I say, knock me here° soundly.

Grumio. Knock you here, sir? Why, sir, what am I,
    sir, that I should knock you here, sir?   *10*

Petruchio. Villain, I say, knock me at this gate°
    And rap me well or I'll knock your knave's pate.°

Grumio. My master is grown quarrelsome. I should
      knock you first,
    And then I know after who comes by the worst.

Petruchio. Will it not be?   *15*
    Faith, sirrah, and° you'll not knock, I'll ring° it;
    I'll try how you can *sol, fa,*° and sing it.
                 He wrings him by the ears.

Grumio. Help, masters, help! My master is mad.

Petruchio. Now, knock when I bid you, sirrah villain.

           Enter Hortensio.

Hortensio. How now, what's the matter? My old   *20*
    friend Grumio, and my good friend Petruchio! How
    do you all at Verona?

Petruchio. Signior Hortensio, come you to part the
      fray?
    Con tutto il cuore ben trovato,° may I say.

Hortensio. Alla nostra casa ben venuto, molto hono-   *25*
    rato signior mio Petruchio.°

---

4 trow think   **7 rebused** (Grumio means *abused*)   **8 knock me
here** knock here for me (Grumio plays game of misunderstanding,
taking "me here" as "my ear")   **11 gate** door   **12 pate** head   16
and if   **16 ring** (pun on *wring*)   **17 sol, fa** go up and down the scales
(possibly with puns on meanings now lost)   **24 Con . . . trovato** with
all [my] heart well found (i.e., welcome)   **25–26 Alla . . . Petruchio**
welcome to our house, my much honored Signior Petruchio

Rise, Grumio, rise. We will compound° this quarrel.

Grumio. Nay, 'tis no matter, sir, what he 'leges° in
Latin.° If this be not a lawful cause for me to leave
30 his service—look you, sir, he bid me knock him and
rap him soundly, sir. Well, was it fit for a servant to
use his master so, being perhaps, for aught I see,
two-and-thirty, a peep out?°
Whom would to God I had well knocked at first,
35 Then had not Grumio come by the worst.

Petruchio. A senseless villain! Good Hortensio,
I bade the rascal knock upon your gate
And could not get him for my heart° to do it.

Grumio. Knock at the gate? O heavens! Spake you
40 not these words plain, "Sirrah, knock me here, rap
me here, knock me well, and knock me soundly"?
And come you now with "knocking at the gate"?

Petruchio. Sirrah, be gone or talk not, I advise you.

Hortensio. Petruchio, patience, I am Grumio's pledge.
45 Why, this's a heavy chance° 'twixt him and you,
Your ancient, trusty, pleasant servant Grumio.
And tell me now, sweet friend, what happy gale
Blows you to Padua here from old Verona?

Petruchio. Such wind as scatters young men through
the world
50 To seek their fortunes farther than at home,
Where small experience grows. But in a few,°
Signior Hortensio, thus it stands with me:
Antonio my father is deceased,
And I have thrust myself into this maze,°
55 Happily° to wive and thrive as best I may.

---

27 **compound** settle   28 **'leges** alleges   29 **Latin** (as if he were English, Grumio does not recognize Italian)   33 **two-and-thirty, a peep
out** (1) an implication that Petruchio is aged (2) a term from cards,
slang for "drunk" (*peep* is an old form of *pip*, a marking on a card)
38 **heart** life   45 **heavy chance** sad happening   51 **few** i.e., words
54 **maze** traveling; uncertain course   55 **Happily** haply, perchance

Crowns in my purse I have and goods at home
And so am come abroad to see the world.

Hortensio. Petruchio, shall I then come roundly° to
thee
And wish thee to a shrewd ill-favored° wife?
Thou'ldst thank me but a little for my counsel—   60
And yet I'll promise thee she shall be rich,
And very rich—but thou'rt too much my friend,
And I'll not wish thee to her.

Petruchio. Signior Hortensio, 'twixt such friends as we
Few words suffice; and therefore if thou know   65
One rich enough to be Petruchio's wife—
As wealth is burthen° of my wooing dance—
Be she as foul° as was Florentius'° love,
As old as Sibyl,° and as curst and shrewd
As Socrates' Xanthippe° or a worse,   70
She moves me not, or not removes, at least,
Affection's edge in me, were she as rough
As are the swelling Adriatic seas.
I come to wive it wealthily in Padua;
If wealthily, then happily in Padua.   75

Grumio. Nay, look you, sir, he tells you flatly what
his mind is. Why, give him gold enough and marry
him to a puppet or an aglet-baby° or an old trot°
with ne'er a tooth in her head, though she have as
many diseases as two-and-fifty horses. Why, nothing   80
comes amiss so money comes withal.°

Hortensio. Petruchio, since we are stepped thus far in,
I will continue that° I broached in jest.
I can, Petruchio, help thee to a wife
With wealth enough and young and beauteous,   85

58 **come roundly** talk frankly   59 **shrewd ill-favored** shrewish,
poorly qualified   67 **burthen** burden (musical accompaniment)   68
foul homely   68 **Florentius** knight in Gower's *Confessio Amantis*
(cf. Chaucer's Wife of Bath's Tale; knight marries hag who turns
into beautiful girl)   69 **Sibyl** prophetess in Greek and Roman myth
70 **Xanthippe** Socrates' wife, legendarily shrewish   78 **aglet-baby**
small female figure forming metal tip of cord or lace (French
aiguillette, point)   78 **trot** hag   81 **withal** with it   83 **that** what

Brought up as best becomes a gentlewoman.
Her only fault—and that is faults enough—
Is that she is intolerable curst°
And shrewd and froward,° so beyond all measure
90 That were my state° far worser than it is,
I would not wed her for a mine of gold.

Petruchio. Hortensio, peace. Thou know'st not gold's
    effect.
Tell me her father's name, and 'tis enough,
For I will board° her though she chide as loud
95 As thunder when the clouds in autumn crack.°

Hortensio. Her father is Baptista Minola,
An affable and courteous gentleman.
Her name is Katherina Minola,
Renowned in Padua for her scolding tongue.

100 *Petruchio.* I know her father though I know not her,
And he knew my deceasèd father well.
I will not sleep, Hortensio, till I see her,
And therefore let me be thus bold with you,
To give you over° at this first encounter
105 Unless you will accompany me thither.

Grumio. I pray you, sir, let him go while the humor°
lasts. A° my word, and° she knew him as well as I
do, she would think scolding would do little good°
upon him. She may perhaps call him half a score
110 knaves or so—why, that's nothing. And he begin
once, he'll rail in his rope-tricks.° I'll tell you what,
sir, and she stand° him but a little, he will throw a
figure in her face and so disfigure her with it that
she shall have no more eyes to see withal than a
115 cat. You know him not, sir.

88 **intolerable curst** intolerably sharp-tempered   89 **froward** willful
90 **state** estate, revenue   94 **board** naval term, with double sense:
(1) accost (2) go on board   95 **crack** make explosive roars   104
give you over leave you   106 **humor** mood   107 **A** on   107 **and** if
(also at lines 110 and 112)   108 **do little good** have little effect   111
rope-tricks (1) Grumio's version of *rhetoric*, going with *figure* just
below (2) rascally conduct, deserving hanging (3) possible sexual
innuendo, as in following lines   112 **stand** withstand

Hortensio. Tarry, Petruchio, I must go with thee,
 For in Baptista's keep° my treasure is.
 He hath the jewel of my life in hold,°
 His youngest daughter, beautiful Bianca,
 And her withholds from me and other more,   120
 Suitors to her and rivals in my love,
 Supposing it a thing impossible,
 For° those defects I have before rehearsed,
 That ever Katherina will be wooed.
 Therefore this order° hath Baptista ta'en,   125
 That none shall have access unto Bianca
 Till Katherine the curst have got a husband.

Grumio. Katherine the curst!
 A title for a maid of all titles the worst.

Hortensio. Now shall my friend Petruchio do me
    grace°   130
 And offer° me, disguised in sober robes,
 To old Baptista as a schoolmaster
 Well seen° in music, to instruct Bianca,
 That so I may, by this device, at least
 Have leave and leisure to make love to her   135
 And unsuspected court her by herself.

        Enter Gremio, and Lucentio disguised
        [as a schoolmaster, Cambio].

Grumio. Here's no knavery! See, to beguile the old
 folks, how the young folks lay their heads together!
 Master, master, look about you. Who goes there,
 ha?   140

Hortensio. Peace, Grumio. It is the rival of my love.
 Petruchio, stand by awhile.   *[They eavesdrop.]*

Grumio. A proper stripling,° and an amorous!

Gremio. O, very well, I have perused the note.°

117 **keep** heavily fortified inner tower of castle 118 **hold** strong-
hold 123 **For** because of 125 **order** step 130 **grace** a favor 131
offer present, introduce 133 **seen** trained 143 **proper stripling**
handsome youth (sarcastic comment on Gremio) 144 **note** memo-
randum (reading list for Bianca)

145   Hark you, sir, I'll have them very fairly bound—
All books of love, see that at any hand,°
And see you read no other lectures° to her.
You understand me. Over and beside
Signior Baptista's liberality,
150   I'll mend it with a largess.° Take your paper° too
And let me have them° very well perfumed,
For she is sweeter than perfume itself
To whom they go to. What will you read to her?

Lucentio. Whate'er I read to her, I'll plead for you
155   As for my patron, stand you so assured,
As firmly as° yourself were still in place°—
Yea, and perhaps with more successful words
Than you unless you were a scholar, sir.

Gremio. O this learning, what a thing it is!

160   *Grumio.* [*Aside*] O this woodcock,° what an ass it is!

Petruchio. Peace, sirrah!

Hortensio. Grumio, mum! [*Coming forward*] God save
you, Signior Gremio.

Gremio. And you are well met, Signior Hortensio.
Trow° you whither I am going? To Baptista Minola.
165   I promised to inquire carefully
About a schoolmaster for the fair Bianca,
And, by good fortune, I have lighted well
On this young man—for° learning and behavior
Fit for her turn,° well read in poetry
170   And other books, good ones I warrant ye.

Hortensio. 'Tis well. And I have met a gentleman
Hath promised me to help me to° another,
A fine musician to instruct our mistress.

---

146 **at any hand** in any case   147 **read no other lectures** assign no
other readings   150 **mend it with a largess** add a gift of money to it
150 **paper** note (line 144)   151 **them** i.e., the books   156 **as** as if you
156 **in place** present   160 **woodcock** bird easily trapped, so consid-
ered silly   164 **Trow** know   168 **for** in   169 **turn** situation (with
unconscious bawdy pun on the sense of "copulation")   172 **help me
to** (1) find (2) become (Hortensio's jest)

   So shall I no whit be behind in duty
   To fair Bianca, so beloved of me.   *175*

Gremio. Beloved of me, and that my deeds shall
   prove.

Grumio. [*Aside*] And that his bags° shall prove.

Hortensio. Gremio, 'tis now no time to vent° our love.
   Listen to me, and if you speak me fair,
   I'll tell you news indifferent° good for either.   *180*
   Here is a gentleman whom by chance I met,
   Upon agreement from us to his liking,°
   Will undertake° to woo curst Katherine,
   Yea, and to marry her if her dowry please.

Gremio. So said, so done, is well.   *185*
   Hortensio, have you told him all her faults?

Petruchio. I know she is an irksome, brawling scold;
   If that be all, masters, I hear no harm.

Gremio. No, say'st me so, friend? What countryman?

Petruchio. Born in Verona, old Antonio's son.   *190*
   My father dead, my fortune lives for me,
   And I do hope good days and long to see.

Gremio. O, sir, such a life with such a wife were
   strange.
   But if you have a stomach,° to't a° God's name;
   You shall have me assisting you in all.   *195*
   But will you woo this wildcat?

Petruchio.   Will I live?

Grumio. [*Aside*] Will he woo her? Ay, or I'll hang her.

Petruchio. Why came I hither but to that intent?
   Think you a little din can daunt mine ears?
   Have I not in my time heard lions roar?
   Have I not heard the sea, puffed up with winds,   *200*
   Rage like an angry boar chafèd with sweat?

177 **bags** i.e., of money   178 **vent** express   180 **indifferent** equally
182 **Upon . . . liking** if we agree to his terms (paying costs)   183
undertake promise   194 **stomach** inclination   194 **a** in

Have I not heard great ordnance° in the field
And heaven's artillery thunder in the skies?
205 Have I not in a pitchèd battle heard
Loud 'larums,° neighing steeds, and trumpets'
clang?
And do you tell me of a woman's tongue,
That gives not half so great a blow to hear
As will a chestnut in a farmer's fire?
Tush, tush, fear° boys with bugs.°

210 *Grumio.* [*Aside*]   For he fears none.

Gremio. Hortensio, hark.
This gentleman is happily arrived,
My mind presumes, for his own good and ours.

Hortensio. I promised we would be contributors
215 And bear his charge of° wooing, whatsoe'er.

Gremio. And so we will, provided that he win her.

Grumio. [*Aside*] I would I were as sure of a good
dinner.

Enter Tranio brave° [as Lucentio] and Biondello.

Tranio. Gentlemen, God save you. If I may be bold,
Tell me, I beseech you, which is the readiest way
220 To the house of Signior Baptista Minola?

Biondello. He that has the two fair daughters? Is't
he you mean?

Tranio. Even he, Biondello.

Gremio. Hark you, sir. You mean not her to—

Tranio. Perhaps, him and her, sir. What have you
to do?°

Petruchio. Not her that chides, sir, at any hand,° I
225 pray.

_____

203 **ordnance** cannon   206 **'larums** calls to arms, sudden attacks
210 **fear** frighten   210 **bugs** bugbears   215 **his charge of** the cost
of his   217s.d. **brave** elegantly attired   224 **to do** i.e., to do with this
225 **at any hand** in any case

Tranio. I love no chiders, sir. Biondello, let's away.

Lucentio. [*Aside*] Well begun, Tranio.

Hortensio.   Sir, a word ere
  you go.
  Are you a suitor to the maid you talk of, yea or no?

Tranio. And if I be, sir, is it any offense?

Gremio. No, if without more words you will get you
  hence.   230

Tranio. Why, sir, I pray, are not the streets as free
  For me as for you?

Gremio.   But so is not she.

Tranio. For what reason, I beseech you?

Gremio. For this reason, if you'll know,
  That she's the choice° love of Signior Gremio.   235

Hortensio. That she's the chosen of Signior Hortensio.

Tranio. Softly, my masters! If you be gentlemen,
  Do me this right: hear me with patience.
  Baptista is a noble gentleman
  To whom my father is not all unknown,   240
  And were his daughter fairer than she is,
  She may more suitors have, and me for one.
  Fair Leda's daughter° had a thousand wooers;
  Then well one more may fair Bianca have.
  And so she shall. Lucentio shall make one,   245
  Though Paris° came° in hope to speed° alone.

Gremio. What, this gentleman will out-talk us all.

Lucentio. Sir, give him head. I know he'll prove a
  jade.°

Petruchio. Hortensio, to what end are all these words?

235 **choice** chosen   243 **Leda's daughter** Helen of Troy   246 **Paris**
lover who took Helen to Troy (legendary cause of Trojan War)
246 **came** should come   246 **speed** succeed   248 **prove a jade** soon
tire (cf. "jaded")

250 *Hortensio.* Sir, let me be so bold as ask you,
    Did you yet ever see Baptista's daughter?

Tranio. No, sir, but hear I do that he hath two,
    The one as famous for a scolding tongue
    As is the other for beauteous modesty.

255 *Petruchio.* Sir, sir, the first's for me; let her go by.

Gremio. Yea, leave that labor to great Hercules,
    And let it be more than Alcides'° twelve.

Petruchio. Sir, understand you this of me in sooth:°
    The youngest daughter, whom you hearken° for,
260 Her father keeps from all access of suitors
    And will not promise her to any man
    Until the elder sister first be wed.
    The younger then is free, and not before.

Tranio. If it be so, sir, that you are the man
265 Must stead° us all, and me amongst the rest,
    And if you break the ice and do this feat,
    Achieve° the elder, set the younger free
    For our access, whose hap° shall be to have her
    Will not so graceless be to be ingrate.°

Hortensio. Sir, you say well, and well you do con-
270   ceive,°
    And since you do profess to be a suitor,
    You must, as we do, gratify° this gentleman
    To whom we all rest° generally beholding.°

Tranio. Sir, I shall not be slack, in sign whereof,
275 Please ye we may contrive° this afternoon
    And quaff carouses° to our mistress' health
    And do as adversaries° do in law,
    Strive mightily but eat and drink as friends.

257 **Alcides** Hercules (after Alcaeus, a family ancestor)   258 **sooth**
truth   259 **hearken** long   265 **stead** aid   267 **Achieve** succeed with
268 **whose hap** the man whose luck   269 **to be ingrate** as to be
ungrateful   270 **conceive** put the case   272 **gratify** compensate
273 **rest** remain   273 **beholding** indebted   275 **contrive** pass   276
quaff carouses empty our cups   277 **adversaries** attorneys

Grumio, Biondello. O excellent motion! Fellows, let's
  be gone.

Hortensio. The motion's good indeed, and be it so.   280
  Petruchio, I shall be your *ben venuto.°*   *Exeunt.*

281 ben venuto welcome (i.e., host)

[ACT II

Scene I. *In Baptista's house.*]

Enter Kate and Bianca [with her hands tied].

Bianca. Good sister, wrong me not nor wrong your-
    self
  To make a bondmaid and a slave of me.
  That I disdain. But for these other gawds,°
  Unbind my hands, I'll pull them off myself,
5 Yea, all my raiment, to my petticoat,
  Or what you will command me will I do,
  So well I know my duty to my elders.

Kate. Of all thy suitors, here I charge thee, tell
  Whom thou lov'st best. See thou dissemble not.

10 *Bianca.* Believe me, sister, of all the men alive
  I never yet beheld that special face
  Which I could fancy more than any other.

Kate. Minion,° thou liest. Is't not Hortensio?

Bianca. If you affect° him, sister, here I swear
15 I'll plead for you myself but you shall have him.

Kate. O then, belike,° you fancy riches more:
  You will have Gremio to keep you fair.°

Bianca. Is it for him you do envy° me so?
  Nay, then you jest, and now I well perceive
20 You have but jested with me all this while.
  I prithee, sister Kate, untie my hands.

II.i.3 **gawds** adornments 13 **Minion** impudent creature 14 **affect**
like 16 **belike** probably 17 **fair** in fine clothes 18 **envy** hate

78

Kate. If that be jest then all the rest was so.

                        Strikes her.

            Enter Baptista.

Baptista. Why, how now, dame, whence grows this
    insolence?
    Bianca, stand aside. Poor girl, she weeps.
    Go ply thy needle; meddle not with her.   25
    For shame, thou hilding° of a devilish spirit,
    Why dost thou wrong her that did ne'er wrong
        thee?
    When did she cross thee with a bitter word?

Kate. Her silence flouts me and I'll be revenged.

                    Flies after Bianca.

Baptista. What, in my sight? Bianca, get thee in.   30

                      Exit [Bianca].

Kate. What, will you not suffer° me? Nay, now I see
    She is your treasure, she must have a husband;
    I must dance barefoot on her wedding day,°
    And, for your love to her, lead apes in hell.°
    Talk not to me; I will go sit and weep   33
    Till I can find occasion of revenge.   [*Exit.*]

Baptista. Was ever gentleman thus grieved as I?
    But who comes here?

    Enter Gremio, Lucentio in the habit of a mean° man
      [Cambio], Petruchio, with [Hortensio as a music
      teacher, Litio, and] Tranio [as Lucentio], with his
      boy [Biondello] bearing a lute and books.

Gremio. Good morrow, neighbor Baptista.

Baptista. Good morrow, neighbor Gremio. God save 40
    you, gentlemen.

Petruchio. And you, good sir. Pray, have you not a
    daughter

26 **hilding** base wretch   31 **suffer** permit (i.e., to deal with you)   33
dance . . . day (expected of older maiden sisters)   34 **lead apes in
hell** (proverbial occupation of old maids; cf. *Much Ado About Nothing*, II.i.41)   38s.d. **mean** lower class

Called Katherina, fair and virtuous?

Baptista. I have a daughter, sir, called Katherina.

45 *Gremio.* [*Aside*] You are too blunt; go to it orderly.°

Petruchio. [*Aside*] You wrong me, Signior Gremio,
    give me leave.
    [*To Baptista*] I am a gentleman of Verona, sir,
    That, hearing of her beauty and her wit,
    Her affability and bashful modesty,
50   Her wondrous qualities and mild behavior,
    Am bold to show myself a forward° guest
    Within your house, to make mine eye the witness
    Of that report which I so oft have heard.
    And, for an entrance to° my entertainment,°
55   I do present you with a man of mine,
                       [*presenting Hortensio*]
    Cunning in music and the mathematics,
    To instruct her fully in those sciences,
    Whereof I know she is not ignorant.
    Accept of him, or else you do me wrong.
60   His name is Litio, born in Mantua.

Baptista. Y'are welcome, sir, and he for your good
    sake.
    But for my daughter Katherine, this I know,
    She is not for your turn,° the more my grief.

Petruchio. I see you do not mean to part with her,
65   Or else you like not of my company.

Baptista. Mistake me not; I speak but as I find.
    Whence are you, sir? What may I call your name?

Petruchio. Petruchio is my name, Antonio's son,
    A man well known throughout all Italy.

Baptista. I know him well. You are welcome for his
70   sake.

Gremio. Saving° your tale, Petruchio, I pray,

---

45 **orderly** gradually 51 **forward** eager 54 **entrance to** price of
admission for 54 **entertainment** reception 63 **turn** purpose (again,
with bawdy pun) 71 **Saving** with all respect for

Let us, that are poor petitioners, speak too.
Backare,° you are marvelous° forward.

Petruchio. O pardon me, Signior Gremio, I would
fain° be doing.°

Gremio. I doubt it not, sir, but you will curse your
wooing.   75
Neighbor, this is a gift very grateful,° I am sure of
it. To express the like kindness myself, that° have
been more kindly beholding to you than any, freely
give unto you this young scholar [*presenting Lu-*
centio] that hath been long studying at Rheims—as   80
cunning in Greek, Latin, and other languages, as
the other in music and mathematics. His name is
Cambio.° Pray accept his service.

Baptista. A thousand thanks, Signior Gremio. Welcome, good Cambio. [*To Tranio*] But, gentle sir,   85
methinks you walk like° a stranger. May I be so
bold to know the cause of your coming?

Tranio. Pardon me, sir, the boldness is mine own,
That,° being a stranger in this city here,
Do make myself a suitor to your daughter,   90
Unto Bianca, fair and virtuous.
Nor is your firm resolve unknown to me
In the preferment of° the eldest sister.
This liberty is all that I request,
That, upon knowledge of my parentage,   95
I may have welcome 'mongst the rest that woo
And free access and favor° as the rest.
And, toward the education of your daughters
I here bestow a simple instrument,°
And this small packet of Greek and Latin books.   100
If you accept them, then their worth is great.

73 **Backare** back (proverbial quasi-Latin)   73 **marvelous** very   74
would fain am eager to   74 **doing** (with a sexual jest)   76 **grateful**
worthy of gratitude   77 **myself, that** I myself, who   83 **Cambio**
(Italian for "exchange")   86 **walk like** have the bearing of   89 **That**
who   93 **preferment of** giving priority to   97 **favor** countenance,
acceptance   99 **instrument** i.e., the lute

Baptista. [*Looking at books*] Lucentio is your name.
    Of whence, I pray?

Tranio. Of Pisa, sir, son to Vincentio.

Baptista. A mighty man of Pisa; by report

105   I know him° well. You are very welcome, sir.
    [*To Hortensio*] Take you the lute, [*to Lucentio*]
    and you the set of books;
    You shall go see your pupils presently.°
    Holla, within!

Enter a Servant.

           Sirrah, lead these gentlemen
    To my daughters and tell them both

110   These are their tutors; bid them use them well.
                [*Exit Servant, with Lucentio,*
            Hortensio, and Biondello following.]
    We will go walk a little in the orchard°
    And then to dinner. You are passing° welcome,
    And so I pray you all to think yourselves.

Petruchio. Signior Baptista, my business asketh haste,

115   And every day I cannot come to woo.
    You knew my father well, and in him me,
    Left solely heir to all his lands and goods,
    Which I have bettered rather than decreased.
    Then tell me, if I get your daughter's love

120   What dowry shall I have with her to wife?

Baptista. After my death the one half of my lands,
    And in possession° twenty thousand crowns.

Petruchio. And, for that dowry, I'll assure her of
    Her widowhood,° be it that she survive me,

125   In all my lands and leases whatsoever.
    Let specialties° be therefore drawn between us
    That covenants may be kept on either hand.

---

105 **him** his name   107 **presently** at once   111 **orchard** garden
112 **passing** very   122 **possession** i.e., at the time of marriage   124
widowhood estate settled on a widow (Johnson)   126 **specialties**
special contracts

Baptista. Ay, when the special thing is well obtained,
That is, her love, for that is all in all.

Petruchio. Why, that is nothing, for I tell you, father,   130
I am as peremptory° as she proud-minded.
And where two raging fires meet together
They do consume the thing that feeds their fury.
Though little fire grows great with little wind,
Yet extreme gusts will blow out fire and all.   135
So I to her, and so she yields to me,
For I am rough and woo not like a babe.

Baptista. Well mayst thou woo, and happy be thy speed!°
But be thou armed for some unhappy words.

Petruchio. Ay, to the proof,° as mountains are for winds
That shakes not, though they blow perpetually.   140

Enter Hortensio with his head broke.

Baptista. How now, my friend, why dost thou look so pale?

Hortensio. For fear, I promise you, if I look pale.

Baptista. What, will my daughter prove a good musician?

Hortensio. I think she'll sooner prove a soldier.   145
Iron may hold with her,° but never lutes.

Baptista. Why, then thou canst not break° her to the lute?

Hortensio. Why, no, for she hath broke the lute to me.
I did but tell her she mistook her frets°
And bowed° her hand to teach her fingering,   150
When, with a most impatient devilish spirit,
"Frets, call you these?" quoth she; "I'll fume with them."

131 **peremptory** resolved   138 **speed** progress   140 **to the proof** in tested steel armor   146 **hold with her** stand her treatment   147 **break** train   149 **frets** ridges where strings are pressed   150 **bowed** bent

And with that word she stroke° me on the head,
And through the instrument my pate made way.
155 And there I stood amazèd for a while
As on a pillory,° looking through the lute,
While she did call me rascal, fiddler,
And twangling Jack,° with twenty such vile terms
As° had she studied° to misuse me so.

160 *Petruchio.* Now, by the world, it is a lusty° wench!
I love her ten times more than e'er I did.
O how I long to have some chat with her!

Baptista. [*To Hortensio*] Well, go with me, and be
   not so discomfited.
Proceed in practice° with my younger daughter;
165 She's apt° to learn and thankful for good turns.
Signior Petruchio, will you go with us
Or shall I send my daughter Kate to you?
           Exit [*Baptista, with Gremio, Tranio, and
                  Hortensio*]. *Manet Petruchio.*°

Petruchio. I pray you do. I'll attend° her here
And woo her with some spirit when she comes.
170 Say that she rail,° why then I'll tell her plain
She sings as sweetly as a nightingale.
Say that she frown, I'll say she looks as clear
As morning roses newly washed with dew.
Say she be mute and will not speak a word,
175 Then I'll commend her volubility
And say she uttereth piercing eloquence.
If she do bid me pack,° I'll give her thanks
As though she bid me stay by her a week.
If she deny° to wed, I'll crave the day
180 When I shall ask the banns° and when be marrièd.
But here she comes, and now, Petruchio, speak.

153 **stroke** struck 156 **pillory** i.e., with a wooden collar (old struc-
ture for public punishment) 158 **Jack** (term of contempt) 159 **As**
as if 159 **studied** prepared 160 **lusty** spirited 164 **practice** instruction 165 **apt** disposed 167s.d. (is in the F position, which
need not be changed; Petruchio speaks to the departing Baptista)
168 **attend** wait for 170 **rail** scold, scoff 177 **pack** go away 179
deny refuse 180 **banns** public announcement in church of intent to
marry

Enter Kate.

Good morrow, Kate, for that's your name, I hear.

Kate. Well have you heard,° but something hard of
hearing.
They call me Katherine that do talk of me.

Petruchio. You lie, in faith, for you are called plain
Kate,   183
And bonny° Kate, and sometimes Kate the curst.
But, Kate, the prettiest Kate in Christendom,
Kate of Kate Hall,° my super-dainty Kate,
For dainties° are all Kates,° and therefore, Kate,
Take this of me, Kate of my consolation.   190
Hearing thy mildness praised in every town,
Thy virtues spoke of, and thy beauty sounded°—
Yet not so deeply as to thee belongs—
Myself am moved to woo thee for my wife.

Kate. Moved! In good time,° let him that moved you
hither   195
Remove you hence. I knew you at the first
You were a movable.°

Petruchio.   Why, what's a movable?

Kate. A joint stool.°

Petruchio   Thou hast hit it; come sit on me.

Kate. Asses are made to bear° and so are you.

Petruchio. Women are made to bear° and so are you.   200

Kate. No such jade° as you, if me you mean.

---

183 **heard** (pun: pronounced like *hard*)   186 **bonny** big, fine (perhaps with pun on *bony*, the F spelling)   188 **Kate Hall** (possible
topical reference; several places have been proposed)   189 **dainties**
delicacies   189 **Kates** i.e., *cates*, delicacies · 192 **sounded** (1) measured (effect of *deeply*) (2) spoken of (pun)   195 **In good time** indeed
197 **movable** article of furniture (with pun)   198 **joint stool** stool
made by a joiner (standard term of disparagement)   199 **bear** carry
200 **bear** i.e., bear children (with second sexual meaning in Petruchio's "I will not burden thee")   201 **jade** worn-out horse (Kate has
now called him both "ass" and "sorry horse")

Petruchio. Alas, good Kate, I will not burden thee,
    For, knowing thee to be but young and light—

Kate. Too light for such a swain° as you to catch
205   And yet as heavy as my weight should be.

Petruchio. Should be!° Should—buzz!

Kate.   Well ta'en, and like a buzzard.°

Petruchio. O slow-winged turtle,° shall a buzzard
    take° thee?

Kate. Ay, for a turtle, as he takes a buzzard.°

Petruchio. Come, come, you wasp, i' faith you are
    too angry.

210 *Kate.* If I be waspish, best beware my sting.

Petruchio. My remedy is then to pluck it out.

Kate. Ay, if the fool could find it where it lies.

Petruchio. Who knows not where a wasp does wear
    his sting?
    In his tail.

Kate.   In his tongue.

Petruchio.   Whose tongue?

215 *Kate.* Yours, if you talk of tales,° and so farewell.

Petruchio. What, with my tongue in your tail? Nay,
    come again.
    Good Kate, I am a gentleman—

Kate.   That I'll try.
                    She strikes him.

Petruchio. I swear I'll cuff you if you strike again.

---

204 **swain** country boy   206 **be** (pun on *bee*; hence *buzz*, scandal,
i.e., about "light" woman)   206 **buzzard** hawk unteachable in falconry (hence idiot)   207 **turtle** turtledove, noted for affectionate-
ness   207 **take** capture (with pun, "mistake for," in next line)   208
buzzard buzzing insect (hence "wasp")   215 **of tales** idle tales (leading to bawdy pun on *tail* = pudend)

Kate. So may you lose your arms:°
If you strike me you are no gentleman,   220
And if no gentleman, why then no arms.

Petruchio. A herald,° Kate? O, put me in thy books.°

Kate. What is your crest?° A coxcomb?°

Petruchio. A combless° cock, so° Kate will be my hen.

Kate. No cock of mine; you crow too like a craven.°   225

Petruchio. Nay, come, Kate, come, you must not look
so sour.

Kate. It is my fashion when I see a crab.°

Petruchio. Why, here's no crab, and therefore look
not sour.

Kate. There is, there is.

Petruchio. Then show it me.

Kate.   Had I a glass° I would.   230

Petruchio. What, you mean my face?

Kate.   Well aimed of°
such a young one.

Petruchio. Now, by Saint George, I am too young
for you.

Kate. Yet you are withered.

Petruchio.   'Tis with cares.

Kate.   I care not.

Petruchio. Nay, hear you, Kate, in sooth° you scape°
not so.

Kate. I chafe° you if I tarry. Let me go.   235

219 **arms** (pun on "coat of arms")   222 **herald** one skilled in heraldry
222 **books** registers of heraldry (with pun on "in your good books")
223 **crest** heraldic device   223 **coxcomb** identifying feature of court
Fool's cap; the cap itself   224 **combless** i.e., unwarlike   224 **so** if
225 **craven** defeated cock   227 **crab** crab apple   230 **glass** mirror
231 **well aimed of** a good shot (in the dark)   234 **sooth** truth   234
scape escape   235 **chafe** (1) annoy (2) warm up

Petruchio. No, not a whit. I find you passing gentle.
    'Twas told me you were rough and coy° and sullen,
    And now I find report a very liar,
    For thou art pleasant, gamesome, passing courteous,
240   But slow in speech, yet sweet as springtime flowers.
    Thou canst not frown, thou canst not look askance,
    Nor bite the lip as angry wenches will,
    Nor hast thou pleasure to be cross in talk,
    But thou with mildness entertain'st thy wooers,
245   With gentle conference,° soft and affable.
    Why does the world report that Kate doth limp?
    O sland'rous world! Kate like the hazel-twig
    Is straight and slender, and as brown in hue
    As hazelnuts and sweeter than the kernels.
250   O, let me see thee walk. Thou dost not halt.°

Kate. Go, fool, and whom thou keep'st° command.

Petruchio. Did ever Dian° so become a grove
    As Kate this chamber with her princely gait?
    O, be thou Dian and let her be Kate,
255   And then let Kate be chaste and Dian sportful!°

Kate. Where did you study all this goodly speech?

Petruchio. It is extempore, from my mother-wit.°

Kate. A witty mother! Witless else° her son.

Petruchio. Am I not wise?

Kate.   Yes,° keep you warm.

Petruchio. Marry, so I mean, sweet Katherine, in thy
260   bed.
    And therefore, setting all this chat aside,
    Thus in plain terms: your father hath consented
    That you shall be my wife, your dowry 'greed on,
    And will you, nill° you, I will marry you.

237 **coy** offish 245 **conference** conversation 250 **halt** limp 251
whom thou keep'st i.e., your servants 252 **Dian** Diana, goddess of
hunting and virginity 255 **sportful** (i.e., in the game of love) 257
mother-wit natural intelligence 258 **else** otherwise would be 259
Yes yes, just enough to (refers to a proverbial saying) 264 **nill**
won't

Now, Kate, I am a husband for your turn,°　　265
For, by this light, whereby I see thy beauty—
Thy beauty that doth make me like thee well—
Thou must be married to no man but me.

Enter Baptista, Gremio, Tranio.

For I am he am born to tame you, Kate,
And bring you from a wild Kate° to a Kate　　270
Conformable° as other household Kates.
Here comes your father. Never make denial;
I must and will have Katherine to my wife.

Baptista. Now, Signior Petruchio, how speed° you
　　with my daughter?

Petruchio. How but well, sir? How but well?　　275
It were impossible I should speed amiss.

Baptista. Why, how now, daughter Katherine, in your
　　dumps?°

Kate. Call you me daughter? Now, I promise° you
You have showed a tender fatherly regard
To wish me wed to one half lunatic,　　280
A madcap ruffian and a swearing Jack
That thinks with oaths to face° the matter out.

Petruchio. Father, 'tis thus: yourself and all the world
That talked of her have talked amiss of her.
If she be curst it is for policy,°　　285
For she's not froward but modest as the dove.
She is not hot° but temperate as the morn;
For patience she will prove a second Grissel°
And Roman Lucrece° for her chastity.
And to conclude, we have 'greed so well together　　290
That upon Sunday is the wedding day.

Kate. I'll see thee hanged on Sunday first.

265 **turn** advantage (with bawdy second meaning)　270 **wild Kate** (pun on "wildcat")　271 **Conformable** submissive　274 **speed** get on　277 **dumps** low spirits　278 **promise** tell　282 **face** brazen 285 **policy** tactics　287 **hot** intemperate　288 **Grissel** Griselda (patient wife in Chaucer's Clerk's Tale)　289 **Lucrece** (killed herself after Tarquin raped her)

Gremio. Hark, Petruchio, she says she'll see thee
   hanged first.

Tranio. Is this your speeding?° Nay, then good night
   our part!

Petruchio. Be patient, gentlemen, I choose her for
295   myself.
   If she and I be pleased, what's that to you?
   'Tis bargained 'twixt us twain, being alone,
   That she shall still be curst in company.
   I tell you, 'tis incredible to believe
300   How much she loves me. O, the kindest Kate,
   She hung about my neck, and kiss on kiss
   She vied° so fast, protesting oath on oath,
   That in a twink° she won me to her love.
   O, you are novices. 'Tis a world° to see
305   How tame, when men and women are alone,
   A meacock° wretch can make the curstest shrew.
   Give me thy hand, Kate. I will unto Venice
   To buy apparel 'gainst° the wedding day.
   Provide the feast, father, and bid the guests;
310   I will be sure my Katherine shall be fine.°

Baptista. I know not what to say, but give me your
   hands.
   God send you joy, Petruchio! 'Tis a match.

Gremio, Tranio. Amen, say we. We will be witnesses.

Petruchio. Father, and wife, and gentlemen, adieu.
315   I will to Venice; Sunday comes apace.
   We will have rings and things and fine array,
   And, kiss me, Kate, "We will be married a Sunday."°

                              Exit Petruchio and Kate.

Gremio. Was ever match clapped° up so suddenly?

---

294 **speeding** success   302 **vied** made higher bids (card-playing
terms), i.e., kissed more frequently   303 **twink** twinkling   304
world wonder   306 **meacock** timid   308 **'gainst** in preparation for
310 **fine** well dressed   317 "**We . . . Sunday**" (line from a ballad)
318 **clapped** fixed

Baptista. Faith, gentlemen, now I play a merchant's
   part
  And venture madly on a desperate mart.°   320

Tranio. 'Twas a commodity° lay fretting° by you;
  'Twill bring you gain or perish on the seas.

Baptista. The gain I seek is quiet in the match.

Gremio. No doubt but he hath got a quiet catch.
  But now, Baptista, to your younger daughter;   325
  Now is the day we long have lookèd for.
  I am your neighbor and was suitor first.

Tranio. And I am one that love Bianca more
  Than words can witness or your thoughts can guess.

Gremio. Youngling, thou canst not love so dear as I. 330

Tranio. Graybeard, thy love doth freeze.

Gremio.   But thine doth fry.
  Skipper,° stand back, 'tis age that nourisheth.

Tranio. But youth in ladies' eyes that flourisheth.

Baptista. Content you, gentlemen; I will compound°
   this strife.
  'Tis deeds must win the prize, and he of both°   335
  That can assure my daughter greatest dower°
  Shall have my Bianca's love.
  Say, Signior Gremio, what can you assure her?

Gremio. First, as you know, my house within the city
  Is richly furnishèd with plate and gold,   340
  Basins and ewers to lave° her dainty hands;
  My hangings all of Tyrian° tapestry;
  In ivory coffers I have stuffed my crowns,
  In cypress chests my arras counterpoints,°

---

320 **mart** "deal"   321 **commodity** (here a coarse term for women;
see Partridge, *Shakespeare's Bawdy*)   321 **fretting** decaying in stor-
age (with pun)   332 **Skipper** skipping (irresponsible) fellow   334
compound settle   335 **he of both** the one of you two   336 **dower**
man's gift to bride   341 **lave** wash   342 **Tyrian** purple   344 **arras
counterpoints** counterpanes woven in Arras

345   Costly apparel, tents,° and canopies,
        Fine linen, Turkey cushions bossed° with pearl,
        Valance° of Venice gold in needlework,
        Pewter and brass, and all things that belongs
        To house or housekeeping. Then, at my farm
350   I have a hundred milch-kine to the pail,°
        Six score fat oxen standing in my stalls
        And all things answerable to this portion.°
        Myself am struck° in years, I must confess,
        And if I die tomorrow, this is hers,
355   If whilst I live she will be only mine.

    Tranio. That "only" came well in. Sir, list to me.
        I am my father's heir and only son.
        If I may have your daughter to my wife,
        I'll leave her houses three or four as good,
360   Within rich Pisa walls, as any one
        Old Signior Gremio has in Padua,
        Besides two thousand ducats° by the year
        Of° fruitful land, all which shall be her jointure.°
        What, have I pinched° you, Signior Gremio?

    Gremio. [Aside] Two thousand ducats by the year of
365   land!
        My land amounts not to so much in all.
        [To others] That she shall have besides an argosy°
        That now is lying in Marcellus' road.°
        What, have I choked you with an argosy?

370 Tranio. Gremio, 'tis known my father hath no less
        Than three great argosies, besides two galliasses°
        And twelve tight° galleys. These I will assure her
        And twice as much, whate'er thou off'rest next.

345 tents bed tester (hanging cover)   346 bossed embroidered   347
Valance bed fringes and drapes   350 milch-kine to the pail cows
producing milk for human use   352 answerable to this portion cor-
responding to this settlement (?)   353 struck advanced   362 ducats
Venetian gold coins   363 Of from   363 jointure settlement   364
pinched put the screws on   367 argosy largest type of merchant
ship   368 Marcellus' road Marseilles' harbor   371 galliasses large
galleys   372 tight watertight

Gremio. Nay, I have off'red all. I have no more,
　And she can have no more than all I have.　375
　If you like me, she shall have me and mine.

Tranio. Why, then the maid is mine from all the world
　By your firm promise. Gremio is outvied.°

Baptista. I must confess your offer is the best,
　And let your father make her the assurance,°　380
　She is your own; else you must pardon me.
　If you should die before him, where's her dower?

Tranio. That's but a cavil.° He is old, I young.

Gremio. And may not young men die as well as old?

Baptista. Well, gentlemen,　385
　I am thus resolved. On Sunday next, you know,
　My daughter Katherine is to be married.
　Now on the Sunday following shall Bianca
　Be bride to you if you make this assurance;
　If not, to Signior Gremio.　390
　And so I take my leave and thank you both.　*Exit.*

Gremio. Adieu, good neighbor. Now I fear thee not.
　Sirrah° young gamester,° your father were° a fool
　To give thee all and in his waning age
　Set foot under thy table.° Tut, a toy!°　395
　An old Italian fox is not so kind, my boy.　*Exit.*

Tranio. A vengeance on your crafty withered hide!
　Yet I have faced it with a card of ten.°
　'Tis in my head to do my master good.
　I see no reason but supposed Lucentio　400
　Must get° a father, called "supposed Vincentio,"
　And that's a wonder. Fathers commonly
　Do get their children, but in this case of wooing
　A child shall get a sire if I fail not of my cunning.
　　　　　　　　　　　　　　　　Exit.

---

378 **outvied** outbid　380 **assurance** guarantee　383 **cavil** small point
393 **Sirrah** (used contemptuously)　393 **gamester** gambler　393
were would be　395 **Set foot under thy table** be dependent on you
395 **a toy** a joke　398 **faced it with a card of ten** bluffed with a ten-
spot　401 **get** beget

ACT III

[Scene I. *Padua. In Baptista's house.*]

Enter Lucentio [as Cambio], Hortensio [as Litio],
and Bianca.

Lucentio. Fiddler, forbear. You grow too forward, sir.
Have you so soon forgot the entertainment°
Her sister Katherine welcomed you withal?

Hortensio. But, wrangling pedant, this is
5   The patroness of heavenly harmony.
Then give me leave to have prerogative,°
And when in music we have spent an hour,
Your lecture° shall have leisure for as much.

Lucentio. Preposterous° ass, that never read so far
10   To know the cause why music was ordained!
Was it not to refresh the mind of man
After his studies or his usual pain?°
Then give me leave to read° philosophy,
And while I pause, serve in your harmony.

Hortensio. Sirrah, I will not bear these braves° of
15   thine.

Bianca. Why, gentlemen, you do me double wrong
To strive for that which resteth in my choice.

III.i.2 **entertainment** i.e., "pillorying" him with the lute   6 **preroga-**
tive priority   8 **lecture** instruction   9 **Preposterous** putting later
things (*post-*) first (*pre-*)   12 **pain** labor   13 **read** give a lesson in
15 **braves** defiances

94

I am no breeching° scholar° in the schools.
I'll not be tied to hours nor 'pointed times,
But learn my lessons as I please myself.   20
And, to cut off all strife, here sit we down.
[*To Hortensio*] Take you your instrument, play you
    the whiles;°
His lecture will be done ere you have tuned.

Hortensio. You'll leave his lecture when I am in tune?

Lucentio. That will be never. Tune your instrument.   25

Bianca. Where left we last?

Lucentio. Here, madam:
    Hic ibat Simois, hic est Sigeia tellus,
        Hic steterat Priami regia celsa senis.°

Bianca. Conster° them.   30

Lucentio. Hic ibat, as I told you before, *Simois,* I am
    Lucentio, *hic est,* son unto Vincentio of Pisa, *Sigeia
    tellus,* disguised thus to get your love, *Hic steterat,*
    and that Lucentio that comes a wooing, *Priami,* is
    my man Tranio, *regia,* bearing my port,° *celsa senis,* 35
    that we might beguile the old pantaloon.°

Hortensio. [*Breaks in*] Madam, my instrument's in
    tune.

Bianca. Let's hear. O fie, the treble jars.°

Lucentio. Spit in the hole, man, and tune again.

Bianca. Now let me see if I can conster it. *Hic ibat*   40
    Simois, I know you not, *hic est Sigeia tellus,* I trust
    you not, *Hic steterat Priami,* take heed he hear us
    not, *regia,* presume not, *celsa senis,* despair not.

Hortensio. [*Breaks in again*] Madam, 'tis now in tune.

---

18 **breeching** (1) in breeches (young) (2) whippable 18 **scholar**
schoolboy 22 **the whiles** meanwhile 28–29 **Hic . . . senis** here
flowed the Simois, here is the Sigeian (Trojan) land, here had stood
old Priam's high palace (Ovid) 30 **Conster** construe 35 **bearing
my port** taking on my style 36 **pantaloon** Gremio (see I.i.47.s.d.
note) 38 **treble jars** highest tone is off

Lucentio.   All but the bass.

Hortensio. The bass is right; 'tis the base knave that
45   jars.
        [*Aside*] How fiery and forward our pedant is!
        Now, for my life, the knave doth court my love.
        Pedascule,° I'll watch you better yet.

Bianca. In time I may believe, yet I mistrust.

50 *Lucentio.* Mistrust it not, for sure Aeacides
        Was Ajax,° called so from his grandfather.

Bianca. I must believe my master; else, I promise you,
        I should be arguing still upon that doubt.
        But let it rest. Now, Litio, to you.
55   Good master, take it not unkindly, pray,
        That I have been thus pleasant° with you both.

Hortensio. [*To Lucentio*] You may go walk and give
        me leave° a while.
        My lessons make no music in three parts.°

Lucentio. Are you so formal, sir? [*Aside*] Well, I
        must wait
60   And watch withal,° for but° I be deceived,
        Our fine musician groweth amorous.

Hortensio. Madam, before you touch the instrument,
        To learn the order of my fingering,
        I must begin with rudiments of art
65   To teach you gamut° in a briefer sort,
        More pleasant, pithy, and effectual,
        Than hath been taught by any of my trade;
        And there it is in writing, fairly drawn.

Bianca. Why, I am past my gamut long ago.

70 *Hortensio.* Yet read the gamut of Hortensio.

48 **Pedascule** little pedant (disparaging quasi-Latin)   50–51 **Aea-
cides/Was Ajax** Ajax, Greek warrior at Troy, was grandson of
Aeacus (Lucentio comments on next passage in Ovid)   56 **pleasant**
merry   57 **give me leave** leave me alone   58 **in three parts** for three
voices   60 **withal** besides   60 **but** unless   65 **gamut** the scale

Bianca. [*Reads*]

> *Gamut* I am, the ground° of all accord.°
>   *A re,* to plead Hortensio's passion:
> *B mi,* Bianca, take him for thy lord,
>   *C fa ut,* that loves with all affection;
> *D sol re,* one clef, two notes have I: 75
>   *E la mi,* show pity or I die.

> Call you this gamut? Tut, I like it not.
> Old fashions please me best; I am not so nice°
> To change true rules for odd inventions.

Enter a Messenger.

Messenger. Mistress, your father prays you leave your
   books   80
And help to dress your sister's chamber up.
You know tomorrow is the wedding day.

Bianca. Farewell, sweet masters both, I must be gone.
            [*Exeunt Bianca and Messenger.*]

Lucentio. Faith, mistress, then I have no cause to stay.
            [*Exit.*]

Hortensio. But I have cause to pry into this pedant.   85
   Methinks he looks as though he were in love.
   Yet if thy thoughts, Bianca, be so humble
   To cast thy wand'ring eyes on every stale,°
   Seize thee that list.° If once I find thee ranging,°
   Hortensio will be quit with thee by changing.° *Exit.*   90

71 **ground** beginning, first note   71 **accord** harmony   78 **nice**
whimsical   88 **stale** lure (as in hunting)   89 **Seize thee that list** let
him who likes capture you   89 **ranging** going astray   90 **changing**
i.e., sweethearts

[Scene II. *Padua. The street in front of
Baptista's house.*]

*Enter Baptista, Gremio, Tranio [as Lucentio], Kate,
Bianca, [Lucentio as Cambio]
and others, Attendants.*

Baptista. [*To Tranio*] Signior Lucentio, this is the
        'pointed day
    That Katherine and Petruchio should be marrièd,
    And yet we hear not of our son-in-law.
    What will be said? What mockery will it be
5   To want° the bridegroom when the priest attends
    To speak the ceremonial rites of marriage!
    What says Lucentio to this shame of ours?

Kate. No shame but mine. I must, forsooth, be forced
    To give my hand opposed against my heart
10 Unto a mad-brain rudesby,° full of spleen,°
    Who wooed in haste and means to wed at leisure.
    I told you, I, he was a frantic fool,
    Hiding his bitter jests in blunt behavior.
    And to be noted for° a merry man,
15 He'll woo a thousand, 'point the day of marriage,
    Make friends, invite,° and proclaim the banns,
    Yet never means to wed where he hath wooed.
    Now must the world point at poor Katherine
    And say, "Lo, there is mad Petruchio's wife,
20 If it would please him come and marry her."

Tranio. Patience, good Katherine, and Baptista too.
    Upon my life, Petruchio means but well,
    Whatever fortune stays° him from his word.

III.ii.5 **want** be without   10 **rudesby** uncouth fellow   10 **spleen**
caprice   14 **noted for** reputed   16 **Make friends, invite** (some editors emend to "Make feast, invite friends")   23 **stays** keeps

    Though he be blunt, I know him passing° wise;
    Though he be merry, yet withal he's honest.   25

Kate. Would Katherine had never seen him though!
    Exit weeping [followed by Bianca and others].

Baptista. Go, girl, I cannot blame thee now to weep.
    For such an injury would vex a very saint,
    Much more a shrew of thy impatient humor.°

         Enter Biondello.

Biondello. Master, master, news! And such old° news   30
    as you never heard of!

Baptista. Is it new and old too? How may that be?

Biondello. Why, is it not news to hear of Petruchio's
    coming?

Baptista. Is he come?   35

Biondello. Why, no, sir.

Baptista. What then?

Biondello. He is coming.

Baptista. When will he be here?

Biondello. When he stands where I am and sees you   40
    there.

Tranio. But, say, what to thine old news?

Biondello. Why, Petruchio is coming in a new hat and
    an old jerkin;° a pair of old breeches thrice turned;°
    a pair of boots that have been candle-cases,° one   45
    buckled, another laced; an old rusty sword ta'en
    out of the town armory, with a broken hilt and
    chapeless;° with two broken points;° his horse
    hipped° (with an old mothy saddle and stirrups of

24 **passing** very   29 **humor** temper   30 **old** strange   44 **jerkin** short
outer coat   44 **turned** i.e., inside out (to conceal wear and tear)   45
candle-cases worn-out boots used to keep candle ends in   48 **chape-**
less lacking the metal mounting at end of scabbard   48 **points** laces
to fasten hose to garment above   49 **hipped** with dislocated hip

50   no kindred),° besides, possessed with the glanders°
      and like to mose in the chine;° troubled with the
      lampass,° infected with the fashions,° full of wind-
      galls,° sped with spavins,° rayed° with the yellows,°
      past cure of the fives,° stark spoiled with the stag-
55   gers,° begnawn with the bots,° swayed° in the
      back, and shoulder-shotten;° near-legged before,°
      and with a half-cheeked° bit and a head-stall° of
      sheep's leather,° which, being restrained° to keep
      him from stumbling, hath been often burst and
60   now repaired with knots; one girth° six times
      pieced,° and a woman's crupper° of velure,° which
      hath two letters for her name fairly set down in
      studs,° and here and there pieced with packthread.°

Baptista. Who comes with him?

65 *Biondello.* O sir, his lackey, for all the world capari-
      soned° like the horse: with a linen stock° on one
      leg and a kersey boot-hose° on the other, gart'red
      with a red and blue list;° an old hat, and the humor
      of forty fancies° pricked° in't for a feather—a mon-
70   ster, a very monster in apparel, and not like a Chris-
      tian footboy° or a gentleman's lackey.

49–50 **of no kindred** not matching   50 **glanders** bacterial disease
affecting mouth and nose   51 **mose in the chine** (1) glanders (2)
nasal discharge   52 **lampass** swollen mouth   52 **fashions** tumors
(related to glanders)   52–53 **windgalls** swellings on lower leg   53
spavins swellings on upper hind leg   53 **rayed** soiled   53 **yellows**
jaundice   54 **fives** vives: swelling of submaxillary glands   54–55
staggers nervous disorder causing loss of balance   55 **begnawn with
the bots** gnawed by parasitic worms (larvae of the botfly)   55
swayed sagging   56 **shoulder-shotten** with dislocated shoulder   56
near-legged before with forefeet knocking together   57 **half-cheeked**
wrongly adjusted to bridle and affording less control   57 **head-stall**
part of bridle which surrounds head   58 **sheep's leather** (weaker
than pigskin)   58 **restrained** pulled back   60 **girth** saddle strap
under belly   61 **pieced** patched   61 **crupper** leather loop under
horse's tail to help steady saddle   61 **velure** velvet   63 **studs** large-
headed nails of brass or silver   63 **pieced with packthread** tied together with coarse thread   65–66 **caparisoned** outfitted   66 **stock**
stocking   67 **kersey boot-hose** coarse stocking worn with riding boot
68 **list** strip of discarded border-cloth   68–69 **humor of forty fancies** fanciful decoration (in place of feather)   69 **pricked** pinned
71 **footboy** page in livery

Tranio. 'Tis some odd humor° pricks° him to this
   fashion,
  Yet oftentimes he goes but mean-appareled.

Baptista. I am glad he's come, howsoe'er he comes.

Biondello. Why, sir, he comes not.   75

Baptista. Didst thou not say he comes?

Biondello. Who? That Petruchio came?

Baptista. Ay, that Petruchio came.

Biondello. No, sir, I say his horse comes, with him
   on his back.   80

Baptista. Why, that's all one.°

Biondello. [*Sings*]

            Nay, by Saint Jamy,
            I hold° you a penny,
            A horse and a man
            Is more than one   85
            And yet not many.

         Enter Petruchio and Grumio.

Petruchio. Come, where be these gallants?° Who's at
   home?

Baptista. You are welcome, sir.

Petruchio.   And yet I come not well.

Baptista. And yet you halt° not.

Tranio.   Not so well appareled
  As I wish you were.   90

Petruchio. Were it better,° I should rush in thus.
  But where is Kate? Where is my lovely bride?
  How does my father? Gentles,° methinks you frown.

72 **humor** mood, fancy   72 **pricks** incites   81 **all one** the same thing
83 **hold** bet   87 **gallants** men of fashion   89 **halt** limp (pun on
come meaning "walk")   91 **Were it better** even if I were better   93
Gentles sirs

And wherefore gaze this goodly company
95   As if they saw some wondrous monument,°
Some comet or unusual prodigy?°

Baptista. Why, sir, you know this is your wedding day.
First were we sad, fearing you would not come,
Now sadder that you come so unprovided.°
100   Fie, doff this habit,° shame to your estate,°
An eyesore to our solemn festival.

Tranio. And tell us what occasion of import°
Hath all so long detained you from your wife
And sent you hither so unlike yourself.

105 *Petruchio.* Tedious it were to tell and harsh to hear.
Sufficeth, I am come to keep my word
Though in some part enforcèd to digress,°
Which, at more leisure, I will so excuse
As you shall well be satisfied with all.
110   But where is Kate? I stay too long from her.
The morning wears, 'tis time we were at church.

Tranio. See not your bride in these unreverent robes.
Go to my chamber; put on clothes of mine.

Petruchio. Not I, believe me; thus I'll visit her.

115 *Baptista.* But thus, I trust, you will not marry her.

Petruchio. Good sooth,° even thus; therefore ha' done
with words.
To me she's married, not unto my clothes.
Could I repair what she will wear° in me
As I can change these poor accoutrements,
120   'Twere well for Kate and better for myself.
But what a fool am I to chat with you
When I should bid good morrow to my bride
And seal the title° with a lovely° kiss.

                               Exit [with Grumio].

95 monument warning sign   **96 prodigy** marvel   **99 unprovided** ill-
outfitted   **100 habit** costume   **100 estate** status   **102 of import** important   **107 enforcèd to digress** forced to depart (perhaps from
his plan to "buy apparel 'gainst the wedding day," II.i.308)   **116
Good sooth** yes indeed   **118 wear** wear out   **123 title** i.e., as of
ownership   **123 lovely** loving

Tranio. He hath some meaning in his mad attire.
　We will persuade him, be it possible,   125
　To put on better ere he go to church.

Baptista. I'll after him and see the event° of this.
　　　　　　Exit [with Gremio and Attendants].

Tranio. But to her love concerneth us to add
　Her father's liking, which to bring to pass,
　As I before imparted to your worship,   130
　I am to get a man—whate'er he be
　It skills° not much, we'll fit him to our turn°—
　And he shall be Vincentio of Pisa,
　And make assurance° here in Padua
　Of greater sums than I have promisèd.   135
　So shall you quietly enjoy your hope
　And marry sweet Bianca with consent.

Lucentio. Were it not that my fellow schoolmaster
　Doth watch Bianca's steps so narrowly,
　'Twere good, methinks, to steal our marriage,°   140
　Which once performed, let all the world say no,
　I'll keep mine own despite of all the world.

Tranio. That by degrees we mean to look into
　And watch our vantage° in this business.
　We'll overreach° the graybeard, Gremio,   145
　The narrow-prying father, Minola,
　The quaint° musician, amorous Litio—
　All for my master's sake, Lucentio.

　　　　　　Enter Gremio.

　Signior Gremio, came you from the church?

Gremio. As willingly as e'er I came from school.   150

Tranio. And is the bride and bridegroom coming
　home?

Gremio. A bridegroom say you? 'Tis a groom° indeed,

127 **event** upshot, outcome   132 **skills** matters   132 **turn** purpose
134 **assurance** guarantee   140 **steal our marriage** elope   144 **vantage** advantage   145 **overreach** get the better of   147 **quaint** artful
152 **groom** menial (i.e., coarse fellow)

A grumbling groom, and that the girl shall find.

Tranio. Curster than she? Why, 'tis impossible.

155 *Gremio.* Why, he's a devil, a devil, a very fiend.

Tranio. Why, she's a devil, a devil, the devil's dam.°

Gremio. Tut, she's a lamb, a dove, a fool to° him.
I'll tell you, Sir Lucentio, when the priest
Should ask, if Katherine should be his wife,
"Ay, by goggs woones!"° quoth he and swore so
160   loud
That, all amazed, the priest let fall the book,
And as he stooped again to take it up,
This mad-brained bridegroom took° him such a cuff
That down fell priest and book and book and priest.
165 "Now, take them up," quoth he, "if any list."°

Tranio. What said the wench when he rose again?

Gremio. Trembled and shook, for why° he stamped
        and swore
As if the vicar meant to cozen° him.
But after many ceremonies done
170 He calls for wine. "A health!" quoth he as if
He had been aboard, carousing° to his mates
After a storm; quaffed off the muscadel°
And threw the sops° all in the sexton's face,
Having no other reason
175 But that his beard grew thin and hungerly,°
And seemed to ask him sops as he was drinking.
This done, he took the bride about the neck
And kissed her lips with such a clamorous smack
That at the parting all the church did echo,
180 And I, seeing this, came thence for very shame.

156 **dam** mother   157 **fool to** harmless person compared with   160
goggs woones by God's wounds (a common oath)   163 **took** gave
165 **list** pleases to   167 **for why** because   168 **cozen** cheat   171
carousing calling "Bottoms up"   172 **muscadel** sweet wine, conven-
tionally drunk after marriage service   173 **sops** pieces of cake
soaked in wine; dregs   175 **hungerly** as if poorly nourished

And after me, I know, the rout° is coming.
Such a mad marriage never was before.
Hark, hark, I hear the minstrels play. *Music plays.*

*Enter Petruchio, Kate, Bianca, Hortensio [as Litio],
Baptista [with Grumio and others].*

Petruchio. Gentlemen and friends, I thank you for
    your pains.
I know you think to dine with me today   185
And have prepared great store of wedding cheer,°
But so it is, my haste doth call me hence
And therefore here I mean to take my leave.

Baptista. Is't possible you will away tonight?

Petruchio. I must away today, before night come.   190
Make it no wonder;° if you knew my business,
You would entreat me rather go than stay.
And, honest company, I thank you all
That have beheld me give away myself
To this most patient, sweet, and virtuous wife.   195
Dine with my father, drink a health to me,
For I must hence, and farewell to you all.

Tranio. Let us entreat you stay till after dinner.

Petruchio. It may not be.

Gremio.   Let me entreat you.

Petruchio. It cannot be.

Kate.   Let me entreat you.   200

Petruchio. I am content.

Kate.   Are you content to stay?

Petruchio. I am content you shall entreat me stay,
    But yet not stay, entreat me how you can.

Kate. Now if you love me, stay.

Petruchio.   Grumio, my horse!°

181 **rout** crowd   186 **cheer** food and drink   191 **Make it no wonder**
don't be surprised   204 **horse** horses

205 *Grumio.* Ay, sir, they be ready; the oats have eaten
the horses.°

Kate. Nay then,
Do what thou canst, I will not go today,
No, nor tomorrow, not till I please myself.
210 The door is open, sir, there lies your way.
You may be jogging whiles your boots are green;°
For me, I'll not be gone till I please myself.
'Tis like you'll prove a jolly° surly groom,
That take it on you° at the first so roundly.°

Petruchio. O Kate, content thee; prithee,° be not
215 angry.

Kate. I will be angry. What hast thou to do?°
Father, be quiet; he shall stay my leisure.°

Gremio. Ay, marry, sir, now it begins to work.

Kate. Gentlemen, forward to the bridal dinner.
220 I see a woman may be made a fool
If she had not a spirit to resist.

Petruchio. They shall go forward, Kate, at thy com-
mand.
Obey the bride, you that attend on her.
Go to the feast, revel and domineer,°
225 Carouse full measure to her maidenhead,
Be mad and merry, or go hang yourselves.
But for my bonny Kate, she must with me.
Nay, look not big,° nor stamp, nor stare,° nor fret;
I will be master of what is mine own.
230 She is my goods, my chattels; she is my house,
My household stuff, my field, my barn,
My horse, my ox, my ass, my anything,°

205–06 **oats have eaten the horses** (1) a slip of the tongue or (2) an
ironic jest   211 **You ... green** (proverbial way of suggesting de-
parture to a guest, *green* = new, cleaned)   213 **jolly** domineering
214 **take it on you** do as you please   214 **roundly** roughly   215
prithee I pray thee   216 **What hast thou to do** what do you have to
do with it   217 **stay my leisure** await my willingness   224 **domineer**
cut up in a lordly fashion   228 **big** challenging   228 **stare** swagger
232 **My horse ... anything** (echoing Tenth Commandment)

And here she stands. Touch her whoever dare,
I'll bring mine action° on the proudest he
That stops my way in Padua. Grumio,   235
Draw forth thy weapon, we are beset with thieves.
Rescue thy mistress, if thou be a man.
Fear not, sweet wench; they shall not touch thee,
    Kate.
I'll buckler° thee against a million.
                Exeunt Petruchio, Kate [and Grumio].

Baptista. Nay, let them go, a couple of quiet ones.   240

Gremio. Went they not quickly, I should die with
    laughing.

Tranio. Of all mad matches never was the like.

Lucentio. Mistress, what's your opinion of your sister?

Bianca. That being mad herself, she's madly mated.

Gremio. I warrant him, Petruchio is Kated.   245

Baptista. Neighbors and friends, though bride and
    bridegroom wants°
For to supply the places at the table,
You know there wants no junkets° at the feast.
[*To Tranio*] Lucentio, you shall supply the bride-
    groom's place,
And let Bianca take her sister's room.   250

Tranio. Shall sweet Bianca practice how to bride it?

Baptista. She shall, Lucentio. Come, gentlemen, let's
    go.   *Exeunt.*

---

234 **action** lawsuit   239 **buckler** shield   246 **wants** are lacking   248
junkets sweetmeats, confections

[ACT IV

Scene I. *Petruchio's country house.*]

Enter Grumio.

Grumio. Fie, fie, on all tired jades,° on all mad masters, and all foul ways!° Was ever man so beaten?
Was ever man so rayed?° Was ever man so weary?
I am sent before to make a fire, and they are coming
after to warm them. Now were not I a little pot and
soon hot,° my very lips might freeze to my teeth,
my tongue to the roof of my mouth, my heart in my
belly, ere I should come by a fire to thaw me. But I
with blowing the fire shall warm myself, for con-
sidering the weather, a taller° man than I will take
cold. Holla, ho, Curtis!

Enter Curtis [a Servant].

Curtis. Who is that calls so coldly?

Grumio. A piece of ice. If thou doubt it, thou mayst
slide from my shoulder to my heel with no greater
a run° but my head and my neck. A fire, good
Curtis.

Curtis. Is my master and his wife coming, Grumio?

IV.i.1 **jades** worthless horses   2 **foul ways** bad roads   3 **rayed** be-
fouled   5–6 **little pot and soon hot** (proverbial for small person of
short temper)   10 **taller** sturdier (with allusion to "little pot")   15
run running start

108

Grumio. O ay, Curtis, ay, and therefore fire, fire;
cast on no water.°

Curtis. Is she so hot a shrew as she's reported?   20

Grumio. She was, good Curtis, before this frost, but
thou know'st winter tames man, woman, and beast;
for it hath tamed my old master, and my new mistress, and myself, fellow Curtis.

Curtis. Away, you three-inch° fool! I am no beast.   25

Grumio. Am I but three inches? Why, thy horn° is a
foot, and so long am I at the least. But wilt thou
make a fire, or shall I complain on thee to our mistress, whose hand—she being now at hand—thou
shalt soon feel, to thy cold comfort, for being slow   30
in thy hot office?°

Curtis. I prithee, good Grumio, tell me, how goes
the world?

Grumio. A cold world, Curtis, in every office but
thine, and therefore, fire. Do thy duty and have thy   35
duty,° for my master and mistress are almost frozen
to death.

Curtis. There's fire ready, and therefore, good Grumio,
the news.

Grumio. Why, "Jack boy, ho boy!"° and as much   40
news as wilt thou.

Curtis. Come, you are so full of cony-catching.°

Grumio. Why therefore fire, for I have caught extreme
cold. Where's the cook? Is supper ready, the house
trimmed, rushes strewed,° cobwebs swept, the serv-   45

---

19 **cast on no water** (alters "Cast on more water" in a well-known
round)   25 **three-inch** (1) another allusion to Grumio's small stature (2) a phallic jest, the first of several   26 **horn** (symbol of cuckold)   31 **hot office** job of making a fire   35–36 **thy duty** what is
due thee   40 **"Jack boy, ho boy!"** (from another round or catch)
42 **cony-catching** rabbit-catching (i.e., tricking simpletons; with pun
on *catch*, the song)   45 **strewed** i.e., on floor (for special occasion)

ingmen in their new fustian,° the white stockings,
and every officer° his wedding garment on? Be the
jacks° fair within, the jills° fair without, the car-
pets° laid and everything in order?

50 *Curtis.* All ready, and therefore, I pray thee, news.

Grumio. First, know my horse is tired, my master and
mistress fall'n out.

Curtis. How?

Grumio. Out of their saddles into the dirt—and
55 thereby hangs a tale.

Curtis. Let's ha't, good Grumio.

Grumio. Lend thine ear.

Curtis. Here.

Grumio. There.   [*Strikes him.*]

60 *Curtis.* This 'tis to feel a tale, not to hear a tale.

Grumio. And therefore 'tis called a sensible° tale, and
this cuff was but to knock at your ear and beseech
list'ning. Now I begin. *Imprimis,*° we came down
a foul° hill, my master riding behind my mistress—

65 *Curtis.* Both of° one horse?

Grumio. What's that to thee?

Curtis. Why, a horse.

Grumio. Tell thou the tale. But hadst thou not
crossed° me thou shouldst have heard how her
70 horse fell and she under her horse. Thou shouldst
hàve heard in how miry a place, how she was bemoiled,° how he left her with the horse upon her,
how he beat me because her horse stumbled, how

46 **fustian** coarse cloth (cotton and flax)   47 **officer** servant   48
jacks (1) menservants (2) half-pint leather drinking cups   48 **jills**
(1) maids (2) gill-size metal drinking cups   48–49 **carpets** table
covers   61 **sensible** (1) rational (2) "feel"-able   63 **Imprimis** first
64 **foul** muddy   65 **of** on   69 **crossed** interrupted   72 **bemoiled**
muddied

she waded through the dirt to pluck him off me;
how he swore, how she prayed that never prayed   *75*
before; how I cried, how the horses ran away, how
her bridle was burst, how I lost my crupper, with
many things of worthy memory which now shall
die in oblivion, and thou return unexperienced° to
thy grave.   *80*

Curtis. By this reck'ning° he is more shrew than she.

Grumio. Ay, and that thou and the proudest of you
all shall find when he comes home. But what° talk
I of this? Call forth Nathaniel, Joseph, Nicholas,
Philip, Walter, Sugarsop, and the rest. Let their   *85*
heads be slickly° combed, their blue° coats brushed,
and their garters of an indifferent° knit. Let them
curtsy with their left legs and not presume to touch
a hair of my master's horsetail till they kiss their
hands. Are they all ready?   *90*

Curtis. They are.

Grumio. Call them forth.

Curtis. Do you hear, ho? You must meet my master
to countenance° my mistress.

Grumio. Why, she hath a face of her own.   *95*

Curtis. Who knows not that?

Grumio. Thou, it seems, that calls for company to
countenance her.

Curtis. I call them forth to credit° her.

Grumio. Why, she comes to borrow nothing of them.   *100*

Enter four or five Servingmen.

Nathaniel. Welcome home, Grumio!

---

79 **unexperienced** uninformed   81 **reck'ning** account   83 **what** why
86 **slickly** smoothly   86 **blue** (usual color of servants' clothing)   87
indifferent matching (?) appropriate (?)   94 **countenance** show respect to (with puns following)   99 **credit** honor

Philip. How now, Grumio?

Joseph. What, Grumio!

Nicholas. Fellow Grumio!

105 *Nathaniel.* How now, old lad!

Grumio. Welcome, you; how now, you; what, you;
   fellow, you; and thus much for greeting. Now, my
   spruce companions, is all ready and all things neat?

Nathaniel. All things is ready. How near is our
110   master?

Grumio. E'en at hand, alighted by this,° and therefore be not—Cock's° passion, silence! I hear my
   master.

Enter Petruchio and Kate.

Petruchio. Where be these knaves? What, no man at
   door
115   To hold my stirrup nor to take my horse?
   Where is Nathaniel, Gregory, Philip?

All Servingmen. Here, here, sir, here, sir.

Petruchio. Here, sir, here, sir, here, sir, here, sir!
   You loggerheaded° and unpolished grooms!
120   What, no attendance? No regard? No duty?
   Where is the foolish knave I sent before?

Grumio. Here, sir, as foolish as I was before.

Petruchio. You peasant swain!° You whoreson° malt-
   horse drudge!°
   Did I not bid thee meet me in the park°
125   And bring along these rascal knaves with thee?

Grumio. Nathaniel's coat, sir, was not fully made
   And Gabrel's pumps were all unpinked° i' th' heel.

---

111 **this** now   112 **Cock's** God's (i.e., Christ's)   119 **loggerheaded**
blockheaded   123 **swain** bumpkin   123 **whoreson** bastardly   123
malt-horse drudge slow horse on brewery treadmill   124 **park** coun-
try-house grounds   127 **unpinked** lacking embellishment made by
pinking (making small holes in leather)

There was no link° to color Peter's hat,
And Walter's dagger was not come from sheathing.°
There were none fine but Adam, Rafe, and Gregory;   130
The rest were ragged, old, and beggarly.
Yet, as they are, here are they come to meet you.

Petruchio. Go, rascals, go, and fetch my supper in.
                              Exeunt Servants.

[*Sings*] "Where is the life that late I led?"°

Where are those°—Sit down, Kate, and welcome.   135
   Soud,° soud, soud, soud!

                Enter Servants with supper.

Why, when,° I say?—Nay, good sweet Kate, be
   merry.—
Off with my boots, you rogues, you villains! When?
[*Sings*] "It was the friar of orders gray,
As he forth walkèd on his way"°—   140
Out, you rogue, you pluck my foot awry!
Take that, and mend° the plucking of the other.
                              [*Strikes him.*]
Be merry, Kate. Some water here! What ho!

                Enter one with water.

Where's my spaniel Troilus? Sirrah, get you hence
And bid my cousin Ferdinand come hither—   145
                              [*Exit Servant.*]
One, Kate, that you must kiss and be acquainted with.
Where are my slippers? Shall I have some water?
Come, Kate, and wash, and welcome heartily.
You whoreson villain, will you let it fall?
                              [*Strikes him.*]

Kate. Patience, I pray you. 'Twas a fault unwilling.   150

Petruchio. A whoreson, beetle-headed,° flap-eared
   knave!

128 **link** torch, providing blacking   129 **sheathing** repairing scabbard   134 **"Where . . . led?"** (from an old ballad)   135 **those**
servants   136 **Soud** (exclamation variously explained; some editors
emend to *Food*)   137 **when** (exclamation of annoyance, as in next
line)   139–40 **"It was . . . his way"** (from another old song)   142
mend improve   151 **beetle-headed** mallet-headed

Come, Kate, sit down; I know you have a stomach.°
Will you give thanks,° sweet Kate, or else shall I?
What's this? Mutton?

First Servingman.　　　Ay.

Petruchio.　　　　　　　Who brought it?

Peter.　　　　　　　　　　　　　　　I.

155　*Petruchio.* 'Tis burnt, and so is all the meat.
　　What dogs are these! Where is the rascal cook?
　　How durst you, villains, bring it from the dresser,°
　　And serve it thus to me that love it not?
　　There, take it to you, trenchers,° cups, and all,
　　　　　　　　　　　[*Throws food and dishes at them.*]
160　You heedless joltheads° and unmannered slaves!
　　What, do you grumble? I'll be with° you straight.°

Kate. I pray you, husband, be not so disquiet.
　　The meat was well if you were so contented.°

Petruchio. I tell thee, Kate, 'twas burnt and dried away,
165　And I expressly am forbid to touch it,
　　For it engenders choler,° planteth anger,
　　And better 'twere that both of us did fast—
　　Since of ourselves, ourselves are choleric°—
　　Than feed it° with such overroasted flesh.
170　Be patient. Tomorrow't shall be mended,°
　　And for this night we'll fast for company.°
　　Come, I will bring thee to thy bridal chamber.
　　　　　　　　　　　　　　　　Exeunt.

Enter Servants severally.

Nathaniel. Peter, didst ever see the like?

Peter. He kills her in her own humor.°

152 **stomach** (1) hunger (2) irascibility　153 **give thanks** say grace
157 **dresser** sideboard　159 **trenchers** wooden platters　160 **jolt-
heads** boneheads (*jolt* is related to *jaw* or *jowl*)　161 **with** even with
161 **straight** directly　163 **so contented** willing to see it as it was
166 **choler** bile, the "humor" (fluid) supposed to produce anger
168 **choleric** bilious, i.e., hot-tempered　169 **it** i.e., their choler　170
't shall be mended things will be better　171 **for company** together
174 **kills her in her own humor** conquers her by using her own disposition

Enter Curtis, a Servant.

Grumio. Where is he?   173

Curtis. In her chamber, making a sermon of continency
    to her,
And rails and swears and rates,° that she, poor soul,
Knows not which way to stand, to look, to speak,
And sits as one new-risen from a dream.   180
Away, away, for he is coming hither.   [*Exeunt.*]

Enter Petruchio.

Petruchio. Thus have I politicly° begun my reign,
And 'tis my hope to end successfully.
My falcon° now is sharp° and passing empty,
And till she stoop° she must not be full gorged,°   185
For then she never looks upon her lure.°
Another way I have to man° my haggard,°
To make her come and know her keeper's call,
That is, to watch° her as we watch these kites°
That bate and beat° and will not be obedient.   190
She eat° no meat today, nor none shall eat.
Last night she slept not, nor tonight she shall not.
As with the meat, some undeservèd fault
I'll find about the making of the bed,
And here I'll fling the pillow, there the bolster,°   195
This way the coverlet, another way the sheets.
Ay, and amid this hurly° I intend°
That all is done in reverent care of her,
And in conclusion she shall watch° all night.
And if she chance to nod I'll rail and brawl   200
And with the clamor keep her still awake.

178 **rates** scolds   182 **politicly** with a calculated plan   184 **falcon**
hawk trained for hunting (falconry figures continue for seven lines)
184 **sharp** pinched with hunger   185 **stoop** (1) obey (2) swoop to
the lure   185 **full gorged** fully fed   186 **lure** device used in training
a hawk to return from flight   187 **man** (1) tame (2) be a man to
187 **haggard** hawk captured after reaching maturity   189 **watch**
keep from sleep   189 **kites** type of small hawk   190 **bate and beat**
flap and flutter (i.e., in jittery resistance to training)   191 **eat** ate
(pronounced *et*, as still in Britain)   195 **bolster** cushion extending
width of bed as under-support for pillows   197 **hurly** disturbance
197 **intend** profess   199 **watch** stay awake

This is a way to kill a wife with kindness,°
And thus I'll curb her mad and headstrong humor.
He that knows better how to tame a shrew,°
205   Now let him speak—'tis charity to show.   *Exit.*

[Scene II. *Padua. The street in front of
Baptista's house.*]

Enter Tranio [as Lucentio] and Hortensio [as Litio].

Tranio. Is't possible, friend Litio, that Mistress Bianca
Doth fancy° any other but Lucentio?
I tell you, sir, she bears me fair in hand.°

Hortensio. Sir, to satisfy you in what I have said,
5   Stand by and mark the manner of his teaching.
                    [*They eavesdrop.*]

Enter Bianca [and Lucentio as Cambio].

Lucentio. Now mistress, profit you in what you read?

Bianca. What, master, read you? First resolve° me that.

Lucentio. I read that° I profess,° the Art to Love.°

Bianca. And may you prove, sir, master of your art.

Lucentio. While you, sweet dear, prove mistress of my
10   heart.   [*They court.*]

Hortensio. Quick proceeders,° marry!° Now, tell me,
        I pray,
You that durst swear that your mistress Bianca
Loved none in the world so well as Lucentio.

202 **kill a wife with kindness** (ironic allusion to proverb on ruining a
wife by pampering) 204 **shrew** (rhymes with "show") IV.ii.2 **fancy**
like 3 **bears me fair in hand** leads me on 7 **resolve** answer 8 **that**
what 8 **profess** avow, practice 8 **Art to Love** (i.e., Ovid's *Ars
Amandi*) 11 **proceeders** (pun on idiom "proceed Master of Arts";
cf. line 9) 11 **marry** by Mary (mild exclamation)

Tranio. O despiteful° love! Unconstant womankind!
I tell thee, Litio, this is wonderful.°   13

Hortensio. Mistake no more. I am not Litio,
Nor a musician, as I seem to be,
But one that scorn to live in this disguise,
For such a one as leaves a gentleman
And makes a god of such a cullion.°   20
Know, sir, that I am called Hortensio.

Tranio. Signior Hortensio, I have often heard
Of your entire affection to Bianca,
And since mine eyes are witness of her lightness,°
I will with you, if you be so contented,   25
Forswear° Bianca and her love forever.

Hortensio. See, how they kiss and court! Signior
    Lucentio,
Here is my hand and here I firmly vow
Never to woo her more, but do forswear her,
As one unworthy all the former favors°   30
That I have fondly° flattered her withal.

Tranio. And here I take the like unfeignèd oath,
Never to marry with her though she would entreat.
Fie on her! See how beastly° she doth court him.

Hortensio. Would all the world but he had quite for-
    sworn.°   35
For me, that I may surely keep mine oath,
I will be married to a wealthy widow
Ere three days pass, which° hath as long loved me
As I have loved this proud disdainful haggard.°
And so farewell, Signior Lucentio.   40
Kindness in women, not their beauteous looks,
Shall win my love, and so I take my leave
In resolution as I swore before.   [*Exit.*]

---

14 **despiteful** spiteful   15 **wonderful** causing wonder   20 **cullion**
low fellow (literally, testicle)   24 **lightness** (cf. "light woman")   26
Forswear "swear off"   30 **favors** marks of esteem   31 **fondly** foolishly   34 **beastly** unashamedly   35 **Would . . . forsworn** i.e., would
she had only one lover   38 **which** who   39 **haggard** (cf. IV.i.187)

Tranio. Mistress Bianca, bless you with such grace
45   As 'longeth to a lover's blessèd case.
      Nay, I have ta'en you napping,° gentle love,
      And have forsworn you with Hortensio.

Bianca. Tranio, you jest. But have you both forsworn
      me?

Tranio. Mistress, we have.

Lucentio.   Then we are rid of Litio.

50   *Tranio.* I' faith, he'll have a lusty° widow now,
      That shall be wooed and wedded in a day.

Bianca. God give him joy!

Tranio. Ay, and he'll tame her.

Bianca.   He says so, Tranio.

Tranio. Faith, he is gone unto the taming school.

Bianca. The taming school! What, is there such a
55   place?

Tranio. Ay, mistress, and Petruchio is the master,
      That teacheth tricks eleven and twenty long°
      To tame a shrew and charm her chattering tongue.

Enter Biondello.

Biondello. O master, master, I have watched so long
60   That I am dog-weary, but at last I spied
      An ancient angel° coming down the hill
      Will serve the turn.°

Tranio.   What° is he, Biondello?

Biondello. Master, a mercatante° or a pedant,°
      I know not what, but formal in apparel,

46 **ta'en you napping** seen you "kiss and court" (line 27)   50 **lusty**
lively   57 **tricks eleven and twenty long** (1) many tricks (2) possibly
an allusion to card game "thirty-one" (cf.I.i.33)   61 **ancient angel**
man of good old stamp (*angel* = coin; cf. "gentleman of the old
school")   62 **Will serve the turn** who will do for our purposes   62
What what kind of man   63 **mercatante** merchant   63 **pedant**
schoolmaster

In gait and countenance° surely like a father.   *65*

Lucentio. And what of him, Tranio?

Tranio. If he be credulous and trust my tale,
I'll make him glad to seem Vincentio,
And give assurance to Baptista Minola
As if he were the right Vincentio.   *70*
Take in your love and then let me alone.
                    [*Exeunt Lucentio and Bianca.*]

                    Enter a Pedant.

Pedant. God save you, sir.

Tranio.   And you, sir. You are welcome.
Travel you far on, or are you at the farthest?

Pedant. Sir, at the farthest for a week or two,
But then up farther and as far as Rome,   *75*
And so to Tripoli if God lend me life.

Tranio. What countryman,° I pray?

Pedant.   Of Mantua.

Tranio. Of Mantua, sir? Marry, God forbid!
And come to Padua, careless of your life?

Pedant. My life, sir? How, I pray? For that goes
hard.°   *80*

Tranio. 'Tis death for anyone in Mantua
To come to Padua. Know you not the cause?
Your ships are stayed° at Venice and the Duke,
For private quarrel 'twixt your duke and him,
Hath published and proclaimed it openly.   *85*
'Tis marvel, but that you are but newly come,
You might have heard it else proclaimed about.

Pedant. Alas, sir, it is worse for me than so,°
For I have bills for money by exchange
From Florence and must here deliver them.   *90*

65 **gait and countenance** bearing and style   77 **What countryman** a
man of what country   80 **goes hard** (cf. "is rough")   83 **stayed** held
88 **than so** than it appears so far

Tranio. Well, sir, to do you courtesy,
    This will I do and this I will advise° you.
    First tell me, have you ever been at Pisa?

Pedant. Ay, sir, in Pisa have I often been—
95   Pisa, renownèd for grave citizens.

Tranio. Among them, know you one Vincentio?

Pedant. I know him not but I have heard of him—
    A merchant of incomparable wealth.

Tranio. He is my father, sir, and, sooth to say,
100   In count'nance somewhat doth resemble you.

Biondello. [*Aside*] As much as an apple doth an oys-
    ter, and all one.°

Tranio. To save your life in this extremity,
    This favor will I do you for his sake,
105   And think it not the worst of all your fortunes
    That you are like to Sir Vincentio.
    His name and credit° shall you undertake,°
    And in my house you shall be friendly lodged.
    Look that you take upon you° as you should.
110   You understand me, sir? So shall you stay
    Till you have done your business in the city.
    If this be court'sy, sir, accept of it.

Pedant. O sir, I do, and will repute° you ever
    The patron of my life and liberty.

115 *Tranio.* Then go with me to make the matter good.
    This, by the way,° I let you understand:
    My father is here looked for every day
    To pass assurance° of a dower in marriage
    'Twixt me and one Baptista's daughter here.
120   In all these circumstances I'll instruct you.
    Go with me to clothe you as becomes you. *Exeunt.*

---

92 **advise** explain to   102 **all one** no difference   107 **credit** standing
107 **undertake** adopt   109 **take upon you** assume your role   113 **re-**
pute esteem   116 **by the way** as we walk along   118 **pass assurance**
give a guarantee

[Scene III. *In Petruchio's house.*]

Enter Kate and Grumio.

Grumio. No, no, forsooth, I dare not for my life.

Kate. The more my wrong,° the more his spite ap-
    pears.
  What, did he marry me to famish me?
  Beggars that come unto my father's door,
  Upon entreaty have a present° alms;   *5*
  If not, elsewhere they meet with charity.
  But I, who never knew how to entreat
  Nor never needed that I should entreat,
  Am starved for meat,° giddy for lack of sleep,
  With oaths kept waking and with brawling fed.   *10*
  And that which spites me more than all these wants,
  He does it under name of perfect love,
  As who should say,° if I should sleep or eat
  'Twere deadly sickness or else present death.
  I prithee go and get me some repast,   *15*
  I care not what, so° it be wholesome food.

Grumio. What say you to a neat's° foot?

Kate. 'Tis passing good; I prithee let me have it.

Grumio. I fear it is too choleric° a meat.
  How say you to a fat tripe finely broiled?   *20*

Kate. I like it well. Good Grumio, fetch it me.

Grumio. I cannot tell, I fear 'tis choleric.
  What say you to a piece of beef and mustard?

IV.iii.2 **The more my wrong** the greater the wrong done me 5
present prompt 9 **meat** food 13 **As who should say** as if to say
16 **so** as long as 17 **neat's** ox's or calf's 19 **choleric** temper-pro-
ducing

Kate. A dish that I do love to feed upon.

25 *Grumio.* Ay, but the mustard is too hot a little.

Kate. Why then, the beef, and let the mustard rest.

Grumio. Nay then, I will not. You shall have the mustard
Or else you get no beef of Grumio.

Kate. Then both or one, or anything thou wilt.

30 *Grumio.* Why then, the mustard without the beef.

Kate. Go, get thee gone, thou false deluding slave,
                                                    Beats him.
That feed'st me with the very name° of meat.
Sorrow on thee and all the pack of you
That triumph thus upon my misery.
35 Go, get thee gone, I say.

        Enter Petruchio and Hortensio with meat.

Petruchio. How fares my Kate? What, sweeting, all
        amort?°

Hortensio. Mistress, what cheer?°

Kate.   Faith, as cold° as can be.

Petruchio. Pluck up thy spirits; look cheerfully upon
        me.
Here, love, thou seest how diligent I am
40 To dress thy meat° myself and bring it thee.
I am sure, sweet Kate, this kindness merits thanks.
What, not a word? Nay then, thou lov'st it not,
And all my pains is sorted to no proof.°
Here, take away this dish.

Kate.   I pray you, let it stand.

45 *Petruchio.* The poorest service is repaid with thanks,
        And so shall mine before you touch the meat.

32 **very name** name only   36 **all amort** depressed, lifeless (cf. "mortified")   37 **what cheer** how are things   37 **cold** (cf. "not so hot"; "cold comfort," IV.i.30)   40 **To dress thy meat** in fixing your food
43 **sorted to no proof** have come to nothing

Kate. I thank you, sir.

Hortensio. Signior Petruchio, fie, you are to blame.
　Come, Mistress Kate, I'll bear you company.

Petruchio. [*Aside*] Eat it up all, Hortensio, if thou
　　lovest me;   *50*
　Much good do it unto thy gentle heart.
　Kate, eat apace. And now, my honey love,
　Will we return unto thy father's house
　And revel it as bravely° as the best,
　With silken coats and caps and golden rings,   *55*
　With ruffs° and cuffs and fardingales° and things,
　With scarfs and fans and double change of brav'ry,°
　With amber bracelets, beads, and all this knav'ry.°
　What, hast thou dined? The tailor stays thy leisure°
　To deck thy body with his ruffling° treasure.   *60*

Enter Tailor.

　Come, tailor, let us see these ornaments.

Enter Haberdasher.

　Lay forth the gown. What news with you, sir?

Haberdasher. Here is the cap your Worship did be-
　speak.°

Petruchio. Why, this was molded on a porringer°—
　A velvet dish. Fie, fie, 'tis lewd° and filthy.   *65*
　Why, 'tis a cockle° or a walnut shell,
　A knack,° a toy, a trick,° a baby's cap.
　Away with it! Come, let me have a bigger.

Kate. I'll have no bigger. This doth fit the time,°
　And gentlewomen wear such caps as these.   *70*

---

54 **bravely** handsomely dressed　56 **ruffs** stiffly starched, wheel-shaped collars　56 **fardingales** farthingales, hooped skirts of petti-coats　57 **brav'ry** handsome clothes　58 **knav'ry** girlish things　59 **stays thy leisure** awaits your permission　60 **ruffling** gaily ruffled　63 **bespeak** order　64 **porringer** soup bowl　65 **lewd** vile　66 **cockle** shell of a mollusk　67 **knack** knickknack　67 **trick** plaything　69 **doth fit the time** is in fashion

Petruchio. When you are gentle you shall have one too,
And not till then.

Hortensio. [*Aside*] That will not be in haste.

Kate. Why, sir, I trust I may have leave to speak,
And speak I will. I am no child, no babe.
75   Your betters have endured me say my mind,
And if you cannot, best you stop your ears.
My tongue will tell the anger of my heart,
Or else my heart, concealing it, will break,
And rather than it shall I will be free
80   Even to the uttermost, as I please, in words.

Petruchio. Why, thou sayst true. It is a paltry cap,
A custard-coffin,° a bauble, a silken pie.°
I love thee well in that thou lik'st it not.

Kate. Love me or love me not, I like the cap,
85   And it I will have or I will have none.
                                        [*Exit Haberdasher.*]

Petruchio. Thy gown? Why, ay. Come, tailor, let us see't.
O mercy, God! What masquing° stuff is here?
What's this? A sleeve? 'Tis like a demi-cannon.°
What, up and down,° carved like an apple tart?
90   Here's snip and nip and cut and slish and slash,
Like to a censer° in a barber's shop.
Why, what, a° devil's name, tailor, call'st thou this?

Hortensio. [*Aside*] I see she's like to have neither cap nor gown.

Tailor. You bid me make it orderly and well,
95   According to the fashion and the time.

Petruchio. Marry, and did, but if you be rememb'red,

---

82 **custard-coffin** custard crust   82 **pie** meat pie   87 **masquing** for masquerades or actors' costumes   88 **demi-cannon** big cannon   89 **up and down** entirely   91 **censer** incense burner with perforated top 92 **a** in the

I did not bid you mar it to the time.°
Go, hop me over every kennel° home,
For you shall hop without my custom, sir.
I'll none of it. Hence, make your best of it.   *100*

Kate. I never saw a better-fashioned gown,
More quaint,° more pleasing, nor more commend-
able.
Belike° you mean to make a puppet of me.

Petruchio. Why, true, he means to make a puppet of
thee.

Tailor. She says your worship means to make a pup-
pet of her.   *105*

Petruchio. O monstrous arrogance!
Thou liest, thou thread, thou thimble,
Thou yard, three-quarters, half-yard, quarter, nail!°
Thou flea, thou nit,° thou winter cricket thou!
Braved° in mine own house with° a skein of thread!   *110*
Away, thou rag, thou quantity,° thou remnant,
Or I shall so bemete° thee with thy yard
As thou shalt think on prating° whilst thou liv'st.
I tell thee, I, that thou hast marred her gown.

Tailor. Your worship is deceived. The gown is made   *115*
Just as my master had direction.°
Grumio gave order how it should be done.

Grumio. I gave him no order; I gave him the stuff.

Tailor. But how did you desire it should be made?

Grumio. Marry, sir, with needle and thread.   *120*

Tailor. But did you not request to have it cut?

Grumio. Thou hast faced° many things.

---

97 **to the time** for all time (cf. line 95, in which "the time" is "the
contemporary style")   98 **kennel** gutter (canal)   102 **quaint** skill-
fully made   103 **Belike** no doubt   108 **nail** 1/16 of a yard   109 **nit**
louse's egg   110 **Braved** defied   110 **with** by   111 **quantity** fragment   112 **bemete** (1) measure (2) beat   113 **think on prating** remember your silly talk   116 **had direction** received orders   122
faced trimmed

Tailor. I have.

Grumio. Face° not me. Thou hast braved° many men;
125   brave° not me. I will neither be faced nor braved. I
say unto thee, I bid thy master cut out the gown,
but I did not bid him cut it to pieces. *Ergo,*° thou
liest.

Tailor. Why, here is the note° of the fashion to testify.

130   *Petruchio.* Read it.

Grumio. The note lies in's throat° if he° say I said so.

Tailor. "*Imprimis,*° a loose-bodied gown."°

Grumio. Master, if ever I said loose-bodied gown, sew
me in the skirts of it and beat me to death with a
135   bottom° of brown thread. I said, a gown.

Petruchio. Proceed.

Tailor. "With a small compassed° cape."

Grumio. I confess the cape.

Tailor. "With a trunk° sleeve."

140   *Grumio.* I confess two sleeves.

Tailor. "The sleeves curiously° cut."

Petruchio. Ay, there's the villainy.

Grumio. Error i' th' bill,° sir, error i' th' bill. I commanded the sleeves should be cut out and sewed
145   up again, and that I'll prove upon° thee, though thy
little finger be armed in a thimble.

Tailor. This is true that I say. And° I had thee in
place where,° thou shouldst know it.

124 **Face** challenge   124 **braved** equipped with finery   125 **brave**
defy   127 **Ergo** therefore   129 **note** written notation   131 **in's
throat** from the heart, with premeditation   131 **he** it   132 **Imprimis**
first   132 **loose-bodied gown** (worn by prostitutes, with *loose* in pun)
135 **bottom** spool   137 **compassed** with circular edge   139 **trunk**
full (cf. line 88)   141 **curiously** painstakingly   143 **bill** i.e., the
"note"   145 **prove upon** test by dueling with   147 **And** if   148
place where the right place

Grumio. I am for° thee straight.° Take thou the bill,°
   give me thy mete-yard,° and spare not me.   *150*

Hortensio. God-a-mercy, Grumio, then he shall have
   no odds.

Petruchio. Well, sir, in brief, the gown is not for me.

Grumio. You are i' th' right, sir; 'tis for my mistress.

Petruchio. Go, take it up unto° thy master's use.°   *155*

Grumio. Villain, not for thy life! Take up my mistress'
   gown for thy master's use!

Petruchio. Why sir, what's your conceit° in that?

Grumio. O sir, the conceit is deeper than you think
   for.
   Take up my mistress' gown to his master's use!   *160*
   O, fie, fie, fie!

Petruchio. [*Aside*] Hortensio, say thou wilt see the
   tailor paid.
   [*To Tailor*] Go take it hence; be gone and say no
   more.

Hortensio. Tailor, I'll pay thee for thy gown tomor-
   row;
   Take no unkindness of his hasty words.   *165*
   Away, I say, commend me to thy master.
                                        Exit Tailor.

Petruchio. Well, come, my Kate, we will unto your
   father's,
   Even in these honest mean habiliments.°
   Our purses shall be proud, our garments poor,
   For 'tis the mind that makes the body rich,   *170*
   And as the sun breaks through the darkest clouds
   So honor peereth° in the meanest habit.°

---

149 **for** ready for   149 **straight** right now   149 **bill** (1) written order
(2)long-handled weapon   150 **mete-yard** yardstick   155 **up unto**
away for   155 **use** i.e., in whatever way he can; Grumio uses these
words for a sex joke   158 **conceit** idea   168 **habiliments** clothes
172 **peereth** is recognized   172 **habit** clothes

What, is the jay more precious than the lark
Because his feathers are more beautiful?
175 Or is the adder better than the eel
Because his painted skin contents the eye?
O no, good Kate, neither art thou the worse
For this poor furniture° and mean array.
If thou account'st it shame, lay° it on me,
180 And therefore frolic. We will hence forthwith
To feast and sport us at thy father's house.
[*To Grumio*] Go call my men, and let us straight
   to him;
And bring our horses unto Long-lane end.
There will we mount, and thither walk on foot.
185 Let's see, I think 'tis now some seven o'clock,
And well we may come there by dinnertime.°

Kate. I dare assure you, sir, 'tis almost two,
And 'twill be suppertime ere you come there.

Petruchio. It shall be seven ere I go to horse.
190 Look what° I speak or do or think to do,
You are still crossing° it. Sirs, let't alone:
I will not go today, and ere I do,
It shall be what o'clock I say it is.

Hortensio. [*Aside*] Why, so this gallant will command
   the sun.   [*Exeunt.*]

---

178 **furniture** outfit   179 **lay** blame   186 **dinnertime** midday   190
Look what whatever   191 **crossing** obstructing, going counter to

[Scene IV. *Padua. The street in front
of Baptista's house.*]

*Enter Tranio [as Lucentio] and the Pedant
dressed like Vincentio.*

Tranio. Sir, this is the house. Please it you that I call?

Pedant. Ay, what else? And but° I be deceived,
Signior Baptista may remember me
Near twenty years ago in Genoa,
Where we were lodgers at the Pegasus.°   *5*

Tranio. 'Tis well, and hold your own° in any case
With such austerity as 'longeth to a father.

Pedant. I warrant° you. But sir, here comes your boy;
'Twere good he were schooled.°

                    Enter Biondello.

Tranio. Fear you not him. Sirrah Biondello,   *10*
Now do your duty throughly,° I advise you.
Imagine 'twere the right Vincentio.

Biondello. Tut, fear not me.

Tranio. But hast thou done thy errand to Baptista?

Biondello. I told him that your father was at Venice   *15*
And that you looked for him this day in Padua.

Tranio. Th' art a tall° fellow. Hold thee that° to drink.
Here comes Baptista. Set your countenance, sir.

IV.iv.2 **but** unless   3–5 **Signior Baptista . . . Pegasus** (the Pedant is
practicing as Vincentio)   5 **Pegasus** common English inn name
(after mythical winged horse symbolizing poetic inspiration)   6 **hold
your own** act your role   8 **warrant** guarantee   9 **schooled** informed
(about his role)   11 **throughly** thoroughly   17 **tall** excellent   17
Hold thee that i.e., take this tip

Enter Baptista and Lucentio [as Cambio].
Pedant booted and bareheaded.°

Signior Baptista, you are happily met.
[*To the Pedant*] Sir, this is the gentleman I told
20   you of.
I pray you, stand good father to me now,
Give me Bianca for my patrimony.

Pedant. Soft,° son.
Sir, by your leave. Having come to Padua
25   To gather in some debts, my son Lucentio
Made me acquainted with a weighty cause°
Of love between your daughter and himself.
And—for the good report I hear of you,
And for the love he beareth to your daughter,
30   And she to him—to stay° him not too long,
I am content, in a good father's care,
To have him matched. And if you please to like°
No worse than I, upon some agreement
Me shall you find ready and willing
35   With one consent to have her so bestowed,
For curious° I cannot be with you,
Signior Baptista, of whom I hear so well.

Baptista. Sir, pardon me in what I have to say.
Your plainness and your shortness° please me well.
40   Right true it is, your son Lucentio here
Doth love my daughter and she loveth him—
Or both dissemble deeply their affections—
And therefore, if you say no more than this,
That like a father you will deal with him
45   And pass° my daughter a sufficient dower,
The match is made, and all is done.
Your son shall have my daughter with consent.

---

18 s.d. **booted and bareheaded** i.e., arriving from a journey and courteously greeting Baptista   23 **Soft** take it easy   26 **weighty cause**
important matter   30 **stay** delay   32 **like** i.e., the match   36 **curi-
ous** overinsistent on fine points   39 **shortness** conciseness   45 **pass**
legally settle upon

Tranio. I thank you, sir. Where, then, do you know°
  best
  We be affied° and such assurance ta'en
  As shall with either part's° agreement stand?   50

Baptista. Not in my house, Lucentio, for you know
  Pitchers have ears, and I have many servants.
  Besides, old Gremio is heark'ning still,°
  And happily° we might be interrupted.

Tranio. Then at my lodging and it like° you.   55
  There doth my father lie,° and there this night
  We'll pass° the business privately and well.
  Send for your daughter by your servant here;
  My boy shall fetch the scrivener° presently.
  The worst is this, that at so slender warning°   60
  You are like to have a thin and slender pittance.°

Baptista. It likes° me well. Cambio, hie you home
  And bid Bianca make her ready straight,
  And, if you will, tell what hath happenèd:
  Lucentio's father is arrived in Padua,   65
  And how she's like to be Lucentio's wife.
                                        [*Exit Lucentio.*]

Biondello. I pray the gods she may with all my heart!
                                                    Exit.

Tranio. Dally not with the gods, but get thee gone.
  Signior Baptista, shall I lead the way?
  Welcome, one mess° is like to be your cheer.°   70
  Come, sir, we will better it in Pisa.

Baptista. I follow you.   *Exeunt.*

     Enter Lucentio [as Cambio] and Biondello.

Biondello. Cambio!

Lucentio. What sayst thou, Biondello?

48 **know** think 49 **affied** formally engaged 50 **part's** party's 53
heark'ning still listening constantly 54 **happily** perchance 55 **and
it like** if it please 56 **lie** stay 57 **pass** settle 59 **scrivener** notary
60 **slender warning** short notice 61 **pittance** meal 62 **likes** pleases
70 **mess** dish 70 **cheer** entertainment

75 *Biondello*. You saw my master° wink and laugh upon
    you?

Lucentio. Biondello, what of that?

Biondello. Faith, nothing, but has° left me here be-
    hind to expound the meaning or moral of his signs
80   and tokens.

Lucentio. I pray thee, moralize° them.

Biondello. Then thus. Baptista is safe, talking with
    the deceiving father of a deceitful son.

Lucentio. And what of him?

85 *Biondello*. His daughter is to be brought by you to
    the supper.

Lucentio. And then?

Biondello. The old priest at Saint Luke's church is at
    your command at all hours.

90 *Lucentio*. And what of all this?

Biondello. I cannot tell, except they are busied about
    a counterfeit assurance.° Take you assurance° of
    her, *"cum previlegio ad impremendum solem."*° To
    th' church! Take the priest, clerk, and some suffi-
95   cient honest witnesses.
    If this be not that you look for, I have no more
        to say,
    But bid Bianca farewell forever and a day.

Lucentio. Hear'st thou, Biondello?

Biondello. I cannot tarry. I knew a wench married
100   in an afternoon as she went to the garden for pars-
    ley to stuff a rabbit. And so may you, sir. And so
    adieu, sir. My master hath appointed me to go to

75 **my master** i.e., Tranio; cf. line 59   78 **has** he has   81 **moraliz***
"expound"   92 **assurance** betrothal document   92 **Take you assur**
ance make sure   93 **cum . . . solem** (Biondello's version of *cum*
previlegio ad imprimendum solum, "with right of sole printing," ⸱
licensing phrase, with sexual pun in *imprimendum*, literally "pressing
upon")

Saint Luke's, to bid the priest be ready to come
against you come° with your appendix.°   *Exit.*

Lucentio. I may, and will, if she be so contented.   *105*
She will be pleased; then wherefore should I doubt?
Hap what hap may, I'll roundly° go about° her.
It shall go hard if Cambio go without her.   *Exit.*

[Scene V. *The road to Padua.*]

Enter Petruchio, Kate, Hortensio
[*with Servants.*]

Petruchio. Come on, a° God's name, once more toward our father's.
Good Lord, how bright and goodly shines the moon.

Kate. The moon? The sun. It is not moonlight now.

Petruchio. I say it is the moon that shines so bright.

Kate. I know it is the sun that shines so bright.   *5*

Petruchio. Now, by my mother's son, and that's my-
self,
It shall be moon or star or what I list,°
Or ere° I journey to your father's house.
[*To Servants*] Go on and fetch our horses back
again.
Evermore crossed and crossed, nothing but crossed!°   *10*

Hortensio. [*To Kate*] Say as he says or we shall never
go.

Kate. Forward, I pray, since we have come so far,
And be it moon or sun or what you please.

---

104 **against you come** in preparing for your coming   104 **appendix**
(1) servant (2) wife (another metaphor from printing)   107 **roundly**
directly   107 **about** after   IV.v.1 a in   7 **list** please   8 **Or ere** before   10 **crossed** opposed, challenged

And if you please to call it a rush-candle,°
15   Henceforth I vow it shall be so for me.

Petruchio. I say it is the moon.

Kate.   I know it is the moon.

Petruchio. Nay, then you lie. It is the blessèd sun.

Kate. Then God be blessed, it is the blessèd sun.
But sun it is not when you say it is not,
20   And the moon changes even as your mind.
What you will have it named, even that it is,
And so it shall be so for Katherine.

Hortensio. [*Aside*] Petruchio, go thy ways. The field
is won.

Petruchio. Well, forward, forward! Thus the bowl°
should run
25   And not unluckily against the bias.°
But soft,° company° is coming here.

Enter Vincentio.

[*To Vincentio*] Good morrow, gentle mistress;
where away?
Tell me, sweet Kate, and tell me truly too,
Hast thou beheld a fresher° gentlewoman?
30   Such war of white and red within her cheeks!
What stars do spangle heaven with such beauty
As those two eyes become that heavenly face?
Fair lovely maid, once more good day to thee.
Sweet Kate, embrace her for her beauty's sake.

35   *Hortensio.* [*Aside*] 'A° will make the man mad, to
make a woman of him.

Kate. Young budding virgin, fair and fresh and sweet,
Whither away, or where is thy abode?

14 **rush-candle** rush dipped in grease and used as candle   24 **bowl**
bowling ball   25 **against the bias** not in the planned curving route,
made possible by a lead insertion (bias) weighting one side of the
ball   26 **soft** hush   26 **company** someone   29 **fresher** more radiant
35 **'A** he

Happy the parents of so fair a child!
Happier the man whom favorable stars   40
Allots thee for his lovely bedfellow!

Petruchio. Why, how now, Kate, I hope thou are not
    mad.
This is a man, old, wrinkled, faded, withered,
And not a maiden, as thou sayst he is.

Kate. Pardon, old father, my mistaking eyes   45
That have been so bedazzled with the sun
That everything I look on seemeth green.°
Now I perceive thou art a reverend father;
Pardon, I pray thee, for my mad mistaking.

Petruchio. Do, good old grandsire, and withal make
    known   50
Which way thou travelest. If along with us,
We shall be joyful of thy company.

Vincentio. Fair sir, and you my merry mistress,
That with your strange encounter° much amazed
    me,
My name is called Vincentio, my dwelling Pisa,   55
And bound I am to Padua, there to visit
A son of mine which long I have not seen.

Petruchio. What is his name?

Vincentio.   Lucentio, gentle sir.

Petruchio. Happily met, the happier for thy son.
And now by law as well as reverend age,   60
I may entitle thee my loving father.
The sister to my wife, this gentlewoman,
Thy son by this° hath married. Wonder not
Nor be not grieved. She is of good esteem,
Her dowry wealthy, and of worthy birth;   65
Beside, so qualified° as may beseem°
The spouse of any noble gentleman.
Let me embrace with old Vincentio

47 green young   54 encounter mode of address   63 this now   66 so
qualified having qualities   66 beseem befit

And wander we to see thy honest son,
70 Who will of thy arrival be full joyous.

Vincentio. But is this true, or is it else your pleasure,
Like pleasant° travelers, to break a jest
Upon the company you overtake?

Hortensio. I do assure thee, father, so it is.

75 *Petruchio.* Come, go along, and see the truth hereof,
For our first merriment hath made thee jealous.°
                    Exeunt [all but Hortensio].

Hortensio. Well, Petruchio, this has put me in heart.
Have to° my widow, and if she be froward,°
Then hast thou taught Hortensio to be untoward.°
                    Exit.

72 **pleasant** addicted to pleasantries   76 **jealous** suspicious · 78 **Have to** on to   78 **froward** fractious   79 **untoward** difficult

[ACT V

Scene I. *Padua. The street in front of
Lucentio's house.*]

Enter Biondello, Lucentio [*as Cambio*], *and
Bianca; Gremio is out before.*°

Biondello. Softly and swiftly, sir, for the priest is
ready.

Lucentio. I fly, Biondello. But they may chance to
need thee at home; therefore leave us.

Exit [*with Bianca*].

Biondello. Nay, faith, I'll see the church a your back,°   5
and then come back to my master's as soon as I
can.   [*Exit.*]

Gremio. I marvel Cambio comes not all this while.

Enter Petruchio, Kate, Vincentio, [*and*] *Grumio,
with Attendants.*

Petruchio. Sir, here's the door, this is Lucentio's
house.
My father's bears° more toward the marketplace;   10
Thither must I, and here I leave you, sir.

Vincentio. You shall not choose but drink before you
go.
I think I shall command your welcome here,
And by all likelihood some cheer is toward.° *Knock.*

V.i.s.d. **out before** precedes, and does not see, the others   5 a **your
back** on your back (see you enter the church? or, married?)   10
bears lies   14 **toward** at hand

137

15 *Gremio.* They're busy within. You were best knock
    louder.

        *Pedant [as Vincentio] looks out of
            the window [above].*

Pedant. What's° he that knocks as he would beat
    down the gate?

Vincentio. Is Signior Lucentio within, sir?

20 *Pedant.* He's within, sir, but not to be spoken withal.°

Vincentio. What if a man bring him a hundred pound
    or two, to make merry withal?

Pedant. Keep your hundred pounds to yourself; he
    shall need none so long as I live.

25 *Petruchio.* Nay, I told you your son was well beloved
    in Padua. Do you hear, sir? To leave frivolous cir-
    cumstances,° I pray you tell Signior Lucentio that
    his father is come from Pisa and is here at the door
    to speak with him.

30 *Pedant.* Thou liest. His father is come from Padua°
    and here looking out at the window.

Vincentio. Art thou his father?

Pedant. Ay sir, so his mother says, if I may believe
    her.

35 *Petruchio.* [*To Vincentio*] Why how now, gentleman?
    Why this is flat° knavery, to take upon you another
    man's name.

Pedant. Lay hands on the villain. I believe 'a° means
    to cozen° somebody in this city under my counte-
40 nance.°

        Enter Biondello.

17 **What's** who is   20 **withal** with   26–27 **frivolous circumstances**
trivial matters   30 **Padua** (perhaps Shakespeare's slip of the pen for
Pisa, home of the real Vincentio, or *Mantua*, where the Pedant
comes from; cf. IV.ii.77)   36 **flat** unvarnished   38 **'a** he   39 **cozen**
defraud   39–40 **countenance** identity

Biondello. I have seen them in the church together;
　God send 'em good shipping!° But who is here?
　Mine old master, Vincentio! Now we are undone°
　and brought to nothing.°

Vincentio. Come hither, crack-hemp.°　　　　　　　45

Biondello. I hope I may choose,° sir.

Vincentio. Come hither, you rogue. What, have you
　forgot me?

Biondello. Forgot you? No, sir. I could not forget you,
　for I never saw you before in all my life.　　　50

Vincentio. What, you notorious° villain, didst thou
　never see thy master's father, Vincentio?

Biondello. What, my old worshipful old master? Yes,
　marry, sir, see where he looks out of the window.

Vincentio. Is't so, indeed?　　　　*He beats Biondello.*　55

Biondello. Help, help, help! Here's a madman will
　murder me.　　　　　　　　　　　　　　　[*Exit.*]

Pedant. Help, son! Help, Signior Baptista!
　　　　　　　　　　　　　　　[*Exit from above.*]

Petruchio. Prithee, Kate, let's stand aside and see the
　end of this controversy.　　　　　　　　　　60
　　　　　　　　　　　　　　　[*They stand aside.*]

　　　*Enter Pedant [below] with Servants, Baptista,
　　　　　　[and] Tranio [as Lucentio].*

Tranio. Sir, what are you that offer° to beat my
　servant?

Vincentio. What am I, sir? Nay, what are you, sir?
　O immortal gods! O fine° villain! A silken doublet,

---

42 **shipping** journey　43 **undone** defeated　44 **brought to nothing**
(cf. "annihilated")　45 **crack-hemp** rope-stretcher (i.e., subject for
hanging)　46 **choose** have some choice (in the matter)　51 **notorious** extraordinary　61 **offer** attempt　64 **fine** well dressed

65 a velvet hose, a scarlet cloak, and a copatain° hat!
O, I am undone, I am undone! While I play the
good husband° at home, my son and my servant
spend all at the university.

Tranio. How now, what's the matter?

70 *Baptista.* What, is the man lunatic?

Tranio. Sir, you seem a sober ancient gentleman by
your habit,° but your words show you a madman.
Why sir, what 'cerns° it you if I wear pearl and
gold? I thank my good father, I am able to main-
75 tain it.

Vincentio. Thy father! O villain, he is a sailmaker in
Bergamo.

Baptista. You mistake, sir, you mistake, sir. Pray,
what do you think is his name?

80 *Vincentio.* His name! As if I knew not his name! I
have brought him up ever since he was three years
old, and his name is Tranio.

Pedant. Away, away, mad ass! His name is Lucentio,
and he is mine only son and heir to the lands of me,
85 Signior Vincentio.

Vincentio. Lucentio! O he hath murd'red his master.
Lay hold on him, I charge you in the Duke's name.
O my son, my son! Tell me, thou villain, where is
my son Lucentio?

90 *Tranio.* Call forth an officer.

[*Enter an Officer.*]

Carry this mad knave to the jail. Father Baptista,
I charge you see that he be forthcoming.°

Vincentio. Carry me to the jail!

Gremio. Stay, officer. He shall not go to prison.

65 **copatain** high conical   67 **husband** manager   72 **habit** manner
73 **'cerns** concerns   92 **forthcoming** available (for trial)

Baptista. Talk not, Signior Gremio. I say he shall go   95
  to prison.

Gremio. Take heed, Signior Baptista, lest you be cony-
  catched° in this business. I dare swear this is the
  right Vincentio.

Pedant. Swear, if thou dar'st.   100

Gremio. Nay, I dare not swear it.

Tranio. Then thou wert best° say that I am not
  Lucentio.

Gremio. Yes, I know thee to be Signior Lucentio.

Baptista. Away with the dotard,° to the jail with him!   105

Vincentio. Thus strangers may be haled° and abused.
  O monstrous villain!

> *Enter Biondello, Lucentio, and Bianca.*

Biondello. O we are spoiled°—and yonder he is. Deny
  him, forswear him, or else we are all undone.
> *Exit Biondello, Tranio, and Pedant as fast*
> *as may be.*

Lucentio. Pardon, sweet father.   *Kneel.*

Vincentio.   Lives my sweet son?   110

Bianca. Pardon, dear father.

Baptista.   How hast thou offended?
  Where is Lucentio?

Lucentio.   Here's Lucentio,
  Right son to the right Vincentio,
  That have by marriage made thy daughter mine
  While counterfeit supposes° bleared thine eyne.°   115

97–98 **cony-catched** fooled   102 **thou wert best** maybe you'll dare
105 **dotard** old fool   106 **haled** pulled about   108 **spoiled** ruined
115 **supposes** pretendings (evidently an allusion to Gascoigne's play
Supposes, one of Shakespeare's sources)   115 **eyne** eyes

Gremio. Here's packing,° with a witness,° to deceive
us all!

Vincentio. Where is that damnèd villain Tranio
That faced and braved° me in this matter so?

120 *Baptista.* Why, tell me, is not this my Cambio?

Bianca. Cambio is changed into Lucentio.

Lucentio. Love wrought these miracles. Bianca's love
Made me exchange my state with Tranio
While he did bear my countenance° in the town,
125 And happily I have arrived at the last
Unto the wishèd haven of my bliss.
What Tranio did, myself enforced him to.
Then pardon him, sweet father, for my sake.

Vincentio. I'll slit the villain's nose that would have
130 sent me to the jail.

Baptista. [*To Lucentio*] But do you hear, sir? Have
you married my daughter without asking my good
will?

Vincentio. Fear not, Baptista; we will content you, go
135 to.° But I will in, to be revenged for this villainy.
                                        Exit.

Baptista. And I, to sound the depth° of this knavery.
                                        Exit.

Lucentio. Look not pale, Bianca. Thy father will not
frown.   *Exeunt [Lucentio and Bianca].*

Gremio. My cake is dough,° but I'll in among the rest
140 Out of hope of all but my share of the feast. [*Exit.*]

Kate. Husband, let's follow, to see the end of this ado.

Petruchio. First kiss me, Kate, and we will.

116 **packing** plotting   116 **with a witness** outright, unabashed   119
faced and braved impudently challenged and defied   124 **bear my
countenance** take on my identity   134–35 **go to** (mild remonstrance;
cf. "go on," "come, come," "don't worry")   136 **sound the depth**
get to the bottom of   139 **cake is dough** project hasn't worked out
(proverbial; cf. I.i.108–09)

Kate. What, in the midst of the street?

Petruchio. What, art thou ashamed of me?

Kate. No sir, God forbid, but ashamed to kiss.   145

Petruchio. Why, then let's home again. [*To Grumio*]
    Come sirrah, let's away.

Kate. Nay, I will give thee a kiss. Now pray thee, love,
    stay.

Petruchio. Is not this well? Come, my sweet Kate.
    Better once° than never, for never too late.° *Exeunt.*

[Scene II. *Padua. In Lucentio's house.*]

*Enter Baptista, Vincentio, Gremio, the Pedant,
Lucentio, and Bianca, [Petruchio, Kate, Hortensio,]
Tranio, Biondello, Grumio, and Widow; the
Servingmen with Tranio bringing in a banquet.°*

Lucentio. At last, though long,° our jarring notes agree,
    And time it is, when raging war is done,
    To smile at 'scapes and perils overblown.°
    My fair Bianca, bid my father welcome
    While I with self-same kindness welcome thine.   5
    Brother Petruchio, sister Katherina,
    And thou, Hortensio, with thy loving widow,
    ·Feast with the best and welcome to my house.
    My banquet is to close our stomachs° up
    After our great good cheer.° Pray you, sit down,   10
    For now we sit to chat as well as eat.

Petruchio. Nothing but sit and sit, and eat and eat.

]

149 once at some time   149 Better . . . late better late than never
V.ii.s.d. banquet dessert   1 At last, though long at long last   3 over-
blown that have blown over   9 stomachs (with pun on "irascibility";
cf. IV.i.152)   10 cheer (reception at Baptista's)

Baptista. Padua affords this kindness, son Petruchio.

Petruchio. Padua affords nothing but what is kind.

Hortensio. For both our sakes I would that word were
15   true.

Petruchio. Now, for my life, Hortensio fears° his
widow.

Widow. Then never trust me if I be afeard.°

Petruchio. You are very sensible and yet you miss my
sense:
I mean Hortensio is afeard of you.

20 *Widow.* He that is giddy thinks the world turns round.

Petruchio. Roundly° replied.

Kate.   Mistress, how mean you that?

Widow. Thus I conceive by° him.

Petruchio. Conceives by° me! How likes Hortensio
that?

Hortensio. My widow says, thus she conceives her
tale.°

Petruchio. Very well mended. Kiss him for that, good
25   widow.

Kate. "He that is giddy thinks the world turns round."
I pray you, tell me what you meant by that.

Widow. Your husband, being troubled with a shrew,
Measures° my husband's sorrow by his° woe,
30   And now you know my meaning.

Kate. A very mean° meaning.

---

16 **fears** is afraid of (the Widow puns on the meaning "frightens")
17 **afeard** (1) frightened (2) suspected   21 **Roundly** outspokenly
22 **conceive by** understand   23 **Conceives by** is made pregnant by
24 **conceives her tale** understands her statement (with another pun)
29 **Measures** estimates   29 **his** his own   31 **mean** paltry

Widow.   Right, I mean you.

Kate. And I am mean° indeed, respecting you.

Petruchio. To her, Kate!

Hortensio. To her, widow!

Petruchio. A hundred marks, my Kate does put her
    down.°   35

Hortensio. That's my office.°

Petruchio. Spoke like an officer. Ha'° to thee, lad.
                          Drinks to Hortensio.

Baptista. How likes Gremio these quick-witted folks?

Gremio. Believe me, sir, they butt° together well.

Bianca. Head and butt!° An hasty-witted body   40
    Would say your head and butt were head and horn.°

Vincentio. Ay, mistress bride, hath that awakened
    you?

Bianca. Ay, but not frighted me; therefore I'll sleep
    again.

Petruchio. Nay, that you shall not. Since you have
    begun,
    Have at you° for a bitter° jest or two.   45

Bianca. Am I your bird?° I mean to shift my bush,
    And then pursue me as you draw your bow.
    You are welcome all.
                    Exit Bianca [with Kate and Widow].

Petruchio. She hath prevented me.° Here, Signior
    Tranio,

32 **am mean** (1) am moderate (2) have a low opinion 35 **put her
down** defeat her (with sexual pun by Hortensio) 36 **office** job
37 **Ha'** here's, hail 39 **butt** (perhaps also "but," i.e., argue or
differ) 40 **butt** (with pun on "bottom") 41 **horn** (1) butting instrument (2) symbol of cuckoldry (3) phallus 45 **Have at you** let's
have 45 **bitter** biting (but good-natured) 46 **bird** prey 49 **prevented me** beaten me to it

50 This bird you aimed at, though you hit her not;
    Therefore a health to all that shot and missed.

Tranio. O sir, Lucentio slipped° me, like his grey-
    hound,
    Which runs himself and catches for his master.

Petruchio. A good swift° simile but something currish.

55 *Tranio.* 'Tis well, sir, that you hunted for yourself;
    'Tis thought your deer° does hold you at a bay.°

Baptista. O, O, Petruchio, Tranio hits you now.

Lucentio. I thank thee for that gird,° good Tranio.

Hortensio. Confess, confess, hath he not hit you here?

60 *Petruchio.* 'A has a little galled° me, I confess,
    And as the jest did glance away from me,
    'Tis ten to one it maimed you two outright.

Baptista. Now, in good sadness,° son Petruchio,
    I think thou hast the veriest° shrew of all.

Petruchio. Well, I say no. And therefore, for assur-
65   ance,°
    Let's each one send unto his wife,
    And he whose wife is most obedient
    To come at first when he doth send for her
    Shall win the wager which we will propose.

Hortensio. Content. What's the wager?

70 *Lucentio.*   Twenty crowns.

Petruchio. Twenty crowns!
    I'll venture so much of° my hawk or hound,
    But twenty times so much upon my wife.

Lucentio. A hundred then.

Hortensio.   Content.°

---

52 **slipped** unleashed   54 **swift** quick-witted   56 **deer** (1) doe (2)
dear   56 **at a bay** at bay (i.e., backed up at a safe distance)   58 **gird**
gibe   60 **galled** chafed   63 **sadness** seriousness   64 **veriest** most
genuine   65 **assurance** proof   72 **of** on   74 **Content** agreed

Petruchio.   A match,° 'tis done.

Hortensio. Who shall begin?

Lucentio.   That will I.   73
   Go Biondello, bid your mistress come to me.

Biondello. I go.   *Exit.*

Baptista. Son, I'll be your half,° Bianca comes.

Lucentio. I'll have no halves; I'll bear it all myself.

                    Enter Biondello.

   How now,° what news?

Biondello.   Sir, my mistress sends you
      word   80
   That she is busy and she cannot come.

Petruchio. How?° She's busy and she cannot come?
   Is that an answer?

Gremio.   Ay, and a kind one too.
   Pray God, sir, your wife send you not a worse.

Petruchio. I hope, better.   85

Hortensio. Sirrah Biondello, go and entreat my wife
   To come to me forthwith.°   *Exit Biondello.*

Petruchio.   O ho, entreat her!
   Nay, then she must needs come.

Hortensio.   I am afraid, sir,
   Do what you can, yours will not be entreated.

                    Enter Biondello.

   Now where's my wife?   90

Biondello. She says you have some goodly jest in hand.
   She will not come. She bids you come to her.

---

74 **A match** (it's) a bet   78 **be your half** assume half your bet   80
How now (mild exclamation; cf. "well")   82 **How** what   87 **forthwith** right away

Petruchio. Worse and worse. She will not come. O vile,

Intolerable, not to be endured!

95   Sirrah Grumio, go to your mistress; say

I command her come to me.   *Exit [Grumio].*

Hortensio. I know her answer.

Petruchio.   What?

Hortensio.   She will not.

Petruchio. The fouler fortune mine, and there an end.

Enter Kate.

Baptista. Now, by my holidame,° here comes Katherina.

100 *Kate.* What is your will, sir, that you send for me?

Petruchio. Where is your sister and Hortensio's wife?

Kate. They sit conferring° by the parlor fire.

Petruchio. Go fetch them hither. If they deny° to come,

Swinge° me them soundly° forth unto their husbands.

103   Away, I say, and bring them hither straight.

                     [Exit Kate.]

Lucentio. Here is a wonder, if you talk of a wonder.

Hortensio. And so it is. I wonder what it bodes.

Petruchio. Marry, peace it bodes, and love, and quiet life,

An awful° rule and right supremacy;

110   And, to be short, what not° that's sweet and happy.

Baptista. Now fair befall° thee, good Petruchio.

---

99 **holidame** holy dame (some editors emend to *halidom,* sacred place or relic) 102 **conferring** conversing 103 **deny** refuse 104 **Swinge** thrash 104 **soundly** thoroughly (cf. "sound beating") 109 **awful** inspiring respect 110 **what not** i.e., everything 111 **fair befall** good luck to

The wager thou hast won, and I will add
Unto their losses twenty thousand crowns,
Another dowry to another daughter,
For she is changed as she had never been.   *115*

Petruchio. Nay, I will win my wager better yet
And show more sign of her obedience,
Her new-built virtue and obedience.

   Enter Kate, Bianca, and Widow.

See where she comes and brings your froward°
   wives
As prisoners to her womanly persuasion.   *120*
Katherine, that cap of yours becomes you not.
Off with that bauble, throw it under foot.
                  [*She throws it.*]

Widow. Lord, let me never have a cause to sigh
Till I be brought to such a silly pass.°

Bianca. Fie, what a foolish—duty call you this?   *125*

Lucentio. I would your duty were as foolish too.
The wisdom of your duty, fair Bianca,
Hath cost me five hundred° crowns since supper-
   time.

Bianca. The more fool you for laying° on my duty.

Petruchio. Katherine, I charge thee, tell these headstrong women
What duty they do owe their lords and husbands.   *130*

Widow. Come, come, you're mocking. We will have
   no telling.

Petruchio. Come on, I say, and first begin with her.

Widow. She shall not.

---

119 **froward** uncooperative 124 **pass** situation 128 **five hundred**
(1) Lucentio makes it look worse than it is, or (2) he made several
bets, or (3) the text errs (some editors emend to "a hundred," assum-
ing that the manuscript's "a" was misread as the Roman numeral v)
129 **laying** betting

135 *Petruchio.* I say she shall—and first begin with her.

Kate. Fie, fie, unknit that threatening unkind° brow
    And dart not scornful glances from those eyes
    To wound thy lord, thy king, thy governor.
    It blots thy beauty as frosts do bite the meads,
    Confounds thy fame° as whirlwinds shake° fair
140   buds,
    And in no sense is meet or amiable.
    A woman moved° is like a fountain troubled,
    Muddy, ill-seeming, thick, bereft of beauty,
    And while it is so, none so dry or thirsty
145   Will deign to sip or touch one drop of it.
    Thy husband is thy lord, thy life, thy keeper,
    Thy head, thy sovereign—one that cares for thee,
    And for thy maintenance commits his body
    To painful labor both by sea and land,
150   To watch° the night in storms, the day in cold,
    Whilst thou li'st warm at home, secure and safe;
    And craves no other tribute at thy hands
    But love, fair looks, and true obedience:
    Too little payment for so great a debt.
155   Such duty as the subject owes the prince,
    Even such a woman oweth to her husband,
    And when she is froward, peevish, sullen, sour,
    And not obedient to his honest° will,
    What is she but a foul contending rebel
160   And graceless traitor to her loving lord?
    I am ashamed that women are so simple°
    To offer war where they should kneel for peace,
    Or seek for rule, supremacy, and sway,
    When they are bound to serve, love, and obey.
165   Why are our bodies soft and weak and smooth,
    Unapt to° toil and trouble in the world,
    But that our soft conditions° and our hearts

---

136 **unkind** hostile   140 **Confounds thy fame** spoils people's opinion
of you   140 **shake** shake off   142 **moved** i.e., by ill temper   150
watch stay awake, be alert during   158 **honest** honorable   161 **simple** silly   166 **Unapt to** unfitted for   167 **conditions** qualities

Should well agree with our external parts?
Come, come, you froward and unable worms,°
My mind hath been as big° as one of yours,   *170*
My heart as great, my reason haply more,
To bandy word for word and frown for frown.
But now I see our lances are but straws,
Our strength as weak, our weakness past compare,
That seeming to be most which we indeed least are.   *175*
Then vail your stomachs,° for it is no boot,°
And place your hands below your husband's foot,
In token of which duty, if he please,
My hand is ready, may it° do him ease.

Petruchio. Why, there's a wench! Come on and kiss
  me, Kate.   *180*

Lucentio. Well, go thy ways, old lad, for thou shalt
  ha't.

Vincentio. 'Tis a good hearing° when children are
  toward.°

Lucentio. But a harsh hearing when women are froward.

Petruchio. Come, Kate, we'll to bed.
  We three are married, but you two are sped.°   *185*
  'Twas I won the wager, [*to Lucentio*] though you
    hit the white,°
  And, being a winner, God give you good night.
                              Exit Petruchio [*with Kate*].

Hortensio. Now, go thy ways; thou hast tamed a curst
  shrow.

Lucentio. 'Tis a wonder, by your leave, she will be
  tamèd so.   [*Exeunt.*]

                              FINIS

169 **unable worms** weak, lowly creatures   170 **big** inflated (cf. "think
big")   176 **vail your stomachs** fell your pride   176 **no boot** useless,
profitless   179 **may it** (1) I hope it may (2) if it may   182 **hearing**
thing to hear; report   182 **toward** tractable   185 **sped** done for
186 **white** (1) bull's eye (2) *Bianca* means white

Textual Note

The authority for the present text is the Folio of 1623 (F). Based on it were the Quarto of 1631 and three later folios. These introduce a number of errors of their own but also make some corrections and some changes accepted by most subsequent editors. The present text adheres as closely as possible to F, accepting standard emendations only when F seems clearly erroneous. These emendations come mainly from such early editors as Rowe, Theobald, and Capell.

F's incomplete division into acts is almost universally altered by modern editors, and the present text conforms to standard practice. F has *"Actus primus. Scoena [sic] Prima"* at the beginning, whereas in modern practice approximately the first 275 lines are placed in an "Induction" with two scenes. F lacks a designation for Act II. F's *"Actus Tertia [sic],"* beginning with Lucentio's "Fiddler, forbear, etc.," is universally accepted. F's *"Actus Quartus. Scena Prima"* generally becomes modern IV.iii, and F's *"Actus Quintus,"* modern V.ii.

F makes a number of erroneous or unclear speech assignments (at one time naming an actor, Sincklo, instead of the character). These are at Ind.i.88; III.i.46ff.; IV.ii.4ff. These are specifically listed below. Names of speakers, nearly always abbreviated in F, are regularly spelled out in the present edition. Speakers in F designated *Beggar*, *Lady*, and *Man* are given as *Sly*, *Page*, and *Servingman*, respectively.

F is not consistent in the spelling of some proper

names. In the stage directions, the shrew, for instance,
appears as *Katerina, Katherina, Katherine* (sometime
with *a* in the second syllable), and *Kate;* she is spoken
to and of as *Katherine* and *Kate;* her speeches are headed
Ka, Kat, and *Kate*. Since *Kate* is the most frequent form,
this edition uses it throughout and does not include the
change in the following list. In F, the name adopted
by Hortensio when he pretends to be a music teacher
appears three times as *Litio,* which we use here, and four
times as *Lisio.* Many editors follow F2 and Rowe in
emending to *Licio.*

Editors vary in the treatment of F's short lines, sometimes letting a short line stand independently, and sometimes joining several short lines into a quasi-pentameter.
The latter practice is generally followed in the present
edition. Modern editors are quite consistent in identifying
as verse a few passages set as prose in F, and vice versa.

Errors in foreign languages in F are allowed to stand
if they are conceivably errors made by the speaker, e.g.
errors in Latin and Spanish. Spellings of English words
are corrected and modernized. The punctuation is modern. Obvious typographical errors, of which there are a
great many, are corrected silently. The following materials,
lacking in F, are given in square brackets in this edition:
cast of characters, missing act and scene designations, indications of place of action, certain stage directions (F
has an unusually copious supply of stage directions, some
of which make interesting references to properties).

The following list includes all significant variations from
F. The reading in the present text is in italics, followed
by the F reading in roman.

Ind.i.s.d. *Hostess and Beggar* Begger and Hostes   12 *thirdborough*
Head-borough   17 *Broach* Brach   82 *A Player* 2. Player   88 *2.*
Player Sincklo

Ind.ii.2 *lordship* Lord   18 *Sly's* Sies   137 *play it. Is* play, it is

I.i.13 *Vincentio* Vincentio's   25 *Mi perdonato* Me Pardonato   47
s.d. *suitor* sister   73 *master* Mr   162 *captum* captam   207 *colored*
Conlord   243 *your* you
I.ii.13 *master* Mr   17s.d. *wrings* rings   18 *masters* mistris   24 *Con*

. . *trovato* Contutti le core bene trobatto 25 *ben* bene 25
molto multo 45 *this's* this 69, 89 *shrewd* shrow'd 70 *Xanthippe*
Xantippe 72 *she* she is 120 *me and other* me. Other 172 *help*
one helpe one 190 *Antonio's* Butonios 213 *ours* yours 266 *feat*
Leeke

I.i.3 *gawds* goods 8 *charge thee* charge 73 *Backare* Bacare
75–76 *wooing. Neighbor,* wooing neighbors: 79 *unto you this*
unto this 104 *Pisa; by report* Pisa by report 158 *vile* vilde 186
bonny bony 241 *askance* a sconce 323 *in me*

II.i.28 *Sigeia* Sigeria (also in 32, 41) 46 [*Aside*] Luc. 49 *Bianca*
F omits] 50 *Lucentio* Bian. 52 *Bianca* Hort. 73 *B mi* Beeme
79 *change* charge 79 *odd* old 80 *Messenger* Nicke

II.ii.29 *of thy* of 30 *such old* such 33 *hear* heard 55 *swayed*
Waid 57 *half-cheeked* halfe-chekt 128 *to her love* sir, Loue
130 *As I* As

IV.i.25 *Curtis* Grumio 100s.d. *Enter . . . Servingmen* [F places
after 99] 174s.d. [in F, after 175] 198 *reverent* reuerend

IV.ii.4 *Hortensio* Luc. 6 *Lucentio* Hor. 8 *Lucentio* Hor. 13
none me 31 *her* them 63 *mercatante* Marcantant 71 *Take in*
Par. Take me.

IV.iii.63 *Haberdasher* Fel. 81 *is a* is 88 *like a* like 179 *account-*
'st accountedst

IV.iv:1 *Sir* Sirs 5 [in F, Tranio's speech begins here] 9s.d. [F
places after 7] 19 *Signior* Tra. Signior 68 [F adds s.d., Enter
Peter] 91 *except* expect

IV.v.18 *is* in 36 *make a* make the 38 *Whither* Whether 38
where whether 41 *Allots* A lots 48 *reverend* reuerent (also in
60) 78 *she be* she

V.i.6 *master's* mistris 52 *master's* Mistris 107s.d. [F places after
105] 145 *No* Mo

V.ii.2 *done* come 37 *thee, lad* the lad 45 *bitter* better 65 *for* sir

A Midsummer Night's Dream

EDITED BY
WOLFGANG CLEMEN

[Dramatis Personae

Theseus, Duke of Athens
Egeus, father to Hermia
Lysander ⎱ in love with Hermia
Demetrius ⎰
Philostrate, Master of the Revels to Theseus
Peter Quince, a carpenter; Prologue in the play
Snug, a joiner; Lion in the play
Nick Bottom, a weaver; Pyramus in the play
Francis Flute, a bellows mender; Thisby in the play
Tom Snout, a tinker; Wall in the play
Robin Starveling, a tailor; Moonshine in the play
Hippolyta, Queen of the Amazons, betrothed to Theseus
Hermia, daughter to Egeus, in love with Lysander
Helena, in love with Demetrius
Oberon, King of the Fairies
Titania, Queen of the Fairies
Puck, or Robin Goodfellow
Peaseblossom ⎫
Cobweb ⎪
Moth ⎬ fairies
Mustardseed ⎭
Other Fairies attending their King and Queen
Attendants on Theseus and Hippolyta

Scene: Athens, and a wood near it]

A Midsummer Night's Dream

[ACT I

Scene I. *The palace of Theseus.*]

Enter Theseus, Hippolyta, [Philostrate,] with others.

Theseus. Now, fair Hippolyta, our nuptial hour
  Draws on apace. Four happy days bring in
  Another moon; but, O, methinks, how slow
  This old moon wanes! She lingers°¹ my desires,
  Like to a stepdame, or a dowager,   5
  Long withering out a young man's revenue.°

Hippolyta. Four days will quickly steep themselves in night,
  Four nights will quickly dream away the time;
  And then the moon, like to a silver bow
  New-bent in heaven, shall behold the night   10
  Of our solemnities.

Theseus.   Go, Philostrate,
  Stir up the Athenian youth to merriments,
  Awake the pert° and nimble spirit of mirth,
  Turn melancholy forth to funerals;

¹ The degree signs (°) indicates a footnote, which is keyed to the
text by line number. Text references are printed in *italic* type; the
annotation follows in roman type.
I.i. 4 *lingers* makes to linger, delays   6 *Long withering out a young
man's revenue* diminishing the young man's money (because she
must be supported by him)   13 *pert* lively

41

15 The pale companion° is not for our pomp.°
                                    [*Exit Philostrate.*]
Hippolyta, I wooed thee with my sword,°
And won thy love, doing thee injuries;
But I will wed thee in another key,
With pomp, with triumph, and with reveling.

*Enter Egeus and his daughter Hermia, and Lysander,
and Demetrius.*

20 *Egeus.* Happy be Theseus, our renownèd Duke!

Theseus. Thanks, good Egeus.° What's the news with
    thee?

Egeus. Full of vexation come I, with complaint
Against my child, my daughter Hermia.
Stand forth, Demetrius. My noble lord,
25 This man hath my consent to marry her.
Stand forth, Lysander. And, my gracious Duke
This man hath bewitched the bosom of my child.
Thou, thou, Lysander, thou hast given her rhymes,
And interchanged love tokens with my child.
30 Thou hast by moonlight at her window sung,
With feigning voice, verses of feigning love,
And stol'n the impression of her fantasy°
With bracelets of thy hair, rings, gauds, conceits,
Knacks,° trifles, nosegays, sweetmeats, messengers
35 Of strong prevailment in unhardened youth.
With cunning hast thou filched my daughter's heart,
Turned her obedience, which is due to me,
To stubborn harshness. And, my gracious Duke,
Be it so she will not here before your Grace
40 Consent to marry with Demetrius,
I beg the ancient privilege of Athens:

15 *companion* fellow (contemptuous)   15 *pomp* festive procession
16 *I wooed thee with my sword* (Theseus had captured Hippolyta
when he conquered the Amazons)   21 *Egeus* (pronounced "E-gé-
us")   32 *stol'n the impression of her fantasy* fraudulently impressed
your image upon her imagination   33–34 *gauds, conceits, Knacks*
trinkets, cleverly devised tokens, knickknacks

As she is mine, I may dispose of her,
Which shall be either to this gentleman
Or to her death, according to our law
Immediately° provided in that case.   45

Theseus. What say you, Hermia? Be advised, fair
   maid.
To you your father should be as a god,
One that composed your beauties; yea, and one
To whom you are but as a form in wax
By him imprinted and within his power   50
To leave the figure or disfigure it.
Demetrius is a worthy gentleman.

Hermia. So is Lysander.

Theseus.   In himself he is;
But in this kind, wanting your father's voice,°
The other must be held the worthier.   55

Hermia. I would my father looked but with my eyes.

Theseus. Rather your eyes must with his judgment
   look.

Hermia. I do entreat your Grace to pardon me.
I know not by what power I am made bold,
Nor how it may concern my modesty,   60
In such a presence here to plead my thoughts;
But I beseech your Grace that I may know
The worst that may befall me in this case,
If I refuse to wed Demetrius.

Theseus. Either to die the death, or to abjure   65
Forever the society of men.
Therefore, fair Hermia, question your desires;
Know of° your youth, examine well your blood,°
Whether, if you yield not to your father's choice,
You can endure the livery of a nun,   70
For aye to be in shady cloister mewed,°
To live a barren sister all your life,

45 *Immediately* expressly 54 *But in . . . father's voice* but in this
particular respect, lacking your father's approval 68 *Know of*
ascertain from 68 *blood* passions 71 *mewed* caged

Chanting faint hymns to the cold fruitless moon.°
Thrice-blessèd they that master so their blood,
75 To undergo such maiden pilgrimage;
But earthlier happy is the rose distilled,°
Than that which, withering on the virgin thorn,
Grows, lives, and dies in single blessedness.

Hermia. So will I grow, so live, so die, my lord,
80 Ere I will yield my virgin patent° up
Unto his lordship, whose unwished yoke
My soul consents not to give sovereignty.

Theseus. Take time to pause; and, by the next new
    moon—
The sealing day betwixt my love and me,
85 For everlasting bond of fellowship—
Upon that day either prepare to die
For disobedience to your father's will,
Or else to wed Demetrius, as he would,
Or on Diana's altar to protest
90 For aye austerity and single life.

Demetrius. Relent, sweet Hermia: and, Lysander,
    yield
Thy crazèd title° to my certain right.

Lysander. You have her father's love, Demetrius;
Let me have Hermia's: do you marry him.

95 *Egeus.* Scornful Lysander! True, he hath my love,
And what is mine my love shall render him.
And she is mine, and all my right of her
I do estate unto° Demetrius.

Lysander. I am, my lord, as well derived as he,
100 As well possessed;° my love is more than his;
My fortunes every way as fairly ranked
(If not with vantage°) as Demetrius';
And, which is more than all these boasts can be,

73 *moon* i.e., Diana, goddess of chastity   76 *distilled* made into
perfumes   80 *patent* privilege   92 *crazèd title* flawed claim   98 *estate unto* settle upon   100 *As well possessed* as rich   102 *If not
with vantage* if not better

   I am beloved of beauteous Hermia.
   Why should not I then prosecute my right?   105
   Demetrius, I'll avouch it to his head,°
   Made love to Nedar's daughter, Helena,
   And won her soul; and she, sweet lady, dotes,
   Devoutly dotes, dotes in idolatry,
   Upon this spotted° and inconstant man.   110

Theseus. I must confess that I have heard so much,
   And with Demetrius thought to have spoke thereof;
   But, being overfull of self-affairs,
   My mind did lose it. But, Demetrius, come;
   And come, Egeus. You shall go with me;   115
   I have some private schooling for you both.
   For you, fair Hermia, look you arm yourself
   To fit your fancies to your father's will;
   Or else the law of Athens yields you up—
   Which by no means we may extenuate—   120
   To death, or to a vow of single life.
   Come, my Hippolyta. What cheer, my love?
   Demetrius and Egeus, go along.
   I must employ you in some business
   Against° our nuptial, and confer with you   125
   Of something nearly° that concerns yourselves.

Egeus. With duty and desire we follow you.
                  Exeunt [all but Lysander and Hermia].

Lysander. How now, my love! Why is your cheek so
      pale?
   How chance° the roses there do fade so fast?

Hermia. Belike° for want of rain, which I could well   130
   Beteem° them from the tempest of my eyes.

Lysander. Ay me! For aught that I could ever read,
   Could ever hear by tale or history,

---

106 *to his head* in his teeth   110 *spotted* i.e., morally stained
125 *Against* in preparation for   126 *nearly* closely   129 *How
chance* how does it come that   130 *Belike* perhaps   131 *Beteem*
bring forth

The course of true love never did run smooth;
135 But, either it was different in blood—

Hermia. O cross! Too high to be enthralled to low!

Lysander. Or else misgraffèd° in respect of years—

Hermia. O spite! Too old to be engaged to young!

Lysander. Or else it stood upon the choice of friends—

140 *Hermia.* O hell! To choose love by another's eyes!

Lysander. Or, if there were a sympathy in choice,
War, death, or sickness did lay siege to it,
Making it momentany° as a sound,
Swift as a shadow, short as any dream,
145 Brief as the lightning in the collied° night,
That, in a spleen,° unfolds both heaven and earth,
And ere a man hath power to say "Behold!"
The jaws of darkness do devour it up:
So quick bright things come to confusion.

150 *Hermia.* If then true lovers have been ever crossed,
It stands as an edict in destiny:
Then let us teach our trial patience,°
Because it is a customary cross,
As due to love as thoughts and dreams and sighs,
155 Wishes and tears, poor Fancy's° followers.

Lysander. A good persuasion.° Therefore, hear me,
    Hermia.
I have a widow aunt, a dowager
Of great revenue, and she hath no child.
From Athens is her house remote seven leagues,
160 And she respects me as her only son.
There, gentle Hermia, may I marry thee,
And to that place the sharp Athenian law
Cannot pursue us. If thou lovest me, then,

---

137 *misgraffèd* ill matched, misgrafted   143 *momentany* momentary,
passing   145 *collied* blackened   146 *spleen* flash   152 *teach our
trial patience* i.e., teach ourselves to be patient   155 *Fancy's* Love's
156 *persuasion* principle

Steal forth thy father's house tomorrow night;
And in the wood, a league without the town,   *165*
Where I did meet thee once with Helena,
To do observance to a morn of May,
There will I stay for thee.

Hermia.   My good Lysander!
I swear to thee, by Cupid's strongest bow,
By his best arrow with the golden head,°   *170*
By the simplicity of Venus' doves,
By that which knitteth souls and prospers loves,
And by that fire which burned the Carthage
    queen,°
When the false Troyan under sail was seen,
By all the vows that ever men have broke,   *175*
In number more than ever women spoke,
In that same place thou hast appointed me,
Tomorrow truly will I meet with thee.

Lysander. Keep promise, love. Look, here comes
    Helena.

Enter Helena.

Hermia. God speed fair Helena! Whither away?   *180*

Helena. Call you me fair? That fair again unsay.
Demetrius loves your fair.° O happy fair!
Your eyes are lodestars,° and your tongue's sweet
    air°
More tunable than lark to shepherd's ear,
When wheat is green, when hawthorn buds appear.   *185*
Sickness is catching. O, were favor° so,
Yours would I catch, fair Hermia, ere I go;
My ear should catch your voice, my eye your eye,

170 *arrow with the golden head* (Cupid's gold-headed arrows caused
love, the leaden ones dislike)   173 *Carthage queen* Dido (who
burned herself on a funeral pyre when the Trojan Aeneas left her)
182 *fair* beauty   183 *lodestars* guiding stars   183 *air* music
186 *favor* looks

My tongue should catch your tongue's sweet mel-
 ody.
190 Were the world mine, Demetrius being bated,°
The rest I'd give to be to you translated.°
O, teach me how you look, and with what art
You sway the motion of Demetrius' heart!

Hermia. I frown upon him, yet he loves me still.

Helena. O that your frowns would teach my smiles
195 such skill!

Hermia. I give him curses, yet he gives me love.

Helena. O that my prayers could such affection move!

Hermia. The more I hate, the more he follows me.

Helena. The more I love, the more he hateth me.

200 *Hermia.* His folly, Helena, is no fault of mine.

Helena. None, but your beauty: would that fault were
 mine!

Hermia. Take comfort. He no more shall see my face;
Lysander and myself will fly this place.
Before the time I did Lysander see,
205 Seemed Athens as a paradise to me.
O, then, what graces in my love do dwell,
That he hath turned a heaven unto a hell!

Lysander. Helen, to you our minds we will unfold.
Tomorrow night, when Phoebe° doth behold
210 Her silver visage in the wat'ry glass,
Decking with liquid pearl the bladed grass,
A time that lovers' flights doth still° conceal,
Through Athens' gates have we devised to steal.

Hermia. And in the wood, where often you and I
215 Upon faint primrose beds were wont to lie,
Emptying our bosoms of their counsel sweet,
There my Lysander and myself shall meet,

190 *bated* excepted 191 *translated* transformed 209 *Phoebe* the
moon 212 *still* always

And thence from Athens turn away our eyes,
To seek new friends and stranger companies.°
Farewell, sweet playfellow. Pray thou for us;   220
And good luck grant thee thy Demetrius!
Keep word, Lysander. We must starve our sight
From lovers' food till tomorrow deep midnight.

ysander. I will, my Hermia.   *Exit Hermia.*
                    Helena, adieu.
As you on him, Demetrius dote on you!   225
                    Exit Lysander.

Ielena. How happy some o'er other some° can be!
  Through Athens I am thought as fair as she.
  But what of that? Demetrius thinks not so;
  He will not know what all but he do know.
  And as he errs, doting on Hermia's eyes,   230
  So I, admiring of his qualities.
  Things base and vile, holding no quantity,°
  Love can transpose to form and dignity.
  Love looks not with the eyes, but with the mind,
  And therefore is winged Cupid painted blind.   235
  Nor hath Love's mind of any judgment taste;
  Wings, and no eyes, figure° unheedy haste:
  And therefore is Love said to be a child,
  Because in choice he is so oft beguiled.
  As waggish boys in game themselves forswear,   240
  So the boy Love is perjured everywhere.
  For ere Demetrius looked on Hermia's eyne,°
  He hailed down oaths that he was only mine;
  And when this hail some heat from Hermia felt,
  So he dissolved, and show'rs of oaths did melt.   245
  I will go tell him of fair Hermia's flight.
  Then to the wood will he tomorrow night
  Pursue her; and for this intelligence°

219 *stranger companies* the company of strangers   226 *some o'er
other some* some in comparison with others   232 *holding no quantity* having no proportion (therefore unattractive)   237 *figure* sym-
bolize   242 *eyne* eyes   248 *intelligence* piece of news

If I have thanks, it is a dear expense:°
250 But herein mean I to enrich my pain,
To have his sight thither and back again.   *Exit*

[Scene II.   *Quince's house.*]

*Enter Quince the Carpenter, and Snug the Joiner
and Bottom the Weaver, and Flute the Bellows
Mender, and Snout the Tinker, and Starveling the
Tailor.°*

Quince. Is all our company here?

Bottom. You were best to call them generally,° man
by man, according to the scrip.

Quince. Here is the scroll of every man's name
5   which is thought fit, through all Athens, to play in
our interlude° before the Duke and the Duchess
on his wedding day at night.

Bottom. First, good Peter Quince, say what the play
treats on; then read the names of the actors; and
10   so grow to a point.

Quince. Marry,° our play is, "The most lamentable
comedy, and most cruel death of Pyramus and
Thisby."

Bottom. A very good piece of work, I assure you,

---

249 *dear expense* (1) expense gladly incurred (2) heavy cost (in
Demetrius' opinion) I.ii.s.d. (the names of the clowns suggest their
trades. *Bottom* skein on which the yarn is wound; *Quince* quines
blocks of wood used for building; *Snug* close-fitting; *Flute* suggesting
fluted bellows [for church organs]; *Snout* spout of a kettle
Starveling an allusion to the proverbial thinness of tailors) 2 *generally* (Bottom means "individually") 6 *interlude* dramatic entertainment 11 *Marry* (an interjection, originally an oath, "By the
Virgin Mary")

and a merry. Now, good Peter Quince, call forth   15
your actors by the scroll. Masters, spread yourselves.

Quince. Answer as I call you. Nick Bottom, the
weaver.

Bottom. Ready. Name what part I am for, and pro-   20
ceed.

Quince. You, Nick Bottom, are set down for Pyramus.

Bottom. What is Pyramus? A lover, or a tyrant?

Quince. A lover that kills himself, most gallant, for
love.   25

Bottom. That will ask some tears in the true per-
forming of it: if I do it, let the audience look to
their eyes. I will move storms, I will condole° in
some measure. To the rest: yet my chief humor°
is for a tyrant. I could play Ercles° rarely, or a   30
part to tear a cat in, to make all split.

> The raging rocks
> And shivering shocks
> Shall break the locks
>   Of prison gates;   35
> And Phibbus' car°
> Shall shine from far,
> And make and mar
>   The foolish Fates.

This was lofty! Now name the rest of the players.   40
This is Ercles' vein, a tyrant's vein. A lover is
more condoling.

Quince. Francis Flute, the bellows mender.

Flute. Here, Peter Quince.

28 *condole* lament   29 *humor* disposition   30 *Ercles* Hercules (a
part notorious for ranting)   36 *Phibbus' car* (mispronunciation for
"Phoebus' car," or chariot, i.e., the sun)

45 *Quince.* Flute, you must take Thisby on you.

Flute. What is Thisby? A wand'ring knight?

Quince. It is the lady that Pyramus must love.

Flute. Nay, faith, let not me play a woman. I have a beard coming.

50 *Quince.* That's all one.° You shall play it in a mask, and you may speak as small° as you will.

Bottom. An° I may hide my face, let me play Thisby too, I'll speak in a monstrous little voice, "Thisne, Thisne!" "Ah Pyramus, my lover dear! Thy Thisby
55 dear, and lady dear!"

Quince. No, no; you must play Pyramus: and, Flute, you Thisby.

Bottom. Well, proceed.

Quince. Robin Starveling, the tailor.

60 *Starveling.* Here, Peter Quince.

Quince. Robin Starveling, you must play Thisby's mother. Tom Snout, the tinker.

Snout. Here, Peter Quince.

Quince. You, Pyramus' father: myself, Thisby's
65 father: Snug, the joiner; you, the lion's part. And I hope here is a play fitted.

Snug. Have you the lion's part written? Pray you, if it be, give it me, for I am slow of study.

Quince. You may do it extempore, for it is nothing
70 but roaring.

Bottom. Let me play the lion too. I will roar that° I will do any man's heart good to hear me. I will roar, that I will make the Duke say, "Let him roar again, let him roar again."

50 *That's all one* it makes no difference   51 *small* softly   52 *An* if
71 *that* so that

Quince. An you should do it too terribly, you would 75
    fright the Duchess and the ladies, that they would
    shriek; and that were enough to hang us all.

All. That would hang us, every mother's son.

Bottom. I grant you, friends, if you should fright the
    ladies out of their wits, they would have no more 80
    discretion but to hang us: but I will aggravate°
    my voice so that I will roar you as gently as any
    sucking dove; I will roar you an 'twere° any night-
    ingale.

Quince. You can play no part but Pyramus; for 85
    Pyramus is a sweet-faced man; a proper° man as
    one shall see in a summer's day; a most lovely,
    gentlemanlike man: therefore you must needs play
    Pyramus.

Bottom. Well, I will undertake it. What beard were 90
    I best to play it in?

Quince. Why, what you will.

Bottom. I will discharge it in either your straw-color
    beard, your orange-tawny beard, your purple-in-
    grain° beard, or your French-crown-color° beard, 95
    your perfit° yellow.

Quince. Some of your French crowns° have no hair
    at all, and then you will play barefaced.° But, mas-
    ters, here are your parts; and I am to entreat you,
    request you, and desire you, to con° them by to- 100
    morrow night; and meet me in the palace wood, a
    mile without the town, by moonlight. There will
    we rehearse, for if we meet in the city, we shall be
    dogged with company, and our devices° known.

---

81 *aggravate* (Bottom means "moderate")   83 *an 'twere* as if it were
86 *proper* handsome   94–95 *purple-in-grain* dyed with a fast purple
95 *French-crown-color* color of French gold coin   96 *perfit* perfect
97 *crowns* (1) gold coins (2) heads bald from the French disease
(syphilis)   98 *barefaced* (1) bald (2) brazen   100 *con* study
104 *devices* plans

105   In the meantime I will draw a bill of properties,
       such as our play wants. I pray you, fail me not.

    Bottom. We will meet; and there we may rehearse
       most obscenely° and courageously. Take pains; be
       perfit: adieu.

110 *Quince.* At the Duke's Oak we meet.

    Bottom. Enough; hold or cut bowstrings.°   *Exeunt*

---

105 *bill of properties* list of stage furnishings   108 *obscenely* (Bottom means "seemly")   111 *hold or cut bowstrings* i.e., keep your word or give it up (?)

[ACT II

Scene I.   *A wood near Athens.*]

Enter a Fairy at one door, and Robin Goodfellow
[Puck] at another.

Puck. How now, spirit! Whither wander you?

Fairy.   Over hill, over dale,
      Thorough bush, thorough brier,
  Over park, over pale,°
      Thorough flood, thorough fire,   *5*
  I do wander everywhere,
  Swifter than the moon's sphere;°
  And I serve the Fairy Queen,
  To dew her orbs° upon the green.
  The cowslips tall her pensioners° be: *10*
  In their gold coats spots you see;
  Those be rubies, fairy favors,°
  In those freckles live their savors.°
  I must go seek some dewdrops here,
  And hang a pearl in every cowslip's ear.   *15*

II.i.4 *pale* enclosed land, park   7 *moon's sphere* (according to the
Ptolemaic system the moon was fixed in a hollow sphere that sur-
rounded and revolved about the earth)   9 *orbs* fairy rings, i.e.,
circles of darker grass   10 *pensioners* bodyguards (referring to
Elizabeth I's bodyguard of fifty splendid young noblemen)
12 *favors* gifts   13 *savors* perfumes

Farewell, thou lob° of spirits; I'll be gone.
Our Queen and all her elves come here anon.

Puck. The King doth keep his revels here tonight.
Take heed the Queen come not within his sight.
20 For Oberon is passing fell and wrath,°
Because that she as her attendant hath
A lovely boy, stolen from an Indian king;
She never had so sweet a changeling.°
And jealous Oberon would have the child
25 Knight of his train, to trace° the forests wild.
But she perforce withholds the lovèd boy,
Crowns him with flowers, and makes him all her
        joy.
And now they never meet in grove or green,
By fountain clear, or spangled starlight sheen,°
30 But they do square,° that all their elves for fear
Creep into acorn cups and hide them there.

Fairy. Either I mistake your shape and making quite,
Or else you are that shrewd and knavish sprite
Called Robin Goodfellow. Are not you he
35 That frights the maidens of the villagery,°
Skim milk, and sometimes labor in the quern,°
And bootless° make the breathless housewife
        churn,
And sometime make the drink to bear no barm,°
Mislead night wanderers, laughing at their harm?
40 Those that Hobgoblin call you, and sweet Puck,
You do their work, and they shall have good luck.
Are not you he?

Puck.   Thou speakest aright;
I am that merry wanderer of the night.
I jest to Oberon, and make him smile,

---

16 *lob* lubber, clumsy fellow   20 *passing fell and wrath* very fierce
and angry   23 *changeling* (usually a child left behind by fairies in
exchange for one stolen, but here applied to the stolen child)   25
trace traverse   29 *starlight sheen* brightly shining starlight   30
square clash, quarrel   35 *villagery* villagers   36 *quern* hand mill for
grinding grain   37 *bootless* in vain   38 *barm* yeast, froth

When I a fat and bean-fed horse beguile,   45
Neighing in likeness of a filly foal:
And sometime lurk I in a gossip's° bowl,
In very likeness of a roasted crab;°
And when she drinks, against her lips I bob
And on her withered dewlap° pour the ale.   50
The wisest aunt, telling the saddest° tale,
Sometime for three-foot stool mistaketh me;
Then slip I from her bum, down topples she,
And "tailor"° cries, and falls into a cough;
And then the whole quire° hold their hips and
    laugh,   55
And waxen° in their mirth, and neeze,° and swear
A merrier hour was never wasted° there.
But, room, fairy! Here comes Oberon.

Fairy. And here my mistress. Would that he were
    gone!

*Enter [Oberon,] the King of Fairies, at one door,
with his train; and [Titania,] the Queen, at another,
with hers.*

Oberon. Ill met by moonlight, proud Titania.   60

Titania. What, jealous Oberon! Fairy, skip hence.
I have forsworn his bed and company.

Oberon. Tarry, rash wanton;° am not I thy lord?

Titania. Then I must be thy lady: but I know
When thou hast stolen away from fairy land   65
And in the shape of Corin° sat all day,
Playing on pipes of corn,° and versing love

47 *gossip's* old woman's   48 *crab* crab apple   50 *dewlap* fold of
skin on the throat   51 *saddest* most serious   54 *tailor* (suggesting
the posture of a tailor squatting; or a term of abuse: Middle English
aillard, "thief")   55 *quire* company, choir   56 *waxen* increase
56 *neeze* sneeze   57 *wasted* passed   63 *rash wanton* hasty willful creature   66 *Corin* (like *Phillida*, line 68, a traditional name for
a lover in pastoral poetry)   67 *pipes of corn* musical instruments
made of grain stalks

To amorous Phillida. Why art thou here,
Come from the farthest steep of India?
70 But that, forsooth, the bouncing° Amazon,
Your buskined° mistress and your warrior love,
To Theseus must be wedded, and you come
To give their bed joy and prosperity.

Oberon. How canst thou thus for shame, Titania,
75 Glance at my credit with Hippolyta,
Knowing I know thy love to Theseus?
Didst not thou lead him through the glimmering
night
From Perigenia, whom he ravishèd?
And make him with fair Aegles break his faith,
80 With Ariadne and Antiopa?°

Titania. These are the forgeries of jealousy:
And never, since the middle summer's spring,°
Met we on hill, in dale, forest, or mead,
By pavèd° fountain or by rushy brook,
85 Or in the beachèd margent° of the sea,
To dance our ringlets to the whistling wind,
But with thy brawls thou hast disturbed our sport.
Therefore the winds, piping to us in vain,
As in revenge, have sucked up from the sea
90 Contagious° fogs; which, falling in the land,
Hath every pelting° river made so proud,
That they have overborne their continents.°
The ox hath therefore stretched his yoke in vain,
The plowman lost his sweat, and the green corn°
95 Hath rotted ere his youth attained a beard;
The fold stands empty in the drownèd field,
And crows are fatted with the murrion flock;°

---

70 *bouncing* swaggering   71 *buskined* wearing a hunter's boot
(buskin)   78–80 *Perigenia, Aegles, Ariadne, Antiopa* (girls Theseus
loved and deserted)   82 *middle summer's spring* beginning of midsummer   84 *pavèd* i.e., with pebbly bottom   85 *margent* margin,
shore   90 *contagious* generating pestilence   91 *pelting* petty   92
continents containers (i.e., banks)   94 *corn* grain   97 *murrion
flock* flock dead of cattle disease (murrain)

The nine men's morris° is filled up with mud;
And the quaint mazes° in the wanton green,°
For lack of tread, are undistinguishable.   100
The human mortals want their winter here;
No night is now with hymn or carol blest.
Therefore the moon, the governess of floods,
Pale in her anger, washes all the air,
That rheumatic diseases do abound.   105
And thorough this distemperature° we see
The seasons alter: hoary-headed frosts
Fall in the fresh lap of the crimson rose,
And on old Hiems'° thin and icy crown
An odorous chaplet° of sweet summer buds   110
Is, as in mockery, set. The spring, the summer,
The childing° autumn, angry winter, change
Their wonted liveries;° and the mazèd° world,
By their increase, now knows not which is which.
And this same progeny of evils comes   115
From our debate,° from our dissension;
We are their parents and original.

Oberon. Do you amend it, then; it lies in you:
Why should Titania cross her Oberon?
I do but beg a little changeling boy,   120
To be my henchman.°

Titania.   Set your heart at rest.
The fairy land buys not° the child of me.
His mother was a vot'ress° of my order,
And, in the spicèd Indian air, by night,
Full often hath she gossiped by my side,   125
And sat with me on Neptune's yellow sands,

98 *nine men's morris* square cut in the turf (for a game in which
each player has nine counters or "men")   99 *quaint mazes* intricate
meandering paths on the grass (kept fresh by running along them)
99 *wanton green* grass growing without check   106 *distemperature*
disturbance in nature   109 *old Hiems'* the winter's   110 *chaplet*
wreath   112 *childing* breeding, fruitful   113 *wonted liveries* accus-
tomed apparel   113 *mazèd* bewildered   116 *debate* quarrel   121
henchman page   122 *The fairy land buys not* i.e., even your whole
domain could not buy   123 *vot'ress* woman who has taken a vow

Marking th' embarkèd traders on the flood;
When we have laughed to see the sails conceive
And grow big-bellied with the wanton wind;
130 Which she, with pretty and with swimming gait
Following—her womb then rich with my young
        squire—
Would imitate, and sail upon the land,
To fetch me trifles, and return again,
As from a voyage, rich with merchandise.
135 But she, being mortal, of that boy did die;
And for her sake do I rear up her boy,
And for her sake I will not part with him.

Oberon. How long within this wood intend you stay?

Titania. Perchance till after Theseus' wedding day.
140 If you will patiently dance in our round,°
And see our moonlight revels, go with us.
If not, shun me, and I will spare° your haunts.

Oberon. Give me that boy, and I will go with thee.

Titania. Not for thy fairy kingdom. Fairies, away!
145 We shall chide downright, if I longer stay.
                    Exeunt [*Titania with her train*].

Oberon. Well, go thy way. Thou shalt not from this
        grove
Till I torment thee for this injury.
My gentle Puck, come hither. Thou rememb'rest
Since° once I sat upon a promontory,
150 And heard a mermaid, on a dolphin's back,
Uttering such dulcet and harmonious breath,
That the rude sea grew civil° at her song,
And certain stars shot madly from their spheres,
· To hear the sea maid's music.

Puck.   I remember.

155 *Oberon.* That very time I saw, but thou couldst not,
Flying between the cold moon and the earth,

---

140 *round* circular dance   142 *spare* keep away from   149 *Since*
when   152 *civil* well behaved

Cupid all armed. A certain aim he took
At a fair vestal° thronèd by the west,
And loosed his love shaft smartly from his bow,
As it should° pierce a hundred thousand hearts.   160
But I might° see young Cupid's fiery shaft
Quenched in the chaste beams of the wat'ry moon,
And the imperial vot'ress passèd on,
In maiden meditation, fancy-free.°
Yet marked I where the bolt of Cupid fell.   165
It fell upon a little western flower,
Before milk-white, now purple with love's wound,
And maidens call it love-in-idleness.°
Fetch me that flow'r; the herb I showed thee once:
The juice of it on sleeping eyelids laid   170
Will make or man or woman° madly dote
Upon the next live creature that it sees.
Fetch me this herb, and be thou here again
Ere the leviathan° can swim a league.

Puck. I'll put a girdle round about the earth   175
In forty minutes.   [*Exit.*]

Oberon.   Having once this juice,
I'll watch Titania when she is asleep,
And drop the liquor of it in her eyes.
The next thing then she waking looks upon,
Be it on lion, bear, or wolf, or bull,   180
On meddling monkey, or on busy° ape,
She shall pursue it with the soul of love.
And ere I take this charm from off her sight,
As I can take it with another herb,
I'll make her render up her page to me.   185
But who comes here? I am invisible,
And I will overhear their conference.

Enter Demetrius, Helena following him.

158 *vestal* virgin (possibly an allusion to Elizabeth, the Virgin
Queen)   160 *As it should* as if it would   161 *might* could   164
fancy-free free from the power of love   168 *love-in-idleness* pansy
171 *or man or woman* either man or woman   174 *leviathan* sea
monster, whale   181 *busy* meddlesome

Demetrius. I love thee not, therefore pursue me not.
Where is Lysander and fair Hermia?
190   The one I'll slay, the other slayeth me.
Thou told'st me they were stol'n unto this wood;
And here am I, and wood° within this wood,
Because I cannot meet my Hermia.
Hence, get thee gone, and follow me no more!

195 *Helena.* You draw me, you hardhearted adamant;°
But yet you draw not iron, for my heart
Is true as steel. Leave you your power to draw,
And I shall have no power to follow you.

Demetrius. Do I entice you? Do I speak you fair?°
200   Or, rather, do I not in plainest truth
Tell you, I do not nor I cannot love you?

Helena. And even for that do I love you the more.
I am your spaniel; and, Demetrius,
The more you beat me, I will fawn on you.
205   Use me but as your spaniel, spurn me, strike me,
Neglect me, lose me; only give me leave,
Unworthy as I am, to follow you.
What worser place can I beg in your love—
And yet a place of high respect with me—
210   Than to be used as you use your dog?

Demetrius. Tempt not too much the hatred of my
spirit,
For I am sick when I do look on thee.

Helena. And I am sick when I look not on you.

Demetrius. You do impeach° your modesty too much,
215   To leave the city, and commit yourself
Into the hands of one that loves you not,
To trust the opportunity of night
And the ill counsel of a desert° place
With the rich worth of your virginity.

192 *wood* out of my mind (with perhaps an additional pun on
"wooed")   195 *adamant* (1) very hard gem (2) loadstone, magnet
199 *speak you fair* speak kindly to you   214 *impeach* expose to
reproach   218 *desert* deserted, uninhabited

Helena. Your virtue is my privilege.° For that   220
　　It is not night when I do see your face,
　　Therefore I think I am not in the night;
　　Nor doth this wood lack worlds of company,
　　For you in my respect° are all the world.
　　Then how can it be said I am alone,   225
　　When all the world is here to look on me?

Demetrius. I'll run from thee and hide me in the
　　brakes,°
　　And leave thee to the mercy of wild beasts.

Helena. The wildest hath not such a heart as you.
　　Run when you will, the story shall be changed: 230
　　Apollo flies, and Daphne° holds the chase;
　　The dove pursues the griffin;° the mild hind°
　　Makes speed to catch the tiger; bootless speed,
　　When cowardice pursues, and valor flies.

Demetrius. I will not stay° thy questions. Let me go!   235
　　Or, if thou follow me, do not believe
　　But I shall do thee mischief in the wood.

Helena. Ay, in the temple, in the town, the field,
　　You do me mischief. Fie, Demetrius!
　　Your wrongs do set a scandal on my sex.   240
　　We cannot fight for love, as men may do;
　　We should be wooed, and were not made to woo.
　　　　　　　　　　　　　　　　[*Exit Demetrius.*]
　　I'll follow thee, and make a heaven of hell,
　　To die upon° the hand I love so well.   [*Exit.*]

Oberon. Fare thee well, nymph: ere he do leave this
　　grove,   245
　　Thou shalt fly him, and he shall seek thy love.

---

220 *Your virtue is my privilege* your inherent power is my warrant
224 *in my respect* in my opinion   227 *brakes* thickets   231 *Daphne*
a nymph who fled from Apollo (at her prayer she was changed into
a laurel tree)   232 *griffin* fabulous monster with an eagle's head
and a lion's body   232 *hind* doe   235 *stay* wait for   244 *To die
upon* dying by

Enter Puck.

Hast thou the flower there? Welcome, wanderer.

Puck. Ay, there it is.

Oberon.   I pray thee, give it me.
I know a bank where the wild thyme blows,
250 Where oxlips and the nodding violet grows,
Quite overcanopied with luscious woodbine,
With sweet musk roses, and with eglantine.
There sleeps Titania sometime of the night,
Lulled in these flowers with dances and delight;
255 And there the snake throws° her enameled skin,
Weed° wide enough to wrap a fairy in.
And with the juice of this I'll streak her eyes,
And make her full of hateful fantasies.
Take thou some of it, and seek through this grove.
260 A sweet Athenian lady is in love
With a disdainful youth. Anoint his eyes;
But do it when the next thing he espies
May be the lady. Thou shalt know the man
By the Athenian garments he hath on.
265 Effect it with some care that he may prove
More fond on her° than she upon her love:
And look thou meet me ere the first cock crow.

Puck. Fear not, my lord, your servant shall do so.
                                                Exeunt.

[Scene II.   *Another part of the wood.*]

Enter Titania, Queen of Fairies, with her train.

Titania. Come, now a roundel° and a fairy song;
Then, for the third part of a minute, hence;

255 *throws* casts off   256 *Weed* garment   266 *fond on her* foolishly
in love with her   II.ii.1 *roundel* dance in a ring

Some to kill cankers in the musk-rose buds,
Some war with reremice° for their leathern wings
To make my small elves coats, and some keep back   5
The clamorous owl, that nightly hoots and wonders
At our quaint° spirits. Sing me now asleep.
Then to your offices, and let me rest.

Fairies sing.

1st   You spotted snakes with double tongue,
Fairy.   Thorny hedgehogs, be not seen;   10
             Newts and blindworms,° do no wrong,
                 Come not near our Fairy Queen.

Chorus.   Philomele,° with melody
                 Sing in our sweet lullaby;
             Lulla, lulla, lullaby, lulla, lulla, lullaby: 15
                     Never harm
                     Nor spell nor charm,
                 Come our lovely lady nigh;
                 So, good night, with lullaby.

1st   Weaving spiders, come not here;   20
Fairy.   Hence, you long-legged spinners, hence!
             Beetles black, approach not near;
                 Worm nor snail, do no offense.

Chorus.   Philomele, with melody, &c.

2nd   Hence, away! Now all is well.   25
Fairy.   One aloof stand sentinel.

                 [*Exeunt Fairies. Titania sleeps.*]

*Enter Oberon [and squeezes the flower on
          Titania's eyelids].*

Oberon.   What thou seest when thou dost wake,
                 Do it for thy truelove take;
                 Love and languish for his sake.
                 Be it ounce,° or cat, or bear,   30

4 *reremice* bats 7 *quaint* dainty 11 *blindworms* small snakes
13 *Philomele* nightingale 30 *ounce* lynx

Pard,° or boar with bristled hair,
In thy eye that shall appear
When thou wak'st, it is thy dear.
Wake when some vile thing is near. [*Exit.*]

Enter Lysander and Hermia.

Lysander. Fair love, you faint with wand'ring in the
35   wood;
And to speak troth,° I have forgot our way.
We'll rest us, Hermia, if you think it good,
And tarry for the comfort of the day.

Hermia. Be't so, Lysander. Find you out a bed;
40   For I upon this bank will rest my head.

Lysander. One turf shall serve as pillow for us both,
One heart, one bed, two bosoms, and one troth.

Hermia. Nay, good Lysander. For my sake, my dear,
Lie further off yet, do not lie so near.

45   *Lysander.* O, take the sense,° sweet, of my innocence!
Love takes the meaning° in love's conference.
I mean, that my heart unto yours is knit,
So that but one heart we can make of it:
Two bosoms interchainèd with an oath;
50   So then two bosoms and a single troth.°
Then by your side no bed-room me deny,
For lying so, Hermia, I do not lie.°

Hermia. Lysander riddles very prettily.
Now much beshrew° my manners and my pride,
55   If Hermia meant to say Lysander lied.
But, gentle friend, for love and courtesy
Lie further off, in human modesty.
Such separation as may well be said

---

31 *Pard* leopard   36 *troth* truth   45 *take the sense* understand the
true meaning   46 *Love takes the meaning* lovers understand the
true meaning of what they say to each other   50 *troth* faithful love
52 *lie* be untrue   54 *beshrew* curse (but commonly, as here, in a
light sense)

Becomes a virtuous bachelor and a maid,
So far be distant; and, good night, sweet friend.   *60*
Thy love ne'er alter till thy sweet life end!

ysander. Amen, amen, to that fair prayer, say I,
And then end life when I end loyalty!
Here is my bed. Sleep give thee all his rest!

Iermia. With half that wish the wisher's eyes be
    pressed!   [*They sleep.*]   *65*

Enter Puck.

uck. Through the forest have I gone,
    But Athenian found I none,
    On whose eyes I might approve°
    This flower's force in stirring love.
    Night and silence.—Who is here?   *70*
    Weeds° of Athens he doth wear:
    This is he, my master said,
    Despisèd the Athenian maid;
    And here the maiden, sleeping sound,
    On the dank and dirty ground.   *75*
    Pretty soul! She durst not lie
    Near this lack-love, this kill-courtesy.
    Churl,° upon thy eyes I throw
    All the power this charm doth owe.°
    When thou wak'st, let love forbid   *80*
    Sleep his seat on thy eyelid.
    So awake when I am gone,
    For I must now to Oberon.   *Exit.*

Enter Demetrius and Helena, running.

Ielena. Stay, though thou kill me, sweet Demetrius.

Demetrius. I charge thee, hence, and do not haunt me
    thus.   *85*

___

58 *approve* try   71 *Weeds* garments   78 *Churl* boorish   fellow
79 *owe* possess

Helena. O, wilt thou darkling° leave me? Do not so.

Demetrius. Stay, on thy peril! I alone will go.   [*Exit.*]

Helena. O, I am out of breath in this fond° chase!
    The more my prayer, the lesser is my grace.
90   Happy is Hermia, wheresoe'er she lies,
    For she hath blessèd and attractive eyes.
    How came her eyes so bright? Not with salt tears.
    If so, my eyes are oft'ner washed than hers.
    No, no, I am as ugly as a bear,
95   For beasts that meet me run away for fear.
    Therefore no marvel though Demetrius
    Do, as a monster, fly my presence thus.
    What wicked and dissembling glass of mine
    Made me compare with Hermia's sphery eyne?°
100   But who is here? Lysander! On the ground!
    Dead? Or asleep? I see no blood, no wound.
    Lysander, if you live, good sir, awake.

Lysander. [*Awaking*] And run through fire I will for
    thy sweet sake.
    Transparent° Helena! Nature shows art,
105   That through thy bosom makes me see thy heart.
    Where is Demetrius? O, how fit a word
    Is that vile name to perish on my sword!

Helena. Do not say so, Lysander, say not so.
    What though he love your Hermia? Lord, what
    though?
110   Yet Hermia still loves you. Then be content.

Lysander. Content with Hermia! No; I do repent
    The tedious minutes I with her have spent.
    Not Hermia but Helena I love:
    Who will not change a raven for a dove?
115   The will° of man is by his reason swayed
    And reason says you are the worthier maid.
    Things growing are not ripe until their season:
    So I, being young, till now ripe not° to reason.

86 *darkling* in the dark   88 *fond* (1) doting (2) foolish   99 *sphery eyne* starry eyes   104 *Transparent* bright   115 *will* desire   118 *ripe not* have not ripened

And touching now the point of human skill,°
Reason becomes the marshal to my will,   120
And leads me to your eyes, where I o'erlook
Love's stories, written in love's richest book.

Helena. Wherefore was I to this keen mockery born?
When at your hands did I deserve this scorn?
Is't not enough, is't not enough, young man,   125
That I did never, no, nor never can,
Deserve a sweet look from Demetrius' eye,
But you must flout° my insufficiency?
Good troth,° you do me wrong, good sooth, you do,
In such disdainful manner me to woo.   130
But fare you well. Perforce I must confess
I thought you lord of more true gentleness.°
O, that a lady, of one man refused,
Should of another therefore be abused!   *Exit.*

Lysander. She sees not Hermia. Hermia, sleep thou
    there,   135
And never mayst thou come Lysander near!
For as a surfeit of the sweetest things
The deepest loathing to the stomach brings,
Or as the heresies that men do leave
Are hated most of those they did deceive,   140
So thou, my surfeit and my heresy,
Of all be hated, but the most of me!
And, all my powers, address° your love and might
To honor Helen and to be her knight!   *Exit.*

Hermia. [*Awaking*] Help me, Lysander, help me! Do
    thy best   145
To pluck this crawling serpent from my breast!
Ay me, for pity! What a dream was here!
Lysander, look how I do quake with fear.
Methought a serpent eat° my heart away,

---

119 *touching now . . . human skill* now reaching the fulness of human
reason   128 *flout* jeer at   129 *Good troth* indeed (an expletive, like
"good sooth")   132 *gentleness* noble character   143 *address* apply
149 *eat* ate (pronounced "et")

150   And you sat smiling at his cruel prey.°
       Lysander! What, removed? Lysander! Lord!
       What, out of hearing? Gone? No sound, no word?
       Alack, where are you? Speak, an if° you hear;
       Speak, of° all loves! I swoon almost with fear.
155   No? Then I well perceive you are not nigh.
       Either death or you I'll find immediately.   *Exit.*

150 *prey* act of preying   153 *an if* if   154 *of* for the sake of

[ACT III

Scene I. *The wood. Titania lying asleep.*]

Enter the clowns: [*Quince, Snug, Bottom, Flute,*
Snout, and Starveling].

Bottom. Are we all met?

Quince. Pat,° pat; and here's a marvail's° convenient
place for our rehearsal. This green plot shall be
our stage, this hawthorn brake° our tiring house,°
and we will do it in action as we will do it before   *5*
the Duke.

Bottom. Peter Quince?

Quince. What sayest thou, bully° Bottom?

Bottom. There are things in this comedy of Pyramus
and Thisby that will never please. First, Pyramus   *10*
must draw a sword to kill himself; which the ladies
cannot abide. How answer you that?

Snout. By'r lakin,° a parlous° fear.

Starveling. I believe we must leave the killing out,
when all is done.   *15*

III.i.2 *Pat* exactly, on the dot   2 *marvail's* (Quince means "marvelous")   4 *brake* thicket   4 *tiring house* attiring house, dressing
room   8 *bully* good fellow   13 *By'r lakin* by our lady (ladykin =
little lady)   13 *parlous* perilous, terrible

Bottom. Not a whit. I have a device to make all well.
Write me a prologue, and let the prologue seem to
say, we will do no harm with our swords, and that
Pyramus is not killed indeed; and, for the more
20   better assurance, tell them that I Pyramus am not
Pyramus, but Bottom the weaver. This will put
them out of fear.

Quince. Well, we will have such a prologue, and it
shall be written in eight and six.°

25   *Bottom.* No, make it two more; let it be written in
eight and eight.

Snout. Will not the ladies be afeared of the lion?

Starveling. I fear it, I promise you.

Bottom. Masters, you ought to consider with your-
30   selves. To bring in—God shield us!—a lion among
ladies, is a most dreadful thing. For there is not a
more fearful wild fowl than your lion living; and
we ought to look to't.

Snout. Therefore another prologue must tell he is not
35   a lion.

Bottom. Nay, you must name his name, and half his
face must be seen through the lion's neck, and he
himself must speak through, saying thus, or to the
same defect—"Ladies"—or, "Fair ladies—I would
40   wish you"—or, "I would request you"—or, "I
would entreat you—not to fear, not to tremble: my
life for yours. If you think I come hither as a lion,
it were pity of my life.° No, I am no such thing.
I am a man as other men are." And there indeed
45   let him name his name, and tell them plainly, he is
Snug the joiner.

Quince. Well, it shall be so. But there is two hard
things; that is, to bring the moonlight into a

---

24 *in eight and six* in alternate lines of eight and six syllables (ballad
stanza)   43 *pity of my life* a bad thing for me

chamber; for, you know, Pyramus and Thisby
meet by moonlight.   50

Snout. Doth the moon shine that night we play our
play?

Bottom. A calendar, a calendar! Look in the almanac;
find out moonshine, find out moonshine.

Quince. Yes, it doth shine that night.   55

Bottom. Why, then may you leave a casement of the
great chamber window, where we play, open, and
the moon may shine in at the casement.

Quince. Ay; or else one must come in with a bush of
thorns° and a lantern, and say he comes to dis-   60
figure,° or to present, the person of Moonshine.
Then, there is another thing: we must have a wall
in the great chamber; for Pyramus and Thisby,
says the story, did talk through the chink of a
wall.   65

Snout. You can never bring in a wall. What say you,
Bottom?

Bottom. Some man or other must present Wall: and
let him have some plaster, or some loam, or some
roughcast° about him, to signify Wall; and let him 70
hold his fingers thus, and through that cranny shall
Pyramus and Thisby whisper.

Quince. If that may be, then all is well. Come, sit
down, every mother's son, and rehearse your parts.
Pyramus, you begin. When you have spoken your   75
speech, enter into that brake; and so everyone according to his cue.

Enter Robin [Puck].

59–60 *bush of thorns* (legend held that the man in the moon had
been placed there for gathering firewood on Sunday)   60-61 *disfigure* (Bottom means "figure," "represent")   70 *roughcast* lime
mixed with gravel to plaster outside walls

Puck. What hempen homespuns° have we swagg'ring here,

    So near the cradle of the Fairy Queen?

80   What, a play toward!° I'll be an auditor;

    An actor too perhaps, if I see cause.

Quince. Speak, Pyramus. Thisby, stand forth.

Pyramus [Bottom]. Thisby, the flowers of odious savors sweet—

Quince. Odors, odors.

85 *Pyramus.* —odors savors sweet:

    So hath thy breath, my dearest Thisby dear.

    But hark, a voice! Stay thou but here awhile,

    And by and by° I will to thee appear.   *Exit.*

Puck. A stranger Pyramus than e'er played here!

                             [Exit.]

90 *Thisby [Flute].* Must I speak now?

Quince. Ay, marry, must you. For you must understand he goes but to see a noise that he heard, and is to come again.

Thisby. Most radiant Pyramus, most lily-white of hue,

95   Of color like the red rose on triumphant brier,

    Most brisky juvenal,° and eke° most lovely Jew,

    As true as truest horse, that yet would never tire,

    I'll meet thee, Pyramus, at Ninny's° tomb.

Quince. "Ninus' tomb," man. Why, you must not

100 speak that yet. That you answer to Pyramus. You speak all your part at once, cues and all. Pyramus enter. Your cue is past; it is "never tire."

Thisby. O—as true as truest horse, that yet would never tire.

---

78 *hempen homespuns* coarse follows (clad in homespun cloth of hemp)   80 *toward* in preparation   88 *by and by* shortly   96 *juvenal* youth   96 *eke* also   98 *Ninny's* (blunder for "Ninus'"; Ninus was the legendary founder of Nineveh)

[*Re-enter Puck, and Bottom with an ass's head.*]

Pyramus. If I were fair, Thisby, I were only thine.

Quince. O monstrous! O strange! We are haunted.   105
Pray, masters! Fly, masters! Help!
> [*Exeunt all the clowns but Bottom.*]

Puck. I'll follow you, I'll lead you about a round,°
 Through bog, through bush, through brake,
  through brier.
Sometime a horse I'll be, sometime a hound,
 A hog, a headless bear, sometime a fire;   110
And neigh, and bark, and grunt, and roar, and
 burn,
Like horse, hound, hog, bear, fire, at every turn.
> *Exit.*

Bottom. Why do they run away? This is a knavery of
them to make me afeard.

Enter Snout.

Snout. O Bottom, thou art changed! What do I see   115
on thee?

Bottom. What do you see? You see an ass head of
your own, do you?   [*Exit Snout.*]

Enter Quince.

Quince. Bless thee, Bottom! Bless thee! Thou art
translated.°   *Exit.*   120

Bottom. I see their knavery. This is to make an ass
of me; to fright me, if they could. But I will not
stir from this place, do what they can. I will walk
up and down here, and will sing, that they shall
hear I am not afraid.   [*Sings.*]   125

107 *about a round* roundabout 120 *translated* transformed

The woosel° cock so black of hue,
    With orange-tawny bill,
The throstle with his note so true,
    The wren with little quill°—

Titania. [*Awaking*] What angel wakes me from my
130   flow'ry bed?

Bottom. [*Sings*] The finch, the sparrow, and the lark,
        The plain-song cuckoo° gray,
            Whose note full many a man doth
            mark,
        And dares not answer nay—
135   for, indeed, who would set his wit° to so foolish
    a bird? Who would give a bird the lie,° though he
    cry "cuckoo" never so?°

Titania. I pray thee, gentle mortal, sing again:
    Mine ear is much enamored of thy note;
140   So is mine eye enthrallèd to thy shape;
    And thy fair virtue's force perforce doth move me
    On the first view to say, to swear, I love thee.

Bottom. Methinks, mistress, you should have little
    reason for that. And yet, to say the truth, reason
145   and love keep little company together nowadays;
    the more the pity, that some honest neighbors will
    not make them friends. Nay, I can gleek° upon
    occasion.

Titania. Thou art as wise as thou art beautiful.

150 Bottom. Not so, neither; but if I had wit enough to
    get out of this wood, I have enough to serve mine
    own turn.

Titania. Out of this wood do not desire to go.

---

126 *woosel* ouzel, blackbird   129 *quill* (literally, "reed pipe"; here, "piping voice")   132 *the plain-song cuckoo* the cuckoo, who sings a simple song   135 *set his wit* use his intelligence to answer   136 *give a bird the lie* contradict a bird (the cuckoo's song supposedly tells a man he is a cuckold)   137 *never so* ever so often   147 *gleek* make a satirical jest

Thou shalt remain here, whether thou wilt or no.
I am a spirit of no common rate.°   155
The summer still doth tend° upon my state;
And I do love thee. Therefore, go with me.
I'll give thee fairies to attend on thee,
And they shall fetch thee jewels from the deep,
And sing, while thou on pressèd flowers dost sleep: 160
And I will purge thy mortal grossness so,
That thou shalt like an airy spirit go.
Peaseblossom! Cobweb! Moth!° And Mustardseed!

Enter four Fairies
[*Peaseblossom, Cobweb, Moth, and Mustardseed*].

Peaseblossom. Ready.

Cobweb.   And I.

Moth.   And I.

Mustardseed.   And I.

All.   Where shall we go.

Titania. Be kind and courteous to this gentleman;   165
        Hop in his walks, and gambol in his eyes;
        Feed him with apricocks and dewberries,°
        With purple grapes, green figs, and mulberries;
        The honey bags steal from the humblebees,°
        And for night tapers crop their waxen thighs,   170
        And light them at the fiery glowworm's eyes,
        To have my love to bed and to arise;
        And pluck the wings from painted butterflies,
        To fan the moonbeams from his sleeping eyes.
        Nod to him, elves, and do him courtesies.   175

Peaseblossom. Hail, mortal!

Cobweb.   Hail!

155 *rate* rank   156 *still doth tend* always waits upon   163 *Moth*
(pronounced "mote," and probably a speck rather than an insect is
denoted)   167 *apricocks and dewberries* apricots and blackberries
169 *humblebees* bumblebees

Moth.   Hail!

Mustardseed.   Hail!

Bottom. I cry your worships mercy,° heartily: I beseech your worship's name.

Cobweb. Cobweb.

180 *Bottom.* I shall desire you of more acquaintance,°
good Master Cobweb: if I cut my finger,° I shall
make bold with you. Your name, honest gentleman?

Peaseblossom. Peaseblossom.

185 *Bottom.* I pray you, commend me to Mistress Squash,°
your mother, and to Master Peascod, your father.
Good Master Peaseblossom. I shall desire you of
more acquaintance too. Your name, I beseech you,
sir?

190 *Mustardseed.* Mustardseed.

Bottom. Good Master Mustardseed, I know your patience well. That same cowardly, giantlike ox-beef
hath devoured° many a gentleman of your house.
I promise you your kindred hath made my eyes
195 water ere now. I desire you of more acquaintance,
good Master Mustardseed.

Titania. Come, wait upon him; lead him to my bower.
The moon methinks looks with a wat'ry eye;
And when she weeps, weeps every little flower,
200   Lamenting some enforcèd° chastity.
Tie up my lover's tongue, bring him silently.
          Exit [Titania with Bottom and Fairies].

---

177 *I cry your worships mercy* I beg pardon of your honors   180 *I
shall desire you of more acquaintance* I shall want to be better
acquainted with you   181 *if I cut my finger* (cobweb was used for
stanching blood)   185 *Squash* unripe pea pod   193 *devoured* (because beef is often eaten with mustard)   200 *enforcèd* violated

[Scene II.   *Another part of the wood.*]

*Enter [Oberon,] King of Fairies, and Robin
Goodfellow [Puck].*

Oberon. I wonder if Titania be awaked;
    Then, what it was that next came in her eye,
    Which she must dote on in extremity.°
    Here comes my messenger. How now, mad spirit!
    What night-rule° now about this haunted grove?   5

Puck. My mistress with a monster is in love.
    Near to her close° and consecrated bower,
    While she was in her dull and sleeping hour,
    A crew of patches,° rude mechanicals,°
    That work for bread upon Athenian stalls,   10
    Were met together to rehearse a play,
    Intended for great Theseus' nuptial day.
    The shallowest thickskin of that barren sort,°
    Who Pyramus presented in their sport,
    Forsook his scene, and entered in a brake.   15
    When I did him at this advantage take,
    An ass's nole° I fixèd on his head.
    Anon° his Thisby must be answerèd,
    And forth my mimic comes. When they him spy,
    As wild geese that the creeping fowler eye,   20
    Or russet-pated choughs, many in sort,°
    Rising and cawing at the gun's report,
    Sever themselves and madly sweep the sky,
    So, at his sight, away his fellows fly;

III.ii.3 *in extremity* to the extreme   5 *night-rule* happenings during
the night   7 *close* private, secret   9 *patches* fools, clowns   9 *rude
mechanicals* uneducated workingmen   13 *barren sort* stupid group
17 *nole* "noodle," head   18 *Anon* presently   21 *russet-pated . . . in
sort* gray-headed jackdaws, many in a flock

25 And, at our stamp, here o'er and o'er one falls;
    He murder cries, and help from Athens calls.
    Their sense thus weak, lost with their fears thus
        strong,
    Made senseless things begin to do them wrong;
    For briers and thorns at their apparel snatch;
30 Some sleeves, some hats, from yielders all things
        catch.
    I led them on in this distracted fear,
    And left sweet Pyramus translated there:
    When in that moment, so it came to pass,
    Titania waked, and straightway loved an ass.

35 *Oberon.* This falls out better than I could devise.
    But hast thou yet latched° the Athenian's eyes
    With the love juice, as I did bid thee do?

    Puck. I took him sleeping—that is finished too—
    And the Athenian woman by his side;
40 That, when he waked, of force° she must be eyed.

                Enter Demetrius and Hermia.

    Oberon. Stand close:° this is the same Athenian.

    Puck. This is the woman, but not this the man.

    Demetrius. O, why rebuke you him that loves you so?
    Lay breath so bitter on your bitter foe.

45 *Hermia.* Now I but chide; but I should use thee worse,
    For thou, I fear, hast given me cause to curse.
    If thou hast slain Lysander in his sleep,
    Being o'er shoes in blood, plunge in the deep,
    And kill me too.
50 The sun was not so true unto the day
    As he to me. Would he have stolen away
    From sleeping Hermia? I'll believe as soon
    This whole° earth may be bored, and that the moon
    May through the center creep, and so displease

36 *latched* fastened (or possibly "moistened")   40 *of force* by
necessity   41 *close* concealed   53 *whole* solid

Her brother's° noontide with th' Antipodes.   55
It cannot be but thou hast murd'red him.
So should a murderer look, so dead,° so grim.

Demetrius. So should the murdered look; and so
    should I,
Pierced through the heart with your stern cruelty.
Yet you, the murderer, look as bright, as clear,   60
As yonder Venus in her glimmering sphere.

Hermia. What's this to my Lysander? Where is he?
Ah, good Demetrius, wilt thou give him me?

Demetrius. I had rather give his carcass to my hounds.

Hermia. Out, dog! Out, cur! Thou driv'st me past the
    bounds   65
Of maiden's patience. Hast thou slain him, then?
Henceforth be never numb'red among men!
O, once tell true! Tell true, even for my sake!
Durst thou have looked upon him being awake?
And hast thou killed him sleeping? O brave touch!°   70
Could not a worm, an adder, do so much?
An adder did it; for with doubler tongue
Than thine, thou serpent, never adder stung.

Demetrius. You spend your passion on a misprised
    mood:°
I am not guilty of Lysander's blood;   75
Nor is he dead, for aught that I can tell.

Hermia. I pray thee, tell me then that he is well.

Demetrius. An if I could, what should I get there-
    fore?°

Hermia. A privilege, never to see me more.
And from thy hated presence part I so.   80
See me no more, whether he be dead or no.   *Exit.*

Demetrius. There is no following her in this fierce vein.

55 *Her brother's* i.e., the sun's   57 *dead* deadly pale   70 *brave
touch* splendid exploit (ironic)   74 *misprised mood* mistaken anger
78 *therefore* in return

Here therefore for a while I will remain.
So sorrow's heaviness doth heavier grow
85 For debt that bankrout sleep doth sorrow owe;°
Which now in some slight measure it will pay,
If for his tender° here I make some stay.

Lie down [and sleep].

Oberon. What hast thou done? Thou hast mistaken quite,
And laid the love juice on some truelove's sight.
90 Of thy misprision° must perforce ensue
Some true love turned, and not a false turned true.

Puck. Then fate o'errules, that, one man holding troth,
A million fail, confounding oath on oath.°

Oberon. About the wood go swifter than the wind,
95 And Helena of Athens look thou find.
All fancy-sick° she is and pale of cheer,°
With sighs of love, that costs the fresh blood dear:
By some illusion see thou bring her here.
I'll charm his eyes against she do appear.°

100 *Puck.* I go, I go; look how I go,
Swifter than arrow from the Tartar's bow.   [*Exit.*]

Oberon. Flower of this purple dye,
Hit with Cupid's archery,
Sink in apple of his eye.
105 When his love he doth espy,
Let her shine as gloriously
As the Venus of the sky.
When thou wak'st, if she be by,
Beg of her for remedy.

Enter Puck.

85 *For debt . . . sorrow owe* because of the debt that bankrupt sleep owes to sorrow   87 *tender* offer   90 *misprision* mistake   93 *confounding oath on oath* breaking oath after oath   96 *fancy-sick* lovesick   96 *cheer* face   99 *against she do appear* in preparation for her appearance

Puck. Captain of our fairy band,   110
    Helena is here at hand;
    And the youth, mistook by me,
    Pleading for a lover's fee.
    Shall we their fond pageant° see?
    Lord, what fools these mortals be!   115

Oberon. Stand aside. The noise they make
    Will cause Demetrius to awake.

Puck. Then will two at once woo one;
    That must needs be sport alone;°
    And those things do best please me   120
    That befall prepost'rously.

Enter Lysander and Helena.

Lysander. Why should you think that I should woo in
    scorn?
    Scorn and derision never come in tears:
Look, when I vow, I weep; and vows so born,
    In their nativity all truth appears.   125
How can these things in me seem scorn to you,
Bearing the badge of faith,° to prove them true?

Helena. You do advance° your cunning more and
    more.
    When truth kills truth, O devilish-holy fray!
These vows are Hermia's: will you give her o'er?   130
    Weigh oath with oath, and you will nothing
    weigh.
Your vows to her and me, put in two scales,
Will even weigh; and both as light as tales.

Lysander. I had no judgment when to her I swore.

Helena. Nor none, in my mind, now you give her o'er.   135

Lysander. Demetrius loves her, and he loves not you.

114 *fond pageant* foolish exhibition   119 *alone* unique, supreme
127 *badge of faith* (Lysander means his tears)   128 *advance* exhibit, display

Demetrius. [*Awaking*] O Helen, goddess, nymph, per-
        fect, divine!
    To what, my love, shall I compare thine eyne?
    Crystal is muddy. O, how ripe in show°
140   Thy lips, those kissing cherries, tempting grow!
    That pure congealèd white, high Taurus'° snow,
    Fanned with the eastern wind, turns to a crow
    When thou hold'st up thy hand: O, let me kiss
    This princess of pure white, this seal of bliss!

145 *Helena.* O spite! O hell! I see you all are bent
    To set against me for your merriment:
    If you were civil° and knew courtesy,
    You would not do me thus much injury.
    Can you not hate me, as I know you do,
150   But you must join in souls to mock me too?
    If you were men, as men you are in show,
    You would not use a gentle° lady so;
    To vow, and swear, and superpraise my parts,°
    When I am sure you hate me with your hearts.
155   You both are rivals, and love Hermia;
    And now both rivals to mock Helena:
    A trim° exploit, a manly enterprise,
    To conjure tears up in a poor maid's eyes
    With your derision! None of noble sort
160   Would so offend a virgin, and extort°
    A poor soul's patience, all to make you sport.

Lysander. You are unkind, Demetrius. Be not so;
    For you love Hermia; this you know I know.
    And here, with all good will, with all my heart,
165   In Hermia's love I yield you up my part;
    And yours of Helena to me bequeath,
    Whom I do love, and will do till my death.

Helena. Never did mockers waste more idle° breath.

Demetrius. Lysander, keep thy Hermia; I will none.

139 *show* appearance   141 *Taurus'* of the Taurus Mountains (in
Turkey)   147 *civil* civilized   152 *gentle* well-born   153 *parts* qualities   157 *trim* splendid (ironical)   160 *extort* wear out by torturing   168 *idle* vain, futile

If e'er I loved her, all that love is gone.   *170*
My heart to her but as guestwise sojourned,
And now to Helen is it home returned,
There to remain.

Lysander.   Helen, it is not so.

Demetrius. Disparage not the faith thou dost not
    know,
Lest, to thy peril, thou aby it dear.°   *175*
Look, where thy love comes; yonder is thy dear.

Enter Hermia.

Hermia. Dark night, that from the eye his° function
    takes,
The ear more quick of apprehension makes;
Wherein it doth impair the seeing sense,
It pays the hearing double recompense.   *180*
Thou art not by mine eye, Lysander, found;
Mine ear, I thank it, brought me to thy sound.
But why unkindly didst thou leave me so?

Lysander. Why should he stay, whom love doth press
    to go?

Hermia. What love could press Lysander from my
    side?   *185*

Lysander. Lysander's love, that would not let him
    bide,
Fair Helena, who more engilds the night
Than all yon fiery oes° and eyes of light.
Why seek'st thou me? Could not this make thee
    know,
The hate I bare thee made me leave thee so?   *190*

Hermia. You speak not as you think: it cannot be.

Helena. Lo, she is one of this confederacy!
Now I perceive they have conjoined all three

175 *aby it dear* pay dearly for it   177 *his* its (the eye's)   188 *oes*
orbs

To fashion this false sport, in spite of me.
195   Injurious° Hermia! Most ungrateful maid!
Have you conspired, have you with these contrived
To bait° me with this foul derision?
Is all the counsel that we two have shared,
The sister's vows, the hours that we have spent,
200   When we have chid the hasty-footed time
For parting us—O, is all forgot?
All school days friendship, childhood innocence?
We, Hermia, like two artificial° gods,
Have with our needles created both one flower,
205   Both on one sampler,° sitting on one cushion,
Both warbling of one song, both in one key;
As if our hands, our sides, voices, and minds,
Had been incorporate.° So we grew together,
Like to a double cherry, seeming parted,
210   But yet an union in partition;
Two lovely berries molded on one stem;
So, with two seeming bodies, but one heart;
Two of the first, like coats in heraldry,
Due but to one, and crownèd with one crest.°
215   And will you rent° our ancient love asunder,
To join with men in scorning your poor friend?
It is not friendly, 'tis not maidenly.
Our sex, as well as I, may chide you for it,
Though I alone do feel the injury.

220   *Hermia.* I am amazèd at your passionate words.
I scorn you not. It seems that you scorn me.

Helena. Have you not set Lysander, as in scorn,
To follow me and praise my eyes and face?
And made your other love, Demetrius
225   (Who even but now did spurn me with his foot),
To call me goddess, nymph, divine and rare,

195 *Injurious* insulting   196–97 *contrived To bait* plotted to assail
203 *artificial* skilled in art   205 *sampler* work of embroidery
208 *incorporate* one body   213–14 *Two of . . . one crest* (Helena
apparently envisages a shield on which the coat of arms appears
twice but which has a single crest; Helena and Hermia have two
bodies but a single heart)   215 *rent* rend, tear

Precious, celestial? Wherefore speaks he this
To her he hates? And wherefore doth Lysander
Deny your love,° so rich within his soul,
And tender me (forsooth) affection,   230
But by your setting on, by your consent?
What though I be not so in grace° as you,
So hung upon with love, so fortunate,
But miserable most, to love unloved?
This you should pity rather than despise.   235

Hermia. I understand not what you mean by this.

Helena. Ay, do! Persever,° counterfeit sad° looks,
Make mouths° upon me when I turn my back;
Wink each at other; hold the sweet jest up.
This sport, well carried, shall be chronicled.   240
If you have any pity, grace, or manners,
You would not make me such an argument.°
But fare ye well. 'Tis partly my own fault,
Which death or absence soon shall remedy.

Lysander. Stay, gentle Helena; hear my excuse: 245
My love, my life, my soul, fair Helena!

Helena. O excellent!

Hermia.   Sweet, do not scorn her so.

Demetrius. If she cannot entreat,° I can compel.

Lysander. Thou canst compel no more than she en-
    treat.
Thy threats have no more strength than her weak
    prayers.   250
Helen, I love thee; by my life, I do!
I swear by that which I will lose for thee,
To prove him false that says I love thee not.

Demetrius. I say I love thee more than he can do.

229 *your love* his love for you   232 *in grace* in favor   237 *persever*
persevere (but accented on second syllable)   237 *sad* grave
238 *Make mouths* make mocking faces   242 *argument* subject (of
scorn)   248 *entreat* prevail by entreating

255 *Lysander.* If thou say so, withdraw and prove it too.

Demetrius. Quick, come!

Hermia.   Lysander, whereto tends all this?

Lysander. Away, you Ethiope!°

Demetrius.   No, no; he'll
  Seem to break loose; take on as° you would follow,
  But yet come not: you are a tame man, go!

Lysander. Hang off, thou cat, thou burr! Vile thing,
260   let loose,
  Or I will shake thee from me like a serpent!

Hermia. Why are you grown so rude! What change is
     this,
  Sweet love?

Lysander.   Thy love! Out, tawny Tartar, out!
  Out, loathèd med'cine! O hated potion, hence!

Hermia. Do you not jest?

265 *Helena.*   Yes, sooth;° and so do you.

Lysander. Demetrius, I will keep my word° with thee.

Demetrius. I would I had your bond, for I perceive
  A weak bond holds you. I'll not trust your word.

Lysander. What, should I hurt her, strike her, kill
     her dead?
270   Although I hate her, I'll not harm her so.

Hermia. What, can you do me greater harm than
     hate?
  Hate me! Wherefore? O me! What news, my love!
  Am not I Hermia? Are not you Lysander?
  I am as fair now as I was erewhile.°

---

257 *Ethiope* blackamoor (brunette)   258 *take on as* make a fuss
as if   265 *sooth* truly   266 *my word* my promise to fight with you
274 *erewhile* a little while ago

Since night° you loved me; yet since night you left
  me.   *275*
Why, then you left me—O, the gods forbid!—
In earnest, shall I say?

Lysander.   Ay, by my life!
And never did desire to see thee more.
Therefore be out of hope, of question, of doubt;
Be certain, nothing truer. 'Tis no jest   *280*
That I do hate thee, and love Helena.

Hermia. O me! You juggler! You canker blossom!°
  You thief of love! What, have you come by night
And stol'n my love's heart from him?

Helena.   Fine, i' faith!
Have you no modesty, no maiden shame,   *285*
No touch of bashfulness? What, will you tear
Impatient answers from my gentle tongue?
Fie, fie! You counterfeit, you puppet, you!

Hermia. Puppet? Why so? Ay, that way goes the
  game.
Now I perceive that she hath made compare°   *290*
Between our statures; she hath urged her height,
And with her personage, her tall personage,
Her height, forsooth, she hath prevailed with him.
And are you grown so high in his esteem,
Because I am so dwarfish and so low?   *295*
How low am I, thou painted maypole? Speak!
How low am I? I am not yet so low
But that my nails can reach unto thine eyes.

Helena. I pray you, though you mock me, gentlemen,
Let her not hurt me. I was never curst;°   *300*
  I have no gift at all in shrewishness;
I am a right maid° for my cowardice.
Let her not strike me. You perhaps may think,

275 *Since night* since the beginning of this night   282 *canker blossom* dog rose (or possibly worm that cankers the blossom)
290 *compare* comparison   300 *curst* quarrelsome   302 *right maid*
true young woman

Because she is something lower than myself,
That I can match her.

305 *Hermia.*   Lower! Hark, again!

Helena. Good Hermia, do not be so bitter with me.
I evermore did love you, Hermia,
Did ever keep your counsels, never wronged you;
Save that, in love unto Demetrius,
310 I told him of your stealth unto this wood.
He followed you; for love I followed him.
But he hath chid me hence, and threatened me
To strike me, spurn me, nay, to kill me too.
And now, so you will let me quiet go,
315 To Athens will I bear my folly back,
And follow you no further. Let me go.
You see how simple and how fond° I am.

Hermia. Why, get you gone. Who is't that hinders you?

Helena. A foolish heart, that I leave here behind.

Hermia. What, with Lysander?

320 *Helena.*   With Demetrius.

Lysander. Be not afraid. She shall not harm thee,
    Helena.

Demetrius. No, sir, she shall not, though you take her
    part.

Helena. O, when she's angry, she is keen and shrewd!°
She was a vixen when she went to school;
325 And though she be but little, she is fierce.

Hermia. "Little" again! Nothing but "low" and "little"!
Why will you suffer her to flout me thus?
Let me come to her.

Lysander.   Get you gone, you dwarf;
You minimus,° of hind'ring knotgrass° made;
You bead, you acorn!

317 *fond* foolish   323 *keen and shrewd* sharp-tongued and shrewish
329 *minimus* smallest thing   329 *knotgrass* (a weed that allegedly
stunted one's growth)

Demetrius.   You are too officious   *330*
  In her behalf that scorns your services.
  Let her alone. Speak not of Helena;
  Take not her part; for, if thou dost intend°
  Never so little show of love to her,
  Thou shalt aby° it.

Lysander.   Now she holds me not.   *335*
  Now follow, if thou dar'st, to try whose right,
  Of thine or mine, is most in Helena.

Demetrius. Follow! Nay, I'll go with thee, cheek by
     jowl.   [*Exeunt Lysander and Demetrius.*]

Hermia. You, mistress, all this coil is 'long of you:°
  Nay, go not back.

Helena.   I will not trust you, I,   *340*
  Nor longer stay in your curst company.
  Your hands than mine are quicker for a fray,
  My legs are longer though, to run away.

Hermia. I am amazed,° and know not what to say.
            Exeunt [*Helena and Hermia*].

Oberon. This is thy negligence. Still thou mistak'st,   *345*
  Or else committ'st thy knaveries willfully.

Puck. Believe me, king of shadows, I mistook.
  Did not you tell me I should know the man
  By the Athenian garments he had on?
  And so far blameless proves my enterprise,   *350*
  That I have 'nointed an Athenian's eyes;
  And so far am I glad it so did sort,°
  As this their jangling I esteem a sport.

Oberon. Thou see'st these lovers seek a place to fight.
  Hie therefore, Robin, overcast the night.   *355*
  The starry welkin° cover thou anon

---

333 *intend* give sign, direct (or possibly "pretend")   335 *aby* pay
for   339 *all this coil is 'long of you* all this turmoil is brought about
by you   344 *amazed* in confusion   352 *sort* turn out   356 *welkin*
sky

With drooping fog, as black as Acheron;°
And lead these testy° rivals so astray,
As° one come not within another's way.
360 Like to Lysander sometime frame thy tongue,
Then stir Demetrius up with bitter wrong;°
And sometime rail thou like Demetrius.
And from each other look thou lead them thus,
Till o'er their brows death-counterfeiting sleep
365 With leaden legs and batty° wings doth creep.
Then crush this herb into Lysander's eye,
Whose liquor hath this virtuous° property,
To take from thence all error with his might,
And make his eyeballs roll with wonted sight.
370 When they next wake, all this derision°
Shall seem a dream and fruitless vision,
And back to Athens shall the lovers wend,
With league whose date° till death shall never end.
Whiles I in this affair do thee employ,
375 I'll to my queen and beg her Indian boy;
And then I will her charmèd eye release
From monster's view, and all things shall be peace.

Puck. My fairy lord, this must be done with haste,
For night's swift dragons cut the clouds full fast,
380 And yonder shines Aurora's harbinger;°
At whose approach, ghosts, wand'ring here and
there,
Troop home to churchyards: damnèd spirits all,
That in crossways and floods have burial,
Already to their wormy beds are gone.
385 For fear lest day should look their shames upon,
They willfully themselves exile from light,
And must for aye consort with black-browed night.

Oberon. But we are spirits of another sort.

357 *Acheron* one of the rivers of the underworld   358 *testy*
excited, angry   359 *As* that   361 *wrong* insult   365 *batty* bat-like
367 *virtuous* potent   370 *derision* i.e., ludicrous delusion   373 *With
league whose date* in union whose term   380 *Aurora's harbinger*
dawn's herald (i.e., the morning star)

I with the Morning's love° have oft made sport;
And, like a forester, the groves may tread,   390
Even till the eastern gate, all fiery-red,
Opening on Neptune with fair blessèd beams,
Turns into yellow gold his salt green streams.
But, notwithstanding, haste; make no delay.
We may effect this business yet ere day.   [*Exit.*] 395

Puck.   Up and down, up and down,
          I will lead them up and down:
          I am feared in field and town:
          Goblin,° lead them up and down.
          Here comes one.   400

Enter Lysander.

Lysander. Where art thou, proud Demetrius? Speak
     thou now.

Puck. Here, villain; drawn° and ready. Where art
     thou?

Lysander. I will be with thee straight.

Puck.   Follow me, then,
     To plainer° ground.   [*Exit Lysander.*]

Enter Demetrius.

Demetrius.   Lysander! Speak again!
     Thou runaway, thou coward, art thou fled?   405
     Speak! In some bush? Where dost thou hide thy
          head?

Puck. Thou coward, art thou bragging to the stars,
     Telling the bushes that thou look'st for wars,
     And wilt not come? Come, recreant! Come, thou
          child!

---

389 *the Morning's love* Aurora (or possibly her lover Cephalus)
399 *Goblin* Hobgoblin (one of Puck's names)   402 *drawn* with
drawn sword   404 *plainer* more level

⁴¹⁰ I'll whip thee with a rod. He is defiled
That draws a sword on thee.

Demetrius.   Yea, art thou there?

Puck. Follow my voice. We'll try no manhood° here.
                                      Exeunt.

[*Enter Lysander.*]

Lysander. He goes before me and still dares me on:
When I come where he calls, then he is gone.
⁴¹⁵ The villain is much lighter-heeled than I.
I followed fast, but faster he did fly,
That fallen am I in dark uneven way,
And here will rest me. [*Lies down.*] Come, thou
    gentle day!
For if but once thou show me thy gray light,
⁴²⁰ I'll find Demetrius, and revenge this spite. [*Sleeps.*]

[*Enter*] *Robin* [*Puck*] *and Demetrius.*

Puck. Ho, ho, ho! Coward, why com'st thou not?

Demetrius. Abide me,° if thou dar'st; for well I wot°
Thou runn'st before me, shifting every place,
And dar'st not stand, nor look me in the face
Where art thou now?

⁴²⁵ *Puck.*   Come hither. I am here.

Demetrius. Nay, then, thou mock'st me. Thou shalt
    buy this dear,°
If ever I thy face by daylight see.
Now, go thy way. Faintness constraineth me
To measure out my length on this cold bed.
⁴³⁰ By day's approach look to be visited.°
                    [*Lies down and sleeps.*]

---

412 *try no manhood* have no test of valor   422 *Abide me* wait for
me   422 *wot* know   426 *buy this dear* pay dearly for this   430 *look
to be visited* be sure to be sought out

Enter Helena.

Helena. O weary night, O long and tedious night,
   Abate° thy hours! Shine comforts from the east,
That I may back to Athens by daylight,
   From these that my poor company detest:
And sleep, that sometimes shuts up sorrow's eye,   435
Steal me awhile from mine own company.   *Sleep.*

   Puck.   Yet but three? Come one more.
             Two of both kinds makes up four.
             Here she comes, curst° and sad:
             Cupid is a knavish lad,   440
             Thus to make poor females mad.

                [*Enter Hermia.*]

Hermia. Never so weary, never so in woe;
   Bedabbled with the dew and torn with briers,
I can no further crawl, no further go;
   My legs can keep no pace with my desires.   445
Here will I rest me till the break of day.
Heavens shield Lysander, if they mean a fray!
                      [*Lies down and sleeps.*]

Puck. On the ground
          Sleep sound:
          I'll apply   450
          To your eye,
       Gentle lover, remedy.
          [*Squeezing the juice on Lysander's eye*]
          When thou wak'st,
          Thou tak'st
          True delight   455
          In the sight
       Of thy former lady's eye:
       And the country proverb known,
       That every man should take his own,

---

432 *Abate* make shorter   439 *curst* cross

460 In your waking shall be shown.
    Jack shall have Jill;
    Nought shall go ill;
The man shall have his mare again, and all shall
  be well.

                        [Exit.]

[ACT IV

Scene I. *The wood. Lysander, Demetrius, Helena,*
and Hermia, lying asleep.]

Enter [Titania,] Queen of Fairies, and [Bottom the]
Clown, and Fairies; and [Oberon,] the King, be-
hind them.

Titania. Come, sit thee down upon this flow'ry bed,
    While I thy amiable cheeks do coy,°
And stick musk roses in thy sleek smooth head,
    And kiss thy fair large ears, my gentle joy.

Bottom. Where's Peaseblossom? 5

Peaseblossom. Ready.

Bottom. Scratch my head, Peaseblossom. Where's
Mounsieur Cobweb?

Cobweb. Ready.

Bottom. Mounsieur Cobweb, good mounsieur, get 10
you your weapons in your hand, and kill me a red-
hipped humblebee on the top of a thistle; and, good
mounsieur, bring me the honey bag. Do not fret
yourself too much in the action, mounsieur; and,
good mounsieur, have a care the honey bag break 15

IV.i.2 *While I . . . do coy* while I caress your lovely cheeks

not; I would be loath to have you overflown with
a honey bag, signior. Where's Mounsieur Mustardseed?

Mustardseed. Ready.

20 *Bottom.* Give me your neaf,° Mounsieur Mustardseed. Pray you, leave your curtsy,° good mounsieur.

Mustardseed. What's your will?

Bottom. Nothing, good mounsieur, but to help Cava-
25 lery° Cobweb to scratch. I must to the barber's,
mounsieur; for methinks I am marvail's° hairy
about the face; and I am such a tender ass, if my
hair do but tickle me, I must scratch.

Titania. What, wilt thou hear some music, my sweet
30 love?

Bottom. I have a reasonable good ear in music. Let's
have the tongs and the bones.°

Titania. Or say, sweet love, what thou desirest to eat.

Bottom. Truly, a peck of provender. I could munch
35 your good dry oats. Methinks I have a great desire
to a bottle° of hay. Good hay, sweet hay, hath no
fellow.°

Titania. I have a venturous fairy that shall seek
The squirrel's hoard, and fetch thee new nuts.

40 *Bottom.* I had rather have a handful or two of dried
peas. But, I pray you, let none of your people stir
me: I have an exposition of° sleep come upon me.

---

20 *neaf* fist, hand   21 *leave your curtsy* i.e., stop bowing, leave your
hat on (a curtsy was any gesture of respect)   24–25 *Cavalery* i.e.,
Cavalier   26 *marvail's* (Bottom means "marvelous")   32 *the tongs
and the bones* rustic music, made by tongs struck with metal and by
bone clappers held between the fingers   36 *bottle* bundle   37 *fellow*
equal   42 *exposition of* (Bottom means "disposition for")

Titania. Sleep thou, and I will wind thee in my arms.
  Fairies, be gone, and be all ways° away.
                    [*Exeunt Fairies.*]
  So doth the woodbine the sweet honeysuckle   45
  Gently entwist; the female ivy° so
  Enrings the barky fingers of the elm.
  O, how I love thee! How I dote on thee!
                    [*They sleep.*]

          Enter Robin Goodfellow [*Puck*].

Oberon. [*Advancing*] Welcome, good Robin. See'st
    thou this sweet sight?
  Her dotage now I do begin to pity: 50
  For, meeting her of late behind the wood,
  Seeking sweet favors° for this hateful fool,
  I did upbraid her, and fall out with her.
  For she his hairy temples then had rounded
  With coronet of fresh and fragrant flowers;   55
  And that same dew, which sometime° on the buds
  Was wont° to swell, like round and orient° pearls,
  Stood now within the pretty flouriets'° eyes,
  Like tears, that did their own disgrace bewail.
  When I had at my pleasure taunted her,   60
  And she in mild terms begged my patience,
  I then did ask of her her changeling child;
  Which straight she gave me, and her fairy sent
  To bear him to my bower in fairy land.
  And now I have the boy, I will undo   65
  This hateful imperfection of her eyes:
  And, gentle Puck, take this transformèd scalp
  From off the head of this Athenian swain,
  That, he awaking when the other° do,
  May all to Athens back again repair,   70
  And think no more of this night's accidents,°

44 *all ways* in every direction 46 *female ivy* (called female because
it clings to the elm and is supported by it) 52 *favors* love tokens
(probably flowers) 56 *sometime* formerly 57 *Was wont* used to
57 *orient* lustrous 58 *flouriets'* flowerets' 69 *other* others 71 *accidents* happenings

But as the fierce vexation of a dream.
But first I will release the Fairy Queen.
        Be as thou wast wont to be;
75   See as thou wast wont to see.
        Dian's bud o'er Cupid's flower
        Hath such force and blessèd power.
Now, my Titania, wake you, my sweet Queen.

Titania. My Oberon, what visions have I seen!
80   Methought I was enamored of an ass.

Oberon. There lies your love.

Titania.   How came these things to pass?
    O, how mine eyes do loathe his visage now!

Oberon. Silence awhile. Robin, take off this head.
    Titania, music call; and strike more dead
85   Than common sleep of all these five the sense.

Titania. Music, ho, music! Such as charmeth sleep!

Puck. Now, when thou wak'st, with thine own fool's
    eyes peep.

Oberon. Sound, music! [*Music*] Come, my Queen,
    take hands with me,
    And rock the ground whereon these sleepers be.
                                        [*Dance*]
90   Now thou and I are new in amity,
    And will tomorrow midnight solemnly°
    Dance in Duke Theseus' house triumphantly,°
    And bless it to all fair prosperity.
    There shall the pairs of faithful lovers be
95   Wedded, with Theseus, all in jollity.

Puck.   Fairy King, attend, and mark:
               I do hear the morning lark.

Oberon.   Then, my Queen, in silence sad,°
               Trip we after night's shade.

91 *solemnly* ceremoniously   92 *triumphantly* in festive procession
98 *sad* serious, solemn

190
We the globe can compass soon,
Swifter than the wand'ring moon.

Titania.   Come, my lord; and in our flight,
Tell me how it came this night,
That I sleeping here was found
With these mortals on the ground.   *105*

         Exeunt.

  Wind horn. Enter Theseus, and all his train;
      [Hippolyta, Egeus].

Theseus. Go, one of you, find out the forester,
For now our observation° is performed;
And since we have the vaward° of the day,
My love shall hear the music of my hounds.
Uncouple in the western valley; let them go.   *110*
Dispatch, I say, and find the forester.
       [Exit an Attendant.]
We will, fair Queen, up to the mountain's top,
And mark the musical confusion
Of hounds and echo in conjunction.

Hippolyta. I was with Hercules and Cadmus once,   *115*
When in a wood of Crete they bayed° the bear
With hounds of Sparta. Never did I hear
Such gallant chiding; for, besides the groves,
The skies, the fountains, every region near
Seemed all one mutual cry. I never heard   *120*
So musical a discord, such sweet thunder.

Theseus. My hounds are bred out of the Spartan kind,
So flewed, so sanded;° and their heads are hung
With ears that sweep away the morning dew;
Crook-kneed, and dew-lapped like Thessalian bulls; *125*
Slow in pursuit, but matched in mouth like bells,

107 *observation* observance, i.e., of the rite of May (cf. I.i.167)
108 *vaward* vanguard, i.e., morning   116 *bayed* brought to bay
123 *So flewed, so sanded* i.e., like Spartan hounds, with hanging
cheeks and of sandy color

Each under each.° A cry° more tunable
Was never holloed to, nor cheered with horn,
In Crete, in Sparta, nor in Thessaly.
Judge when you hear. But, soft!° What nymphs
130   are these?

Egeus. My lord, this is my daughter here asleep;
And this, Lysander; this Demetrius is;
This Helena, old Nedar's Helena:
I wonder of their being here together.

135 *Theseus.* No doubt they rose up early to observe
The rite of May; and, hearing our intent,
Came here in grace of our solemnity.°
But speak, Egeus. Is not this the day
That Hermia should give answer of her choice?

140 *Egeus.* It is, my lord.

Theseus. Go, bid the huntsmen wake them with their
horns.

        Shout within. They all start up. Wind horns.

Good morrow, friends. Saint Valentine is past:
Begin these wood birds but to couple now?°

Lysander. Pardon, my lord.

Theseus.   I pray you all, stand up.
145 I know you two are rival enemies.
How comes this gentle concord in the world,
That hatred is so far from jealousy,°
To sleep by hate, and fear no enmity?

Lysander. My lord, I shall reply amazedly,°
150 Half sleep, half waking: but as yet, I swear,
I cannot truly say how I came here.

127 *Each under each* of different tone (like the chime of bells)
127 *cry* pack of hounds   130 *soft* stop   137 *in grace of our solemnity* in honor of our festival   143 *Begin these . . . couple now* (it
was supposed that birds began to mate on February 14, St. Valentine's Day)   147 *jealousy* suspicion   149 *amazedly* confusedly

But, as I think—for truly would I speak,
And now I do bethink me, so it is—
I came with Hermia hither. Our intent
Was to be gone from Athens, where we might,   155
Without° the peril of the Athenian law—

Egeus. Enough, enough, my lord; you have enough.
I beg the law, the law, upon his head.
They would have stol'n away; they would, Deme-
    trius,
Thereby to have defeated° you and me,   160
You of your wife and me of my consent,
Of my consent that she should be your wife.

Demetrius. My lord, fair Helen told me of their
    stealth,°
Of this their purpose hither to this wood,
And I in fury hither followed them,   165
Fair Helena in fancy° following me.
But, my good lord, I wot not by what power—
But by some power it is—my love to Hermia,
Melted as the snow, seems to me now
As the remembrance of an idle gaud,°   170
Which in my childhood I did dote upon;
And all the faith, the virtue° of my heart,
The object and the pleasure of mine eye,
Is only Helena. To her, my lord,
Was I betrothed ere I saw Hermia: 175
But, like a sickness,° did I loathe this food;
But, as in health, come to my natural taste,
Now I do wish it, love it, long for it,
And will for evermore be true to it.

Theseus. Fair lovers, you are fortunately met.   180
Of this discourse we more will hear anon.
Egeus, I will overbear your will,
For in the temple, by and by,° with us

---

156 *Without* outside of   160 *defeated* deprived by fraud   163
stealth stealthy flight   166 *in fancy* in love, doting   170 *idle gaud*
worthless trinket   172 *virtue* power   176 *like a sickness* like one
who is sick   183 *by and by* shortly

These couples shall eternally be knit;
185 And, for the morning now is something worn,°
Our purposed hunting shall be set aside.
Away with us to Athens! Three and three,
We'll hold a feast in great solemnity.
Come, Hippolyta.
         [*Exeunt Theseus, Hippolyta, Egeus, and train.*]

Demetrius. These things seem small and undistin-
190   guishable,
Like far-off mountains turnèd into clouds.

Hermia. Methinks I see these things with parted eye,°
When everything seems double.

Helena.   So methinks:
And I have found Demetrius like a jewel,
Mine own, and not mine own.

195 *Demetrius.*   Are you sure
That we are awake? It seems to me
That yet we sleep, we dream. Do not you think
The Duke was here, and bid us follow him?

Hermia. Yea, and my father.

Helena.   And Hippolyta.

200 *Lysander.* And he did bid us follow to the temple.

Demetrius. Why, then, we are awake. Let's follow
      him,
And by the way let us recount our dreams.
                              [*Exeunt.*]

Bottom. [*Awaking*] When my cue comes, call me,
and I will answer. My next is, "Most fair Pyramus."
205   Heigh-ho! Peter Quince? Flute, the bellows
mender? Snout, the tinker? Starveling? God's my
life,° stol'n hence, and left me asleep? I have had
a most rare vision. I have had a dream, past the

---

185 *something worn* somewhat spent   192 *with parted eye* i.e., with
the eyes out of focus   206–07 *God's my life* an oath (possibly from
"God bless my life")

wit of man to say what dream it was. Man is but
an ass, if he go about° to expound this dream.   210
Methought I was—there is no man can tell what.
Methought I was—and methought I had—but man
is but a patched° fool if he will offer to say what
methought I had. The eye of man hath not heard,
the ear of man hath not seen, man's hand is not   215
able to taste, his tongue to conceive, nor his heart
to report, what my dream was. I will get Peter
Quince to write a ballet° of this dream. It shall
be called "Bottom's Dream," because it hath no
bottom; and I will sing it in the latter end of a   220
play, before the Duke. Peradventure to make it
the more gracious, I shall sing it at her death.°

[Exit.]

[Scene II.   *Athens. Quince's house.*]

Enter Quince, Flute,° Thisby and the rabble
[Snout, Starveling].

Quince. Have you sent to Bottom's house? Is he come
home yet?

Starveling. He cannot be heard of. Out of doubt he
is transported.°

Flute. If he come not, then the play is marred. It   *5*
goes not forward, doth it?

Quince. It is not possible. You have not a man in all

---

210 *go about* endeavor   213 *patched* (referring to the patchwork
dress of jesters)   218 *ballet* ballad   222 *her death* i.e., Thisby's
death in the play   IV.ii.s.d. *Flute* (Shakespeare seems to have for-
gotten that Flute and Thisby are the same person)   4 *transported*
carried off (by the fairies)

Athens able to discharge° Pyramus but he.

Flute. No, he hath simply the best wit of any handi-
craft man in Athens.

Quince. Yea, and the best person too; and he is a
very paramour for a sweet voice.

Flute. You must say "paragon." A paramour is, God
bless us, a thing of nought.°

Enter Snug the Joiner.

Snug. Masters, the Duke is coming from the temple,
and there is two or three lords and ladies more
married. If our sport had gone forward, we had
all been made men.°

Flute. O sweet bully Bottom! Thus hath he lost sixpence a day° during his life. He could not have
scaped sixpence a day. An the Duke had not given
him sixpence a day for playing Pyramus, I'll be
hanged. He would have deserved it. Sixpence a
day in Pyramus, or nothing.

Enter Bottom.

Bottom. Where are these lads? Where are these
hearts?

Quince. Bottom! O most courageous° day! O most
happy hour!

Bottom. Masters, I am to discourse wonders: but ask
me not what; for if I tell you, I am not true
Athenian. I will tell you everything, right as it fell
out.

Quince. Let us hear, sweet Bottom.

---

8 *discharge* play   14 *a thing of nought* a wicked thing   18 *made*
men men whose fortunes are made   19–20 *sixpence a day* (a pension)   27 *courageous* brave, splendid

Bottom. Not a word of me.° All that I will tell you
   is, that the Duke hath dined. Get your apparel   35
   together, good strings to your beards, new ribbons
   to your pumps; meet presently° at the palace; every
   man look o'er his part; for the short and the long
   is, our play is preferred.° In any case, let Thisby
   have clean linen; and let not him that plays the   40
   lion pare his nails, for they shall hang out for the
   lion's claws. And, most dear actors, eat no onions
   nor garlic, for we are to utter sweet breath,° and
   I do not doubt but to hear them say it is a sweet
   comedy. No more words. Away! Go, away!   45

                                     [Exeunt.]

---

34 *of me* from me   37 *presently* immediately   39 *preferred* put
forward, recommended   43 *breath* (1) exhalation (2) words

[ACT V

Scene I. *Athens. The palace of Theseus.*]

*Enter Theseus, Hippolyta, and Philostrate, [Lords,
and Attendants].*

Hippolyta. 'Tis strange, my Theseus, that these lovers
    speak of.

Theseus. More strange than true. I never may believe
    These antique° fables, nor these fairy toys.°
    Lovers and madmen have such seething brains,
5   Such shaping fantasies,° that apprehend
    More than cool reason ever comprehends.
    The lunatic, the lover and the poet
    Are of imagination all compact.°
    One sees more devils than vast hell can hold,
10   That is the madman. The lover, all as frantic,
    Sees Helen's beauty in a brow of Egypt.°
    The poet's eye, in a fine frenzy rolling,
    Doth glance from heaven to earth, from earth to
      heaven;
    And as imagination bodies forth
15   The forms of things unknown, the poet's pen
    Turns them to shapes, and gives to airy nothing
    A local habitation and a name.

V.i.3 *antique* (1) ancient (2) grotesque (antic)   3 *fairy toys* trifles
about fairies 5 *fantasies* imagination 8 *compact* composed 11
brow of Egypt face of a gypsy

Such tricks hath strong imagination,
That, if it would but apprehend some joy,
It comprehends some bringer of that joy;°   20
Or in the night, imagining some fear,°
How easy is a bush supposed a bear!

Hippolyta. But all the story of the night told over,
And all their minds transfigured so together,
More witnesseth than fancy's images,   25
And grows to something of great constancy;°
But, howsoever, strange and admirable.°

*Enter Lovers: Lysander, Demetrius, Hermia and
Helena.*

Theseus. Here come the lovers, full of joy and mirth.
Joy, gentle friends! Joy and fresh days of love
Accompany your hearts!

Lysander.   More than to us   30
Wait in your royal walks, your board, your bed!

Theseus. Come now, what masques,° what dances
     shall we have,
To wear away this long age of three hours
Between our aftersupper° and bedtime?
Where is our usual manager of mirth?   35
What revels are in hand? Is there no play,
To ease the anguish of a torturing hour?
Call Philostrate.

Philostrate.   Here, mighty Theseus.

Theseus. Say, what abridgment° have you for this
     evening?

20 *It comprehends . . . that joy* it includes an imagined bringer of
the joy   21 *fear* object of fear   26 *constancy* consistency (and
reality)   27 *admirable* wonderful   32 *masques* courtly entertain-
ments with masked dancers   34 *aftersupper* refreshment served
after early supper   39 *abridgment* entertainment (to abridge or
shorten the time)

40   What masque? What music? How shall we beguile
      The lazy time, if not with some delight?

      Philostrate. There is a brief° how many sports are
          ripe:°
      Make choice of which your Highness will see first.
                                    [*Giving a paper*]

      Theseus. "The battle with the Centaurs, to be sung
45   By an Athenian eunuch to the harp."
      We'll none of that. That have I told my love,
      In glory of my kinsman Hercules.
      "The riot of the tipsy Bacchanals,
      Tearing the Thracian singer° in their rage."
50   That is an old device;° and it was played
      When I from Thebes came last a conqueror.
      "The thrice three Muses mourning for the death
      Of Learning, late deceased in beggary."
      That is some satire, keen and critical,
55   Not sorting with° a nuptial ceremony.
      "A tedious brief scene of young Pyramus
      And his love Thisby; very tragical mirth."
      Merry and tragical? Tedious and brief?
      That is, hot ice and wondrous strange snow.
60   How shall we find the concord of this discord?

      Philostrate. A play there is, my lord, some ten words
          long,
      Which is as brief as I have known a play;
      But by ten words, my lord, it is too long,
      Which makes it tedious. For in all the play
65   There is not one word apt, one player fitted.
      And tragical, my noble lord, it is,
      For Pyramus therein doth kill himself.
      Which, when I saw rehearsed, I must confess,
      Made mine eyes water; but more merry tears
70   The passion° of loud laughter never shed.

      Theseus. What are they that do play it?

      42 *brief* written list   42 *ripe* ready to be presented   49 *Thracian
      singer* Orpheus   50 *device* show   55 *sorting with* suited to   70 *pas-
      sion* strong emotion

Philostrate. Hard-handed men, that work in Athens
   here,
   Which never labored in their minds till now;
   And now have toiled their unbreathed° memories
   With this same play, against° your nuptial.   75

Theseus. And we will hear it.

Philostrate.   No, my noble lord;
   It is not for you. I have heard it over,
   And it is nothing, nothing in the world;
   Unless you can find sport in their intents,
   Extremely stretched and conned with cruel pain,   80
   To do you service.

Theseus.   I will hear that play;
   For never anything can be amiss,
   When simpleness and duty tender it.
   Go, bring them in: and take your places, ladies.
                              [*Exit Philostrate.*]

Hippolyta. I love not to see wretchedness o'ercharged,°   85
   And duty in his service perishing.

Theseus. Why, gentle sweet, you shall see no such
   thing.

Hippolyta. He says they can do nothing in this kind.°

Theseus. The kinder we, to give them thanks for
   nothing.
   Our sport shall be to take what they mistake: 90
   And what poor duty cannot do, noble respect
   Takes it in might,° not merit.
   Where I have come, great clerks° have purposèd
   To greet me with premeditated welcomes;
   Where I have seen them shiver and look pale,   95
   Make periods in the midst of sentences,
   Throttle their practiced accent in their fears,

---

74 *unbreathed* unexercised 75 *against* in preparation for 85
wretchedness o'ercharged lowly people overburdened 88 *in this
kind* in this kind of thing (i.e., acting) 92 *Takes it in might* con-
siders the ability and the effort made 93 *clerks* scholars

And, in conclusion, dumbly have broke off,
Not paying me a welcome. Trust me, sweet,
100 Out of this silence yet I picked a welcome;
And in the modesty of fearful duty
I read as much as from the rattling tongue
Of saucy and audacious eloquence.
    Love, therefore, and tongue-tied simplicity
105   In least speak most, to my capacity.°

[Enter Philostrate.]

Philostrate. So please your Grace, the Prologue is
    addressed.°

Theseus. Let him approach.   *[Flourish trumpets.]*

Enter the Prologue [Quince].

Prologue. If we offend, it is with our good will.
    That you should think, we come not to offend,
110 But with good will. To show our simple skill,
    That is the true beginning of our end.°
Consider, then, we come but in despite.
    We do not come, as minding to content you,
Our true intent is. All for your delight,
115   We are not here. That you should here repent
        you,
The actors are at hand; and, by their show,°
You shall know all, that you are like to know.

Theseus. This fellow doth not stand upon points.°

Lysander. He hath rid his prologue like a rough colt;
120 he knows not the stop.° A good moral, my lord:
it is not enough to speak, but to speak true.

105 *to my capacity* according to my understanding   106 *addressed*
ready   111 *end* aim   116 *show* (probably referring to a kind of
pantomime—"dumb show"—that was to follow, in which the
action of the play was acted without words while the Prologue gave
his account)   118 *stand upon points* (1) care about punctuation
(2) worry about niceties   120 *stop* (1) technical term for the check-
ing of a horse (2) mark of punctuation

Hippolyta. Indeed he hath played on this prologue
  like a child on a recorder;° a sound, but not in
  government.°

Theseus. His speech was like a tangled chain; noth-   125
  ing impaired, but all disordered. Who is next?

*Enter Pyramus and Thisby and Wall and Moonshine
      and Lion [as in dumbshow].*

Prologue. Gentles, perchance you wonder at this show;
      But wonder on, till truth make all things plain.
  This man is Pyramus, if you would know;
      This beauteous lady Thisby is certain.   130
  This man, with lime and roughcast, doth present
      Wall, that vile Wall which did these lovers
        sunder;
  And through Wall's chink, poor souls, they are
        content
      To whisper. At the which let no man wonder.
  This man, with lantern, dog, and bush of thorn,   135
      Presenteth Moonshine; for, if you will know,
  By moonshine did these lovers think no scorn
      To meet at Ninus' tomb, there, there to woo.
  This grisly beast, which Lion hight° by name,
      The trusty Thisby, coming first by night,   140
  Did scare away, or rather did affright;
      And, as she fled, her mantle she did fall,°
  Which Lion vile with bloody mouth did stain.
  Anon comes Pyramus, sweet youth and tall,°
      And finds his trusty Thisby's mantle slain: 145
  Whereat, with blade, with bloody blameful blade,
      He bravely broached° his boiling bloody breast;
  And Thisby, tarrying in mulberry shade,
      His dagger drew, and died. For all the rest,

---

123 *recorder* flutelike instrument 124 *government* control 139
hight is called 142 *fall* let fall 144 *tall* brave 147 *bravely
broached* gallantly stabbed

150   Let Lion, Moonshine, Wall, and lovers twain
    At large° discourse, while here they do remain.

Theseus. I wonder if the lion be to speak.

Demetrius. No wonder, my lord. One lion may, when many asses do.

       Exit Lion, Thisby and Moonshine.

155   *Wall.* In this same interlude it doth befall
    That I, one Snout by name, present a wall;
    And such a wall, as I would have you think,
    That had in it a crannied hole or chink,
    Through which the lovers, Pyramus and Thisby,
160   Did whisper often very secretly.
    This loam, this roughcast, and this stone, doth show
    That I am that same wall; the truth is so;
    And this the cranny is, right and sinister,°
    Through which the fearful lovers are to whisper.

165   *Theseus.* Would you desire lime and hair to speak better?

Demetrius. It is the wittiest partition° that ever I heard discourse, my lord.

Theseus. Pyramus draws near the wall. Silence!

Pyramus. O grim-looked night! O night with hue so
170   black!
    O night, which ever art when day is not!
    O night, O night! Alack, alack, alack,
    I fear my Thisby's promise is forgot!
    And thou, O wall, O sweet, O lovely wall,
    That stand'st between her father's ground and
175   mine!
    Thou wall, O wall, O sweet and lovely wall,

---

151 *At large* at length   163 *right and sinister* i.e., running right and left, horizontal   167 *wittiest partition* most intelligent wall (with a pun on "partition," a section of a book or of an oration)

Show me thy chink, to blink through with mine
eyne!

> [*Wall holds up his fingers.*]

Thanks, courteous wall. Jove shield thee well for
this!
But what see I? No Thisby do I see.
O wicked wall, through whom I see no bliss!   *180*
Cursed be thy stones for thus deceiving me!

Theseus. The wall, methinks, being sensible,° should
curse again.°

Pyramus. No, in truth, sir, he should not. "Deceiving
me" is Thisby's cue. She is to enter now, and I   *185*
am to spy her through the wall. You shall see it
will fall pat° as I told you. Yonder she comes.

Enter Thisby.

Thisby. O wall, full often hast thou heard my moans,
For parting my fair Pyramus and me!
My cherry lips have often kissed thy stones,   *190*
Thy stones with lime and hair knit up in thee.

Pyramus. I see a voice: now will I to the chink,
To spy an I can hear my Thisby's face.
Thisby!

Thisby. My love thou art, my love I think.   *195*

Pyramus. Think what thou wilt, I am thy lover's
grace;°
And, like Limander,° am I trusty still.

Thisby. And I like Helen,° till the Fates me kill.

Pyramus. Not Shafalus to Procrus° was so true.

---

182 *sensible* conscious   183 *again* in return   187 *pat* exactly   196
thy lover's grace thy gracious lover   197 *Limander* (Bottom means
Leander, but blends him with Alexander)   198 *Helen* (Hero, beloved of Leander, is probably meant)   199 *Shafalus to Procrus*
(Cephalus and Procris are meant, legendary lovers)

200 *Thisby.* As Shafalus to Procrus, I to you.

Pyramus. O kiss me through the hole of this vile wall!

Thisby. I kiss the wall's hole, not your lips at all.

Pyramus. Wilt thou at Ninny's tomb meet me straight-
way?

Thisby. 'Tide life, 'tide death,° I come without delay.
[*Exeunt Pyramus and Thisby.*]

205 *Wall.* Thus have I, Wall, my part dischargèd so;
And, being done, thus wall away doth go.   [*Exit.*]

Theseus. Now is the moon used° between the two
neighbors.

Demetrius. No remedy, my lord, when walls are so
210   willful to hear without warning.°

Hippolyta. This is the silliest stuff that ever I heard.

Theseus. The best in this kind° are but shadows; and
the worst are no worse, if imagination amend them.

Hippolyta. It must be your imagination then, and
215   not theirs.

Theseus. If we imagine no worse of them than they
of themselves, they may pass for excellent men.
Here come two noble beasts in, a man and a lion.

Enter Lion and Moonshine.

Lion. You, ladies, you, whose gentle hearts do fear
The smallest monstrous mouse that creeps on
220   floor,

____

204 *'Tide life, 'tide death* come (betide) life or death   207 *moon
used* (the quartos read thus, the Folio reads *morall downe.* Among
suggested emendations are "mural down," and "moon to see")
209–10 *when walls . . . without warning* i.e., when walls are so eager
to listen without warning the parents (?)   212 *in this kind* of this
sort, i.e., plays (or players?)

May now perchance both quake and tremble here,
  When lion rough in wildest rage doth roar.
Then know that I, as Snug the joiner, am
A lion fell,° nor else no lion's dam;
For, if I should as lion come in strife   225
Into this place, 'twere pity on my life.°

Theseus. A very gentle° beast, and of a good conscience.

Demetrius. The very best at a beast, my lord, that
  e'er I saw.   230

Lysander. This lion is a very fox for his valor.

Theseus. True; and a goose for his discretion.

Demetrius. Not so, my lord; for his valor cannot
  carry° his discretion, and the fox carries the goose.

Theseus. His discretion, I am sure, cannot carry his   235
  valor; for the goose carries not the fox. It is well.
  Leave it to his discretion, and let us listen to the
  moon.

Moonshine. This lanthorn° doth the hornèd moon
  present—

Demetrius. He should have worn the horns on his
  head.°   240

Theseus. He is no crescent, and his horns are invisible
  within the circumference.

Moonshine. This lanthorn doth the hornèd moon
  present;
  Myself the man i' th' moon do seem to be.   245

Theseus. This is the greatest error of all the rest.

---

224 *lion fell* fierce lion (perhaps with a pun on *fell* = "skin")
226 *pity on my life* a dangerous thing for me   227 *gentle* gentle-
manly, courteous   234 *carry* carry away   239 *lanthorn* (so spelled,
and perhaps pronounced "lant-horn," because lanterns were commonly made of horn)   240 *horns on his head* (cuckolds were said
to have horns)

The man should be put into the lanthorn. How is
it else the man i' th' moon?

Demetrius. He dares not come there for the candle;
250   for, you see, it is already in snuff.°

Hippolyta. I am aweary of this moon. Would he would
change!

Theseus. It appears, by his small light of discretion,
that he is in the wane; but yet, in courtesy, in all
255   reason, we must stay the time.

Lysander. Proceed, Moon.

Moonshine. All that I have to say is to tell you that
the lanthorn is the moon; I, the man i' th' moon;
this thorn bush, my thorn bush; and this dog, my
260   dog.

Demetrius. Why, all these should be in the lanthorn;
for all these are in the moon. But, silence! Here
comes Thisby.

Enter Thisby.

Thisby. This is old Ninny's tomb. Where is my love?

265 *Lion.* Oh—   [*The lion roars. Thisby runs off.*]

Demetrius. Well roared, Lion.

Theseus. Well run, Thisby.

Hippolyta. Well shone, Moon. Truly, the moon shines
with a good grace.
    [*The Lion shakes Thisby's mantle, and exit.*]

270 *Theseus.* Well moused,° Lion.

Demetrius. And then came Pyramus.

Lysander. And so the lion vanished.

---

250 *in snuff* (1) in need of snuffing (2) resentful   270 *moused*
shaken (like a mouse)

Enter Pyramus.

Pyramus. Sweet Moon, I thank thee for thy sunny
    beams;
  I thank thee, Moon, for shining now so bright;
  For, by thy gracious, golden, glittering gleams,   275
      I trust to take of truest Thisby sight.
        But stay, O spite!°
        But mark, poor knight,
      What dreadful dole° is here!
        Eyes, do you see?   280
        How can it be?
      O dainty duck! O dear!
        Thy mantle good,
        What, stained with blood!
      Approach, ye Furies fell!°   285
        O Fates, come, come,
        Cut thread and thrum;°
      Quail,° crush, conclude, and quell!°

Theseus. This passion, and the death of a dear friend,
  would go near to make a man look sad.   290

Hippolyta. Beshrew° my heart, but I pity the man.

Pyramus. O wherefore, Nature, didst thou lions frame?
  Since lion vile hath here deflow'red my dear:
  Which is—no, no—which was the fairest dame
    That lived, that loved, that liked, that looked
    with cheer.°   295
        Come, tears, confound;
        Out, sword, and wound
      The pap of Pyramus;
        Ay, that left pap,
        Where heart doth hop. [*Stabs himself.*]   300
      Thus die I, thus, thus, thus.
        Now am I dead,

---

277 *spite* vexation 279 *dole* sorrowful thing 285 *fell* fierce
287 *thread and thrum* i.e., everything (*thrum* = the end of the
warp thread) 288 *Quail* destroy 288 *quell* kill 291 *Beshrew*
curse (but a mild word) 295 *cheer* countenance

> Now am I fled;
> My soul is in the sky.
305   Tongue, lose thy light;
> Moon, take thy flight.
>
>   *[Exit Moonshine.]*
> Now die, die, die, die, die.   *[Dies.]*

Demetrius. No die, but an ace,° for him; for he is but one.

310 *Lysander.* Less than an ace, man; for he is dead, he is nothing.

Theseus. With the help of a surgeon he might yet recover, and yet prove an ass.

Hippolyta. How chance° Moonshine is gone before
315   Thisby comes back and finds her lover?

Theseus. She will find him by starlight. Here she comes; and her passion° ends the play.

[Enter Thisby.]

Hippolyta. Methinks she should not use a long one for such a Pyramus. I hope she will be brief.

320 *Demetrius.* A mote will turn the balance, which Pyramus, which Thisby, is the better; he for a man, God warr'nt us; she for a woman, God bless us!

Lysander. She hath spied him already with those sweet eyes.

325 *Demetrius.* And thus she means,° videlicet:

Thisby.   Asleep, my love?
> What, dead, my dove?
> O Pyramus, arise!
> Speak, speak. Quite dumb?
330   Dead, dead? A tomb

---

308 *No die, but an ace* not a die (singular of "dice"), but a one-spot on a die   314 *How chance* how does it come that · 317 *passion* passionate speech   325 *means* laments

        Must cover thy sweet eyes.
          These lily lips,
          This cherry nose,
        These yellow cowslip cheeks,
          Are gone, are gone.   335
          Lovers, make moan.
        His eyes were green as leeks.
          O Sisters Three,°
          Come, come to me,
        With hands as pale as milk;   340
          Lay them in gore,
          Since you have shore°
        With shears his thread of silk.
          Tongue, not a word.
          Come, trusty sword,   345
        Come, blade, my breast imbrue!°
                                    [*Stabs herself.*]
          And, farewell, friends.
          Thus Thisby ends.
        Adieu, adieu, adieu.   [*Dies.*]

Theseus. Moonshine and Lion are left to bury the   350
    dead.

Demetrius. Ay, and Wall too.

Bottom. [*Starting up*] No, I assure you; the wall is
    down that parted their fathers. Will it please you
    to see the epilogue, or to hear a Bergomask dance°   355
    between two of our company?

Theseus. No epilogue, I pray you; for your play needs
    no excuse. Never excuse, for when the players are
    all dead, there need none to be blamed. Marry, if
    he that writ it had played Pyramus and hanged   360
    himself in Thisby's garter, it would have been a
    fine tragedy: and so it is, truly; and very notably
    discharged. But, come, your Bergomask. Let your
    epilogue alone.   [*A dance.*]

---

338 *Sisters Three* i.e., the three Fates   342 *shore* shorn   346 *imbrue*
stain with blood   355 *Bergomask dance* rustic dance

365   The iron tongue of midnight hath told° twelve.
      Lovers, to bed; 'tis almost fairy time.
      I fear we shall outsleep the coming morn,
      As much as we this night have overwatched.
      This palpable-gross° play hath well beguiled
370   The heavy gait of night. Sweet friends, to bed.
      A fortnight hold we this solemnity,
      In nightly revels and new jollity.   *Exeunt.*

            Enter Puck [with a broom].

      Puck. Now the hungry lion roars,
            And the wolf behowls the moon;
375   Whilst the heavy plowman snores,
            All with weary task fordone.°
      Now the wasted° brands do glow,
            Whilst the screech owl, screeching loud,
      Puts the wretch that lies in woe
380   In remembrance of a shroud.
      Now it is the time of night,
            That the graves, all gaping wide,
      Every one lets forth his sprite,
            In the churchway paths to glide:
385   And we fairies, that do run
            By the triple Hecate's team,°
      From the presence of the sun,
            Following darkness like a dream,
      Now are frolic.° Not a mouse
390   Shall disturb this hallowed house:
      I am sent, with broom, before,
      To sweep the dust behind the door.°

---

365 *told* counted, tolled   369 *palpable-gross* obviously grotesque
376 *fordone* worn out   377 *wasted* used-up   386 *triple Hecate's
team* i.e., because she had three names: Phoebe in Heaven, Diana
on Earth, Hecate in Hades. (Like her chariot—drawn by black
horses or dragons—the elves were abroad only at night; but
III.ii.388–91 says differently)   389 *frolic* frolicsome   392 *behind
the door* i.e., from behind the door (Puck traditionally helped with
household chores)

Enter King and Queen of Fairies with all their train.

Oberon. Through the house give glimmering light,
    By the dead and drowsy fire:
  Every elf and fairy sprite   *395*
    Hop as light as bird from brier;
  And this ditty, after me,
  Sing, and dance it trippingly.

Titania. First, rehearse your song by rote,
  To each word a warbling note: *400*
  Hand in hand, with fairy grace,
  Will we sing, and bless this place.
                          [Song and dance.]

Oberon. Now, until the break of day,
  Through this house each fairy stray.
  To the best bride-bed will we,   *405*
  Which by us shall blessèd be;
  And the issue there create°
  Ever shall be fortunate.
  So shall all the couples three
  Ever true in loving be;   *410*
  And the blots of Nature's hand
  Shall not in their issue stand.
  Never mole, harelip, nor scar,
  Nor mark prodigious,° such as are
  Despisèd in nativity,   *415*
  Shall upon their children be.
  With this field-dew consecrate,
  Every fairy take his gait,°
  And each several° chamber bless,
  Through this palace, with sweet peace,   *420*
  And the owner of it blest
  Ever shall in safety rest.
  Trip away; make no stay;
  Meet me all by break of day.
                   Exeunt [all but Puck].

---

407 *create* created   414 *mark prodigious* ominous birthmark   418
take his gait proceed   419 *several* individual

425 *Puck.* If we shadows have offended,
       Think but this, and all is mended:
       That you have but slumb'red here,
       While these visions did appear.
       And this weak and idle° theme,
430   No more yielding but° a dream,
       Gentles, do not reprehend:
       If you pardon, we will mend.
       And, as I am an honest Puck,
       If we have unearnèd luck
435   Now to scape the serpent's tongue,°
       We will make amends ere long;
       Else the Puck a liar call:
       So, good night unto you all.
       Give me your hands,° if we be friends,
440   And Robin shall restore amends.°   [*Exit.*]

FINIS

429 *idle* foolish   430 *No more yielding but* yielding no more than
435 *to scape the serpent's tongue* i.e., to escape hisses from the
audience   439 *Give me your hands* applaud   440 *restore amends*
make amends

Textual Note

Our chief authority for the text of *A Midsummer Night's Dream* is the First Quarto of 1600 (Q1), possibly printed from Shakespeare's own manuscript. The Second Quarto of 1619 (Q2), fraudulently dated 1600, and the First Folio of 1623 (F) correct a few obvious mistakes of Q1 and add some new ones. The Folio introduces division into acts. The present text follows Q1 as closely as possible, but modernizes punctuation and spelling (and prints "and" as "an" when it means "if"), occasionally alters the lineation (e.g., prints as prose some lines that were mistakenly set as verse), expands and regularizes the speech prefixes, slightly alters the position of stage directions where necessary, and corrects obvious typographical errors. Other departures from Q1 are listed below, the adopted reading first in italics, and then Q1's reading in roman. If the adopted reading is derived from Q2 or from F, the fact is noted in a bracket following the reading.

I.i.4 *wanes* [Q2] waues 10 *New-bent* Now bent 19 s.d. *Lysander* [F] Lysander and Helena 24 *Stand forth, Demetrius* [printed as s.d. in Q1, Q2, F] 26 *Stand forth, Lysander* [printed as s.d. in Q1, Q2, F] 102 *Demetrius'* Demetrius 136 *low* loue 187 *Yours would* Your words 191 *I'd* ile 216 *sweet* sweld 219 *stranger companies* strange companions

II.i.69 *steep* [Q2] steppe 79 *Aegles* Eagles 109 *thin* chinne 158 *the west* [F] west 190 *slay . . . slayeth* stay . . . stayeth 201 *not nor* [F] not not

II.ii.9, 13, 24 [speech prefixes added by editor]   39 *Be't* Bet it   47 *is* [Q2] it

III.i.13 *By'r lakin* Berlakin   29–30 *yourselves* [F] your selfe   56 *Bottom* [Q2] Cet   70 *and let* or let   84 *Odors, odors* [F] odours, odorous   89 *Puck* [F] Quin   164 *Peaseblossom . . . All* [Q1, Q2, and F print as a single speech, attributed to "Fairies"]   176 *Peaseblossom . . . Mustardseed. Hail* [Q1, Q2, and F print thus: 1 Fai. Haile mortall, haile./2. Fai. Haile./3. Fai. Haile]   195 *you of* you

III.ii.19 *mimic* [F] Minnick   80 *part I so* part I   85 *sleep* slippe   213 *first, like* first life   220 *passionate words* [F] words   250 *prayers* praise   299 *gentlemen* [Q2] gentleman   323 *she's* [Q2] she is   406 *Speak! In some bush?* Speake in some bush   426 *shalt* [Q2] shat   451 *To your eye* your eye

IV.i.76 *o'er* or   85 *sleep of all these five* sleepe: of all these, fine   120 *seemed* seeme   131 *this is my* [Q2] this my   175 *saw* see   202 *let us* [Q2] lets   210 *to expound* [Q2] expound   213 *a patched* [F] patcht a

IV.ii.3 *Starveling* [F] Flute

V.i.34 *our* [F] or   156 *Snout* [F] Flute   191 *up in thee* [F] now againe   275 *gleams* beams   320 *mote* moth   353 *Bottom* [F] Lion   373 *lion* Lyons   374 *behowls* beholds   421–22 *And the owner . . . rest* [these two lines are transposed in Q1, Q2, and F]

Twelfth Night,
or, What You Will

EDITED BY
HERSCHEL BAKER

Dramatis Personae

Orsino, Duke of Illyria
Sebastian, brother of Viola
A Sea Captain, friend to Viola
Antonio, a sea captain, friend to Sebastian
Valentine ⎤
Curio   ⎦ gentlemen attending on the Duke
Sir Toby Belch, uncle to Olivia
Sir Andrew Aguecheek
Malvolio, steward to Olivia
Fabian   ⎤
Feste, a clown ⎦ servants to Olivia
Olivia, a countess
Viola, sister to Sebastian
Maria, Olivia's woman
Lords, a Priest, Sailors, Officers, Musicians, and
   Attendants

Scene: Illyria

Twelfth Night,
or, What You Will

ACT I

Scene I. [*The Duke's palace.*]

Enter Orsino, Duke of Illyria, Curio, and other Lords,
[with Musicians].

Duke. If music be the food of love, play on,
    Give me excess of it, that, surfeiting,
    The appetite°¹ may sicken, and so die.
    That strain again! It had a dying fall;°
    O, it came o'er my ear like the sweet sound   5
    That breathes upon a bank of violets,
    Stealing and giving odor. Enough, no more!
    'Tis not so sweet now as it was before.
    O spirit of love, how quick and fresh° art thou,
    That,° notwithstanding thy capacity,   10
    Receiveth as the sea. Nought enters there,°
    Of what validity and pitch° soe'er,
    But falls into abatement and low price°

---

¹ The degree sign (°) indicates a footnote, which is keyed to the
text by line number. Text references are printed in **boldface** type;
the annotation follows in roman type.
I.i.3 **appetite** i.e., the lover's appetite for music   4 **fall** cadence
9 **quick and fresh** lively and eager   10 **That** in that   11 **there** i.e.,
in the lover's "capacity"   12 **validity and pitch** value and superiority
(in falconry, pitch is the highest point of a bird's flight)   13 **price**
esteem

Even in a minute. So full of shapes° is fancy°
15 That it alone is high fantastical.°

Curio. Will you go hunt, my lord?

Duke. What, Curio?

Curio. The hart.

Duke. Why, so I do, the noblest that I have.
20 O, when mine eyes did see Olivia first,
Methought she purged the air of pestilence.
That instant was I turned into a hart,
And my desires, like fell° and cruel hounds,
E'er since pursue me.°

Enter Valentine.

How now? What news from her?

25 *Valentine.* So please my lord, I might not be admitted;
But from her handmaid do return this answer:
The element° itself, till seven years' heat,°
Shall not behold her face at ample view;
But like a cloistress she will veilèd walk,
30 And water once a day her chamber round
With eye-offending brine: all this to season°
A brother's dead love, which she would keep fresh
And lasting in her sad remembrance.°

Duke. O, she that hath a heart of that fine frame
35 To pay this debt of love but to a brother,
How will she love when the rich golden shaft°
Hath killed the flock of all affections else°

14 **shapes** fantasies   14 **fancy** love   15 **high fantastical** preeminently
imaginative   23 **fell** fierce   22–24 **That instant ... pursue me** (Orsino's mannered play on "hart-heart"—which exemplifies the lover's
"high fantastical" wit—derives from the story of Actaeon, a famous
hunter who, having seen Diana bathing, was transformed into a stag
and torn to pieces by his hounds)   27 **element** sky   27 **heat** course
31 **season** preserve (by the salt in her tears)   33 **remembrance** (pronounced with four syllables, "re-mem-ber-ance")   36 **golden shaft**
(the shaft, borne by Cupid, that causes love, as distinguished from the
leaden shaft, which causes aversion and disdain)   37 **all affections**
else i.e., all other emotions but love

That live in her; when liver, brain, and heart,°
These sovereign thrones, are all supplied and filled,
Her sweet perfections,° with one self° king.   40
Away before me to sweet beds of flow'rs;
Love-thoughts lie rich when canopied with bow'rs.

Exeunt.

Scene II. [*The seacoast.*]

Enter Viola, a Captain, and Sailors.

Viola. What country, friends, is this?

Captain. This is Illyria,° lady.

Viola. And what should I do in Illyria?
My brother he is in Elysium.°
Perchance he is not drowned. What think you, sailors?   5

Captain. It is perchance that you yourself were saved.

Viola. O my poor brother, and so perchance may he be.

Captain. True, madam; and, to comfort you with
    chance,°
Assure yourself, after our ship did split,
When you, and those poor number saved with you,   10
Hung on our driving° boat, I saw your brother,
Most provident in peril, bind himself
(Courage and hope both teaching him the practice)°
To a strong mast that lived° upon the sea;
Where, like Arion° on the dolphin's back,   15

38 **liver, brain, and heart** (the seats respectively of sexual desire, thought, and feeling) 40 **perfections** (pronounced with four syllables) 40 **self** sole I.ii.2 **Illyria** region bordering the east coast of the Adriatic 4 **Elysium** heaven (in classical mythology, the abode of the happy dead) 8 **chance** possibility 11 **driving** drifting 13 **practice** procedure 14 **lived** i.e., floated 15 **Arion** (in classical mythology, a bard who, having leapt into the sea to escape from murderous sailors, was borne to shore by a dolphin that he charmed by his songs)

I saw him hold acquaintance with the waves
So long as I could see.

Viola. For saying so, there's gold.
Mine own escape unfoldeth to my hope,°
20   Whereto thy speech serves for authority°
The like of him. Know'st thou this country?

Captain. Ay, madam, well, for I was bred and born
Not three hours' travel from this very place.

Viola. Who governs here?

25 *Captain.* A noble duke, in nature as in name.

Viola. What is his name?

Captain. Orsino.

Viola. Orsino! I have heard my father name him.
He was a bachelor then.

30 *Captain.* And so is now, or was so very late;
For but a month ago I went from hence,
And then 'twas fresh in murmur° (as you know
What great ones do, the less will prattle of)
That he did seek the love of fair Olivia.

35 *Viola.* What's she?

Captain. A virtuous maid, the daughter of a count
That died some twelvemonth since, then leaving her
In the protection of his son, her brother,
Who shortly also died; for whose dear love,
40   They say, she hath abjured the sight
And company of men.

Viola.   O that I served that lady,
And might not be delivered° to the world,
Till I had made mine own occasion mellow,
What my estate is.°

Captain.   That were hard to compass,°

---

19 **unfoldeth to my hope** i.e., reinforces my hope for my brother's
safety   20 **serves for authority** i.e., tends to justify   32 **fresh in
murmur** i.e., being rumored   42 **delivered** disclosed   43–44 **made
mine . . . estate is** found an appropriate time to reveal my status
44 **compass** effect

Because she will admit no kind of suit,　　　45
No, not° the Duke's.

Viola. There is a fair behavior in thee, captain,
And though that° nature with a beauteous wall
Doth oft close in° pollution, yet of thee
I will believe thou hast a mind that suits　　　50
With this thy fair and outward character.°
I prithee (and I'll pay thee bounteously)
Conceal me what I am, and be my aid
For such disguise as haply shall become
The form of my intent.° I'll serve this duke.　　　55
Thou shalt present me as an eunuch to him;
It may be worth thy pains. For I can sing,
And speak to him in many sorts of music
That will allow° me very worth his service.
What else may hap, to time I will commit;　　　60
Only shape thou thy silence to my wit.°

Captain. Be you his eunuch,° and your mute I'll be;
When my tongue blabs, then let mine eyes not see.

Viola. I thank thee. Lead me on.　　　　　*Exeunt.*

Scene III. [*Olivia's house.*]

Enter Sir Toby and Maria.

Toby. What a plague means my niece to take the death
of her brother thus? I am sure care's an enemy to
life.

Maria. By my troth, Sir Toby, you must come in

46 **not** not even　48 **though that** even though　49 **close in** conceal
51 **character** i.e., appearance and demeanor　54–55 **become/The
form of my intent** i.e., suit my purpose　59 **allow** certify　61 **wit**
i.e., skill in carrying out my plan　62 **Be you his eunuch** (this part of
the plan was not carried out)

5   earlier a' nights. Your cousin,° my lady, takes great
       exceptions to your ill hours.

       Toby. Why, let her except before excepted.°

       Maria. Ay, but you must confine yourself within the
       modest limits of order.°

10   *Toby.* Confine? I'll confine° myself no finer than I am.
       These clothes are good enough to drink in, and so
       be these boots too. And° they be not, let them hang
       themselves in their own straps.

       Maria. That quaffing and drinking will undo you. I
15   heard my lady talk of it yesterday; and of a foolish
       knight that you brought in one night here to be her
       wooer.

       Toby. Who? Sir Andrew Aguecheek?

       Maria. Ay, he.

20   *Toby.* He's as tall° a man as any's in Illyria.

       Maria. What's that to th' purpose?

       Toby. Why, he has three thousand ducats a year.

       Maria. Ay, but he'll have but a year in all these ducats.
       He's a very fool and a prodigal.

25   *Toby.* Fie that you'll say so! He plays o' th' viol-de-
       gamboys,° and speaks three or four languages word
       for word without book, and hath all the good gifts
       of nature.

       Maria. He hath indeed all, most natural;° for, besides
30   that he's a fool, he's a great quarreler; and but that
       he hath the gift of a coward to allay the gust° he
       hath in quarreling, 'tis thought among the prudent
       he would quickly have the gift of a grave.

I.iii.5 **cousin** (a term indicating various degrees of kinship; here,
niece) 7 **except before excepted** (Sir Toby parodies the legal jargon
exceptis exceptiendis ["with the exceptions previously noted"] commonly used in leases and contracts) 9 **modest limits of order** reasonable limits of good behavior 10 **confine** i.e., clothe 12 **And if** (a
common Elizabethan usage) 20 **tall** i.e., bold and handsome 25–
26 **viol-de-gamboys** bass viol 29 **natural** i.e., like a natural fool or
idiot 31 **gust** gusto

Toby. By this hand, they are scoundrels and sub-
stractors° that say so of him. Who are they?   *35*

Maria. They that add, moreover, he's drunk nightly in
your company.

Toby. With drinking healths to my niece. I'll drink to
her as long as there is a passage in my throat and
drink in Illyria. He's a coward and a coistrel° that   *40*
will not drink to my niece till his brains turn o' th'
toe like a parish top.° What, wench? *Castiliano
vulgo;*° for here comes Sir Andrew Agueface.

Enter Sir Andrew.

Andrew. Sir Toby Belch. How now, Sir Toby Belch?

Toby. Sweet Sir Andrew.   *45*

Andrew. Bless you, fair shrew.

Maria. And you too, sir.

Toby. Accost, Sir Andrew, accost.

Andrew. What's that?

Toby. My niece's chambermaid.°   *50*

Andrew. Good Mistress Accost, I desire better acquaintance.

Maria. My name is Mary, sir.

Andrew. Good Mistress Mary Accost.

34–35 **substractors** slanderers   40 **coistrel** knave (literally, a groom
who takes care of a knight's horse)   42 **parish top** (according to
George Steevens, a large top "formerly kept in every village, to be
whipped in frosty weather, that the peasants might be kept warm
by exercise, and out of mischief while they could not work"; however, the allusion may be to the communal top-spinning whose
origins are buried in religious ritual)   42–43 **Castiliano vulgo** (a
phrase of uncertain meaning; perhaps Sir Toby is suggesting that
Maria assume a grave and ceremonial manner—like that of the
notoriously formal Castilians—for Sir Andrew's benefit)   49–50
What's that?/My niece's chambermaid (Sir Andrew asks the meaning of the word "accost," but Sir Toby thinks that he is referring to
Maria. Actually, she was not Olivia's chambermaid, but rather her
companion, or lady in waiting, as is made clear at I.v.162)

55 *Toby.* You mistake, knight. "Accost" is front her, board her, woo her, assail her.

Andrew. By my troth, I would not undertake her in this company. Is that the meaning of "accost"?

Maria. Fare you well, gentlemen.

60 *Toby.* And thou let part so,° Sir Andrew, would thou mightst never draw sword again.

Andrew. And you part so, mistress, I would I might never draw sword again! Fair lady, do you think you have fools in hand?°

65 *Maria.* Sir, I have not you by th' hand.

Andrew. Marry,° but you shall have, and here's my hand.

Maria. Now, sir, thought is free. I pray you, bring your hand to th' butt'ry° bar and let it drink.

70 *Andrew.* Wherefore, sweetheart? What's your metaphor?

Maria. It's dry,° sir.

Andrew. Why, I think so. I am not such an ass but I can keep my hand dry. But what's your jest?

75 *Maria.* A dry jest, sir.

Andrew. Are you full of them?

Maria. Ay, sir, I have them at my finger's ends. Marry, now I let go your hand, I am barren.° *Exit Maria.*

Toby. O knight, thou lack'st a cup of canary!° When
80 did I see thee so put down?

Andrew. Never in your life, I think, unless you see canary put me down. Methinks sometimes I have

60 **so** i.e., without ceremony   64 **have fools in hand** i.e., are dealing with fools   66 **Marry** indeed (a mild interjection, originally an oath by the Virgin Mary)   69 **butt'ry** buttery, a storeroom for butts or casks of liquor   72 **dry** (1) thirsty (2) indicative of impotence 78 **barren** (1) without more jests (2) dull-witted   79 **canary** a sweet wine from the Canary Islands

no more wit than a Christian or an ordinary man
has. But I am a great eater of beef, and I believe
that does harm to my wit.   85

Toby. No question.

Andrew. And I thought that, I'd forswear it. I'll ride
home tomorrow, Sir Toby.

Toby. Pourquoi,° my dear knight?

Andrew. What is *"pourquoi"*? Do, or not do? I would   90
I had bestowed that time in the tongues that I have
in fencing, dancing, and bearbaiting. O, had I but
followed the arts!

Toby. Then hadst thou had an excellent head of hair.°

Andrew. Why, would that have mended my hair?   95

Toby. Past question, for thou seest it will not curl by
nature.

Andrew. But it becomes me well enough, does't not?

Toby. Excellent. It hangs like flax on a distaff;° and
I hope to see a huswife° take thee between her legs   100
and spin it off.

Andrew. Faith, I'll home tomorrow, Sir Toby. Your
niece will not be seen; or if she be, it's four to one
she'll none of me. The Count himself here hard by
woos her.   105

Toby. She'll none o' th' Count. She'll not match above
her degree, neither in estate,° years, nor wit; I have
heard her swear't. Tut, there's life in't,° man.

Andrew. I'll stay a month longer. I am a fellow o' th'
strangest mind i' th' world. I delight in masques and 110
revels sometimes altogether.

Toby. Art thou good at these kickshawses,° knight?

89 **Pourquoi** why (French)   94 **Then hadst thou had an excellent
head of hair** (perhaps Sir Toby is punning on Sir Andrew's "tongues"
[line 91] as "tongs" or curling irons)   99 **distaff** stick used in spinning   100 **huswife** housewife   107 **estate** fortune   108 **there's life
in't** i.e., there's hope for you yet   112 **kickshawses** trifles (French
quelque chose)

Andrew. As any man in Illyria, whatsoever he be, under the degree of my betters,° and yet I will no compare with an old° man.

Toby. What is thy excellence in a galliard,° knight?

Andrew. Faith, I can cut a caper.°

Toby. And I can cut the mutton to't.

Andrew. And I think I have the back-trick° simply as strong as any man in Illyria.

Toby. Wherefore are these things hid? Wherefore have these gifts a curtain before 'em? Are they like to take° dust, like Mistress Mall's picture? Why dost thou not go to church in a galliard and come home in a coranto?° My very walk should be a jig. would not so much as make water but in a sink-a-pace.° What dost thou mean? Is it a world to hide virtues° in? I did think, by the excellent constitution of thy leg, it was formed under the star of a galliard.°

Andrew. Ay, 'tis strong, and it does indifferent well in a damned-colored stock.° Shall we set about some revels?

Toby. What shall we do else? Were we not born under Taurus?°

Andrew. Taurus? That's sides and heart.

114 **under the degree of my betters** i.e., so long as he is not my social superior   115 **old** i.e., experienced (?)   116 **galliard** lively dance in triple time   117 **caper** (1) frisky leap (2) spice used to season mutton (hence Sir Toby's remark in the next line)   119 **back-trick** reverse step in dancing   123 **take** gather   125 **coranto** quick running dance   126–27 **sink-a-pace** cinquepace (French *cinque pas*), a kind of galliard of five steps (but there is also a scatological pun here)   128 **virtues** talents, accomplishments   129–30 **the star of a galliard** i.e., a dancing star   132 **damned-colored stock** (of the many emendations proposed for this stocking of uncertain color—"damasked colored," "dun-colored," "dove-colored," "damson-colored," and the like—Rowe's "flame-colored" has been most popular)   135 **Taurus** the Bull (one of the twelve signs of the zodiac, each of which was thought to influence a certain part of the human body. Most authorities assigned Taurus to neither "sides and heart" nor "legs and thighs," but to neck and throat)

oby. No, sir; it is legs and thighs. Let me see thee
caper. Ha, higher; ha, ha, excellent!　*Exeunt.*

Scene IV. [*The Duke's palace.*]

Enter Valentine, and Viola in man's attire.

Valentine. If the Duke continue these favors towards
you, Cesario, you are like to be much advanced.
He hath known you but three days and already you
are no stranger.

Viola. You either fear his humor° or my negligence,　*5*
that° you call in question the continuance of his
love. Is he inconstant, sir, in his favors?

Valentine. No, believe me.

Enter Duke, Curio, and Attendants.

Viola. I thank you. Here comes the Count.

Duke. Who saw Cesario, ho?　*10*

Viola. On your attendance, my lord, here.

Duke. Stand you awhile aloof. Cesario,
Thou know'st no less but all.° I have unclasped
To thee the book even of my secret soul.
Therefore, good youth, address thy gait° unto her;　*15*
Be not denied access, stand at her doors,
And tell them there thy fixèd foot shall grow
Till thou have audience.

Viola.　　　　　　　Sure, my noble lord,
If she be so abandoned to her sorrow
As it is spoke, she never will admit me.　*20*

I.iv.5 **humor** changeable disposition　6 **that** in that　13 **no less but
all** i.e., everything　15 **address thy gait** direct your steps

Duke. Be clamorous and leap all civil bounds
        Rather than make unprofited° return.

Viola. Say I do speak with her, my lord, what thēn?

Duke. O, then unfold the passion of my love;
25   Surprise her with discourse of my dear° faith;
        It shall become thee well to act my woes.
        She will attend it better in thy youth
        Than in a nuncio's° of more grave aspect.°

Viola. I think not so, my lord.

Duke.   Dear lad, believe it;
30   For they shall yet belie thy happy years
        That say thou art a man. Diana's lip
        Is not more smooth and rubious;° thy small pipe°
        Is as the maiden's organ, shrill and sound,°
        And all is semblative° a woman's part.
35   I know thy constellation° is right apt°
        For this affair. Some four or five attend him,
        All, if you will; for I myself am best
        When least in company. Prosper well in this,
        And thou shalt live as freely as thy lord
        To call his fortunes thine.

40 *Viola.*   I'll do my best
        To woo your lady. [*Aside*] Yet a barful° strife!
        Whoe'er I woo, myself would be his wife. *Exeunt*

---

22 **unprofited** unsuccessful   25 **dear** intense   28 **nuncio's** messenger's   28 **aspect** (accent on second syllable)   32 **rubious** ruby-re
32 **pipe** voice   33 **shrill and sound** high and clear   34 **semblativ**
like   35 **constellation** predetermined qualities   35 **apt** suitabl
41 **barful** full of impediments

Scene V. [*Olivia's house.*]

Enter Maria and Clown.

Maria. Nay, either tell me where thou hast been, or I will not open my lips so wide as a bristle may enter in way of thy excuse. My lady will hang thee for thy absence.

Clown. Let her hang me. He that is well hanged in   *5* this world needs to fear no colors.°

Maria. Make that good.°

Clown. He shall see none to fear.

Maria. A good lenten° answer. I can tell thee where that saying was born, of "I fear no colors."   *10*

Clown. Where, good Mistress Mary?

Maria. In the wars; and that may you be bold to say in your foolery.

Clown. Well, God give them wisdom that have it, and those that are fools, let them use their talents.°   *15*

Maria. Yet you will be hanged for being so long absent, or to be turned away. Is not that as good as a hanging to you?

Clown. Many a good hanging prevents a bad marriage, and for turning away, let summer bear it out.°   *20*

I.v.6 **fear no colors** i.e., fear nothing (with a pun on "color" meaning "flag" and "collar" meaning "hangman's noose") 7 **Make that good** i.e., explain it 9 **lenten** thin, meager (perhaps an allusion to the colorless, unbleached linen that replaced the customary liturgical purple or violet during Lent) 15 **talents** native intelligence (with perhaps a pun on "talons" meaning "claws") 20 **let summer bear it out** i.e., let the warm weather make it endurable

Maria. You are resolute then?

Clown. Not so, neither; but I am resolved on two
    points.°

Maria. That if one break, the other will hold; or if
25   both break, your gaskins° fall.

Clown. Apt, in good faith; very apt. Well, go thy way!
    If Sir Toby would leave drinking, thou wert as
    witty a piece of Eve's flesh° as any in Illyria.

Maria. Peace, you rogue; no more o' that. Here comes
30   my lady. Make your excuse wisely, you were best.°
                                                    [*Exit.*]

            Enter Lady Olivia with Malvolio
            [*and other Attendants*].

Clown. Wit, and't° be thy will, put me into good
    fooling. Those wits that think they have thee do
    very oft prove fools, and I that am sure I lack thee
    may pass for a wise man. For what says Quina-
35   palus?° "Better a witty fool than a foolish wit."
    God bless thee, lady.

Olivia. Take the fool away.

Clown. Do you not hear, fellows? Take away the lady.

Olivia. Go to,° y' are a dry° fool! I'll no more of you.
40   Besides, you grow dishonest.°

Clown. Two faults, madonna,° that drink and good
    counsel will amend. For give the dry° fool drink,
    then is the fool not dry. Bid the dishonest man
    mend himself: if he mend, he is no longer dishonest;
45   if he cannot, let the botcher° mend him. Anything

23 **points** counts (but Maria takes it in the sense of tagged laces
serving as suspenders)   25 **gaskins** loose breeches   27-28 **thou wert
as witty a piece of Eve's flesh** i.e., you would make as clever a wife
30 **you were best** it would be best for you   31 **and't** if it   34-35 **Quin-
apalus** (a sage of the Clown's invention)   39 **Go to** enough   39 **dry**
stupid   40 **dishonest** unreliable   41 **madonna** my lady   42 **dry**
thirsty   45 **botcher** mender of clothes

that's mended is but patched; virtue that trans-
gresses is but patched with sin, and sin that amends
is but patched with virtue. If that this simple syllo-
gism will serve, so; if it will not, what remedy? As
there is no true cuckold but calamity,° so beauty's   50
a flower. The lady bade take away the fool; therefore, I say again, take her away.

Olivia. Sir, I bade them take away you.

Clown. Misprision in the highest degree.° Lady, *cucullus non facit monachum.*° That's as much to say   55
as, I wear not motley in my brain. Good madonna,
give me leave to prove you a fool.

Olivia. Can you do it?

Clown. Dexteriously,° good madonna.

Olivia. Make your proof.   60

Clown. I must catechize you for it, madonna. Good
my mouse of virtue,° answer me.

Olivia. Well, sir, for want of other idleness,° I'll bide
your proof.

Clown. Good madonna, why mourn'st thou?   65

Olivia. Good fool, for my brother's death.

Clown. I think his soul is in hell, madonna.

Olivia. I know his soul is in heaven, fool.

Clown. The more fool, madonna, to mourn for your
brother's soul, being in heaven. Take away the fool,   70
gentlemen.

50 **there is no true cuckold but calamity** (although the Clown's chat-
ter should not be pressed too hard for significance, Kittredge's para-
phrase of this difficult passage is perhaps the least unsatisfactory:
"Every man is wedded to fortune; hence, when one's fortune is unfaithful, one may in very truth be called a cuckold—the husband of
an unfaithful wife")   54 **Misprision in the highest degree** i.e., an
egregious error in mistaken identity   54–55 **cucullus non facit
monachum** a cowl does not make a monk   59 **Dexteriously** dexter-
ously   61–62 **Good my mouse of virtue** my good virtuous mouse (a
term of playful affection)   63 **idleness** trifling

Olivia. What think you of this fool, Malvolio? Doth
he not mend?

Malvolio. Yes, and shall do till the pangs of death
75   shake him. Infirmity, that decays the wise, doth
ever make the better fool.

Clown. God send you, sir, a speedy infirmity, for the
better increasing your folly. Sir Toby will be sworn
that I am no fox,° but he will not pass his word for
80   twopence that you are no fool.

Olivia. How say you to that, Malvolio?

Malvolio. I marvel your ladyship takes delight in such
a barren° rascal. I saw him put down the other day
with° an ordinary fool that has no more brain than
85   a stone. Look you now, he's out of his guard°
already. Unless you laugh and minister occasion°
to him, he is gagged. I protest I take these wise men
that crow° so at these set° kind of fools no better
than the fools' zanies.°

90 *Olivia.* O, you are sick of self-love, Malvolio, and
taste with a distempered appetite. To be generous,°
guiltless, and of free disposition, is to take those
things for birdbolts° that you deem cannon bullets.
There is no slander in an allowed° fool, though
95   he do nothing but rail; nor no railing in a known
discreet man, though he do nothing but reprove.

Clown. Now Mercury indue thee with leasing,° for
thou speak'st well of fools.

Enter Maria.

Maria. Madam, there is at the gate a young gentleman
100   much desires to speak with you.

79 **I am no fox** i.e., sly and dangerous (like you)   83 **barren** stupid
83–84 **put down ... with** bested ... by   85 **out of his guard** defense-
less   86 **minister occasion** afford opportunity (for his fooling)
88 **crow** i.e., with laughter   88 **set** artificial   89 **zanies** inferior buf-
foons   91 **generous** liberal-minded   93 **birdbolts** blunt arrows   94
allowed licensed, privileged   97 **Mercury indue thee with leasing**
may the god of trickery endow you with the gift of deception

Olivia. From the Count Orsino, is it?

Maria. I know not, madam. 'Tis a fair young man, and well attended.

Olivia. Who of my people hold him in delay?

Maria. Sir Toby, madam, your kinsman.   *105*

Olivia. Fetch him off, I pray you. He speaks nothing but madman. Fie on him! [*Exit Maria.*] Go you, Malvolio. If it be a suit from the Count, I am sick, or not at home. What you will, to dismiss it. *(Exit Malvolio.)* Now you see, sir, how your fooling *110* grows old,° and people dislike it.

Clown. Thou hast spoke for us, madonna, as if thy eldest son should be a fool; whose skull Jove° cram with brains, for—here he comes—one of thy kin has a most weak pia mater.°   *115*

Enter Sir Toby.

Olivia. By mine honor, half drunk. What is he at the gate, cousin?

Toby. A gentleman.

Olivia. A gentleman? What gentleman?

Toby. 'Tis a gentleman here. A plague o' these pickle- *120* herring!° How now, sot?°

Clown. Good Sir Toby.

Olivia. Cousin,° cousin, how have you come so early by this lethargy?

Toby. Lechery? I defy lechery. There's one at the gate. *125*

Olivia. Ay, marry, what is he?

---

111 **old** stale, tedious   113 **Jove** (if, as is likely, Shakespeare here and elsewhere wrote "God," the printed text reflects the statute of 1606 that prohibited profane stage allusions to the deity)   115 **pia mater** brain   120–21 **pickle-herring** (to which the drunken Sir Toby attributes his hiccoughing)   121 **sot** fool   123 **Cousin** i.e., uncle (see I.iii.5)

Toby. Let him be the devil and he will, I care not.
Give me faith,° say I. Well, it's all one.   *Exit.*

Olivia. What's a drunken man like, fool?

130 *Clown.* Like a drowned man, a fool, and a madman.
One draught above heat° makes him a fool, the
second mads him, and a third drowns him.

Olivia. Go thou and seek the crowner,° and let him
sit o' my coz;° for he's in the third degree of drink—
135 he's drowned. Go look after him.

Clown. He is but mad yet, madonna, and the fool
shall look to the madman.   [*Exit.*]

Enter Malvolio.

Malvolio. Madam, yond young fellow swears he will
speak with you. I told him you were sick; he takes
140 on him to understand so much, and therefore comes
to speak with you. I told him you were asleep; he
seems to have a foreknowledge of that too, and
therefore comes to speak with you. What is to be
said to him, lady? He's fortified against any denial.

145 *Olivia.* Tell him he shall not speak with me.

Malvolio. H'as° been told so; and he says he'll stand
at your door like a sheriff's post,° and be the sup-
porter to a bench, but° he'll speak with you.

Olivia. What kind o' man is he?

150 *Malvolio.* Why, of mankind.°

Olivia. What manner of man?

Malvolio. Of very ill manner. He'll speak with you,
will you or no.

128 **faith** (in order to resist the devil)   131 **above heat** i.e., above
what is required to make a man normally warm   133 **crowner**
coroner   134 **sit o' my coz** hold an inquest on my kinsman   146 **H'as**
he has   147 **sheriff's post** post set up before a sheriff's door for
placards, notices, and such   148 **but** except   150 **of mankind** i.e.,
like other men

Olivia. Of what personage and years is he?

Malvolio. Not yet old enough for a man nor young 155
 enough for a boy; as a squash° is before 'tis a
 peascod, or a codling° when 'tis almost an apple.
 'Tis with him in standing water,° between boy and
 man. He is very well-favored and he speaks very
 shrewishly.° One would think his mother's milk 160
 were scarce out of him.

Olivia. Let him approach. Call in my gentlewoman.

Malvolio. Gentlewoman, my lady calls.   *Exit.*

Enter Maria.

Olivia. Give me my veil; come, throw it o'er my face.
 We'll once more hear Orsino's embassy.   165

Enter Viola.

Viola. The honorable lady of the house, which is she?

Olivia. Speak to me; I shall answer for her. Your will?

Viola. Most radiant, exquisite, and unmatchable beauty
 —I pray you tell me if this be the lady of the house,
 for I never saw her. I would be loath to cast away 170
 my speech; for, besides that it is excellently well
 penned, I have taken great pains to con° it. Good
 beauties, let me sustain no scorn. I am very comptible,° even to the least sinister° usage.

Olivia. Whence came you, sir?   175

Viola. I can say little more than I have studied, and
 that question's out of my part. Good gentle one,
 give me modest° assurance if you be the lady of the
 house, that I may proceed in my speech.

---

156 **squash** unripe peascod (pea pod)   157 **codling** unripe apple
158 **standing water** i.e., at the turning of the tide, between ebb and
flood, when it flows neither way   160 **shrewishly** tartly   172 **con**
learn   173–74 **comptible** sensitive   174 **sinister** discourteous   178
modest reasonable

180 *Olivia.* Are you a comedian?°

Viola. No, my profound heart;° and yet (by the very
fangs of malice I swear) I am not that° I play.
Are you the lady of the house?

Olivia. If I do not usurp° myself, I am.

185 *Viola.* Most certain, if you are she, you do usurp
yourself; for what° is yours to bestow is not yours
to reserve. But this is from my commission.° I will
on with my speech in your praise and then show
you the heart of my message.

190 *Olivia.* Come to what is important in't. I forgive you°
the praise.

Viola. Alas, I took great pains to study it, and 'tis
poetical.

Olivia. It is the more like to be feigned; I pray you
195 keep it in. I heard you were saucy at my gates; and
allowed your approach rather to wonder at you
than to hear you. If you be not mad, be gone; if
you have reason, be brief. 'Tis not that time of
moon with me to make one in so skipping a dia-
200 logue.°

Maria. Will you hoist sail, sir? Here lies your way.

Viola. No, good swabber; I am to hull° here a little
longer. Some mollification for your giant,° sweet
lady. Tell me your mind. I am a messenger.°

205 *Olivia.* Sure you have some hideous matter to deliver,
when the courtesy of it is so fearful.° Speak your
office.°

180 **comedian** actor (because he has had to "con" a "part")   181 **my
profound heart** my sagacious lady (a bantering compliment)
182 **that** that which   184 **usurp** counterfeit (but Viola takes it in the
sense "betray," "wrong")   186 **what** i.e., your hand in marriage
187 **from my commission** beyond my instructions   190 **forgive you**
excuse you from repeating   198–200 **'Tis not ... dialogue** i.e., I am
not in the mood to sustain such aimless banter   202 **hull** lie adrift
203 **giant** (an ironical reference to Maria's small size)   204 **Tell me
your mind. I am a messenger.** (Many editors have divided these
sentences, assigning the first to Olivia and the second to Viola)
206 **when the courtesy of it is so fearful** i.e., since your manner is so
truculent   207 **office** business

Viola. It alone concerns your ear. I bring no overture
of war, no taxation of° homage. I hold the olive°
in my hand. My words are as full of peace as   *210*
matter.°

Olivia. Yet you began rudely. What are you? What
would you?

Viola. The rudeness that hath appeared in me have I
learned from my entertainment.° What I am, and   *215*
what I would, are as secret as maidenhead:° to
your ears, divinity;° to any other's, profanation.

Olivia. Give us the place alone; we will hear this
divinity. [*Exit Maria and Attendants.*] Now, sir,
what is your text?   *220*

Viola. Most sweet lady—

Olivia. A comfortable° doctrine, and much may be
said of it. Where lies your text?

Viola. In Orsino's bosom.

Olivia. In his bosom? In what chapter of his bosom?   *225*

Viola. To answer by the method,° in the first of his
heart.

Olivia. O, I have read it; it is heresy. Have you no
more to say?

Viola. Good madam, let me see your face.   *230*

Olivia. Have you any commission from your lord to
negotiate with my face? You are now out of your
text.° But we will draw the curtain and show you
the picture. [*Unveils.*] Look you, sir, such a one I
was this present.° Is't not well done?   *235*

209 **taxation of** demand for   209 **olive** (the symbol of peace)
211 **matter** significant content   215 **entertainment** reception   216
maidenhead maidenhood   217 **divinity** i.e., a sacred message
222 **comfortable** comforting   226 **method** i.e., in the theological
style suggested by "divinity," "profanation," "text," and "doctrine"
232–33 **You are now out of your text** i.e., you have shifted from
talking of your master's heart to asking about my face   235 **this
present** just now (like portrait painters, Olivia gives the age of the
subject of the "picture" she has just revealed by drawing the "curtain" of a veil from her face)

Viola. Excellently done, if God did all.

Olivia. 'Tis in grain,° sir; 'twill endure wind and
weather.

Viola. 'Tis beauty truly blent, whose red and white
240 Nature's own sweet and cunning° hand laid on.
Lady, you are the cruel'st she alive
If you will lead these graces to the grave,
And leave the world no copy.

Olivia. O, sir, I will not be so hard-hearted. I will give
245 out divers schedules° of my beauty. It shall be in-
ventoried, and every particle and utensil° labeled
to my will:° as, item,° two lips, indifferent red;
item, two gray eyes, with lids to them; item, one
neck, one chin, and so forth. Were you sent hither
250 to praise° me?

Viola. I see you what you are; you are too proud;
But if° you were the devil, you are fair.
My lord and master loves you. O, such love
Could be but recompensed though you were crowned
The nonpareil of beauty.

255 *Olivia.*   How does he love me?

Viola. With adorations, with fertile° tears,
With groans that thunder love, with sighs of fire.

Olivia. Your lord does know my mind; I cannot love
him.
Yet I suppose him virtuous, know him noble,
260 Of great estate, of fresh and stainless youth;
In voices well divulged,° free, learned, and valiant,
And in dimension° and the shape of nature
A gracious person. But yet I cannot love him.
He might have took his answer long ago.

265 *Viola.* If I did love you in my master's flame,

237 **in grain** fast-dyed, indelible 240 **cunning** skillful 245 **sched-
ules** statements 246 **utensil** article 246–47 **labeled to my will** i.e.,
added as a codicil 247 **item** also 250 **praise** appraise 252 **if** even
if 256 **fertile** copious 261 **well divulged** i.e., of good repute
262 **dimension** physique

With such a suff'ring, such a deadly° life,
In your denial I would find no sense;
I would not understand it.

Olivia.   Why, what would you?

Viola. Make me a willow° cabin at your gate
And call upon my soul° within the house;   270
Write loyal cantons° of contemnèd° love
And sing them loud even in the dead of night;
Hallo your name to the reverberate° hills
And make the babbling gossip of the air°
Cry out "Olivia!" O, you should not rest   275
Between the elements of air and earth
But° you should pity me.

Olivia. You might do much. What is your parentage?

Viola. Above my fortunes, yet my state° is well.
I am a gentleman.

Olivia.   Get you to your lord.   280
I cannot love him. Let him send no more,
Unless, perchance, you come to me again
To tell me how he takes it. Fare you well.
I thank you for your pains. Spend this for me.

Viola. I am no fee'd post,° lady; keep your purse;   285
My master, not myself, lacks recompense.
Love make his heart of flint that you shall love;°
And let your fervor, like my master's, be
Placed in contempt. Farewell, fair cruelty.   *Exit.*

Olivia. "What is your parentage?"   290
"Above my fortunes, yet my state is well.
I am a gentleman." I'll be sworn thou art.
Thy tongue, thy face, thy limbs, actions, and spirit

---

266 **deadly** doomed to die   269 **willow** (emblem of a disconsolate lover)   270 **my soul** i.e., Olivia   271 **cantons** songs   271 **contemnèd** rejected   273 **reverberate** reverberating   274 **babbling gossip of the air** i.e., echo   277 **But** but that   279 **state** status   285 **fee'd post** i.e., lackey to be tipped   287 **Love make . . . love** may Love make the heart of him you love like flint

Do give thee fivefold blazon.° Not too fast; soft,°
   soft,
295 Unless the master were the man. How now?
Even so quickly may one catch the plague?
Methinks I feel this youth's perfections
With an invisible and subtle stealth
To creep in at mine eyes. Well, let it be.
What ho, Malvolio!

Enter Malvolio.

300 *Malvolio.*   Here, madam, at your service.

Olivia. Run after that same peevish° messenger,
   The County's° man. He left this ring behind him,
   Would I or not. Tell him I'll none of it.
   Desire him not to flatter with° his lord
305 Nor hold him up with hopes. I am not for him.
   If that the youth will come this way tomorrow,
   I'll give him reasons for't. Hie thee, Malvolio.

Malvolio. Madam, I will.   *Exit.*

Olivia. I do I know not what, and fear to find
310 Mine eye too great a flatterer for my mind.°
   Fate, show thy force; ourselves we do not owe.°
   What is decreed must be—and be this so!   *[Exit.]*

---

294 **blazon** heraldic insignia   294 **soft** i.e., take it slowly   301 **peevish** truculent impertinent   302 **County's** Count's   304 **flatter with** encourage   310 **Mine eye . . . mind** i.e., my eye, so susceptible to external attractions, will betray my judgment   311 **owe** own

ACT II

Scene I. [*The seacoast*.]

Enter Antonio and Sebastian.

Antonio. Will you stay no longer? Nor will you not
   that I go with you?

Sebastian. By your patience,° no. My stars shine darkly
   over me; the malignancy of my fate might perhaps
   distemper° yours. Therefore I shall crave of you   5
   your leave, that I may bear my evils alone. It were
   a bad recompense for your love to lay any of them
   on you.

Antonio. Let me yet know of you whither you are
   bound.   10

Sebastian. No, sooth,° sir. My determinate° voyage is
   mere extravagancy.° But I perceive in you so excellent a touch of modesty that you will not extort
   from me what I am willing to keep in; therefore it
   charges me in manners the rather to express myself.° 15
   You must know of me then, Antonio, my name is
   Sebastian, which I called Roderigo. My father was
   that Sebastian of Messaline whom I know you have
   heard of. He left behind him myself and a sister,
   both born in an hour.° If the heavens had been   20

II.i.3 **patience** permission   5 **distemper** disorder   11 **sooth** truly
11 **determinate** intended   12 **extravagancy** wandering   14–15 **it
charges me . . . myself** i.e., civility requires that I give some account
of myself   20 **in an hour** in the same hour

59

pleased, would we had so ended! But you, sir,
altered that, for some hour before you took me
from the breach° of the sea was my sister drowned.

Antonio. Alas the day!

25 *Sebastian.* A lady, sir, though it was said she much
resembled me, was yet of many accounted beautiful.
But though I could not with such estimable wonder°
overfar believe that, yet thus far I will boldly
publish° her: she bore a mind that envy could not
30 but call fair. She is drowned already, sir, with salt
water, though I seem to drown her remembrance
again with more.

Antonio. Pardon me, sir, your bad entertainment.°

Sebastian. O good Antonio, forgive me your trouble.°

35 *Antonio.* If you will not murder me° for my love, let
me be your servant.

Sebastian. If you will not undo what you have done,
that is, kill him whom you have recovered,° desire
it not. Fare ye well at once. My bosom is full of
40 kindness, and I am yet so near the manners of my
mother that, upon the least occasion more, mine
eyes will tell tales of me.° I am bound to the Count
Orsino's court. Farewell.   *Exit.*

Antonio. The gentleness of all the gods go with thee.
45 I have many enemies in Orsino's court,
Else would I very shortly see thee there.
But come what may, I do adore thee so
That danger shall seem sport, and I will go.   *Exit.*

---

23 **breach** breakers   27 **with such estimable wonder** i.e., with so
much esteem in my appraisal   29 **publish** describe   33 **bad entertainment** i.e., poor reception at my hands   34 **your trouble** the
trouble I have given you   35 **murder me** i.e., by forcing me to part
from you   38 **recovered** saved   40–42 **so near . . . tales of me** i.e.,
so overwrought by my sorrow that, like a woman, I shall weep

Scene II. [*A street near Olivia's house.*]

Enter Viola and Malvolio at several° doors.

Malvolio. Were not you ev'n now with the Countess
　　Olivia?

Viola. Even now, sir. On a moderate pace I have since
　　arrived but hither.

Malvolio. She returns this ring to you, sir. You might　　*5*
　　have saved me my pains, to have taken it away
　　yourself. She adds, moreover, that you should put
　　your lord into a desperate assurance° she will none
　　of him. And one thing more, that you be never so
　　hardy to come again in his affairs, unless it be to　　*10*
　　report your lord's taking of this. Receive it so.

Viola. She took the ring of me.° I'll none of it.

Malvolio. Come, sir, you peevishly threw it to her,
　　and her will is, it should be so returned. If it be
　　worth stooping for, there it lies, in your eye;° if　　*15*
　　not, be it his that finds it.　　　　　　　　　*Exit.*

Viola. I left no ring with her. What means this lady?
　　Fortune forbid my outside have not charmed her.
　　She made good view of me; indeed, so much
　　That sure methought° her eyes had lost her tongue,°　　*20*
　　For she did speak in starts distractedly.
　　She loves me sure; the cunning° of her passion

II.ii.s.d. **several** separate　　8 **desperate assurance** hopeless certainty
12 **She took the ring of me** (of the various emendations proposed for
this puzzling line, Malone's "She took no ring of me" is perhaps the
most attractive)　　15 **eye** sight　　20 **sure methought** ("sure," which
repairs the defective meter of this line, has been adopted from the
Second Folio. Another common emendation is "as methought")
20 **her eyes had lost her tongue** i.e., her fixed gaze made her lose the
power of speech　　22 **cunning** craftiness

Invites me in this churlish messenger.
None of my lord's ring? Why, he sent her none.
25   I am the man.° If it be so, as 'tis,
Poor lady, she were better love a dream.
Disguise, I see thou art a wickedness
Wherein the pregnant enemy° does much.
How easy is it for the proper false°
30   In women's waxen hearts to set their forms!
Alas, our frailty is the cause, not we,
For such as we are made of, such we be.
How will this fadge?° My master loves her dearly;
And I (poor monster)° fond° as much on him;
35   And she (mistaken) seems to dote on me.
What will become of this? As I am man,
My state is desperate° for my master's love.
As I am woman (now alas the day!),
What thriftless° sighs shall poor Olivia breathe?
40   O Time, thou must untangle this, not I;
It is too hard a knot for me t' untie.   [*Exit.*]

Scene III. [*A room in Olivia's house.*]

Enter Sir Toby and Sir Andrew.

Toby. Approach, Sir Andrew. Not to be abed after
midnight is to be up betimes; and *"Deliculo surgere,"*° thou know'st.

Andrew. Nay, by my troth, I know not, but I know
5   to be up late is to be up late.

25 **I am the man** i.e., whom she loves   28 **pregnant enemy** crafty
fiend (i.e., Satan)   29 **proper false** i.e., attractive but deceitful suitors
33 **fadge** turn out   34 **monster** (because of her equivocal position as
both man and woman)   34 **fond** dote   37 **desperate** hopeless   39
thriftless unavailing   II.iii.2–3 **Deliculo surgere** i.e., *Diluculo surgere
saluberrimum est,* "it is most healthful to rise early" (a tag from
William Lily's Latin grammar, which was widely used in sixteenth-
century schools)

Toby. A false conclusion; I hate it as an unfilled can.° To be up after midnight, and to go to bed then, is early; so that to go to bed after midnight is to go to bed betimes. Does not our lives consist of the four elements?°　　　　　　　　　　　　　　*10*

Andrew. Faith, so they say; but I think it rather consists of eating and drinking.

Toby. Th' art a scholar! Let us therefore eat and drink. Marian I say, a stoup° of wine!

Enter Clown.

Andrew. Here comes the fool, i' faith.　　　　　　*15*

Clown. How now, my hearts? Did you never see the picture of We Three?°

Toby. Welcome, ass. Now let's have a catch.°

Andrew. By my troth, the fool has an excellent breast.° I had rather than forty shillings I had such *20* a leg,° and so sweet a breath to sing, as the fool has. In sooth, thou wast in very gracious° fooling last night, when thou spok'st of Pigrogromitus,° of the Vapians° passing the equinoctial of Queubus.° 'Twas very good, i' faith. I sent thee sixpence for *25* thy leman.° Hadst it?

Clown. I did impeticos thy gratillity,° for Malvolio's nose is no whipstock. My lady has a white hand, and the Myrmidons are no bottle-ale houses.°

6 can tankard　9–10 the four elements i.e., air, fire, earth, and water, which were thought to be the basic ingredients of all things　14 stoup cup　16–17 the picture of We Three i.e., a picture of two asses, the spectator making the third　18 catch round, a simple polyphonic song for several voices　20 breast voice　21 leg i.e., skill in bowing (?)　22 gracious delightful　23–24 Pigrogromitus, Vapians, Queubus (presumably words invented by the Clown as specimens of his "gracious fooling" in mock learning)　26 leman sweetheart　27 impeticos thy gratillity (more of the Clown's fooling, which perhaps means something like "pocket your gratuity")　27–29 Malvolio's nose . . . bottle-ale houses (probably mere nonsense)

30 *Andrew.* Excellent. Why, this is the best fooling, when all is done. Now a song!

Toby. Come on, there is sixpence for you. Let's have a song.

Andrew. There's a testril° of me too. If one knight
35 give a—°

Clown. Would you have a love song, or a song of good life?°

Toby. A love song, a love song.

Andrew. Ay, ay, I care not for good life.

Clown sings.

40 O mistress mine, where are you roaming?
 O, stay and hear, your true-love's coming,
  That can sing both high and low.
 Trip no further, pretty sweeting;
 Journeys end in lovers meeting,
45 Every wise man's son doth know.

Andrew. Excellent good, i' faith.

Toby. Good, good.

Clown [sings].

 What is love? 'Tis not hereafter;
 Present mirth hath present laughter;
50 What's to come is still° unsure:
 In delay there lies no plenty;
 Then come kiss me, sweet, and twenty,°
  Youth's a stuff will not endure.

---

34 **testril** tester, sixpence 34–35 **If one knight give a—** (some editors have tried to supply what seems to be a missing line here, but it is probable that the Clown breaks in without permitting Sir Andrew to finish his sentence) 36–37 **of good life** i.e., moral, edifying (?)
50 **still** always 52 **Then come kiss me, sweet, and twenty** i.e., so kiss me, my sweet, and then kiss me twenty times again (some editors, taking "twenty" as an intensive, read the line as "so kiss me then, my very sweet one")

Andrew. A mellifluous voice, as I am true knight.

Toby. A contagious breath.°   55

Andrew. Very sweet and contagious, i' faith.

Toby. To hear by the nose, it is dulcet in contagion.°
But shall we make the welkin° dance indeed? Shall
we rouse the night owl in a catch that will draw
three souls out of one weaver?° Shall we do that?   60

Andrew. And you love me, let's do't. I am dog° at a
catch.

Clown. By'r Lady, sir, and some dogs will catch well.

Andrew. Most certain. Let our catch be "Thou knave."

Clown. "Hold thy peace, thou knave,"° knight? I   65
shall be constrained in't to call thee knave, knight.

Andrew. 'Tis not the first time I have constrained one
to call me knave. Begin, fool. It begins, "Hold thy
peace."

Clown. I shall never begin if I hold my peace.   70

Andrew. Good, i' faith! Come, begin.

                 Catch sung. Enter Maria.

Maria. What a caterwauling do you keep here? If my
lady have not called up her steward Malvolio and
bid him turn you out of doors, never trust me.

Toby. My lady's a Cataian, we are politicians,° Mal-   75

55 **contagious breath** catchy song   57 **to hear by the nose, it is dulcet
in contagion** i.e., if we could hear through the nose, the Clown's
"breath" would be sweet and not malodorous, as "contagious"
breaths usually are   58 **welkin** sky   60 **weaver** (weavers were noted
for their singing)   61 **dog** clever (but in the next line the Clown
puns on **dog** i.e., latch, gripping device)   65 **Hold thy peace, thou
knave** (a line from the round proposed by Sir Andrew)   75 **My
lady's a Cataian, we are politicians** (because Sir Toby and his companions are "politicians" [i.e., tricksters, intriguers] they recognize
Maria's warning of Olivia's anger as the ruse of a "Cataian" [i.e.,
native of Cathay, cheater]; hence "Tilly-vally, lady" [line 78], which
means something like "Fiddlesticks, lady")

volio's a Peg-a-Ramsey,° and [*sings*] "Three merry
men be we."° Am not I consanguineous?° Am I
not of her blood? Tilly-vally, lady. [*Sings*] "There
dwelt a man in Babylon, lady, lady."

80 *Clown.* Beshrew° me, the knight's in admirable fooling.

Andrew. Ay, he does well enough if he be disposed,
and so do I too. He does it with a better grace, but
I do it more natural.°

85 *Toby.* [*Sings*] "O the twelfth day of December."

Maria. For the love o' God, peace!

Enter Malvolio.

Malvolio. My masters, are you mad? Or what are you?
Have you no wit,° manners, nor honesty,° but to
gabble like tinkers at this time of night? Do ye
90 make an alehouse of my lady's house, that ye squeak
out your coziers'° catches without any mitigation
or remorse° of voice? Is there no respect of place,
persons, nor time in you?

Toby. We did keep time, sir, in our catches. Sneck up.°

95 *Malvolio.* Sir Toby, I must be round° with you. My
lady bade me tell you that, though she harbors
you as her kinsman, she's nothing allied to your
disorders. If you can separate yourself and your
misdemeanors, you are welcome to the house. If
100 not, and it would please you to take leave of her,
she is very willing to bid you farewell.

---

76 **Peg-a-Ramsey** (character in an old song whose name Sir Toby
uses apparently as a term of contempt) 76–77 **Three merry men be
we** (like Sir Toby's other snatches, a fragment of an old song)
77 **consanguineous** related, kin (to Olivia) 80 **Beshrew** curse
84 **natural** (with an unintentional pun on "natural" as a term for fool
or idiot; see I.iii.29) 88 **wit** sense 88 **honesty** decency 91 **coziers'**
cobblers' 91–92 **mitigation or remorse** i.e., lowering 94 **Sneck up**
go hang 95 **round** blunt

Toby. [*Sings*] "Farewell, dear heart since I must needs be gone."°

Maria. Nay, good Sir Toby.

Clown. [*Sings*] "His eyes do show his days are almost done."

Malvolio. Is't even so?   *105*

Toby. [*Sings*] "But I will never die."

Clown. [*Sings*] Sir Toby, there you lie.

Malvolio. This is much credit to you.

Toby. [*Sings*] "Shall I bid him go?"

Clown. [*Sings*] "What and if you do?"   *110*

Toby. [*Sings*] "Shall I bid him go, and spare not?"

Clown. [*Sings*] "O, no, no, no, no, you dare not!"

Toby. Out o' tune, sir? Ye lie.° Art any more than a steward? Dost thou think, because thou art virtuous, there shall be no more cakes and ale?   *115*

Clown. Yes, by Saint Anne, and ginger° shall be hot i' th' mouth too.

Toby. Th' art i' th' right. —Go, sir, rub your chain with crumbs.° A stoup of wine, Maria!

Malvolio. Mistress Mary, if you prized my lady's favor   *120* at anything more than contempt, you would not give means for this uncivil rule.° She shall know of it, by this hand.   *Exit.*

Maria. Go shake your ears.°

102 **Farewell . . . gone** (what follows, in crude antiphony between Sir Toby and the Clown, is adapted from a ballad, "Corydon's Farewell to Phyllis")   113 **Out o' tune, sir? Ye lie** (Sir Toby accuses the Clown of being out of tune, it seems, because he had added an extra "no" and thus an extra note in line 112, and of lying because he had questioned his valor in "you dare not." Then he turns to berating Malvolio)   116 **ginger** (commonly used to spice ale)   118–19 **rub your chain with crumbs** i.e., polish your steward's chain, your badge of office   122 **give means for this uncivil rule** i.e., provide liquor for this brawl   124 **Go shake your ears** i.e., like the ass you are (?)

125 *Andrew.* 'Twere as good a deed as to drink when a
       man's ahungry,° to challenge him the field,° and
       then to break promise with him and make a fool
       of him.

     Toby. Do't, knight. I'll write thee a challenge; or I'll
130   deliver thy indignation to him by word of mouth.

     Maria. Sweet Sir Toby, be patient for tonight. Since
       the youth of the Count's was today with my lady,
       she is much out of quiet. For Monsieur Malvolio,
       let me alone with him. If I do not gull him into a
135   nayword,° and make him a common recreation, do
       not think I have wit enough to lie straight in my
       bed. I know I can do it.

     Toby. Possess° us, possess us. Tell us something of
       him.

140 *Maria.* Marry, sir, sometimes he is a kind of Puritan.°

     Andrew. O, if I thought that, I'd beat him like a dog.

     Toby. What, for being a Puritan? Thy exquisite
       reason, dear knight.

     Andrew. I have no exquisite reason for't, but I have
145   reason good enough.

     Maria. The devil a Puritan that he is, or anything
       constantly° but a time-pleaser;° an affectioned° ass,
       that cons state without book° and utters it by great
       swarths;° the best persuaded of himself;° so
150   crammed, as he thinks, with excellencies that it is
       his grounds of faith that all that look on him love
       him; and on that vice in him will my revenge find
       notable cause to work.

126 **ahungry** (characteristically, Sir Andrew confuses hunger and
thirst and thus perverts the proverbial expression)   126 **the field** i.e.,
to a duel   135 **nayword** byword   138 **Possess** inform   140 **Puritan**
i.e., a straight-laced, censorious person (in lines 146–47 Maria makes
it clear that she is not using the label in a strict ecclesiastical sense, as
Sir Andrew [line 141] thinks)   147 **constantly** consistently   147
time-pleaser sycophant   147 **affectioned** affected   148 **cons state
without book** i.e., memorizes stately gestures and turns of phrase
149 **swarths** swaths, quantities   149 **the best persuaded of himself**
i.e., who thinks most highly of himself

Toby. What wilt thou do?

Maria. I will drop in his way some obscure epistles of   155
    love, wherein by the color of his beard, the shape of
    his leg, the manner of his gait, the expressure° of
    his eye, forehead, and complexion, he shall find
    himself most feelingly personated.° I can write very
    like my lady your niece; on a forgotten matter we   160
    can hardly make distinction of our hands.

Toby. Excellent. I smell a device.

Andrew. I have't in my nose too.

Toby. He shall think by the letters that thou wilt drop
    that they come from my niece, and that she's in love   165
    with him.

Maria. My purpose is indeed a horse of that color.

Andrew. And your horse now would make him an
    ass.

Maria. Ass, I doubt not.   170

Andrew. O, 'twill be admirable.

Maria. Sport royal, I warrant you. I know my physic
    will work with him. I will plant you two, and let
    the fool make a third,° where he shall find the
    letter. Observe his construction° of it. For this   175
    night, to bed, and dream on the event.° Farewell.

                                        Exit.

Toby. Good night, Penthesilea.°

Andrew. Before me,° she's a good wench.

Toby. She's a beagle° true-bred, and one that adores
    me. What o' that?   180

157 **expressure** expression   159 **personated** represented   173–74 **let
the fool make a third** (like the plan to have Viola present herself to
Duke Orsino as a eunuch [I.ii.62], this plot device was abandoned; it
is Fabian, not the Clown, who makes the third spectator to Malvolio's exposé)   175 **construction** interpretation   176 **event** outcome
177 **Penthesilea** (in classical mythology, the queen of the Amazons)
178 **Before me** i.e., I swear, with myself as witness   179 **beagle** (one
of several allusions to Maria's small stature)

Andrew. I was adored once too.

Toby. Let's to bed, knight. Thou hadst need send for
more money.

Andrew. If I cannot recover° your niece, I am a foul
185   way out.°

Toby. Send for money, knight. If thou hast her not
i' th' end, call me Cut.°

Andrew. If I do not, never trust me, take it how you
will.

190 *Toby.* Come, come; I'll go burn some sack.° 'Tis too
late to go to bed now. Come, knight; come, knight.
                                    Exeunt.

Scene IV. [*The Duke's palace.*]

Enter Duke, Viola, Curio, and others.

Duke. Give me some music. Now good morrow, friends.
Now, good Cesario, but that piece of song,
That old and antic° song we heard last night.
Methought it did relieve my passion° much,
5   More than light airs and recollected terms°
Of these most brisk and giddy-pacèd times.
Come, but one verse.

Curio. He is not here, so please your lordship, that
should sing it.

10 *Duke.* Who was it?

Curio. Feste the jester, my lord, a fool that the Lady

184 **recover** win   184–85 **a foul way out** i.e., badly out of pocket
187 **Cut** i.e., a dock-tailed horse   190 **burn some sack** heat and
spice some Spanish wine   II.iv.3 **antic** quaint   4 **passion** suffering
(from unrequited love)   5 **recollected terms** studied phrases

Olivia's father took much delight in. He is about the
house.

Duke. Seek him out, and play the tune the while.
　　　　　　　　　　[*Exit Curio.*] *Music plays.*
　Come hither, boy. If ever thou shalt love,　　　　　　15
　In the sweet pangs of it remember me;
　For such as I am all true lovers are,
　Unstaid and skittish in all motions° else
　Save in the constant image of the creature
　That is beloved. How dost thou like this tune?　　　20

Viola. It gives a very echo to the seat°
　Where Love is throned.

Duke.　　　　　　　　Thou dost speak masterly.
　My life upon't, young though thou art, thine eye
　Hath stayed upon some favor° that it loves.
　Hath it not, boy?

Viola.　　　　　　A little, by your favor.　　　　　25

Duke. What kind of woman is't?

Viola.　　　　　　　　Of your complexion.°

Duke. She is not worth thee then. What years, i' faith?

Viola. About your years, my lord.

Duke. Too old, by heaven. Let still° the woman take
　An elder than herself: so wears she° to him,　　　　30
　So sways she level in her husband's heart;°
　For, boy, however we do praise ourselves,
　Our fancies° are more giddy and unfirm,
　More longing, wavering, sooner lost and worn,°
　Than women's are.

Viola.　　　　　I think it well, my lord.　　　　35

Duke. Then let thy love be younger than thyself,

---

18 **motions** emotions　21 **seat** i.e., the heart (see I.i.38–39)　24 **favor**
face　26 **complexion** temperament　29 **still** always　30 **wears she**
she adapts herself　31 **sways she . . . heart** i.e., she keeps steady in
her husband's affections　33 **fancies** loves　34 **worn** (many editors
have adopted the reading "won" from the Second Folio)

Or thy affection cannot hold the bent;°
For women are as roses, whose fair flow'r,
Being once displayed, doth fall that very hour.

40 *Viola.* And so they are; alas, that they are so.
To die, even when they to perfection grow.

Enter Curio and Clown.

Duke. O, fellow, come, the song we had last night.
Mark it, Cesario; it is old and plain.
The spinsters° and the knitters in the sun,
And the free° maids that weave their thread with
45   bones,°
Do use to chant it. It is silly sooth,°
And dallies° with the innocence of love,
Like the old age.°

Clown. Are you ready, sir?

50 *Duke.* I prithee sing.   *Music.*

The Song.

Come away, come away, death,
And in sad cypress° let me be laid.
Fly away, fly away, breath;
I am slain by a fair cruel maid.
55 My shroud of white, stuck all with yew,
O, prepare it.
My part of death, no one so true
Did share it.

Not a flower, not a flower sweet,
60 On my black coffin let there be strown;
Not a friend, not a friend greet
My poor corpse, where my bones shall be
thrown.

37 **hold the bent** i.e., maintain its strength and tension (the image is that of a bent bow)   44 **spinsters** spinners   45 **free** carefree   45 **bones** i.e., bone bobbins   46 **silly sooth** simple truth   47 **dallies** deals movingly   48 **the old age** i.e., the good old times   52 **cypress** a coffin made of cypress wood

A thousand thousand sighs to save,
    Lay me, O, where
Sad true lover never find my grave,   65
    To weep there.

Duke. There's for thy pains.

Clown. No pains, sir. I take pleasure in singing, sir.

Duke. I'll pay thy pleasure then.

Clown. Truly, sir, and pleasure will be paid one time   70
or another.

Duke. Give me now leave to leave thee.

Clown. Now the melancholy god protect thee, and the
tailor make thy doublet of changeable° taffeta, for
thy mind is a very opal. I would have men of such   75
constancy put to sea, that their business might be
everything, and their intent everywhere; for that's
it that always makes a good voyage of nothing.
Farewell.   *Exit.*

Duke. Let all the rest give place.°
                [*Exeunt Curio and Attendants.*]
                        Once more, Cesario,   80
Get thee to yond same sovereign cruelty.°
Tell her my love, more noble than the world,
Prizes not quantity of dirty lands;
The parts° that fortune hath bestowed upon her
Tell her I hold as giddily° as fortune,   85
But 'tis that miracle and queen of gems°
That nature pranks her in° attracts my soul.

Viola. But if she cannot love you, sir?

Duke. I cannot be so answered.

Viola.   Sooth,° but you must.

74 **changeable** i.e., with shifting lights and colors   80 **give place**
withdraw   81 **sovereign cruelty** i.e., peerless and disdainful lady
84 **parts** gifts (of wealth and social status)   85 **giddily** indifferently
86 **queen of gems** i.e., Olivia's beauty   87 **pranks her in** adorns her
with   89 **Sooth** truly

90   Say that some lady, as perhaps there is,
      Hath for your love as great a pang of heart
      As you have for Olivia. You cannot love her.
      You tell her so. Must she not then be answered?

      Duke. There is no woman's sides
95   Can bide° the beating of so strong a passion
      As love doth give my heart; no woman's heart
      So big to hold so much; they lack retention.°
      Alas, their love may be called appetite,
      No motion° of the liver° but the palate,
100   That suffer surfeit, cloyment, and revolt;°
      But mine is all as hungry as the sea
      And can digest as much. Make no compare
      Between that love a woman can bear me
      And that I owe Olivia.

      Viola.   Ay, but I know—

105   *Duke.* What dost thou know?

      Viola. Too well what love women to men may owe.
      In faith, they are as true of heart as we.
      My father had a daughter loved a man
      As it might be perhaps, were I a woman,
      I should your lordship.

110   *Duke.*   And what's her history?

      Viola. A blank, my lord. She never told her love,
      But let concealment, like a worm i' th' bud,
      Feed on her damask° cheek. She pined in thought;°
      And, with a green and yellow melancholy,
115   She sat like Patience on a monument,
      Smiling at grief. Was not this love indeed?
      We men may say more, swear more; but indeed
      Our shows are more than will;° for still we prove
      Much in our vows but little in our love.

120   *Duke.* But died thy sister of her love, my boy?

95 **bide** endure   97 **retention** i.e., the ability to retain   99 **motion**
stirring, prompting   99 **liver** (seat of passion)   100 **revolt** revulsion
113 **damask** i.e., like a pink and white damask rose   113 **thought**
brooding   118 **Our shows are more than will** i.e., what we show is
greater than the passion that we feel

Viola. I am all the daughters of my father's house,
      And all the brothers too, and yet I know not.°
      Sir, shall I to this lady?

Duke.   Ay, that's the theme.
      To her in haste. Give her this jewel. Say
      My love can give no place,° bide no denay.°   125
                                    Exeunt.

Scene V. [*Olivia's garden.*]

Enter Sir Toby, Sir Andrew, and Fabian.

Toby. Come thy ways, Signior Fabian.

Fabian. Nay, I'll come. If I lose a scruple° of this
      sport, let me be boiled° to death with melancholy.

Toby. Wouldst thou not be glad to have the niggardly
      rascally sheep-biter° come by some notable shame?   5

Fabian. I would exult, man. You know he brought me
      out o' favor with my lady about a bearbaiting here.

Toby. To anger him we'll have the bear again, and we
      will fool him black and blue. Shall we not, Sir
      Andrew?   10

Andrew. And we do not, it is pity of our lives.

Enter Maria.

Toby. Here comes the little villain. How now, my
      metal of India?°

122 **I know not** (because she thinks that her brother may be still
alive) 125 **can give no place** cannot yield 125 **denay** denial II.v.2
scruple smallest part 3 **boiled** (pronounced "biled," quibbling on
"bile," which was thought to be the cause of melancholy) 5 **sheep-
biter** i.e., sneaky dog 13 **metal of India** i.e., golden girl

Maria. Get ye all three into the box tree. Malvolio's
15   coming down this walk. He has been yonder i' the
sun practicing behavior to his own shadow this half
hour. Observe him, for the love of mockery; for I
know this letter will make a contemplative° idiot of
of him. Close,° in the name of jesting. [*The others*
20   *hide.*] Lie thou there [*throws down a letter*]; for
here comes the trout that must be caught with
tickling.°   *Exit.*

Enter Malvolio.

Malvolio. 'Tis but fortune; all is fortune. Maria once
told me she did affect me;° and I have heard herself
25   come thus near, that, should she fancy,° it should
be one of my complexion. Besides, she uses me with
a more exalted respect than anyone else that
follows° her. What should I think on't?

Toby. Here's an overweening rogue.

30   *Fabian.* O, peace! Contemplation makes a rare turkey
cock of him. How he jets° under his advanced°
plumes!

Andrew. 'Slight,° I could so beat the rogue.

Toby. Peace, I say.°

35   *Malvolio.* To be Count Malvolio.

Toby. Ah, rogue!

Andrew. Pistol him, pistol him.

Toby. Peace, peace.

Malvolio. There is example for't. The Lady of the
40   Strachy° married the yeoman of the wardrobe.

18 **contemplative** i.e., self-centered 19 **Close** hide 22 **tickling**
stroking, i.e., flattery 24 **she did affect me** i.e., Olivia liked me
25 **fancy** love 28 **follows** serves 31 **jets** struts 31 **advanced** uplifted 33 **'Slight** by God's light (a mild oath) 34 **Peace, I say**
(many editors assign this and line 38 to Fabian on the ground that
it is his function throughout the scene to restrain Sir Toby and Sir
Andrew) 39–40 **The Lady of the Strachy** (an unidentified allusion
to a great lady who married beneath her)

Andrew. Fie on him, Jezebel.°

Fabian. O, peace! Now he's deeply in. Look how imagination blows him.°

Malvolio. Having been three months married to her, sitting in my state—　　45

Toby. O for a stonebow,° to hit him in the eye!

Malvolio. Calling my officers about me, in my branched° velvet gown; having come from a day-bed,° where I have left Olivia sleeping—

Toby. Fire and brimstone!　　50

Fabian. O, peace, peace!

Malvolio. And then to have the humor of state;° and after a demure travel of regard,° telling them I know my place, as I would they should do theirs, to ask for my kinsman Toby—　　55

Toby. Bolts and shackles!

Fabian. O peace, peace, peace, now, now.

Malvolio. Seven of my people, with an obedient start, make out for° him. I frown the while, and per-chance wind up my watch, or play with my—some　　60 rich jewel.° Toby approaches; curtsies there to me—

Toby. Shall this fellow live?

Fabian. Though our silence be drawn from us with cars, yet peace.

Malvolio. I extend my hand to him thus, quenching　　65 my familiar smile with an austere regard of con-trol°—

41 **Jezebel** (the proud and wicked queen of Ahab, King of Israel, whom Sir Andrew, muddled as usual, regards as Malvolio's proto-type in arrogance) 43 **blows him** puffs him up 46 **stonebow** crossbow that shoots stones 48 **branched** embroidered 48–49 **daybed** sofa 52 **to have the humor of state** i.e., to assume an imperious manner 53 **after a demure travel of regard** i.e., having glanced gravely over my retainers 59 **make out for** i.e., go to fetch 60–61 **play with my—some rich jewel** (Malvolio automatically reaches for his steward's chain and then catches himself) 66–67 **an austere regard of control** i.e., a stern look of authority

Toby. And does not Toby take° you a blow o' the
lips then?

70 *Malvolio*. Saying, "Cousin Toby, my fortunes having
cast me on your niece, give me this prerogative of
speech."

Toby. What, what?

Malvolio. "You must amend your drunkenness."

75 *Toby*. Out, scab!

Fabian. Nay, patience, or we break the sinews of our
plot.

Malvolio. "Besides, you waste the treasure of your
time with a foolish knight"—

80 *Andrew*. That's me, I warrant you.

Malvolio. "One Sir Andrew"—

Andrew. I knew 'twas I, for many do call me fool.

Malvolio. What employment° have we here?
                                [*Takes up the letter*.]

Fabian. Now is the woodcock° near the gin.°

85 *Toby*. O, peace, and the spirit of humors intimate
reading aloud to him!

Malvolio. By my life, this is my lady's hand. These be
her very C's, her U's, and her T's; and thus makes
she her great P's. It is, in contempt of° question,
90 her hand.

Andrew. Her C's, her U's, and her T's? Why that?

Malvolio. [*Reads*] "To the unknown beloved, this,
and my good wishes." Her very phrases! By your
leave, wax.° Soft,° and the impressure her Lucrece,°

68 **take** give   83 **employment** business   84 **woodcock** (a proverbially
stupid bird)   84 **gin** snare   89 **in contempt of** beyond   93–94 **By
your leave, wax** i.e., excuse me for breaking the seal   94 **Soft** i.e.,
take it slowly   94 **the impressure her Lucrece** i.e., the seal depicts
Lucrece (noble Roman matron who stabbed herself after she was
raped by Tarquin, hence a symbol of chastity)

with which she uses to seal.° 'Tis my lady. To   95
whom should this be?

Fabian. This wins him, liver and all.

Malvolio. [*Reads*]
> "Jove knows I love,
>   But who?
> Lips, do not move;   100
>   No man must know."

"No man must know." What follows? The numbers
altered!° "No man must know." If this should be
thee, Malvolio?

Toby. Marry, hang thee, brock!°   105

Malvolio. [*Reads*]
> "I may command where I adore,
>   But silence, like a Lucrece knife,
> With bloodless stroke my heart doth gore.
>   M. O. A. I. doth sway my life."

Fabian. A fustian° riddle.   110

Toby. Excellent wench,° say I.

Malvolio. "M. O. A. I. doth sway my life." Nay, but
first, let me see, let me see, let me see.

Fabian. What dish o' poison has she dressed° him!

Toby. And with what wing the staniel checks at it!° 115

Malvolio. "I may command where I adore." Why, she
may command me: I serve her; she is my lady.
Why, this is evident to any formal capacity.° There
is no obstruction° in this. And the end; what should
that alphabetical position portend? If I could make 120
that resemble something in me! Softly, "M. O. A. I."

Toby. O, ay, make up that. He is now at a cold scent.

95 **uses to seal** customarily seals   102–103 **The numbers altered** the
meter changed (in the stanza that follows)   105 **brock** badger
110 **fustian** i.e., foolish and pretentious   111 **wench** i.e., Maria
114 **dressed** prepared for   115 **with what wing the staniel checks at
it** i.e., with what speed the kestrel (a kind of hawk) turns to snatch
at the wrong prey   118 **formal capacity** normal intelligence   119
obstruction difficulty

Fabian. Sowter will cry upon't for all this, though i̇
be as rank as a fox.°

125 *Malvolio.* M.—Malvolio. M.—Why, that begins my
name.

Fabian. Did not I say he would work it out? The cur
is excellent at faults.°

Malvolio. M.—But then there is no consonancy in the
130 sequel.° That suffers under probation.° A should
follow, but O does.

Fabian. And O° shall end, I hope.

Toby. Ay, or I'll cudgel him, and make him cry O.

Malvolio. And then I comes behind.

135 *Fabian.* Ay, and you had any eye behind you, you
might see more detraction at your heels than
fortunes before you.

Malvolio. M, O, A, I. This simulation° is not as the
former; and yet, to crush° this a little, it would bow
140 to me, for every one of these letters are in my name.
Soft, here follows prose.

[*Reads*] "If this fall into thy hand, revolve.° In my
stars° I am above thee, but be not afraid of greatness. Some are born great, some achieve greatness,
145 and some have greatness thrust upon 'em. Thy
Fates open their hands; let thy blood and spirit
embrace them; and to inure° thyself to what thou
art like to be, cast thy humble slough° and appear
fresh. Be opposite with° a kinsman, surly with
150 servants. Let thy tongue tang arguments of state;°
put thyself into the trick of singularity.° She thus

123–24 **Sowter will cry . . . as a fox** i.e., the hound will bay after the
false scent even though the deceit is gross and clear   128 **faults**
breaks in the scent   129–30 **consonancy in the sequel** consistency
in what follows   130 **suffers under probation** does not stand up
under scrutiny   132 **O** i.e., sound of lamentation   138 **simulation**
hidden significance   139 **crush** force   142 **revolve** reflect   143 **stars**
fortune   147 **inure** accustom   148 **slough** skin (of a snake)   149
opposite with hostile to   150 **tang arguments of state** i.e., resound
with topics of statecraft   151 **trick of singularity** affectation of
eccentricity

advises thee that sighs for thee. Remember who
commended thy yellow stockings and wished to see
thee ever cross-gartered.° I say, remember. Go to,
thou art made, if thou desir'st to be so. If not, let   155
me see thee a steward still, the fellow of servants,
and not worthy to touch Fortune's fingers. Farewell.
She that would alter services with thee,
                    THE FORTUNATE UNHAPPY."

Daylight and champian° discovers° not more. This   160
is open. I will be proud, I will read politic authors,°
I will baffle° Sir Toby, I will wash off gross° acquaintance, I will be point-devise,° the very man.
I do not now fool myself, to let imagination jade°
me, for every reason excites to this,° that my lady   165
loves me. She did commend my yellow stockings of
late, she did praise my leg being cross-gartered; and
in this she manifests herself to my love, and with
a kind of injunction drives me to these habits of her
liking.° I thank my stars, I am happy. I will be   170
strange,° stout,° in yellow stockings, and cross-
gartered, even with the swiftness of putting on. Jove
and my stars be praised. Here is yet a postscript.
[Reads] "Thou canst not choose but know who I
am. If thou entertain'st° my love, let it appear in   175
thy smiling. Thy smiles become thee well. Therefore in my presence still smile, dear my sweet, I
prithee."
Jove, I thank thee. I will smile; I will do everything
that thou wilt have me.   Exit.   180

Fabian. I will not give my part of this sport for a
pension of thousands to be paid from the Sophy.°

154 cross-gartered i.e., with garters crossed above and below the
knee   160 champian champaign, open country   160 discovers reveals   161 politic authors writers on politics   162 baffle publicly
humiliate   162 gross low   163 be point-devise i.e., follow the advice
in the letter in every detail   164 jade trick   165 excites to this
i.e., enforces this conclusion   169–170 these habits of her liking
this clothing that she likes   171 strange haughty   171 stout proud
175 entertain'st accept   182 Sophy Shah of Persia (perhaps with
reference to Sir Anthony Shirley's visit to the Persian court in 1599,
from which he returned laden with gifts and honors)

Toby. I could marry this wench for this device.

Andrew. So could I too.

185 *Toby.* And ask no other dowry with her but such another jest.

Enter Maria.

Andrew. Nor I neither.

Fabian. Here comes my noble gull-catcher.°

Toby. Wilt thou set thy foot o' my neck?

190 *Andrew.* Or o' mine either?

Toby. Shall I play° my freedom at tray-trip° and become thy bondslave?

Andrew. I' faith, or I either?

Toby. Why, thou hast put him in such a dream that, 195 when the image of it leaves him, he must run mad.

Maria. Nay, but say true, does it work upon him?

Toby. Like aqua-vitae° with a midwife.

Maria. If you will, then, see the fruits of the sport, mark his first approach before my lady. He will 200 come to her in yellow stockings, and 'tis a color she abhors, and cross-gartered, a fashion she detests; and he will smile upon her which will now be so unsuitable to her disposition, being addicted to a melancholy as she is, that it cannot but turn him 205 into a notable contempt. If you will see it, follow me.

Toby. To the gates of Tartar,° thou most excellent devil of wit.

Andrew. I'll make one° too. *Exeunt.*

188 **gull-catcher** fool-catcher 191 **play** gamble 191 **tray-trip** (a dice game) 197 **aqua-vitae** distilled liquors 207 **Tartar** Tartarus (in classical mythology, the infernal regions) 209 **make one** i.e., come

ACT III

Scene I. [*Olivia's garden.*]

Enter Viola and Clown [with a tabor].

Viola. Save thee,° friend, and thy music. Dost thou
live by° thy tabor?°

Clown. No, sir, I live by the church.

Viola. Art thou a churchman?

Clown. No such matter, sir. I do live by the church;   5
for I do live at my house, and my house doth stand
by the church.

Viola. So thou mayst say, the king lies° by a beggar,
if a beggar dwell near him; or, the church stands
by° thy tabor, if thy tabor stand by the church.   10

Clown. You have said, sir. To see this age! A sentence is but a chev'ril° glove to a good wit. How
quickly the wrong side may be turned outward!

Viola. Nay, that's certain. They that dally nicely°
with words may quickly make them wanton.°   15

Clown. I would therefore my sister had had no name,
sir.

III.i.1 **Save thee** i.e., God save you   2 **live by** gain a living from (but
the Clown takes it in the sense of "reside near")   2 **tabor** (1) drum
(2) taborn, tavern   8 **lies** sojourns   9-10 **stands by** (1) stands near
(2) upholds   12 **chev'ril** cheveril (i.e., soft kid leather)   14 **dally
nicely** play subtly   15 **wanton** i.e., equivocal in meaning (but the
Clown takes it in the sense of "unchaste")

Viola. Why, man?

Clown. Why, sir, her name's a word, and to dally with
20   that word might make my sister wanton. But indeed
words are very rascals since bonds disgraced them.°

Viola. Thy reason, man?

Clown. Troth,° sir, I can yield you none without
words, and words are grown so false I am loath to
25   prove reason with them.

Viola. I warrant thou art a merry fellow and car'st
for nothing.

Clown. Not so, sir; I do care for something; but in my
conscience, sir, I do not care for you. If that be to
30   care for nothing, sir, I would it would make you
invisible.

Viola. Art not thou the Lady Olivia's fool?

Clown. No, indeed, sir. The Lady Olivia has no folly.
She will keep no fool, sir, till she be married; and
35   fools are as like husbands as pilchers° are to her-
rings—the husband's the bigger. I am indeed not
her fool, but her corrupter of words.

Viola. I saw thee late at the Count Orsino's.

Clown. Foolery, sir, does walk about the orb° like
40   the sun; it shines everywhere. I would be sorry, sir,
but° the fool should be as oft with your master as
with my mistress. I think I saw your wisdom there.

Viola. Nay, and thou pass upon me,° I'll no more
with thee. Hold, there's expenses for thee.

                                [Gives a coin.]

45 *Clown.* Now Jove, in his next commodity° of hair,
send thee a beard.

21 **since bonds disgraced them** i.e., since it was required that a man's
word be guaranteed by a bond (?)   23 **Troth** by my troth
35 **pilchers** pilchards (a kind of small herring)   39 **orb** earth
41 **but** but that   43 **pass upon me** i.e., make me the butt of your
witticisms   45 **commodity** lot, consignment

Viola. By my troth, I'll tell thee, I am almost sick
for one, though I would not have it grow on my
chin. Is thy lady within?

Clown. Would not a pair of these° have bred, sir?   50

Viola. Yes, being kept together and put to use.°

Clown. I would play Lord Pandarus of Phrygia, sir,
to bring a Cressida to this Troilus.°

Viola. I understand you, sir. 'Tis well begged.
                              [*Gives another coin.*]

Clown. The matter, I hope, is not great, sir, begging   55
but a beggar: Cressida was a beggar.° My lady is
within, sir. I will conster° to them whence you
come. Who you are and what you would are out of
my welkin;° I might say "element," but the word is
overworn.°   *Exit.*   60

Viola. This fellow is wise enough to play the fool,
And to do that well craves° a kind of wit.°
He must observe their mood on whom he jests,
The quality of persons, and the time;
And,° like the haggard,° check at° every feather   65
That comes before his eye. This is a practice°
As full of labor as a wise man's art;
For folly that he wisely shows, is fit;
But wise men, folly-fall'n,° quite taint their wit.°

---

50 **these** i.e., coins of the sort that Viola had just given him   51 **put
to use** put out at interest   52–53 **I would play . . . this Troilus** (in
the story of Troilus and Cressida, which supplied both Chaucer and
Shakespeare the plot for major works, Pandarus was the go-between
in the disastrous love affair)   56 **Cressida was a beggar** (in Robert
Henryson's *Testament of Cressida,* a kind of sequel to Chaucer's
poem, the faithless heroine became a harlot and a beggar)
57 **conster** explain   59 **welkin** sky   59–60 **I might say . . . overworn**
(perhaps a thrust at Ben Jonson, whose fondness for the word "element" had been ridiculed by other writers)   62 **craves** requires
62 **wit** intelligence   65 **And** (many editors, following Johnson, have
emended this to "not")   65 **haggard** untrained hawk   65 **check at**
leave the true course and pursue   66 **practice** skill   69 **folly-fall'n**
having fallen into folly   69 **taint their wit** i.e., betray their common
sense

Enter Sir Toby and [Sir] Andrew.

70 *Toby.* Save you, gentleman.

Viola. And you, sir.

Andrew. Dieu vous garde, monsieur.

Viola. Et vous aussi; votre serviteur.°

Andrew. I hope, sir, you are, and I am yours.

75 *Toby.* Will you encounter° the house? My niece is
desirous you should enter, if your trade be to° her.

Viola. I am bound to° your niece, sir; I mean, she is
the list° of my voyage.

Toby. Taste° your legs, sir; put them to motion.

80 *Viola.* My legs do better understand° me, sir, than I
understand what you mean by bidding me taste my
legs.

Toby. I mean, to go, sir, to enter.

Viola. I will answer you with gait and entrance.° But
85 we are prevented.°

Enter Olivia and Gentlewoman [Maria].

Most excellent accomplished lady, the heavens rain
odors on you.

Andrew. That youth's a rare courtier. "Rain odors"—
well!°

90 *Viola.* My matter hath no voice,° lady, but to your
own most pregnant and vouchsafed ear.

72–73 **Dieu vous garde . . . votre serviteur** God protect you, sir./And
you also; your servant   75 **encounter** approach   76 **trade be to**
business be with   77 **bound to** bound for (carrying on the metaphor
in "trade")   78 **list** destination   79 **Taste** try   80 **understand** i.e.,
stand under, support   84 **with gait and entrance** by going and enter-
ing (with a pun on "gate")   85 **prevented** anticipated   89 **well**
i.e., well put   90 **matter hath no voice** i.e., business must not be
revealed

Andrew. "Odors," "pregnant," and "vouchsafed"—
　I'll get 'em all three all ready.

Olivia. Let the garden door be shut, and leave me to
　my hearing. [*Exeunt Sir Toby, Sir Andrew, and*　95
　Maria.] Give me your hand, sir.

Viola. My duty, madam, and most humble service.

Olivia. What is your name?

Viola. Cesario is your servant's name, fair princess.

Olivia. My servant, sir? 'Twas never merry world　100
　Since lowly feigning° was called compliment.
　Y' are servant to the Count Orsino, youth.

Viola. And he is yours, and his must needs be yours.
　Your servant's servant is your servant, madam.

Olivia. For° him, I think not on him; for his thoughts,　105
　Would they were blanks, rather than filled with me.

Viola. Madam, I come to whet your gentle thoughts
　On his behalf.

Olivia.　　　　　　O, by your leave, I pray you.
　I bade you never speak again of him;
　But, would you undertake another suit,　　　　110
　I had rather hear you to solicit that
　Than music from the spheres.°

Viola.　　　　　　　　　　Dear lady—

Olivia. Give me leave,° beseech you. I did send,
　After the last enchantment you did here,
　A ring in chase of you. So did I abuse°　　　115
　Myself, my servant, and, I fear me, you.
　Under your hard construction° must I sit,
　To force that on you in a shameful cunning
　Which you knew none of yours. What might you
　　think?

101 **lowly feigning** affected humility　105 **For** as for　112 **music from the spheres** i.e., the alleged celestial harmony of the revolving stars and planets　113 **Give me leave** i.e., do not interrupt me　115 **abuse** deceive　117 **hard construction** harsh interpretation

120 Have you not set mine honor at the stake
And baited it with all th' unmuzzled thoughts°
That tyrannous heart can think? To one of your
    receiving°
Enough is shown; a cypress,° not a bosom,
Hides my heart. So, let me hear you speak.

Viola. I pity you.

125 *Olivia.*   That's a degree° to love.

Viola. No, not a grize;° for 'tis a vulgar proof°
That very oft we pity enemies.

Olivia. Why then, methinks 'tis time to smile again.
O world, how apt the poor are to be proud.
130 If one should be a prey, how much the better
To fall before the lion than the wolf.   *Clock strikes.*
The clock upbraids me with the waste of time.
Be not afraid, good youth, I will not have you,
And yet, when wit and youth is come to harvest,°
135 Your wife is like to reap a proper° man.
There lies your way, due west.°

Viola.   Then westward ho!°
Grace and good disposition° attend your ladyship.
You'll nothing, madam, to my lord by me?

Olivia. Stay.
140 I prithee tell me what thou think'st of me.

Viola. That you do think you are not what you are.°

Olivia. If I think so, I think the same of you.°

120–121 **set mine honor . . . unmuzzled thoughts** (the metaphor is
from the Elizabethan sport of bearbaiting, in which a bear was tied
to a stake and harassed by savage dogs)   122 **receiving** i.e., per-
ception   123 **cypress** gauzelike material   125 **degree** step   126 **grize**
step   126 **vulgar proof** i.e., common knowledge   134 **when wit and
youth is come to harvest** i.e., when you are mature   135 **proper**
handsome   136 **due west** (Olivia is perhaps implying that the sun
of her life—Cesario's love—is about to vanish)   136 **westward ho**
(cry of Thames watermen)   137 **good disposition** i.e., tranquillity
of mind   141 **That you do think you are not what you are** i.e., that
you think you are in love with a man, and are not   142 **If I think
so, I think the same of you** (Olivia misconstrues Viola's remark to
mean that she is out of her mind)

Viola. Then think you right. I am not what I am.

Olivia. I would you were as I would have you be.

Viola. Would it be better, madam, than I am?   *145*
  I wish it might, for now I am your fool.°

Olivia. O, what a deal of scorn looks beautiful
  In the contempt and anger of his lip.
  A murd'rous guilt shows not itself more soon
  Than love that would seem hid: love's night is
    noon.°   *150*
  Cesario, by the roses of the spring,
  By maidhood,° honor, truth, and everything,
  I love thee so that, maugre° all thy pride,
  Nor wit nor reason can my passion hide.
  Do not extort thy reasons from this clause,°   *155*
  For that° I woo, thou therefore hast no cause;°
  But rather reason thus with reason fetter,
  Love sought is good, but given unsought is better.

Viola. By innocence I swear, and by my youth,
  I have one heart, one bosom, and one truth,   *160*
  And that no woman has; nor never none
  Shall mistress be of it, save I alone.
  And so adieu, good madam. Never more
  Will I my master's tears to you deplore.

Olivia. Yet come again; for thou perhaps mayst move *165*
  That heart which now abhors to like his love.
                                        Exeunt.

146 **I am your fool** i.e., you are making a fool of me   150 **love's
night is noon** i.e., love is apparent even when it is hidden   152 **maidhood** maidenhood   153 **maugre** despite   155 **clause** premise   156
For that that because   156 **cause** i.e., to accept my love

Scene II. [*Olivia's house.*]

Enter Sir Toby, Sir Andrew, and Fabian.

Andrew. No, faith, I'll not stay a jot longer.

Toby. Thy reason, dear venom; give thy reason.

Fabian. You must needs yield° your reason, Sir
Andrew.

5   *Andrew.* Marry, I saw your niece do more favors to
the Count's servingman than ever she bestowed
upon me. I saw't i' th' orchard.

Toby. Did she see thee the while, old boy? Tell me
that.

10 *Andrew.* As plain as I see you now.

Fabian. This was a great argument° of love in her
toward you.

Andrew. 'Slight, will you make an ass o' me?

Fabian. I will prove it legitimate,° sir, upon the oaths
15   of judgment and reason.

Toby. And they have been grand-jurymen since
before Noah was a sailor.

Fabian. She did show favor to the youth in your sight
only to exasperate you, to awake your dormouse°
20   valor, to put fire in your heart and brimstone in
your liver. You should then have accosted her, and
with some excellent jests, fire-new from the mint,
you should have banged the youth into dumbness.
This was looked for at your hand, and this was

III.ii.3 **yield** give   11 **great argument** strong evidence   14 **legitimate**
valid   19 **dormouse** i.e., sleepy

balked.° The double gilt° of this opportunity you   25
let time wash off, and you are now sailed into the
North of my lady's opinion,° where you will hang
like an icicle on a Dutchman's beard° unless you do
redeem it by some laudable attempt either of valor
or policy.°   30

Andrew. And't be any way, it must be with valor; for
policy I hate. I had as lief be a Brownist° as a
politician.°

Toby. Why then, build me thy fortunes upon the basis
of valor. Challenge me the Count's youth to fight   35
with him; hurt him in eleven places. My niece shall
take note of it, and assure thyself there is no love-
broker in the world can° more prevail in man's
commendation with woman than report of valor.

Fabian. There is no way but this, Sir Andrew.   40

Andrew. Will either of you bear me a challenge to
him?

Toby. Go, write it in a martial hand. Be curst° and
brief; it is no matter how witty, so it be eloquent
and full of invention. Taunt him with the license of 45
ink.° If thou thou'st° him some thrice, it shall not
be amiss; and as many lies as will lie in thy sheet
of paper, although the sheet were big enough for
the bed of Ware° in England, set 'em down. Go
about it. Let there be gall enough in thy ink, though 50
thou write with a goose-pen, no matter. About it!

Andrew. Where shall I find you?

25 **balked** let slip   25 **gilt** plating   26–27 **the North of my lady's
opinion** i.e., her frosty disdain   28 **an icicle on a Dutchman's beard**
(perhaps an allusion to the arctic voyage [1596–97] of the Dutchman
Willem Barents, an account of which was registered for publication
in 1598)   30 **policy** intrigue, trickery   32 **Brownist** follower of
William Browne, a reformer who advocated the separation of church
and state   33 **politician** schemer   38 **can** i.e., that can   43 **curst**
petulant   45–46 **the license of ink** i.e., the freedom that writing
permits   46 **thou'st** i.e., use the familiar "thou" instead of the more
formal "you"   49 **the bed of Ware** a famous bedstead, almost eleven
feet square, formerly in an inn at Ware in Herfordshire

Toby. We'll call thee at the cubiculo.° Go.

Exit Sir Andrew.

Fabian. This is a dear manikin° to you, Sir Toby.

55 *Toby.* I have been dear to him,° lad, some two thousand strong or so.

Fabian. We shall have a rare letter from him, but you'll not deliver't?

Toby. Never trust me then; and by all means stir on
60 the youth to an answer. I think oxen and wainropes° cannot hale them together. For Andrew, if he were opened, and you find so much blood in his liver as will clog the foot of a flea, I'll eat the rest of th' anatomy.°

65 *Fabian.* And his opposite,° the youth, bears in his visage no great presage of cruelty.

Enter Maria.

Toby. Look where the youngest wren° of mine° comes.

Maria. If you desire the spleen,° and will laugh yourselves into stitches, follow me. Yond gull Malvolio
70 is turned heathen, a very renegado; for there is no Christian that means to be saved by believing rightly can ever believe such impossible passages of grossness.° He's in yellow stockings.

Toby. And cross-gartered?

75 *Maria.* Most villainously; like a pedant that keeps a school i' th' church. I have dogged him like his murderer. He does obey every point of the letter that I dropped to betray him. He does smile his face into more lines than is in the new map with

53 **cubiculo** little chamber   54 **manikin** puppet   55 **been dear to him** i.e., spent his money   60–61 **wainropes** wagon ropes   64 **anatomy** cadaver   65 **opposite** adversary   67 **youngest wren** i.e., smallest of small birds   67 **mine** (most editors adopt Theobald's emendation "nine")   68 **spleen** i.e., a fit of laughter   72–73 **impossible passages of grossness** i.e., improbabilities

the augmentation of the Indies.° You have not seen   80
such a thing as 'tis. I can hardly forbear hurling
things at him. I know my lady will strike him. If
she do, he'll smile, and take't for a great favor.

Toby. Come bring us, bring us where he is.

                                        Exeunt omnes.

Scene III. [*A street.*]

Enter Sebastian and Antonio.

Sebastian. I would not by my will have troubled you;
  But since you make your pleasure of your pains,
  I will no further chide you.

Antonio. I could not stay behind you. My desire
  (More sharp than filèd steel) did spur me forth;   5
  And not all love to see you (though so much
  As might have drawn one to a longer voyage)
  But jealousy° what might befall your travel,
  Being skilless in° these parts; which to a stranger,
  Unguided and unfriended, often prove   10
  Rough and unhospitable. My willing love,
  The rather by these arguments of fear,°
  Set forth in your pursuit.

Sebastian.   My kind Antonio,
  I can no other answer make but thanks,
  And thanks, and ever oft good turns°   15

79–80 **the new map with the augmentation of the Indies** (presumably a map, prepared under the supervision of Richard Hakluyt and others and published about 1600, that employed the principles of projection and showed North America and the East Indies in fuller detail than any earlier map. It was conspicuous for the rhumb lines marking the meridians)   III.iii.8 **jealousy** anxiety   9 **skilless in** unacquainted with   12 **The rather by these arguments of fear** i.e., reinforced by my solicitude for your safety   15 **And thanks, and ever oft good turns** (the fact that this line is a foot too short has prompted a wide variety of emendations, the most popular of which has been Theobald's "And thanks, and ever thanks; and oft good turns." Later Folios omit this and the following line altogether)

Are shuffled off with such uncurrent° pay.
But, were my worth° as is my conscience firm,
You should find better dealing. What's to do?
Shall we go see the relics of this town?

20 *Antonio.* Tomorrow, sir; best first go see your lodging.

Sebastian. I am not weary, and 'tis long to night.
I pray you let us satisfy our eyes
With the memorials and the things of fame
That do renown this city.

Antonio.   Would you'ld pardon° me.
25 I do not without danger walk these streets.
Once in a sea-fight 'gainst the Count his galleys°
I did some service; of such note indeed
That, were I ta'en here, it would scarce be answered.°

Sebastian. Belike you slew great number of his people?

30 *Antonio.* Th' offense is not of such a bloody nature,
Albeit the quality° of the time and quarrel
Might well have given us bloody argument.°
It might have since been answered° in repaying
What we took from them, which for traffic's° sake
35 Most of our city did. Only myself stood out;
For which, if I be lapsèd° in this place,
I shall pay dear.

Sebastian.   Do not then walk too open.

Antonio. It doth not fit me. Hold, sir, here's my purse.
In the south suburbs at the Elephant°
40 Is best to lodge. I will bespeak our diet,°
Whiles° you beguile the time and feed your knowledge
With viewing of the town. There shall you have°
me.

16 **uncurrent** worthless 17 **worth** resources 24 **pardon** excuse
26 **the Count his galleys** the Count's warships 28 **answered** defended 31 **quality** circumstances 32 **argument** cause 33 **answered** compensated 34 **traffic's** trade's 36 **lapsèd** surprised and apprehended 39 **Elephant** an inn 40 **bespeak our diet** i.e., arrange for our meals 41 **Whiles** while 42 **have** find

Sebastian. Why I your purse?

Antonio. Haply your eye shall light upon some toy°
   You have desire to purchase, and your store°   *45*
   I think is not for idle markets,° sir.

Sebastian. I'll be your purse-bearer, and leave you for
  An hour.

Antonio.   To th' Elephant.

Sebastian.   I do remember. *Exeunt.*

Scene IV. [*Olivia's garden.*]

Enter Olivia and Maria.

Olivia. I have sent after him. He says he'll come:°
   How shall I feast him? What bestow of° him?
   For youth is bought more oft than begged or bor-
     rowed.
   I speak too loud. Where's Malvolio? He is sad and
     civil,°
   And suits well for a servant with my fortunes.   *5*
   Where is Malvolio?

Maria. He's coming, madam, but in very strange manner. He is sure possessed,° madam.

Olivia. Why, what's the matter? Does he rave?

Maria. No, madam, he does nothing but smile. Your *10*
   ladyship were best to have some guard about you
   if he come, for sure the man is tainted in 's wits.

Olivia. Go call him hither. I am as mad as he,
   If sad and merry madness equal be.

44 **toy** trifle 45 **store** wealth 46 **idle markets** unnecessary pur-
chases III.iv.1 **He says he'll come** suppose he says he'll come 2 **of**
on 4 **sad and civil** grave and formal 8 **possessed** i.e., with a devil,
mad

Enter Malvolio.

15   How now, Malvolio?

Malvolio. Sweet lady, ho, ho!

Olivia. Smil'st thou? I sent for thee upon a sad° occasion.

Malvolio. Sad, lady? I could be sad. This does make
20   some obstruction in the blood, this cross-gartering;
       but what of that? If it please the eye of one, it is
       with me as the very true sonnet° is, "Please one,
       and please all."°

Olivia. Why, how dost thou, man? What is the matter
25   with thee?

Malvolio. Not black in my mind, though yellow in my
       legs. It did come to his hands, and commands shall
       be executed. I think we do know the sweet Roman
       hand.°

30   *Olivia.* Wilt thou go to bed, Malvolio?

Malvolio. To bed? Ay, sweetheart, and I'll come to
       thee.

Olivia. God comfort thee. Why dost thou smile so,
       and kiss thy hand so oft?

35   *Maria.* How do you, Malvolio?

Malvolio. At your request? Yes, nightingales answer
       daws!°

Maria. Why appear you with this ridiculous boldness
       before my lady?

40   *Malvolio.* "Be not afraid of greatness." 'Twas well writ.

17 **sad** serious   22 **sonnet** (any short lyric poem)   22–23 **Please
one, and please all** i.e., so long as I please the one I love I do not
care about the rest (from "A prettie newe Ballad, intytuled: The
Crow sits vpon the wall, Please one and please all")   28–29 **the
sweet Roman hand** i.e., italic writing, an elegant cursive script more
fashionable than the crabbed "secretary hand" commonly used in
Shakespeare's time   36–37 **At . . . daws** i.e., should I reply to a
mere servant like you? Yes, for sometimes nightingales answer jackdaws

Olivia. What mean'st thou by that, Malvolio?

Malvolio. "Some are born great."

Olivia. Ha?

Malvolio. "Some achieve greatness."

Olivia. What say'st thou?   45

Malvolio. "And some have greatness thrust upon them."

Olivia. Heaven restore thee!

Malvolio. "Remember who commended thy yellow stockings."   50

Olivia. Thy yellow stockings?

Malvolio. "And wished to see thee cross-gartered."

Olivia. Cross-gartered?

Malvolio. "Go to, thou art made, if thou desir'st to be so."   55

Olivia. Am I made?

Malvolio. "If not, let me see thee a servant still."

Olivia. Why, this is very midsummer madness.°

Enter Servant.

Servant. Madam, the young gentleman of the Count Orsino's is returned. I could hardly entreat him   60
back. He attends your ladyship's pleasure.

Olivia. I'll come to him. [*Exit Servant.*] Good Maria, let this fellow be looked to. Where's my cousin Toby? Let some of my people have a special care of him. I would not have him miscarry° for the   65
half of my dowry.

Exit [Olivia, accompanied by Maria].

58 **midsummer madness** extreme folly, Midsummer Eve (June 23)
being traditionally associated with irresponsible and eccentric behavior   65 **miscarry** come to harm

Malvolio. O ho, do you come near me° now? No
worse man than Sir Toby to look to me. This con-
curs directly with the letter. She sends him on pur-
70   pose, that I may appear stubborn° to him; for she
incites me to that in the letter. "Cast thy humble
slough," says she; "be opposite with a kinsman,
surly with servants; let thy tongue tang with arguments of state; put thyself into the trick of singu-
75   larity." And consequently sets down the manner
how: as, a sad face, a reverend carriage, a slow
tongue, in the habit° of some sir° of note, and so
forth. I have limed° her; but it is Jove's doing, and
Jove make me thankful. And when she went away
80   now, "Let this fellow° be looked to." "Fellow."
Not "Malvolio," nor after my degree,° but "fellow." Why, everything adheres together, that no
dram° of a scruple,° no scruple of a scruple, no
obstacle, no incredulous or unsafe° circumstance—
85   what can be said? Nothing that can be can come
between me and the full prospect of my hopes.
Well, Jove, not I, is the doer of this, and he is to
be thanked.

Enter [Sir] Toby, Fabian, and Maria.

Toby. Which way is he, in the name of sanctity? If
90   all the devils of hell be drawn in little,° and
Legion° himself possessed him, yet I'll speak to
him.

Fabian. Here he is, here he is! How is't with you, sir?

---

67 come near me i.e., begin to understand my importance   **70 stubborn** hostile   **77 habit** clothing   **77 sir** personage   **78 limed** caught
(as birds are caught with sticky birdlime)   **80 fellow** (1) menial
(2) associate (the sense in which Malvolio takes the word)   **81 after
my degree** according to my status   **83 dram** (1) minute part (2)
apothecary's measure for one-eighth of an ounce   **83 scruple** (1)
doubt (2) apothecary's measure for one-third of a dram   **84 incredulous or unsafe** incredible or doubtful   **90 in little** in small
compass   **91 Legion** a group of devils (see Mark 5:8–9)

Toby. How is't with you, man?°

Malvolio. Go off; I discard you. Let me enjoy my 95
private.° Go off.

Maria. Lo, how hollow the fiend speaks within him!
Did not I tell you? Sir Toby, my lady prays you
to have a care of him.

Malvolio. Aha, does she so? 100

Toby. Go to, go to; peace, peace; we must deal gently
with him. Let me alone. How do you, Malvolio?
How is't with you? What, man, defy the devil?
Consider, he's an enemy to mankind.

Malvolio. Do you know what you say? 105

Maria. La you, and you speak ill of the devil, how he
takes it at heart. Pray God he be not bewitched.

Fabian. Carry his water to th' wise woman.°

Maria. Marry, and it shall be done tomorrow morning if I live. My lady would not lose him for more 110
than I'll say.

Malvolio. How now, mistress?

Maria. O Lord.

Toby. Prithee hold thy peace. This is not the way. Do
you not see you move° him? Let me alone with him. 115

Fabian. No way but gentleness; gently, gently. The
fiend is rough° and will not be roughly used.

Toby. Why, how now, my bawcock?° How dost thou,
chuck?°

Malvolio. Sir. 120

Toby. Ay, biddy, come with me. What, man, 'tis not

94 **How is't with you, man** (the Folio implausibly assigns this speech
to Fabian, but the contemptuous "man" suggests that the speaker
must be Malvolio's social superior)   96 **private** privacy   108 **Carry
his water to th' wise woman** i.e., for analysis   115 **move** agitate
117 **rough** violent   118 **bawcock** fine fellow (French *beau coq*)
119 **chuck** chick

for gravity to play at cherry-pit with Satan.° Hang
him, foul collier!°

Maria. Get him to say his prayers; good Sir Toby, get
125 him to pray.

Malvolio. My prayers, minx?

Maria. No, I warrant you, he will not hear of godli-
ness.

Malvolio. Go hang yourselves all! You are idle° shal-
130 low things; I am not of your element.° You shall
know more hereafter.   *Exit.*

Toby. Is't possible?

Fabian. If this were played upon a stage now, I could
condemn it as an improbable fiction.

135 *Toby.* His very genius° hath taken the infection of the
device, man.

Maria. Nay, pursue him now, lest the device take air
and taint.°

Fabian. Why, we shall make him mad indeed.

140 *Maria.* The house will be the quieter.

Toby. Come, we'll have him in a dark room and
bound. My niece is already in the belief that he's
mad. We may carry it° thus, for our pleasure and
his penance, till our very pastime, tired out of
145 breath, prompt us to have mercy on him; at which
time we will bring the device to the bar and crown
thee for a finder of madmen. But see, but see.

Enter Sir Andrew.

Fabian. More matter for a May morning.°

121–22 'tis not for gravity . . . Satan i.e., it is unsuitable for a man of
your dignity to play a children's game with Satan   123 collier vendor
of coals   129 idle trifling   130 element sphere   135 genius nature,
personality   137–138 take air and taint be exposed and spoiled
143 carry it i.e., go on with the joke   148 More matter for a May
morning i.e., another subject for a May-Day pageant

Andrew. Here's the challenge; read it. I warrant there's
vinegar and pepper in't.   150

Fabian. Is't so saucy?°

Andrew. Ay, is't, I warrant him. Do but read.

Toby. Give me. [*Reads*] "Youth, whatsoever thou art,
thou art but a scurvy fellow."

Fabian. Good, and valiant.   155

Toby. [*Reads*] "Wonder not nor admire° not in thy
mind why I do call thee so, for I will show thee no
reason for't."

Fabian. A good note that keeps you from the blow of
the law.   160

Toby. [*Reads*] "Thou com'st to the Lady Olivia, and
in my sight she uses thee kindly. But thou liest in
thy throat; that is not the matter I challenge thee
for."

Fabian. Very brief, and to exceeding good sense—   165
less.

Toby. [*Reads*] "I will waylay thee going home; where
if it be thy chance to kill me"—

Fabian. Good.

Toby. [*Reads*] "Thou kill'st me like a rogue and a   170
villain."

Fabian. Still you keep o' th' windy side of the law.°
Good.

Toby. [*Reads*] "Fare thee well, and God have mercy
upon one of our souls. He may have mercy upon   175
mine, but my hope is better, and so look to thyself.
Thy friend, as thou usest him, and thy sworn enemy,
                         ANDREW AGUECHEEK."
If this letter move him not, his legs cannot. I'll give't
him.   180

151 **saucy** i.e., with "vinegar and pepper"   156 **admire** marvel
172 **o' th' windy side of the law** i.e., safe from prosecution

Maria. You may have very fit occasion for't. He is now in some commerce° with my lady and will by and by depart.

Toby. Go, Sir Andrew. Scout me for him at the corner
185 of the orchard like a bum-baily.° So soon as ever thou seest him, draw; and as thou draw'st, swear horrible; for it comes to pass oft that a terrible oath, with a swaggering accent sharply twanged off, gives manhood more approbation° than ever
190 proof° itself would have earned him. Away!

Andrew. Nay, let me alone for swearing.°   *Exit.*

Toby. Now will not I deliver his letter; for the behavior of the young gentleman gives him out to be of good capacity and breeding; his employment
195 between his lord and my niece confirms no less. Therefore this letter, being so excellently ignorant, will breed no terror in the youth. He will find it comes from a clodpoll.° But, sir, I will deliver his challenge by word of mouth, set upon Aguecheek
200 a notable report of valor, and drive the gentleman (as I know his youth will aptly receive it) into a most hideous opinion of his rage, skill, fury, and impetuosity. This will so fright them both that they will kill one another by the look, like cockatrices.°

Enter Olivia and Viola.

205 *Fabian.* Here he comes with your niece. Give them way till he take leave, and presently after him.°

Toby. I will meditate the while upon some horrid message for a challenge.
            [*Exeunt Sir Toby, Fabian, and Maria.*]
Olivia. I have said too much unto a heart of stone

---

182 **commerce** conversation   185 **bum-baily** bailiff, sheriff's officer
189 **approbation** attestation   190 **proof** actual trial   191 **let me alone for swearing** i.e., do not worry about my ability at swearing
198 **clodpoll** dunce   204 **cockatrices** fabulous serpents that could kill with a glance   205–206 **Give them way . . . after him** i.e., do not interrupt them until he goes, and then follow him at once

And laid mine honor too unchary° on't.   210
There's something in me that reproves my fault;
But such a headstrong potent fault it is
That it but mocks reproof.

Viola. With the same havior° that your passion bears
Goes on my master's griefs.   215

Olivia. Here, wear this jewel° for me; 'tis my picture.
Refuse it not; it hath no tongue to vex you.
And I beseech you come again tomorrow.
What shall you ask of me that I'll deny,
That honor, saved, may upon asking give?   220

Viola. Nothing but this: your true love for my master.

Olivia. How with mine honor may I give him that
Which I have given to you?

Viola.   I will acquit you.

Olivia. Well, come again tomorrow. Fare thee well.
A fiend like thee° might bear my soul to hell.   225
                                              [*Exit.*]

Enter [Sir] Toby and Fabian.

Toby. Gentleman, God save thee.

Viola. And you, sir.

Toby. That defense thou hast, betake thee to't. Of
what nature the wrongs are thou hast done him,
I know not; but thy intercepter, full of despite,°   230
bloody as the hunter,° attends° thee at the orchard
end. Dismount thy tuck,° be yare° in thy preparation, for thy assailant is quick, skillful, and deadly.

Viola. You mistake, sir. I am sure no man hath any
quarrel to me. My remembrance is very free and   235
clear from any image of offense done to any man.

210 **unchary** carelessly   214 **havior** behavior   216 **jewel** i.e., jeweled
locket (?)   225 **like thee** i.e., with your attractions   230 **despite**
defiance   231 **bloody as the hunter** i.e., bloodthirsty as a hunting
dog   231 **attends** awaits   232 **Dismount thy tuck** unsheathe your
rapier   232 **yare** quick, prompt

Toby. You'll find it otherwise, I assure you. Therefore, if you hold your life at any price, betake you to your guard; for your opposite° hath in him what
240 youth, strength, skill, and wrath can furnish man withal.°

Viola. I pray you, sir, what is he?

Toby. He is knight, dubbed with unhatched° rapier and on carpet consideration,° but he is a devil in
245 private brawl. Souls and bodies hath he divorced three; and his incensement at this moment is so implacable that satisfaction can be none but by pangs of death and sepulcher. "Hob, nob"° is his word; "give't or take't."

250 *Viola.* I will return again into the house and desire some conduct° of the lady. I am no fighter. I have heard of some kind of men that put quarrels purposely on others to taste° their valor. Belike this is a man of that quirk.

255 *Toby.* Sir, no. His indignation derives itself out of a very competent° injury; therefore get you on and give him his desire. Back you shall not to the house, unless you undertake that with me which with as much safety you might answer him. There-
260 fore on, or strip your sword stark naked; for meddle° you must, that's certain, or forswear to wear iron about you.

Viola. This is as uncivil as strange. I beseech you do me this courteous office, as to know of the knight
265 what my offense to him is. It is something of my negligence,° nothing of my purpose.

Toby. I will do so. Signior Fabian, stay you by this gentleman till my return.   *Exit [Sir] Toby.*

Viola. Pray you, sir, do you know of this matter?

239 **opposite** adversary   241 **withal** with   243 **unhatched** unhacked
244 **on carpet consideration** i.e., not because of his exploits in the
field but through connections at court   248 **Hob, nob** have it, or
have it not   251 **conduct** escort   253 **taste** test   256 **competent**
sufficient   261 **meddle** engage him, fight   265–66 **of my negligence**
unintentional

Fabian. I know the knight is incensed against you, 270
even to a mortal arbitrament;° but nothing of the
circumstance more.

Viola. I beseech you, what manner of man is he?

Fabian. Nothing of that wonderful promise, to read
him by his form, as you are like to find him in the 275
proof of his valor. He is indeed, sir, the most skillful, bloody, and fatal opposite that you could possibly have found in any part of Illyria. Will you
walk towards him? I will make your peace with
him if I can. 280

Viola. I shall be much bound to you for't. I am one
that had rather go with sir priest than sir knight. I
care not who knows so much of my mettle.°
                                          Exeunt.°

        Enter [Sir] Toby and [Sir] Andrew.

Toby. Why, man, he's a very devil; I have not seen
such a firago.° I had a pass° with him, rapier, scab- 285
bard, and all, and he gives me the stuck-in° with
such a mortal motion° that it is inevitable; and on
the answer° he pays you as surely as your feet hits
the ground they step on. They say he has been
fencer to the Sophy.° 290

Andrew. Pox on't, I'll not meddle with him.

Toby. Ay, but he will not now be pacified. Fabian
can scarce hold him yonder.

Andrew. Plague on't, and I thought he had been
valiant, and so cunning in fence,° I'd have seen 295

---

271 **mortal arbitrament** deadly trial   283 **mettle** character, disposition   283 s.d. **Exeunt** (this stage direction, which leaves the stage
empty, properly marks the ending of the scene, but the new scene
that opens with the entrance of Sir Toby and Sir Andrew is not
indicated as such in the Folio)   285 **firago** virago (probably a
phonetic spelling)   285 **pass** bout   286 **stuck-in** stoccado, thrust
287 **mortal motion** deadly pass   288 **answer** return   290 **Sophy**
Shah   295 **in fence** at fencing

him damned ere I'd have challenged him. Let him
let the matter slip, and I'll give him my horse,
gray Capilet.

Toby. I'll make the motion.° Stand here; make a good
300   show on't. This shall end without the perdition of
souls.° [*Aside*] Marry, I'll ride your horse as well
as I ride you.

Enter Fabian and Viola.

I have his horse to take up° the quarrel. I have
persuaded him the youth's a devil.

305 *Fabian.* He is as horribly conceited of him,° and pants
and looks pale, as if a bear were at his heels.

Toby. There's no remedy, sir; he will fight with you
for's oath° sake. Marry, he hath better bethought
him of his quarrel,° and he finds that now scarce
310   to be worth talking of. Therefore draw for the supportance of his vow.° He protests he will not hurt
you.

Viola. [*Aside*] Pray God defend me! A little thing
would make me tell them how much I lack of a
315   man.

Fabian. Give ground if you see him furious.

Toby. Come, Sir Andrew, there's no remedy. The
gentleman will for his honor's sake have one bout
with you; he cannot by the duello° avoid it; but he
320   has promised me, as he is a gentleman and a
soldier, he will not hurt you. Come on, to't.

Andrew. Pray God he keep his oath!   [*Draws.*]

299 **motion** proposal   300–01 **perdition of souls** i.e., loss of life
303 **take up** settle   305 **He is as horribly conceited of him** i.e.,
Cesario has just as terrifying a notion of Sir Andrew   308 **oath**
oath's   309 **his quarrel** the cause of his resentment   310–11 **Therefore draw for the supportance of his vow** i.e., make a show of valor
merely for the satisfaction of his oath   319 **duello** duelling code

Enter Antonio.

Viola. I do assure you 'tis against my will.   [*Draws.*]

Antonio. Put up your sword. If this young gentleman
   Have done offense, I take the fault on me;   325
   If you offend him, I for him defy you.

Toby. You, sir? Why, what are you?

Antonio. [*Draws*] One, sir, that for his love dares yet
   do more
   Than you have heard him brag to you he will.

Toby. Nay, if you be an undertaker,° I am for you.   330
                                              [*Draws.*]

Enter Officers.

Fabian. O good Sir Toby, hold. Here come the officers.

Toby. [*To Antonio*] I'll be with you anon.

Viola. [*To Sir Andrew*] Pray, sir, put your sword up,
   if you please.

Andrew. Marry, will I, sir; and for that° I promised   335
   you, I'll be as good as my word. He will bear you
   easily, and reins well.

First Officer. This is the man; do thy office.°

Second Officer. Antonio, I arrest thee at the suit
   Of Count Orsino.

Antonio.   You do mistake me, sir.   340

First Officer. No, sir, no jot. I know your favor°
   well,
   Though now you have no sea-cap on your head.
   Take him away. He knows I know him well.

Antonio. I must obey. [*To Viola*] This comes with
   seeking you.

330 **an undertaker** one who takes up a challenge for another (with
perhaps a pun on "undertaker" as a government agent, i.e., scoun-
drel)   335 **for that** as for what (i.e., his horse, "gray Capilet")
338 **office** duty   341 **favor** face

345   But there's no remedy; I shall answer it.°
   What will you do, now my necessity
   Makes me to ask you for my purse? It grieves me
   Much more for what I cannot do for you
   Than what befalls myself. You stand amazed,
350   But be of comfort.

Second Officer. Come, sir, away.

Antonio. I must entreat of you some of that money.

Viola. What money, sir?
   For the fair kindness you have showed me here,
355   And part° being prompted by your present trouble,
   Out of my lean and low ability
   I'll lend you something. My having is not much.
   I'll make division of my present° with you.
   Hold, there's half my coffer.°

Antonio.   Will you deny me now?
360   Is't possible that my deserts to you
   Can lack persuasion?° Do not tempt my misery,
   Lest that it make me so unsound° a man
   As to upbraid you with those kindnesses
   That I have done for you.

Viola.   I know of none,
365   Nor know I you by voice or any feature.
   I hate ingratitude more in a man
   Than lying, vainness,° babbling, drunkenness,
   Or any taint of vice whose strong corruption
   Inhabits our frail blood.

Antonio.   O heavens themselves!

370 *Second Officer.* Come, sir, I pray you go.

Antonio. Let me speak a little. This youth that you
   see here
   I snatched one half out of the jaws of death;

---

345 **answer it** i.e., try to defend myself against the accusation
355 **part** partly 358 **present** present resources 359 **coffer** chest,
i.e., money 360–61 **deserts to you/Can lack persuasion** claims on
you can fail to be persuasive 362 **unsound** weak, unmanly
367 **vainness** (1) falseness (2) boasting

Relieved him with such sanctity of love,
And to his image, which methought did promise
Most venerable° worth, did I devotion.   375

First Officer. What's that to us? The time goes by.
   Away.

Antonio. But, O, how vild° an idol proves this god!
   Thou hast, Sebastian, done good feature° shame.
   In nature there's no blemish but the mind;°
   None can be called deformed but the unkind.°   380
   Virtue is beauty; but the beauteous evil
   Are empty trunks,° o'erflourished° by the devil.

First Officer. The man grows mad; away with him!
   Come, come, sir.

Antonio. Lead me on.   *Exit [with Officers].*

Viola. Methinks his words do from such passion fly   385
   That he believes himself; so do not I.
   Prove true, imagination, O, prove true,
   That I, dear brother, be now ta'en for you!

Toby. Come hither, knight; come hither, Fabian. We'll
   whisper o'er a couplet or two of most sage saws.°   390

Viola. He named Sebastian. I my brother know
   Yet living in my glass.° Even such and so
   In favor was my brother, and he went
   Still in this fashion, color, ornament,
   For him I imitate. O, if it prove,   395
   Tempests are kind, and salt waves fresh in love!
                                             [Exit.]

Toby. A very dishonest° paltry boy, and more a
   coward than a hare. His dishonesty appears in
   leaving his friend here in necessity and denying
   him; and for his cowardship, ask Fabian.   400

375 **venerable** worthy of veneration   377 **vild** vile   378 **feature**
shape, external appearance   379 **mind** (as distinguished from body
or "feature")   380 **unkind** unnatural   382 **trunks** chests   382 **o'er-
flourished** decorated with carving and painting   390 **sage saws** wise
maxims   392 **living in my glass** i.e., staring at me from my mirror
397 **dishonest** dishonorable

Fabian. A coward, a most devout coward; religious in it.°

Andrew. 'Slid,° I'll after him again and beat him.

405 *Toby.* Do; cuff him soundly, but never draw thy sword.

Andrew. And I do not—   [*Exit.*]

Fabian. Come, let's see the event.°

Toby. I dare lay any money 'twill be nothing yet.°
                    Exit [*with Sir Andrew and Fabian*].

401–02 **religious in it** i.e., dedicated to his cowardice (following "devout")   403 **'Slid** by God's eyelid   407 **event** outcome   408 **yet** after all

ACT IV

Scene I. [*Before Olivia's house.*]

Enter Sebastian and Clown.

Clown. Will you make me believe that I am not sent
  for you?

Sebastian. Go to, go to, thou art a foolish fellow. Let
  me be clear of thee.

Clown. Well held out,° i' faith! No, I do not know   5
  you; nor I am not sent to you by my lady, to bid
  you come speak with her; nor your name is not
  Master Cesario; nor this is not my nose neither.
  Nothing that is so is so.

Sebastian. I prithee vent thy folly somewhere else.   10
  Thou know'st not me.

Clown. Vent my folly! He has heard that word of
  some great man, and now applies it to a fool. Vent
  my folly! I am afraid this great lubber,° the world,
  will prove a cockney.° I prithee now, ungird thy   15
  strangeness,° and tell me what I shall vent° to my
  lady. Shall I vent to her that thou art coming?

Sebastian. I prithee, foolish Greek,° depart from me.

IV.i.5 **held out** maintained   14 **lubber** lout   15 **cockney** affected
fop   15–16 **ungird thy strangeness** i.e., abandon your silly pretense
(of not recognizing me)   16 **vent** say   18 **Greek** buffoon

111

There's money for thee. If you tarry longer, I shall
20   give worse payment.

Clown. By my troth, thou hast an open hand. These
wise men that give fools money get themselves a
good report—after fourteen years' purchase.°

Enter [Sir] Andrew, [Sir] Toby, and Fabian.

Andrew. Now, sir, have I met you again? There's for
25   you!   [*Strikes Sebastian.*]

Sebastian. Why, there's for thee, and there, and there!
                               [*Strikes Sir Andrew.*]
Are all the people mad?

Toby. Hold, sir, or I'll throw your dagger o'er the
house.   [*Seizes Sebastian.*]

30 *Clown.* This will I tell my lady straight.° I would not
be in some of your coats for twopence.   [*Exit.*]

Toby. Come on, sir; hold.

Andrew. Nay, let him alone. I'll go another way to
work with him. I'll have an action of battery against
35   him,° if there be any law in Illyria. Though I
stroke° him first, yet it's no matter for that.

Sebastian. Let go thy hand.

Toby. Come, sir, I will not let you go. Come, my
young soldier, put up your iron. You are well
40   fleshed.° Come on.

Sebastian. I will be free from thee. [*Frees himself.*]
What wouldst thou now?
If thou dar'st tempt me further, draw thy sword.

Toby. What, what? Nay then, I must have an ounce
or two of this malapert° blood from you. [*Draws.*]

23 **after fourteen years' purchase** i.e., after a long delay, at a high
price   30 **straight** straightaway, at once   34–35 **have an action of
battery against him** charge him with assaulting me   36 **stroke**
struck   39–40 **well fleshed** i.e., made eager for fighting by having
tasted blood   44 **malapert** saucy

Enter Olivia.

Olivia. Hold, Toby! On thy life I charge thee hold!   *45*

Toby. Madam.

Olivia. Will it be ever thus? Ungracious wretch,
    Fit for the mountains and the barbarous caves,
    Where manners ne'er were preached! Out of my
      sight!
    Be not offended, dear Cesario.   *50*
    Rudesby,° begone.
           [Exeunt Sir Toby, Sir Andrew, and Fabian.]
                I prithee gentle friend,
    Let thy fair wisdom, not thy passion, sway°
    In this uncivil° and unjust extent°
    Against thy peace. Go with me to my house,
    And hear thou there how many fruitless pranks   *55*
    This ruffian hath botched up,° that thou thereby
    Mayst smile at this. Thou shalt not choose but go.
    Do not deny. Beshrew° his soul for me.
    He started° one poor heart° of mine, in thee.

Sebastian. What relish is in this?° How runs the
    stream?   *60*
    Or° I am mad, or else this is a dream.
    Let fancy still my sense in Lethe° steep;
    If it be thus to dream, still let me sleep!

Olivia. Nay, come, I prithee. Would thou'dst be ruled
    by me!

Sebastian. Madam, I will.

Olivia.   O, say so, and so be.   *65*
                          Exeunt.

---

51 **Rudesby** ruffian   52 **sway** rule   53 **uncivil** barbarous   53 **extent**
display   56 **botched up** clumsily contrived   58 **Beshrew** curse
59 **started** roused   59 **heart** (with a pun on "hart")   60 **What relish
is in this?** i.e., what does this mean?   61 **Or** either   62 **Lethe** in
classical mythology, the river of oblivion in Hades

Scene II. [*Olivia's house.*]

Enter Maria and Clown.

Maria. Nay, I prithee put on this gown and this beard;
make him believe thou art Sir Topas° the curate;
do it quickly. I'll call Sir Toby the whilst.° [*Exit.*]

Clown. Well, I'll put it on, and I will dissemble° my-
5　　self in't, and I would I were the first that ever dis-
sembled in such a gown. I am not tall enough to
become the function° well, nor lean enough to be
thought a good student;° but to be said an honest
man and a good housekeeper° goes as fairly as to
10　　say a careful° man and a great scholar. The com-
petitors° enter.

Enter [*Sir*] *Toby* [*and Maria*].

Toby. Jove bless thee, Master Parson.

Clown. Bonos· dies,° Sir Toby; for, as the old hermit
of Prague,° that never saw pen and ink, very wit-
15　　tily said to a niece of King Gorboduc,° "That that
is is"; so, I, being Master Parson, am Master Parson; for what is "that" but that, and "is" but is?

Toby. To him, Sir Topas.

Clown. What ho, I say. Peace in this prison!

20　　*Toby.* The knave counterfeits well; a good knave.°

IV.ii.2 **Sir Topas** (the ridiculous hero of Chaucer's *Rime of Sir
Thopas,* a parody of chivalric romances)　3 **the whilst** meanwhile
4 **dissemble** disguise　7 **function** clerical office　8 **student** student
9 **good housekeeper** solid citizen　10 **careful** painstaking　10-11
competitors confederates　13 **Bonos dies** good day　13-14 **the old
hermit of Prague** (apparently the Clown's nonsensical invention)
15 **King Gorboduc** (a legendary king of Britain)　20 **knave** fellow

Malvolio within.

Malvolio. Who calls there?

Clown. Sir Topas the curate, who comes to visit Malvolio the lunatic.

Malvolio. Sir Topas, Sir Topas, good Sir Topas, go to my lady.   *25*

Clown. Out, hyperbolical° fiend! How vexest thou this man! Talkest thou nothing but of ladies?

Toby. Well said, Master Parson.

Malvolio. Sir Topas, never was man thus wronged. Good Sir Topas, do not think I am mad. They have *30* laid me here in hideous darkness.

Clown. Fie, thou dishonest Satan. I call thee by the most modest° terms, for I am one of those gentle ones that will use the devil himself with courtesy. Say'st thou that house° is dark?   *35*

Malvolio. As hell, Sir Topas.

Clown. Why, it hath bay windows transparent as barricadoes,° and the clerestories° toward the south north are as lustrous as ebony; and yet complainest thou of obstruction?   *40*

Malvolio. I am not mad, Sir Topas. I say to you this house is dark.

Clown. Madman, thou errest. I say there is no darkness but ignorance, in which thou art more puzzled than the Egyptians in their fog.°   *45*

Malvolio. I say this house is as dark as ignorance, though ignorance were as dark as hell; and I say there was never man thus abused. I am no more

26 **hyperbolical** boisterous (a term from rhetoric meaning "exaggerated in style")   33 **most modest** mildest   35 **house** madman's cell   37–38 **barricadoes** barricades   38 **clerestories** upper windows   45 **Egyptians in their fog** (to plague the Egyptians Moses brought a "thick darkness" that lasted three days; see Exodus 10:21–23)

mad than you are. Make the trial of it in any con-
50 stant question.°

Clown. What is the opinion of Pythagoras° concerning
wild fowl?

Malvolio. That the soul of our grandam might hap-
pily° inhabit a bird.

55 Clown. What think'st thou of his opinion?

Malvolio. I think nobly of the soul and no way approve
his opinion.

Clown. Fare thee well. Remain thou still in darkness.
Thou shalt hold th' opinion of Pythagoras ere I
60 will allow of thy wits,° and fear to kill a woodcock,° lest thou dispossess the soul of thy grandam.
Fare thee well.

Malvolio. Sir Topas, Sir Topas!

Toby. My most exquisite Sir Topas!

65 Clown. Nay, I am for all waters.°

Maria. Thou mightst have done this without thy beard
and gown. He sees thee not.

Toby. To him in thine own voice, and bring me word
how thou find'st him. [To Maria] I would we were
70 well rid of this knavery. If he may be conveniently
delivered,° I would he were; for I am now so far
in offense with my niece that I cannot pursue with
any safety this sport to the upshot.° [To the Clown]
Come by and by to my chamber. Exit [with Maria].

75 Clown. [Sings] "Hey, Robin, jolly Robin,
                    Tell me how thy lady does."°

49–50 **constant question** consistent topic, normal conversation
51 **Pythagoras** (ancient Greek philosopher who expounded the doctrine of the transmigration of souls)   53–54 **happily** haply, perhaps
60 **allow of thy wits** acknowledge your sanity   60–61 **woodcock** (a
proverbially stupid bird)   65 **I am for all waters** i.e., I can turn my
hand to any trade   71 **delivered** released   73 **upshot** conclusion
75–76 **Hey, Robin . . . lady does** (the Clown sings an old ballad)

Malvolio. Fool.

Clown. "My lady is unkind, perdie."°

Malvolio. Fool.

Clown. "Alas, why is she so?"   *80*

Malvolio. Fool, I say.

Clown. "She loves another." Who calls, ha?

Malvolio. Good fool, as ever thou wilt deserve well
at my hand, help me to a candle, and pen, ink, and
paper. As I am a gentleman, I will live to be thank-   *85*
ful to thee for't.

Clown. Master Malvolio?

Malvolio. Ay, good fool.

Clown. Alas, sir, how fell you besides your five wits?°

Malvolio. Fool, there was never man so notoriously°   *90*
abused. I am as well in my wits, fool, as thou art.

Clown. But as well? Then you are mad indeed, if you
be no better in your wits than a fool.

Malvolio. They have here propertied° me; keep me in
darkness, send ministers to me, asses, and do all   *95*
they can to face me out of my wits.°

Clown. Advise you° what you say. The minister is
here.°— Malvolio, Malvolio, thy wits the heavens
restore. Endeavor thyself to sleep and leave thy
vain bibble babble.   *100*

Malvolio. Sir Topas.

Clown. Maintain no words with him, good fellow.

---

78 **perdie** certainly / 89 **how fell you besides your five wits?** i.e., how
did you happen to become mad?   90 **notoriously** outrageously
94 **propertied** i.e., used me as a mere object, not a human being
96 **face me out of my wits** i.e., impudently insist that I am mad
97 **Advise you** consider carefully   97–98 **The minister is here** (for
the next few lines the Clown uses two voices, his own and that of Sir
Topas)

—Who, I, sir? Not I, sir. God buy you,° good Sir
Topas.—Marry, amen.—I will, sir, I will.

105 *Malvolio.* Fool, fool, fool, I say!

Clown. Alas, sir, be patient. What say you, sir? I am
shent° for speaking to you.

Malvolio. Good fool, help me to some light and some
paper. I tell thee, I am as well in my wits as any
110   man in Illyria.

Clown. Well-a-day that you were,° sir.

Malvolio. By this hand, I am. Good fool, some ink,
paper, and light; and convey what I will set down
to my lady. It shall advantage thee more than ever
115   the bearing of letter did.

Clown. I will help you to't. But tell me true, are you
not mad indeed, or do you but counterfeit?°

Malvolio. Believe me, I am not. I tell thee true.

Clown. Nay, I'll ne'er believe a madman till I see his
120   brains. I will fetch you light and paper and ink.

Malvolio. Fool, I'll requite it in the highest degree. I
prithee be gone.

Clown. [*Sings*]   I am gone, sir.
                          And anon, sir,
125   I'll be with you again,
                          In a trice,
                          Like to the old Vice,°
                  Your need to sustain.°
                  Who with dagger of lath,
130   In his rage and his wrath,
                          Cries "Ah ha" to the devil.
                  Like a mad lad,

103 **God buy you** God be with you, i.e., good-bye   107 **shent** re-
buked   111 **Well-a-day that you were** alas, if only you were   117
counterfeit pretend   127 **Vice** (in the morality plays, a stock mis-
chievous character who usually carried a wooden dagger)   128 **Your
need to sustain** i.e., in order to help you resist the Devil

"Pare thy nails, dad."
            Adieu, goodman devil.°   *Exit.*

Scene III. [*Olivia's garden.*]

Enter Sebastian.

Sebastian. This is the air; that is the glorious sun;
    This pearl she gave me, I do feel't and see't;
    And though 'tis wonder that enwraps me thus,
    Yet 'tis not madness. Where's Antonio then?
    I could not find him at the Elephant;   5
    Yet there he was,° and there I found this credit,°
    That he did range the town to seek me out.
    His counsel now might do me golden service;
    For though my soul disputes well with my sense°
    That this may be some error, but no madness,   10
    Yet doth this accident and flood of fortune
    So far exceed all instance,° all discourse,°
    That I am ready to distrust mine eyes
    And wrangle with my reason that persuades me
    To any other trust° but that I am mad,   15
    Or else the lady's mad. Yet, if 'twere so,
    She could not sway° her house, command her
        followers,
    Take and give back affairs and their dispatch°
    With such a smooth, discreet, and stable bearing
    As I perceive she does. There's something in't   20
    That is deceivable.° But here the lady comes.

---

134 **Adieu, goodman devil** (a much emended line; "goodman" [Folio
"good man"], a title for a yeoman or any man of substance not of
gentle birth, roughly corresponds to our "mister")   IV.iii.6 **was** had
been   6 **credit** belief   9 **my soul disputes well with my sense** my
reason agrees with the evidence of my senses   12 **instance** precedent
12 **discourse** reason   15 **trust** belief   17 **sway** rule   18 **Take and
give ... their dispatch** i.e., assume and discharge the management of
affairs   21 **deceivable** deceptive

Enter Olivia and Priest.

Olivia. Blame not this haste of mine. If you mean well,
 Now go with me and with this holy man
 Into the chantry by.° There, before him,
25 And underneath that consecrated roof,
 Plight me the full assurance of your faith,
 That my most jealous° and too doubtful soul
 May live at peace. He shall conceal it
 Whiles° you are willing it shall come to note,°
30 What time we will our celebration keep°
 According to my birth. What do you say?

Sebastian. I'll follow this good man and go with you
 And having sworn truth, ever will be true.

Olivia. Then lead the way, good father, and heavens
  so shine
35 That they may fairly note° this act of mine.
            Exeunt.

24 **chantry by** nearby chapel 27 **jealous** jealous, anxious 29 **Whiles**
until 29 **come to note** be made public 30 **our celebration keep**
celebrate our marriage ceremony (as distinguished from the formal
compact of betrothal) 35 **fairly note** look with favor on

ACT V

Scene I. [*Before Olivia's house.*]

Enter Clown and Fabian.

Fabian. Now as thou lov'st me, let me see his° letter.

Clown. Good Master Fabian, grant me another request.

Fabian. Anything.

Clown. Do not desire to see this letter.   5

Fabian. This is to give a dog, and in recompense desire my dog again.

    Enter Duke, Viola, Curio, and Lords.

Duke. Belong you to the Lady Olivia, friends?

Clown. Ay, sir, we are some of her trappings.

Duke. I know thee well. How dost thou, my good   10
fellow?

Clown. Truly, sir, the better for my foes, and the worse for my friends.

V.i.1 his i.e., Malvolio's

Duke. Just the contrary: the better for thy friends.

15 *Clown.* No, sir, the worse.

Duke. How can that be?

Clown. Marry, sir, they praise me and make an ass of
me. Now my foes tell me plainly I am an ass; so
that by my foes, sir, I profit in the knowledge of
20 myself, and by my friends I am abused;° so that,
conclusions to be as kisses,° if your four negatives°
make your two affirmatives,° why then, the worse
for my friends, and the better for my foes.

Duke. Why, this is excellent.

25 *Clown.* By my troth, sir, no, though it please you to
be one of my friends.

Duke. Thou shalt not be the worse for me. There's
gold.

Clown. But that it would be double-dealing,° sir, I
30 would you could make it another.

Duke. O, you give me ill counsel.

Clown. Put your grace° in your pocket, sir, for this
once, and let your flesh and blood obey it.

Duke. Well, I will be so much a sinner to be a double-
35 dealer. There's another.°

Clown. Primo, secundo, tertio° is a good play;° and
the old saying is "The third pays for all." The
triplex,° sir, is a good tripping measure; or the
bells of Saint Bennet,° sir, may put you in mind—
40 one, two, three.

Duke. You can fool no more money out of me at this

20 **abused** deceived 21 **conclusions to be as kisses** i.e., if conclusions
may be compared to kisses (when a coy girl's repeated denials really
mean assent) 21 **negatives** i.e., lips (?) 22 **affirmatives** i.e., mouths
(?) 29 **double-dealing** (1) giving twice (2) duplicity 32 **grace** (1)
title of nobility (2) generosity 35 **another** i.e., coin 36 **Primo,
secundo, tertio** one, two, three 36 **play** child's game (?) 38 **triplex**
triple time in dancing 39 **Saint Bennet** St. Benedict (a church)

throw.° If you will let your lady know I am here
to speak with her, and bring her along with you, it
may awake my bounty further.

Clown. Marry, sir, lullaby to your bounty till I come   45
again. I go, sir; but I would not have you to think
that my desire of having is the sin of covetousness.
But, as you say, sir, let your bounty take a nap; I
will awake it anon.   *Exit.*

Enter Antonio and Officers.

Viola. Here comes the man, sir, that did rescue me.   50

Duke. That face of his I do remember well;
Yet when I saw it last, it was besmeared
As black as Vulcan° in the smoke of war.
A baubling° vessel was he captain of,
For shallow draught and bulk unprizable,°   55
With which such scathful° grapple did he make
With the most noble bottom° of our fleet
That very envy and the tongue of loss°
Cried fame and honor on him. What's the matter?

First Officer. Orsino, this is that Antonio   60
That took the *Phoenix* and her fraught° from
    Candy;°
And this is he that did the *Tiger* board
When your young nephew Titus lost his leg.
Here in the streets, desperate of shame and state,°
In private brabble° did we apprehend him.   65

Viola. He did me kindness, sir; drew on my side;°
But in conclusion put strange speech upon me.°
I know not what 'twas but distraction.°

42 **throw** throw of the dice 53 **Vulcan** Roman god of fire and
patron of blacksmiths 54 **baubling** insignificant 55 **For shallow
draught and bulk unprizable** i.e., virtually worthless on account of
its small size 56 **scathful** destructive 57 **bottom** ship 58 **very
envy and the tongue of loss** even enmity and the voice of the losers
61 **fraught** freight, cargo 61 **Candy** Candia, Crete 64 **desperate
of shame and state** i.e., recklessly disregarding his shameful past
behavior and the requirements of public order 65 **brabble** brawl
66 **drew on my side** i.e., drew his sword in my defense 67 **put
strange speech upon me** spoke to me so oddly 68 **distraction** madness

Duke. Notable° pirate, thou salt-water thief,
70   What foolish boldness brought thee to their mercies
      Whom thou in terms so bloody and so dear°
      Hast made thine enemies?

Antonio.   Orsino, noble sir,
      Be pleased that I shake off these names you give me.
      Antonio never yet was thief or pirate,
75   Though I confess, on base and ground enough,
      Orsino's enemy. A witchcraft drew me hither.
      That most ingrateful boy there by your side
      From the rude sea's enraged and foamy mouth
      Did I redeem. A wrack° past hope he was.
80   His life I gave him, and did thereto add
      My love without retention or restraint,
      All his in dedication. For his sake
      Did I expose myself (pure° for his love)
      Into the danger of this adverse° town;
85   Drew to defend him when he was beset;
      Where being apprehended, his false cunning
      (Not meaning to partake with me in danger)
      Taught him to face me out of his acquaintance,°
      And grew a twenty years removèd thing
90   While one would wink; denied me mine own purse,
      Which I had recommended° to his use
      Not half an hour before.

Viola.   How can this be?

Duke. When came he to this town?

Antonio. Today, my lord; and for three months before,
95   No int'rim, not a minute's vacancy,
      Both day and night did we keep company.

                Enter Olivia and Attendants.

Duke. Here comes the Countess; now heaven walks on
      earth.

---

69 **Notable** notorious   71 **dear** grievous   79 **wrack** wreck   83 **pure**
purely   84 **adverse** unfriendly   88 **to face me out of his acquaintance** i.e., brazenly to deny any knowledge of me   91 **recommended**
given

But for° thee, fellow: fellow, thy words are madness.
Three months this youth hath tended upon me;
But more of that anon. Take him aside.   *100*

Olivia. What would my lord, but that° he may not have,
Wherein Olivia may seem serviceable?
Cesario, you do not keep promise with me.

Viola. Madam?

Duke. Gracious Olivia—   *105*

Olivia. What do you say, Cesario?—Good my lord°—

Viola. My lord would speak; my duty hushes me.

Olivia. If it be aught to the old tune, my lord,
It is as fat and fulsome° to mine ear
As howling after music.

Duke.   Still so cruel?   *110*

Olivia. Still so constant, lord.

Duke. What, to perverseness? You uncivil lady,
To whose ingrate and unauspicious° altars
My soul the faithfull'st off'rings have breathed out
That e'er devotion tendered. What shall I do?   *115*

Olivia. Even what it please my lord, that shall become him.

Duke. Why should I not, had I the heart to do it,
Like to th' Egyptian thief° at point of death,
Kill what I love?—a savage jealousy
That sometime savors nobly. But hear me this: *120*
Since you to non-regardance° cast my faith,

98 **But for** as for   101 **but that** except that which (i.e., my love)
106 **Good my lord** i.e., please be silent (so Cesario may speak)
109 **fat and fulsome** gross and repulsive   113 **ingrate and unauspicious** ungrateful and unpropitious   118 **th' Egyptian thief** (in Heliodorus' *Ethiopica*, a Greek romance translated by Thomas Underdown about 1569, the bandit Thyamis, besieged in a cave, plans to kill the captive princess Clariclea, the object of his hopeless love; but in the darkness he kills another woman instead)   121 **non-regardance** neglect

And that° I partly know the instrument
That screws° me from my true place in your favor,
Live you the marble-breasted tyrant still.
125 But this your minion, whom I know you love,
And whom, by heaven I swear, I tender° dearly,
Him will I tear out of that cruel eye
Where he sits crownèd in his master's spite.
Come, boy, with me. My thoughts are ripe in
  mischief.
130 I'll sacrifice the lamb that I do love
To spite a raven's heart within a dove.   [Going.]

Viola. And I, most jocund, apt,° and willingly,
To do you rest° a thousand deaths would die.
                                              [Following.]

Olivia. Where goes Cesario?

Viola.   After him I love
135 More than I love these eyes, more than my life,
More, by all mores,° than e'er I shall love wife.
If I do feign, you witnesses above
Punish my life for tainting of my love!

Olivia. Ay me detested, how am I beguiled!

Viola. Who does beguile you? Who does do you
140   wrong?

Olivia. Hast thou forgot thyself? Is it so long?
Call forth the holy father.   [Exit an Attendant.]

Duke.   [To Viola] Come, away!

Olivia. Whither, my lord? Cesario, husband, stay.

Duke. Husband?

Olivia.   Ay, husband. Can he that deny?

Duke. Her husband, sirrah?°

145 *Viola.*   No, my lord, not I.

---

122 **that** since   123 **screws** forces   126 **tender** hold   132 **apt** readily
133 **do you rest** give you peace   136 **mores** i.e., possible comparisons
144 **sirrah** (customary form of address to a menial)

Olivia. Alas, it is the baseness of thy fear
That makes thee strangle thy propriety.°
Fear not, Cesario; take thy fortunes up;
Be that thou know'st thou art, and then thou art
As great as that° thou fear'st.

Enter Priest.

                     O, welcome, father!   *150*
Father, I charge thee by thy reverence
Here to unfold—though lately we intended
To keep in darkness what occasion now
Reveals before 'tis ripe—what thou dost know
Hath newly passed between this youth and me.   *155*

Priest. A contract° of eternal bond of love,
Confirmed by mutual joinder of your hands,
Attested by the holy close of lips,
Strength'ned by interchangement of your rings;
And all the ceremony of this compact°   *160*
Sealed in my function,° by my testimony;
Since when, my watch hath told me, toward my
    grave
I have traveled but two hours.

Duke. O thou dissembling cub, what wilt thou be
When time hath sowed a grizzle on thy case?°   *165*
Or will not else thy craft° so quickly grow
That thine own trip° shall be thine overthrow?
Farewell, and take her; but direct thy feet
Where thou and I, henceforth, may never meet.

Viola. My lord, I do protest.

Olivia.   O, do not swear.   *170*
Hold little° faith, though thou hast too much fear.

Enter Sir Andrew.

---

147 **strangle thy propriety** deny your identity   150 **that** him who
(i.e., the Duke)   156 **contract** betrothal   160 **compact** (accent on
second syllable)   161 **Sealed in my function** i.e., ratified by me in
my priestly office   165 **a grizzle on thy case** gray hairs on your skin
166 **craft** duplicity   167 **trip** craftiness   171 **little** i.e., at least a little

Andrew. For the love of God, a surgeon! Send one
presently° to Sir Toby.

Olivia. What's the matter?

175 *Andrew.* H'as° broke my head across, and has given
Sir Toby a bloody coxcomb° too. For the love of
God, your help! I had rather than forty pound I
were at home.

Olivia. Who has done this, Sir Andrew?

180 *Andrew.* The Count's gentleman, one Cesario. We
took him for a coward, but he's the very devil
incardinate.°

Duke. My gentleman Cesario?

Andrew. Od's lifelings,° here he is! You broke my
185   head for nothing; and that that I did, I was set on
to do't by Sir Toby.

Viola. Why do you speak to me? I never hurt you.
You drew your sword upon me without cause,
But I bespake you fair° and hurt you not.

Enter [Sir] Toby and Clown.

190 *Andrew.* If a bloody coxcomb be a hurt, you have
hurt me. I think you set nothing by a bloody coxcomb. Here comes Sir Toby halting;° you shall hear
more. But if he had not been in drink, he would
have tickled you othergates° than he did.

195 *Duke.* How now, gentleman? How is't with you?

Toby. That's all one! Has hurt me, and there's th'
end on't. Sot,° didst see Dick Surgeon, sot?

Clown. O, he's drunk, Sir Toby, an hour agone. His
eyes were set° at eight i' th' morning.

173 **presently** immediately   175 **H'as** he has   176 **coxcomb** pate
182 **incardinate** incarnate   184 **Od's lifelings** by God's life   189 **bespake you fair** addressed you courteously   192 **halting** limping
194 **othergates** otherwise   197 **Sot** fool   199 **set** closed

Toby. Then he's a rogue and a passy measures   200
pavin.° I hate a drunken rogue.

Olivia. Away with him! Who hath made this havoc
with them?

Andrew. I'll help you, Sir Toby, because we'll be
dressed° together.   205

Toby. Will you help—an ass-head and a coxcomb
and a knave, a thin-faced knave, a gull?

Olivia. Get him to bed, and let his hurt be looked to.
                    [*Exeunt Clown, Fabian, Sir Toby,
                              and Sir Andrew.*]

              Enter Sebastian.

Sebastian. I am sorry, madam, I have hurt your
kinsman;
But had it been the brother of my blood,   210
I must have done no less with wit and safety.°
You throw a strange regard° upon me, and by that
I do perceive it hath offended you.
Pardon me, sweet one, even for the vows
We made each other but so late ago.   215

Duke. One face, one voice, one habit,° and two
persons—
A natural perspective° that is and is not.

Sebastian. Antonio, O my dear Antonio,
How have the hours racked and tortured me
Since I have lost thee!   220

Antonio. Sebastian are you?

Sebastian.   Fear'st thou° that, Antonio?

200–01 **passy measures pavin** i.e., *passamezzo* pavan, a slow and
stately dance of eight bars (hence its relevance to the surgeon whose
eyes had "set at eight")   204–05 **be dressed** have our wounds dressed
211 **with wit and safety** i.e., with a sensible regard for my safety
212 **strange regard** unfriendly look   216 **habit** costume   217 **A
natural perspective** i.e., a natural optical illusion (like that produced
by a stereoscope, which converts two images into one)   221 **Fear'st
thou** do you doubt

Antonio. How have you made division of yourself?
　　An apple cleft in two is not more twin
　　Than these two creatures. Which is Sebastian?

225 *Olivia.* Most wonderful.

Sebastian. Do I stand there? I never had a brother;
　　Nor can there be that deity in my nature
　　Of here and everywhere.° I had a sister,
　　Whom the blind waves and surges have devoured.
230　　Of charity,° what kin are you to me?
　　What countryman? What name? What parentage?

Viola. Of Messaline; Sebastian was my father;
　　Such a Sebastian was my brother too;
　　So went he suited° to his watery tomb.
235　　If spirits can assume both form and suit,°
　　You come to fright us.

Sebastian.　　　　　　　A spirit I am indeed,
　　But am in that dimension grossly clad
　　Which from the womb I did participate.°
　　Were you a woman, as the rest goes even,°
240　　I should my tears let fall upon your cheek
　　And say, "Thrice welcome, drownèd Viola!"

Viola. My father had a mole upon his brow.

Sebastian. And so had mine.

Viola. And died that day when Viola from her birth
245　　Had numb'red thirteen years.

Sebastian. O, that record° is lively in my soul!
　　He finishèd indeed his mortal act
　　That day that made my sister thirteen years.

Viola. If nothing lets° to make us happy both
250　　But this my masculine usurped attire,

227–28 **Nor can there be . . . everywhere** i.e., nor can I, like God, be
everywhere at once　230 **Of charity** out of simple kindness　234
suited clothed　235 **form and suit** body and clothing　237–38 **am
in that dimension . . . participate** i.e., clothed in the bodily form that,
like other mortals, I acquired at birth　239 **as the rest goes even** i.e.,
as other circumstances seem to indicate　246 **record** history (accent
on second syllable)　249 **lets** interferes

Do not embrace me till each circumstance
Of place, time, fortune do cohere and jump°
That I am Viola; which to confirm,
I'll bring you to a captain in this town,
Where lie my maiden weeds;° by whose gentle help   255
I was preserved to serve this noble Count.
All the occurrence of my fortune since
Hath been between this lady and this lord.

Sebastian. [*To Olivia*] So comes it, lady, you have
    been mistook.
But nature to her bias drew° in that.   260
You would have been contracted to a maid;
Nor are you therein, by my life, deceived:
You are betrothed both to a maid and man.

Duke. Be not amazed; right noble is his blood.
If this be so, as yet the glass° seems true,   265
I shall have share in this most happy wrack.
[*To Viola*] Boy, thou hast said to me a thousand
    times
Thou never shouldst love woman like to me.

Viola. And all those sayings will I over° swear,
And all those swearings keep as true in soul   270
As doth that orbèd continent° the fire
That severs day from night.

Duke.   Give me thy hand,
And let me see thee in thy woman's weeds.

Viola. The captain that did bring me first on shore
Hath my maid's garments. He upon some action   275
Is now in durance, at Malvolio's suit,°
A gentleman, and follower of my lady's.

Olivia. He shall enlarge° him. Fetch Malvolio hither.

252 **cohere and jump** i.e., fall together and agree   255 **weeds** clothes
260 **nature to her bias drew** i.e., nature followed her normal inclination   265 **glass** i.e., the "natural perspective" of line 217   269 **over**
repeatedly   271 **orbèd continent** in Ptolemaic astronomy, the sphere
of the sun   275–76 **He upon some action . . . Malvolio's suit** i.e.,
at Malvolio's instigation he is now imprisoned upon some legal
charge   278 **enlarge** release

And yet alas, now I remember me,
280   They say, poor gentleman, he's much distract.

Enter Clown with a letter, and Fabian.

A most extracting° frenzy of mine own
From my remembrance clearly banished his.
How does he, sirrah?

Clown. Truly, madam, he holds Belzebub at the
285   stave's end° as well as a man in his case° may do.
Has here writ a letter to you; I should have given't
you today morning. But as a madman's epistles are
no gospels, so it skills° not much when they are
delivered.

290 *Olivia.* Open't and read it.

Clown. Look then to be well edified, when the fool
delivers the madman. [*Reads in a loud voice*] "By
the Lord, madam"—

Olivia. How now? Art thou mad?

295 *Clown.* No, madam, I do but read madness. And your
ladyship will have it as it ought to be, you must
allow *vox.*°

Olivia. Prithee read i' thy right wits.

Clown. So I do, madonna; but to read his right wits is
300   to read thus. Therefore perpend,° my princess, and
give ear.

Olivia. [*To Fabian*] Read it you, sirrah.

Fabian. (*Reads*) "By the Lord, madam, you wrong
me, and the world shall know it. Though you have
305   put me into darkness, and given your drunken
cousin rule over me, yet have I the benefit of my
senses as well as your ladyship. I have your own
letter that induced me to the semblance I put on;

281 **extracting** i.e., obliterating (in that it draws me from all thoughts
of Malvolio's "frenzy")   284–85 **he holds Belzebub at the stave's
end** i.e., he keeps the fiend at a distance   285 **case** condition
288 **skills** matters   297 **vox** i.e., an appropriately loud voice   300
perpend pay attention

with the which I doubt not but to do myself much
right, or you much shame. Think of me as you   310
please. I leave my duty a little unthought of, and
speak out of my injury.

                THE MADLY USED MALVOLIO."

Olivia. Did he write this?

Clown. Ay, madam.   315

Duke. This savors not much of distraction.

Olivia. See him delivered, Fabian; bring him hither.
                                   [*Exit Fabian.*]
My lord, so please you, these things further thought
   on,
To think me as well a sister as a wife,
One day shall crown th' alliance on't, so please you,   320
Here at my house and at my proper° cost.

Duke. Madam, I am most apt° t' embrace your offer.
   [*To Viola*] Your master quits° you; and for your
     service done him,
So much against the mettle of your sex,
So far beneath your soft and tender breeding,   325
And since you called me master for so long,
Here is my hand; you shall from this time be
Your master's mistress.

Olivia.   A sister; you are she.

        Enter [*Fabian, with*] *Malvolio.*

Duke. Is this the madman?

Olivia.   Ay, my lord, this same.
How now, Malvolio?

Malvolio.   Madam, you have done me wrong,   330
Notorious° wrong.

Olivia.   Have I, Malvolio? No.

Malvolio. Lady, you have. Pray you peruse that letter.
You must not now deny it is your hand.

---

321 **proper** own   322 **apt** ready   323 **quits** releases   331 **Notorious**
notable

Write from it° if you can, in hand or phrase,
335   Or say 'tis not your seal, not your invention.°
You can say none of this. Well, grant it then,
And tell me, in the modesty of honor,°
Why you have given me such clear lights of favor,
Bade me come smiling and cross-gartered to you,
340   To put on yellow stockings, and to frown
Upon Sir Toby and the lighter° people;
And, acting this in an obedient hope,
Why have you suffered me to be imprisoned,
Kept in a dark house, visited by the priest,
345   And made the most notorious geck and gull°
That e'er invention played on? Tell me why.

Olivia. Alas, Malvolio, this is not my writing,
Though I confess much like the character;
But, out of° question, 'tis Maria's hand.
350   And now I do bethink me, it was she
First told me thou wast mad; then cam'st in smiling,
And in such forms which here were presupposed°
Upon thee in the letter. Prithee be content.
This practice hath most shrewdly passed° upon thee;
355   But when we know the grounds and authors of it,
Thou shalt be both the plaintiff and the judge
Of thine own cause.

Fabian.   Good madam, hear me speak,
And let no quarrel, nor no brawl to come,
Taint the condition of this present hour,
360   Which I have wond'red at. In hope it shall not,
Most freely I confess myself and Toby
Set this device against Malvolio here,
Upon some stubborn and uncourteous parts°
We had conceived against him. Maria writ
365   The letter, at Sir Toby's great importance,°

334 **from it** differently   335 **invention** composition   336 **in the
modesty of honor** i.e., with a proper regard to your own honor
341 **lighter** lesser   345 **geck and gull** fool and dupe   349 **out of**
beyond   352 **presupposed** imposed   354 **This practice hath most
shrewdly passed** i.e., this trick has most mischievously worked   363
Upon some stubborn and uncourteous parts i.e., because of some
unyielding and discourteous traits of character   365 **importance** im-
portunity

In recompense whereof he hath married her.
How with a sportful malice it was followed
May rather pluck on° laughter than revenge,
If that° the injuries be justly weighed
That have on both sides passed.   370

Olivia. Alas, poor fool,° how have they baffled° thee!

Clown. Why, "some are born great, some achieve
greatness, and some have greatness thrown upon
them." I was one, sir, in this interlude,° one Sir
Topas, sir; but that's all one. "By the Lord, fool, I   375
am not mad!" But do you remember, "Madam, why
laugh you at such a barren rascal? And you smile
not, he's gagged"? And thus the whirligig of time
brings in his revenges.

Malvolio. I'll be revenged on the whole pack of you!   380
                                        [*Exit.*]

Olivia. He hath been most notoriously abused.

Duke. Pursue him and entreat him to a peace.
He hath not told us of the captain yet.
When that is known, and golden time convents,°
A solemn combination shall be made   385
Of our dear souls. Meantime, sweet sister,
We will not part from hence. Cesario, come—
For so you shall be while you are a man,
But when in other habits you are seen,
Orsino's mistress and his fancy's° queen.   390
                        Exeunt [*all but the Clown*].

                    Clown sings.°

When that I was and a° little tiny boy,
    With hey, ho, the wind and the rain,
A foolish thing was but a toy,°

___

368 **pluck on** prompt 369 **If that** if 371 **fool** (here, a term of affection and compassion) 371 **baffled** publicly humiliated 374 **interlude** little play 384 **convents** is suitable (?) 390 **fancy's** love's
s.d. **Clown sings** (since no source has been found for the Clown's
song—which certain editors have inexplicably denounced as dog-
gerel—we may assume that it is Shakespeare's) 391 **and** a a
393 **toy** trifle

For the rain it raineth every day.

395 But when I came to man's estate,
  With hey, ho, the wind and the rain,
'Gainst knaves and thieves men shut their gate,
  For the rain it raineth every day.

But when I came, alas, to wive,
400 With hey, ho, the wind and the rain,
By swaggering could I never thrive,
  For the rain it raineth every day.

But when I came unto my beds,
  With hey, ho, the wind and the rain,
405 With tosspots° still had drunken heads,
  For the rain it raineth every day.

A great while ago the world begun,
  Hey, ho, the wind and the rain;
But that's all one, our play is done,
410 And we'll strive to please you every day.

[*Exit.*]

FINIS.

405 tosspots sots

Textual Note

The text of *Twelfth Night,* for which the sole source is the Folio of 1623, is, if not immaculate, so clean and tidy that it presents almost no problems. Apparently set up from the prompt copy or a transcript of it, the Folio of course contains a few misprints (like *incardinatc* for *incardinate* at V.i.182), a few presumed or obvious errors in speech-headings (like those at II.v.34, 38, where Sir Toby is perhaps confused with Fabian, or at III.iv.24, where Malvolio is assigned a speech that clearly is not his), and a few lines (for example, II.ii.12 and III.iii.15) that seem to need some sort of emendation. Moreover, the fact that the Clown is given all the lovely songs that were perhaps originally Viola's (as suggested at I.ii.57–59 and II.iv.42–43) has been cited as a token of revision. In general, however, the text, as all its editors have gratefully conceded, is one of almost unexampled purity.

In the present edition, therefore, it is followed very closely, even in such forms as *studient, jealious, wrack* (for *wreck*) and *vild,* which preserve, we may suppose, not only Shakespeare's spelling but also his pronunciation. But *prethee, divil, murther, Sathan* (for *Satan*), *Anthonio,* and *berd* (which occurs once for *beard*) are given in modern spelling. A few emendations sanctioned by long and universal approbation—like Pope's *Arion* for *Orion* at I.ii.15, Theobald's inspired *curl by* for *coole my* at I.iii.96, and Hanmer's *staniel* for *stallion* at II.v.115—have been admitted here, as have one or two superior readings from the later Folios (for example, *tang* for *langer* at III.iv.73). However, such attractive but unnecessary emendations as Pope's *south* for *sound* at I.i.5 have been rejected, and the few real cruxes have been allowed to stand, so that each reader must struggle all alone with Sir Andrew's *damned colored stock* at I.iii.132, make what he can of the mysterious Lady of the Strachy at II.v.39–40, and unravel Viola's puzzling pronouncement at II.ii.12 without the aid of emendation.

In this edition the spelling has been modernized (with the exceptions noted above), the Latin act and scene divisions of the Folio translated, the punctuation brought into conformity with modern usage, a few lines that through compositorial error were printed as prose restored to verse (IV.ii.75–76), and a few stage directions (like the one at III.iv.14) shifted to accommodate the text. At the conclusion of the first, second, and fourth acts, the Folio has *"Finis Actus . . . ,"* here omitted. All editorial interpolations such as the list of characters, indications of place, and stage directions implied by the text but not indicated in the Folio are enclosed in square brackets. Other material departures from the copy text (excluding obvious typographical errors) are listed below in italic type, followed in roman by the Folio reading. It will be apparent that most of them required no agonizing reappraisal.

I.ii.15 *Arion* Orion

I.iii.29 *all most,* almost   51 *Andrew* Ma.   96 *curl by* coole my   98 *me* we   112 *kickshawses* kicke-chawses   132 *set* sit   136 *That's* That

I.iv.28 *nuncio's* Nuntio's

I.v.146 *H'as* Ha's   165 s.d. *Viola* Uiolenta   256 *with fertile tears* fertill teares   302 *County's* Countes

II.ii.20 *That sure methought* That me thought   31 *our frailty* O frailtie   32 *of* if

II.iii.26 *leman* Lemon   35 *give a—* giue a   134–35 *a nayword* an ayword

II.iv.53 *Fly . . . fly* Fye . . . fie   55 *yew* Ew   89 *I* It   104 *know—* know.

II.v.13 *metal* Mettle 115 *staniel* stallion 144 *born* become 144 *achieve* atcheeues 159-60 *thee,* THE FORTUNATE UNHAPPY./ *Daylight* thee, tht fortunate vnhappy daylight 177 *dear* deero

III.i.8 *king lies* Kings lyes 69 *wise men* wisemens 84 *gait* gate 93 *all ready* already 114 *here* heare

III.ii.8 *see thee the* see the 70 *renegado* Renegatho

III.iv.24 *Olivia* Mal. 73 *tang* langer 94 *How is't with you, man* [The Folio assigns this speech to Fabian] 121 *Ay, biddy* I biddy 152 *Ay, is't,* I, ist? 181 *You . . . for't* Yon . . . fot't 256 *competent* computent

IV.ii.6 *in* in in 15 *Gorboduc* Gorbodacke 38 *clerestories* cleere stores 73 *sport to the* sport the

V.i.201 *pavin* panyn

The Tempest

EDITED BY
ROBERT LANGBAUM

The Scene: An uninhabited island.

Names of the Actors

Alonso, King of Naples
Sebastian, his brother
Prospero, the right Duke of Milan
Antonio, his brother, the usurping Duke of Milan
Ferdinand, son to the King of Naples
Gonzalo, an honest old councilor
Adrian and Francisco, lords
Caliban, a savage and deformed slave
Trinculo, a jester
Stephano, a drunken butler
Master of a ship
Boatswain
Mariners
Miranda, daughter to Prospero
Ariel, an airy spirit
Iris ⎫
Ceres ⎪
Juno ⎬ [presented by] spirits
Nymphs ⎪
Reapers ⎭
[Other Spirits attending on Prospero]

The Tempest

ACT I

Scene I. [*On a ship at sea.*]

A tempestuous noise of thunder and lightning heard. Enter a Shipmaster and a Boatswain.

Master. Boatswain!

Boatswain. Here, master. What cheer?

Master. Good,°1 speak to th' mariners! Fall to't yarely,° or we run ourselves aground. Bestir, bestir!
Exit.

Enter Mariners.

Boatswain. Heigh, my hearts! Cheerly, cheerly, my 5
hearts! Yare, yare! Take in the topsail! Tend to th'
master's whistle! Blow till thou burst thy wind, if
room enough!°

Enter Alonso, Sebastian, Antonio, Ferdinand, Gonzalo, and others.

Alonso. Good boatswain, have care. Where's the
master? Play the men.° 10

Boatswain. I pray now, keep below.

1 The degree sign (°) indicates a footnote, which is keyed to the text by line number. Text references are printed in *italic* type; the annotation follows in roman type.
I.i.3. *Good* good fellow   4 *yarely* briskly   7–8 *Blow till . . . room enough* the storm can blow and split itself as long as there is open sea without rocks to maneuver in   10 *Play the men* act like men

37

Antonio. Where is the master, bos'n?

Boatswain. Do you not hear him? You mar our labor. Keep your cabins; you do assist the storm.

15 *Gonzalo.* Nay, good, be patient.

Boatswain. When the sea is. Hence! What cares these roarers for the name of king? To cabin! Silence! Trouble us not!

Gonzalo. Good, yet remember whom thou hast
20   aboard.

Boatswain. None that I more love than myself. You are a councilor; if you can command these elements to silence and work the peace of the present,° we will not hand° a rope more. Use your authority.
25   If you cannot, give thanks you have lived so long, and make yourself ready in your cabin for the mischance of the hour, if it so hap. Cheerly, good hearts! Out of our way, I say.   *Exit.*

Gonzalo. I have great comfort from this fellow. Me-
30   thinks he hath no drowning mark upon him; his complexion is perfect gallows.° Stand fast, good Fate, to his hanging! Make the rope of his destiny our cable, for our own doth little advantage.° If he be not born to be hanged, our case is miserable.
                    Exit [with the rest].

Enter Boatswain.

35 *Boatswain.* Down with the topmast! Yare! Lower, lower! Bring her to try with main course!° (*A cry within.*) A plague upon this howling! They are louder than the weather or our office.°

23 *work the peace of the present* restore the present to peace (since as a councilor his job is to quell disorder)   24 *hand* handle   30–31 *no drowning mark . . . gallows* (alluding to the proverb, "He that's born to be hanged need fear no drowning")   33 *doth little advantage* gives us little advantage   36 *Bring her to try with main course* heave to, under the mainsail   37–38 *They are louder . . . office* these passengers make more noise than the tempest or than we do at our work

Enter Sebastian, Antonio, and Gonzalo.

Yet again? What do you here? Shall we give o'er°
and drown? Have you a mind to sink?   40

Sebastian. A pox o' your throat, you bawling, blas-
phemous, incharitable dog!

Boatswain. Work you, then.

Antonio. Hang, cur! Hang, you whoreson, insolent
noisemaker! We are less afraid to be drowned than   45
thou art.

Gonzalo. I'll warrant him for° drowning, though the
ship were no stronger than a nutshell and as leaky
as an unstanched° wench.

Boatswain. Lay her ahold, ahold! Set her two   50
courses!° Off to sea again! Lay her off!°

Enter Mariners wet.

Mariners. All lost! To prayers, to prayers! All lost!
                                              [*Exeunt.*]

Boatswain. What, must our mouths be cold?

Gonzalo. The King and Prince at prayers! Let's assist
them,
For our case is as theirs.

Sebastian.   I am out of patience.   55

Antonio. We are merely° cheated of our lives by
drunkards.
This wide-chopped° rascal—would thou mightst lie
drowning
The washing of ten tides!°

39 *give o'er* give up trying to run the ship   47 *warrant him for*
guarantee him against   49 *unstanched* wide-open   50–51 *Lay her
ahold. . . . courses* (the ship is still being blown dangerously to shore,
so the boatswain orders that the foresail be set in addition to the
mainsail; but the ship still moves toward shore)   51 *Lay her off* i.e.,
away from the shore   56 *merely* completely   57 *wide-chopped* big-
mouthed   58 *ten tides* (pirates were hanged on the shore and left
there until three tides had washed over them)

Gonzalo.   He'll be hanged yet,
Though every drop of water swear against it
And gape at wid'st to glut him.

60   *A confused noise within:* "Mercy on us!"
"We split, we split!" "Farewell, my wife and chil-
     dren!"
"Farewell, brother!" "We split, we split, we split!"
                         [*Exit Boatswain.*]

Antonio. Let's all sink wi' th' King.

Sebastian.   Let's take leave of him.
                         Exit [*with Antonio*].

Gonzalo. Now would I give a thousand furlongs of
65   sea for an acre of barren ground—long heath,°
brown furze, anything. The wills above be done,
but I would fain die a dry death.   *Exit.*

Scene II. [*The island. In front of Prospero's cell.*]

Enter Prospero and Miranda.

Miranda. If by your art, my dearest father, you have
Put the wild waters in this roar, allay them.
The sky, it seems, would pour down stinking pitch
But that the sea, mounting to th' welkin's cheek,°
5   Dashes the fire out. O, I have suffered
With those that I saw suffer! A brave° vessel
(Who had no doubt some noble creature in her)
Dashed all to pieces! O, the cry did knock

65 *heath* heather   I.ii.4 *welkin's cheek* face of the sky   6 *brave* fine,
gallant (the word often has this meaning in the play)

 Against my very heart! Poor souls, they perished!
 Had I been any god of power, I would   10
 Have sunk the sea within the earth or ere
 It should the good ship so have swallowed and
 The fraughting° souls within her.

Prospero.   Be collected.
 No more amazement.° Tell your piteous heart
 There's no harm done.

Miranda.   O, woe the day!

Prospero.   No harm. 15
 I have done nothing but in care of thee,
 Of thee my dear one, thee my daughter, who
 Art ignorant of what thou art, naught knowing
 Of whence I am, nor that I am more better
 Than Prospero, master of a full poor cell,   20
 And thy no greater father.°

Miranda.   More to know
 Did never meddle° with my thoughts.

Prospero.   'Tis time
 I should inform thee farther. Lend thy hand
 And pluck my magic garment from me. So.
        [Lays down his robe.]
 Lie there, my art. Wipe thou thine eyes; have
  comfort.   25
 The direful spectacle of the wrack, which touched
 The very virtue° of compassion in thee,
 I have with such provision° in mine art
 So safely ordered that there is no soul—
 No, not so much perdition° as an hair   30
 Betid° to any creature in the vessel
 Which thou heard'st cry, which thou saw'st sink.
  Sit down;
 For thou must now know farther.

---

13 *fraughting* forming her freight 14 *amazement* consternation
21 *thy no greater father* i.e., thy father, no greater than the Prospero
just described 22 *meddle* mingle 27 *virtue* essence 28 *provision*
foresight 30 *perdition* loss 31 *Betid* happened

Miranda.   You have often
   Begun to tell me what I am; but stopped
35 And left me to a bootless inquisition,
   Concluding, "Stay; not yet."

Prospero.   The hour's now come;
   The very minute bids thee ope thine ear.
   Obey, and be attentive. Canst thou remember
   A time before we came unto this cell?
40 I do not think thou canst, for then thou wast not
   Out° three years old.

Miranda.   Certainly, sir, I can.

Prospero. By what? By any other house or person?
   Of anything the image tell me that
   Hath kept with thy remembrance.

Miranda.   'Tis far off,
45 And rather like a dream than an assurance
   That my remembrance warrants.° Had I not
   Four or five women once that tended me?

Prospero. Thou hadst, and more, Miranda. But how
      is it
   That this lives in thy mind? What seest thou else
50 In the dark backward and abysm of time?
   If thou rememb'rest aught ere thou cam'st here,
   How thou cam'st here thou mayst.

Miranda.   But that I do not.

Prospero. Twelve year since, Miranda, twelve year
      since,
   Thy father was the Duke of Milan° and
   A prince of power.

55 *Miranda.*   Sir, are not you my father?

Prospero. Thy mother was a piece° of virtue, and
   She said thou wast my daughter; and thy father
   Was Duke of Milan; and his only heir

41 *Out* fully   46 *remembrance warrants* memory guarantees   54
Milan (pronounced "Mílan")   56 *piece* masterpiece

And princess, no worse issued.°

Miranda.   O the heavens!
What foul play had we that we came from thence?   60
Or blessèd was't we did?

Prospero.   Both, both, my girl!
By foul play, as thou say'st, were we heaved thence,
But blessedly holp° hither.

Miranda.   O, my heart bleeds
To think o' th' teen that I have turned you to,°
Which is from° my remembrance! Please you,
     farther.   65

Prospero. My brother and thy uncle, called
     Antonio—
I pray thee mark me—that a brother should
Be so perfidious!—he whom next thyself
Of all the world I loved, and to him put
The manage of my state,° as at that time   70
Through all the signories° it was the first,
And Prospero the prime duke, being so reputed
In dignity, and for the liberal arts
Without a parallel. Those being all my study,
The government I cast upon my brother   75
And to my state grew stranger, being transported
And rapt in secret studies. Thy false uncle—
Dost thou attend me?

Miranda.   Sir, most heedfully.

Prospero. Being once perfected° how to grant suits,
How to deny them, who t' advance, and who   80
To trash for overtopping,° new-created
The creatures that were mine, I say—or changed
     'em,

59 *no worse issued* of no meaner lineage than he   63 *holp* helped
64 *teen that I have turned you to* sorrow I have caused you to remember   65 *from* out of   70 *manage of my state* management of
my domain   71 *signories* lordships (of Italy)   79 *perfected* grown
skillful   81 *trash for overtopping* (1) check the speed of (as of
hounds) (2) cut down to size (as of overtall trees) the aspirants
for political favor who are growing too bold

Or else new-formed 'em°——having both the key°
Of officer and office, set all hearts i' th' state
85   To what tune pleased his ear, that now he was
The ivy which had hid my princely trunk
And sucked my verdure out on't. Thou attend'st
   not?

Miranda. O, good sir, I do.

Prospero.   I pray thee mark me.
I thus neglecting worldly ends, all dedicated
90   To closeness° and the bettering of my mind—
With that which, but by being so retired,
O'erprized all popular rate, in my false brother
Awaked an evil nature,° and my trust,
Like a good parent,° did beget of him
95   A falsehood in its contrary as great
As my trust was, which had indeed no limit,
A confidence sans bound. He being thus lorded—
Not only with what my revenue° yielded
But what my power might else exact, like one
100 Who having into truth—by telling of it,°
Made such a sinner of his memory
To° credit his own lie, he did believe
He was indeed the Duke, out o' th' substitution
And executing th' outward face of royalty
With all prerogative.° Hence his ambition
105   growing—
Dost thou hear?

81–83 *new-created/The creatures . . . new-formed 'em* i.e., he re-
created my following—either exchanging my adherents for his
own, or else transforming my adherents into different people
83 *key* (a pun leading to the musical metaphor)   90 *closeness* se-
clusion   91–93 *With that . . . evil nature* i.e., with that dedication
to the mind which, were it not that it kept me from exercising the
duties of my office would surpass in value all ordinary estimate, I
awakened evil in my brother's nature   94 *good parent* (alluding to
the proverb cited by Miranda in line 120)   98 *revenue* (pronounced
"revènue")   99–100 *like one/Who having . . . of it* i.e., like one
who really had these things—by repeatedly saying he had them
(*into* = unto)   102 *To* as to   103–05 *out o' th' substitution . . .
all prerogative* i.e., as a result of his acting as my substitute and per-
forming the outward functions of royalty with all its prerogatives

Miranda.   Your tale, sir, would cure deafness.

Prospero. To have no screen between this part he
       played
   And him he played it for, he needs will be
   Absolute Milan.° Me (poor man) my library
   Was dukedom large enough. Of temporal royalties   *110*
   He thinks me now incapable; confederates
   (So dry° he was for sway) wi' th' King of Naples
   To give him annual tribute, do him homage,
   Subject his coronet to his crown, and bend
   The dukedom, yet unbowed (alas, poor Milan!),   *115*
   To most ignoble stooping.

Miranda.   O the heavens!

Prospero. Mark his condition,° and th' event;° then
       tell me
   If this might be a brother.

Miranda.   I should sin
   To think but nobly of my grandmother.
   Good wombs have borne bad sons.

Prospero.   Now the condition.   *120*
   This King of Naples, being an enemy
   To me inveterate, hearkens my brother's suit;
   Which was, that he, in lieu o' th' premises°
   Of homage and I know not how much tribute,
   Should presently extirpate me and mine   *125*
   Out of the dukedom and confer fair Milan,
   With all the honors, on my brother. Whereon,
   A treacherous army levied, one midnight
   Fated to th' purpose, did Antonio open
   The gates of Milan; and, i' th' dead of darkness,   *130*
   The ministers° for th' purpose hurried thence
   Me and thy crying self.

Miranda.   Alack, for pity!

109 *Absolute Milan* Duke of Milan in fact   112 *dry* thirsty
117 *condition* terms of his pact with Naples   117 *event* outcome
123 *in lieu o' th' premises* in return for the guarantees   131 *ministers* agents

I, not rememb'ring how I cried out then,
Will cry it o'er again; it is a hint°
That wrings mine eyes to't.

135 *Prospero.*   Hear a little further,
And then I'll bring thee to the present business
Which now's upon's; without the which this story
Were most impertinent.°

Miranda.   Wherefore did they not
That hour destroy us?

Prospero.   Well demanded, wench.
My tale provokes that question. Dear, they durst
140   not,
So dear the love my people bore me; nor set
A mark so bloody on the business; but,
With colors fairer, painted their foul ends.
In few,° they hurried us aboard a bark;
145 Bore us some leagues to sea, where they prepared
A rotten carcass of a butt,° not rigged,
Nor tackle, sail, nor mast; the very rats
Instinctively have quit it. There they hoist us,
To cry to th' sea that roared to us; to sigh
150 To th' winds, whose pity, sighing back again,
Did us but loving wrong.

Miranda.   Alack, what trouble
Was I then to you!

Prospero.   O, a cherubin
Thou wast that did preserve me! Thou didst smile,
Infusèd with a fortitude from heaven,
155 When I have decked° the sea with drops full salt,
Under my burden groaned; which° raised in me
An undergoing stomach,° to bear up
Against what should ensue.
Miranda.   How came we ashore?

---

134 *hint* occasion 138 *impertinent* inappropriate 144 *few* few
words 146 *butt* tub 155 *decked* covered (wept salt tears into the
sea) 156 *which* i.e., Miranda's smile 157 *undergoing stomach*
spirit of endurance

Prospero. By providence divine.
Some food we had, and some fresh water, that   *160*
A noble Neapolitan, Gonzalo,
Out of his charity, who being then appointed
Master of this design, did give us, with
Rich garments, linens, stuffs, and necessaries
Which since have steaded° much. So, of his gentle-
          ness,   *165*
Knowing I loved my books, he furnished me
From mine own library with volumes that
I prize above my dukedom.

Miranda.   Would I might
But ever see that man!

Prospero.   Now I arise.
Sit still, and hear the last of our sea sorrow.   *170*
Here in this island we arrived; and here
Have I, thy schoolmaster, made thee more profit
Than other princess' can,° that have more time
For vainer hours, and tutors not so careful.

Miranda. Heavens thank you for't! And now I pray
          you, sir—   *175*
For still 'tis beating in my mind—your reason
For raising this sea storm?

Prospero.   Know thus far forth.
By accident most strange, bountiful Fortune
(Now my dear lady)° hath mine enemies
Brought to this shore; and by my prescience   *180*
I find my zenith° doth depend upon
A most auspicious star, whose influence
If now I court not, but omit,° my fortunes
Will ever after droop. Here cease more questions.
Thou art inclined to sleep. 'Tis a good dullness,   *185*
And give it way. I know thou canst not choose.
                              [*Miranda sleeps.*]

165 *steaded* been of use   173 *princess' can* princesses can have
179 *Now my dear lady* i.e., formerly my foe, now my patroness
181 *zenith* apex of fortune   183 *omit* neglect

Come away,° servant, come! I am ready now.
Approach, my Ariel! Come!

Enter Ariel.

Ariel. All hail, great master! Grave sir, hail! I come
190 To answer thy best pleasure; be't to fly,
To swim, to dive into the fire, to ride
On the curled clouds. To thy strong bidding task°
Ariel and all his quality.°

Prospero.   Hast thou, spirit,
Performed, to point,° the tempest that I bade thee?

195 *Ariel.* To every article.
I boarded the King's ship. Now on the beak,°
Now in the waist,° the deck,° in every cabin,
I flamed amazement.° Sometime I'd divide
And burn in many places; on the topmast,
200 The yards, and boresprit° would I flame distinctly,°
Then meet and join. Jove's lightnings, the precursors
O' th' dreadful thunderclaps, more momentary
And sight-outrunning were not. The fire and cracks
Of sulfurous roaring the most mighty Neptune
205 Seem to besiege, and make his bold waves tremble;
Yea, his dread trident shake.

Prospero.   My brave spirit!
Who was so firm, so constant, that this coil°
Would not infect his reason?

Ariel.   Not a soul
But felt a fever of the mad and played
210 Some tricks of desperation. All but mariners
Plunged in the foaming brine and quit the vessel,
Then all afire with me. The King's son Ferdinand,

---

187 *Come away* i.e., come from where you are; come here   192 *task*
tax to the utmost   193 *quality* cohorts (Ariel is leader of a band of
spirits)   194 *to point* in every detail   196 *beak* prow   197 *waist*
amidships   197 *deck* poop   198 *flamed amazement* struck terror
by appearing as (St. Elmo's) fire   200 *boresprit* bowsprit   200 *distinctly* in different places   207 *coil* uproar

With hair up-staring° (then like reeds, not hair),
Was the first man that leapt; cried "Hell is empty,
And all the devils are here!"

Prospero.   Why, that's my spirit! 215
But was not this nigh shore?

Ariel.   Close by, my master.

Prospero. But are they, Ariel, safe?

Ariel.   Not a hair perished.
On their sustaining° garments not a blemish,
But fresher than before; and as thou bad'st me,
In troops I have dispersed them 'bout the isle.   220
The King's son have I landed by himself,
Whom I left cooling of the air with sighs
In an odd angle of the isle, and sitting,
His arms in this sad knot.
                         [*Illustrates with a gesture.*]

Prospero.   Of the King's ship,
The mariners, say how thou hast disposed,   225
And all the rest o' th' fleet.

Ariel.   Safely in harbor
Is the King's ship; in the deep nook where once
Thou call'dst me up at midnight to fetch dew
From the still-vexed Bermoothes,° there she's hid;
The mariners all under hatches stowed,   230
Who, with a charm joined to their suff'red° labor,
I have left asleep. And for the rest o' th' fleet,
Which I dispersed, they all have met again,
And are upon the Mediterranean flote°
Bound sadly home for Naples,   235
Supposing that they saw the King's ship wracked
And his great person perish.

Prospero.   Ariel, thy charge
Exactly is performed; but there's more work.

213 *up-staring* standing on end 218 *sustaining* buoying them up
229 *Bermoothes* Bermudas 231 *suff'red* undergone 234 *flote* sea

What is the time o' th' day?

Ariel.   Past the mid season.°

Prospero. At least two glasses.° The time 'twixt six
240   and now
Must by us both be spent most preciously.

Ariel. Is there more toil? Since thou dost give me
pains,°
Let me remember° thee what thou hast promised,
Which is not yet performed me.

Prospero.   How now? Moody?
What is't thou canst demand?

245 *Ariel.*   My liberty.

Prospero. Before the time be out? No more!

Ariel.   I prithee,
Remember I have done thee worthy service,
Told thee no lies, made thee no mistakings, served
Without or grudge or grumblings. Thou did
promise
To bate me° a full year.

250 *Prospero.*   Dost thou forget
From what a torment I did free thee?

Ariel.   No.

Prospero. Thou dost; and think'st it much to tread
the ooze
Of the salt deep,
To run upon the sharp wind of the North,
255   To do me business in the veins° o' th' earth
When it is baked° with frost.

Ariel.   I do not, sir.

Prospero. Thou liest, malignant thing! Hast thou
forgot

239 *mid season* noon   240 *two glasses* two o'clock   242 *pains* hard
tasks   243 *remember* remind   250 *bate me* reduce my term of
service   255 *veins* streams   256 *baked* caked

The foul witch Sycorax,° who with age and envy°
Was grown into a hoop? Hast thou forgot her?

Ariel. No, sir.

Prospero.   Thou hast. Where was she born? Speak!
Tell me!   260

Ariel. Sir, in Argier.°

Prospero.   O, was she so? I must
Once in a month recount what thou hast been,
Which thou forget'st. This damned witch Sycorax,
For mischiefs manifold, and sorceries terrible
To enter human hearing, from Argier,   265
Thou know'st, was banished. For one thing she did
They would not take her life. Is not this true?

Ariel. Ay, sir.

Prospero. This blue-eyed° hag was hither brought
with child
And here was left by th' sailors. Thou, my slave,   270
As thou report'st thyself, wast then her servant.
And, for thou wast a spirit too delicate
To act her earthy and abhorred commands,
Refusing her grand hests,° she did confine thee,
By help of her more potent ministers,°   275
And in her most unmitigable rage,
Into a cloven pine; within which rift
Imprisoned thou didst painfully remain
A dozen years; within which space she died
And left thee there, where thou didst vent thy
groans   280
As fast as millwheels strike. Then was this island
(Save for the son that she did litter here,
A freckled whelp, hagborn) not honored with
A human shape.

258 *Sycorax* (name not found elsewhere; probably derived from
Greek *sys*, "sow," and *korax*, which means both "raven"—see line
322—and "hook"—hence perhaps "hoop")   258 *envy* malice   261
Argier Algiers   269 *blue-eyed* (referring to the livid color of the
eyelid, a sign of pregnancy)   274 *hests* commands   275 *her more
potent ministers* her agents, spirits more powerful than thou

Ariel.   Yes, Caliban her son.

285 *Prospero.* Dull thing, I say so! He, that Caliban
        Whom now I keep in service. Thou best know'st
        What torment I did find thee in; thy groans
        Did make wolves howl and penetrate the breasts
        Of ever-angry bears. It was a torment
290   To lay upon the damned, which Sycorax
        Could not again undo. It was mine art,
        When I arrived and heard thee, that made gape
        The pine, and let thee out.

Ariel.   I thank thee, master.

Prospero. If thou more murmur'st, I will rend an oak
295   And peg thee in his° knotty entrails till
        Thou hast howled away twelve winters.

Ariel.   Pardon, master.
        I will be correspondent° to command
        And do my spriting gently.°

Prospero.   Do so; and after two days
        I will discharge thee.

Ariel.   That's my noble master!
300   What shall I do? Say what? What shall I do?

Prospero. Go make thyself like a nymph o' th' sea. Be
        subject
        To no sight but thine and mine, invisible
        To every eyeball else.° Go take this shape
        And hither come in't. Go! Hence with diligence!
                                Exit [Ariel].
305   Awake, dear heart, awake! Thou hast slept well.
        Awake!

Miranda. The strangeness of your story put
        Heaviness in me.

295 *his* its   297 *correspondent* obedient   298 *do my spriting gently*
render graciously my services as a spirit   302–03 *invisible/To
every eyeball else* (Ariel is invisible to everyone in the play except
Prospero; Henslowe's *Diary*, an Elizabethan stage account, lists
"a robe for to go invisible")

Prospero.   Shake it off. Come on.
  We'll visit Caliban, my slave, who never
  Yields us kind answer.

Miranda.   'Tis a villain, sir,
  I do not love to look on.

Prospero.   But as 'tis,   310
  We cannot miss° him. He does make our fire,
  Fetch in our wood, and serves in offices
  That profit us. What, ho! Slave! Caliban!
  Thou earth, thou! Speak!

Caliban. (*Within*)   There's wood enough within.

Prospero. Come forth, I say! There's other business   315
     for thee.
  Come, thou tortoise! When?°

             Enter Ariel like a water nymph.

  Fine apparition! My quaint° Ariel,
  Hark in thine ear.   [*Whispers.*]

Ariel.   My lord, it shall be done. *Exit.*

Prospero. Thou poisonous slave, got by the devil
     himself
  Upon thy wicked dam, come forth!   320

                    Enter Caliban.

Caliban. As wicked dew as e'er my mother brushed
  With raven's feather from unwholesome fen
  Drop on you both! A southwest blow on ye
  And blister you all o'er!

Prospero. For this, be sure, tonight thou shalt have
     cramps,   325
  Side-stitches that shall pen thy breath up. Urchins°
  Shall, for that vast of night that they may work,°

311 *miss* do without   316 *When* (expression of impatience)   317
quaint ingenious   326 *Urchins* goblins in the shape of hedgehogs
327 *vast of night . . . work* (the long, empty stretch of night during
which malignant spirits are allowed to be active)

All exercise on thee; thou shalt be pinched
As thick as honeycomb, each pinch more stinging
Than bees that made 'em.

330 *Caliban.*   I must eat my dinner.
This island's mine by Sycorax my mother,
Which thou tak'st from me. When thou cam'st first,
Thou strok'st me and made much of me; wouldst
     give me
Water with berries in't; and teach me how
335 To name the bigger light, and how the less,
That burn by day and night. And then I loved thee
And showed thee all the qualities o' th' isle,
The fresh springs, brine pits, barren place and
     fertile.
Cursed be I that did so! All the charms
340 Of Sycorax—toads, beetles, bats, light on you!
For I am all the subjects that you have,
Which first was mine own king; and here you sty
     me
In this hard rock, whiles you do keep from me
The rest o' th' island.

Prospero.   Thou most lying slave,
Whom stripes° may move, not kindness! I have
345   used thee
(Filth as thou art) with humane care, and lodged
     thee
In mine own cell till thou didst seek to violate
The honor of my child.

Caliban. O ho, O ho! Would't had been done!
350 Thou didst prevent me; I had peopled else
This isle with Calibans.

Miranda.°   Abhorrèd slave,
Which any print of goodness wilt not take,
Being capable of all ill!° I pitied thee,

---

345 *stripes* lashes   351 (many editors transfer this speech to Prospero as inappropriate to Miranda)   353 *capable of all ill* susceptible only to evil impressions

Took pains to make thee speak, taught thee each
hour
One thing or other. When thou didst not, savage,   355
Know thine own meaning, but wouldst gabble like
A thing most brutish, I endowed thy purposes
With words that made them known. But thy vile
race,
Though thou didst learn, had that in't which good
natures
Could not abide to be with. Therefore wast thou   360
Deservedly confined into this rock, who hadst
Deserved more than a prison.

Caliban. You taught me language, and my profit on't
Is, I know how to curse. The red plague rid° you
For learning me your language!

Prospero.   Hagseed, hence!   365
Fetch us in fuel. And be quick, thou'rt best,°
To answer other business. Shrug'st thou, malice?
If thou neglect'st or dost unwillingly
What I command, I'll rack thee with old° cramps,
Fill all thy bones with aches,° make thee roar   370
That beasts shall tremble at thy din.

Caliban.   No, pray thee.
[*Aside*] I must obey. His art is of such pow'r
It would control my dam's god, Setebos,
And make a vassal of him.

Prospero.   So, slave; hence!   *Exit Caliban.*

*Enter Ferdinand; and Ariel (invisible), playing
    and singing.*

Ariel's song.

Come unto these yellow sands,   375

364 *rid* destroy   366 *thou'rt best* you'd better   369 *old* plenty of
(with an additional suggestion, "such as old people have")   370
aches (pronounced "aitches")

And then take hands.
Curtsied when you have and kissed
    The wild waves whist,°
Foot it featly° here and there;
And, sweet sprites, the burden bear.
    Hark, hark!
        Burden, dispersedly.° Bow, wow!
    The watchdogs bark.
        [*Burden, dispersedly.*] Bow, wow!
    Hark, hark! I hear
    The strain of strutting chanticleer
        Cry cock-a-diddle-dow.

Ferdinand. Where should this music be? I' th' air or
    th' earth?
It sounds no more; and sure it waits upon
Some god o' th' island. Sitting on a bank,
Weeping again the King my father's wrack,
This music crept by me upon the waters,
Allaying both their fury and my passion°
With its sweet air. Thence I have followed it,
Or it hath drawn me rather; but 'tis gone.
No, it begins again.

Ariel's song.

Full fathom five thy father lies;
    Of his bones are coral made;
Those are pearls that were his eyes;
    Nothing of him that doth fade
But doth suffer a sea change
Into something rich and strange.
Sea nymphs hourly ring his knell:
        Burden. Ding-dong.
    Hark! Now I hear them—ding-dong bell.

377–78 *kissed/The wild waves whist* i.e., when you have, through
the harmony of kissing in the dance, kissed the wild waves into
silence (?); when you have kissed in the dance, the wild waves being
silenced (?)   379 *featly* nimbly   382 *Burden, dispersedly* (an un-
dersong, coming from all parts of the stage; it imitates the barking
of dogs and perhaps in the end the crowing of a cock)   393 *passion*
grief

Ferdinand. The ditty does remember my drowned
    father.
  This is no mortal business, nor no sound
  That the earth owes.° I hear it now above me.

Prospero. The fringèd curtains of thine eye advance°
  And say what thou seest yond.

Miranda.   What is't? A spirit? *410*
  Lord, how it looks about! Believe me, sir,
  It carries a brave form. But 'tis a spirit.

Prospero. No, wench; it eats, and sleeps, and hath
    such senses
  As we have, such. This gallant which thou seest
  Was in the wrack; and, but he's something stained *415*
  With grief (that's beauty's canker), thou mightst
    call him
  A goodly person. He hath lost his fellows
  And strays about to find 'em.

Miranda.   I might call him
  A thing divine; for nothing natural
  I ever saw so noble.

Prospero.   [*Aside*] It goes on, I see,   *420*
  As my soul prompts it. Spirit, fine spirit, I'll free
    thee
  Within two days for this.

Ferdinand.   Most sure, the goddess
  On whom these airs attend! Vouchsafe my prayer
  May know if you remain° upon this island,
  And that you will some good instruction give   *425*
  How I may bear me° here. My prime request,
  Which I do last pronounce, is (O you wonder!)
  If you be maid or no?

Miranda.   No wonder, sir,
  But certainly a maid.

---

408 *owes* owns   409 *advance* raise   423–24 *Vouchsafe my prayer
. . . remain* may my prayer induce you to inform me whether you
dwell   426 *bear me* conduct myself

Ferdinand.   My language? Heavens!
430   I am the best of them that speak this speech,
      Were I but where 'tis spoken.

Prospero.   How? The best?
      What wert thou if the King of Naples heard thee?

Ferdinand. A single° thing, as I am now, that won-
      ders
      To hear thee speak of Naples. He does hear me;
435   And that he does I weep. Myself am Naples,
      Who with mine eyes, never since at ebb, beheld
      The King my father wracked.

Miranda.   Alack, for mercy!

Ferdinand. Yes, faith, and all his lords, the Duke of
      Milan
      And his brave son° being twain.°

Prospero.   [*Aside*] The Duke of Milan
440   And his more braver daughter could control° thee,
      If now 'twere fit to do't. At the first sight
      They have changed eyes.° Delicate Ariel,
      I'll set thee free for this. [*To Ferdinand*] A word,
      good sir.
      I fear you have done yourself some wrong.° A
      word!

445   *Miranda.* Why speaks my father so ungently? This
      Is the third man that e'er I saw; the first
      That e'er I sighed for. Pity move my father
      To be inclined my way!

Ferdinand.   O, if a virgin,
      And your affection not gone forth, I'll make you
      The Queen of Naples.

450   *Prospero.*   Soft, sir! One word more.
      [*Aside*] They are both in either's pow'rs. But this
      swift business

433 *single* (1) solitary (2) helpless   439 *son* (the only time Antonio's son is mentioned)   439 *twain* two (of these lords)   440
control refute   442 *changed eyes* i.e., fallen in love   444 *done*
yourself some wrong said what is not so

I must uneasy make, lest too light winning
Make the prize light. [*To Ferdinand*] One word
   more! I charge thee
That thou attend me. Thou dost here usurp
The name thou ow'st° not, and hast put thyself   455
Upon this island as a spy, to win it
From me, the lord on't.

Ferdinand.   No, as I am a man!

Miranda. There's nothing ill can dwell in such a
   temple.
If the ill spirit have so fair a house,
Good things will strive to dwell with't.

Prospero.   Follow me.   460
[*To Miranda*] Speak not you for him; he's a traitor.
[*To Ferdinand*] Come!
I'll manacle thy neck and feet together;
Sea water shalt thou drink; thy food shall be
The fresh-brook mussels, withered roots, and husks
Wherein the acorn cradled. Follow!

Ferdinand.   No.   465
I will resist such entertainment till
Mine enemy has more pow'r.
       He draws, and is charmed from moving.

Miranda.   O dear father,
Make not too rash a trial of him, for
He's gentle and not fearful.°

Prospero.   What, I say,
My foot my tutor?° [*To Ferdinand*] Put thy sword
   up, traitor—   470
Who mak'st a show but dar'st not strike, thy con-
   science
Is so possessed with guilt! Come, from thy ward!°
For I can here disarm thee with this stick°
And make thy weapon drop.

---

455 *ow'st* ownest   469 *gentle and not fearful* of noble birth and
no coward   470 *My foot my tutor* am I to be instructed by my inferior   472 *ward* fighting posture   473 *stick* i.e., his wand

Miranda.   Beseech you, father!

Prospero. Hence! Hang not on my garments.

475 *Miranda.*   Sir, have pity.
    I'll be his surety.

Prospero.   Silence! One word more
    Shall make me chide thee, if not hate thee. What,
    An advocate for an impostor? Hush!
    Thou think'st there is no more such shapes as he,
480   Having seen but him and Caliban. Foolish wench!
    To th' most of men this is a Caliban,
    And they to him are angels.

Miranda.   My affections
    Are then most humble. I have no ambition
    To see a goodlier man.

Prospero. [*To Ferdinand*] Come on, obey!
485   Thy nerves° are in their infancy again
    And have no vigor in them.

Ferdinand.   So they are.
    My spirits, as in a dream, are all bound up.
    My father's loss, the weakness which I feel,
    The wrack of all my friends, nor this man's threats
490   To whom I am subdued, are but light to me,
    Might I but through my prison once a day
    Behold this maid. All corners else o' th' earth
    Let liberty make use of. Space enough
    Have I in such a prison.

Prospero. [*Aside*] It works. [*To Ferdinand*] Come on.
    [*To Ariel*] Thou hast done well, fine Ariel! [*To*
495   *Ferdinand*] Follow me.
    [*To Ariel*] Hark what thou else shalt do me.

Miranda.   Be of comfort.
    My father's of a better nature, sir,
    Than he appears by speech. This is unwonted
    Which now came from him.

'85 *nerves* sinews

Prospero.   Thou shalt be as free
    As mountain winds; but then° exactly do   *500*
    All points of my command.

Ariel.   To th' syllable.

Prospero. [*To Ferdinand*] Come, follow. [*To Mi-
    randa*] Speak not for him.   *Exeunt.*

ACT II

Scene I. [*Another part of the island.*]

*Enter Alonso, Sebastian, Antonio, Gonzalo,
    Adrian, Francisco, and others.*

Gonzalo. Beseech you, sir, be merry. You have cause
    (So have we all) of joy; for our escape
    Is much beyond our loss. Our hint of° woe
    Is common; every day some sailor's wife,
    The master of some merchant,° and the merchant,   *5*
    Have just our theme of woe. But for the miracle,
    I mean our preservation, few in millions
    Can speak like us. Then wisely, good sir, weigh
    Our sorrow with° our comfort.

Alonso.   Prithee, peace.

Sebastian. [*Aside to Antonio*] He receives comfort   *10*
    like cold porridge.°

Antonio. [*Aside to Sebastian*] The visitor° will not
    give him o'er so.°

Sebastian. Look, he's winding up the watch of his
    wit; by and by it will strike.   *15*

500 *then* till then II.i.3 *hint of* occasion for 5 *master of some
merchant* captain of some merchant ship 9 *with* against 10-11 *He
receives comfort like cold porridge* ("He" is Alonso; pun on
"peace," since porridge contained peas) 12 *visitor* spiritual comforter 13 *give him o'er so* release him so easily

Gonzalo. Sir—

Sebastian. [*Aside to Antonio*] One. Tell.°

Gonzalo. When every grief is entertained, that's°
   offered
   Comes to th' entertainer—

20 *Sebastian.* A dollar.

Gonzalo. Dolor comes to him, indeed. You have
   spoken truer than you purposed.

Sebastian. You have taken it wiselier° than I meant
   you should.

25 *Gonzalo.* Therefore, my lord—

Antonio. Fie, what a spendthrift is he of his tongue!

Alonso. I prithee, spare.°

Gonzalo. Well, I have done. But yet—

Sebastian. He will be talking.

30 *Antonio.* Which, of he or Adrian, for a good wager,
   first° begins to crow?

Sebastian. The old cock.°

Antonio. The cock'rel.°

Sebastian. Done! The wager?

35 *Antonio.* A laughter.°

Sebastian. A match!

Adrian. Though this island seem to be desert—

Antonio. Ha, ha, ha!

Sebastian. So, you're paid.

17 *One. Tell* he has struck one; keep count   18 *that's* that which is
23 *wiselier* i.e., understood my pun   27 *spare* spare your words
30-31 *Which, of he or Adrian . . . first* let's wager which of the two,
Gonzalo or Adrian, will first   32 *old cock* i.e., Gonzalo   33
cock'rel young cock; i.e., Adrian   35 *laughter* the winner will have
the laugh on the loser

Adrian. Uninhabitable and almost inaccessible—   40

Sebastian. Yet—

Adrian. Yet—

Antonio. He could not miss't.

Adrian. It must needs be of subtle, tender, and delicate temperance.°   45

Antonio. Temperance was a delicate wench.

Sebastian. Ay, and a subtle, as he most learnedly delivered.

Adrian. The air breathes upon us here most sweetly.

Sebastian. As if it had lungs, and rotten ones.   50

Antonio. Or as 'twere perfumed by a fen.

Gonzalo. Here is everything advantageous to life.

Antonio. True; save means to live.

Sebastian. Of that there's none, or little.

Gonzalo. How lush and lusty the grass looks! How   55
green!

Antonio. The ground indeed is tawny.

Sebastian. With an eye° of green in't.

Antonio. He misses not much.

Sebastian. No; he doth but mistake the truth totally.   60

Gonzalo. But the rarity of it is—which is indeed almost beyond credit—

Sebastian. As many vouched rarities are.

Gonzalo. That our garments, being, as they were, drenched in the sea, hold, notwithstanding, their   65
freshness and glosses, being rather new-dyed than stained with salt water.

45 *temperance* climate (in the next line, a girl's name)   58 *eye*
spot (also perhaps Gonzalo's eye)

Antonio. If but one of his pockets could speak, would it not say he lies?°

70 *Sebastian.* Ay, or very falsely pocket up his report.°

Gonzalo. Methinks our garments are now as fresh as when we put them on first in Afric, at the marriage of the King's fair daughter Claribel to the King of Tunis.

75 *Sebastian.* 'Twas a sweet marriage, and we prosper well in our return.

Adrian. Tunis was never graced before with such a paragon to° their queen.

Gonzalo. Not since widow Dido's time.

80 *Antonio.* Widow? A pox o' that! How came that "widow" in? Widow Dido!

Sebastian. What if he had said "widower Aeneas"° too? Good Lord, how you take it!

Adrian. "Widow Dido," said you? You make me
85 study of that. She was of Carthage, not of Tunis.

Gonzalo. This Tunis, sir, was Carthage.

Adrian. Carthage?

Gonzalo. I assure you, Carthage.

Antonio. His word is more than the miraculous
90 harp.°

Sebastian. He hath raised the wall and houses too.

Antonio. What impossible matter will he make easy next?

68–69 *If but . . . he lies* i.e., the inside of Gonzalo's pockets are stained   70 *Ay, or . . . his report* unless the pocket were, like a false knave, to receive without resentment the imputation that it is unstained   78 *to* for   81–82 *Widow Dido . . . "widower Aeneas"* (the point of the joke is that Dido was a widow, but one doesn't ordinarily think of her that way; and the same with Aeneas)   89–90 *miraculous harp* (of Amphion, which only raised the *walls* of Thebes; whereas Gonzalo has rebuilt the whole ancient city of Carthage by identifying it mistakenly with modern Tunis)

Sebastian. I think he will carry this island home in his
    pocket and give it his son for an apple.   *95*

Antonio. And, sowing the kernels of it in the sea,
    bring forth more islands.

Gonzalo. Ay!

Antonio. Why, in good time.°

Gonzalo. [*To Alonso*] Sir, we were talking that our   *100*
    garments seem now as fresh as when we were at
    Tunis at the marriage of your daughter, who is now
    Queen.

Antonio. And the rarest that e'er came there.

Sebastian. Bate,° I beseech you, widow Dido.   *105*

Antonio. O, widow Dido? Ay, widow Dido!

Gonzalo. Is not, sir, my doublet as fresh as the first
    day I wore it? I mean, in a sort.°

Antonio. That "sort" was well fished for.

Gonzalo. When I wore it at your daughter's marriage.   *110*

Alonso. You cram these words into mine ears against
    The stomach of my sense.° Would I had never
    Married my daughter there! For, coming thence,
    My son is lost; and, in my rate,° she too,
    Who is so far from Italy removed   *115*
    I ne'er again shall see her. O thou mine heir
    Of Naples and of Milan, what strange fish
    Hath made his meal on thee?

Francisco.   Sir, he may live.
    I saw him beat the surges under him
    And ride upon their backs. He trod the water,   *120*
    Whose enmity he flung aside, and breasted

99 *Why, in good time* (hearing Gonzalo reaffirm his false statement
about Tunis and Carthage, Antonio suggests that Gonzalo will indeed, at the first opportunity, carry this island home in his pocket)
105 *Bate* except   108 *in a sort* so to speak   111–12 *against/The
stomach of my sense* i.e., though my mind (or feelings) have no
appetite for them   114 *rate* opinion

The surge most swol'n that met him. His bold head
'Bove the contentious waves he kept, and oared
Himself with his good arms in lusty stroke
To th' shore, that o'er his° wave-worn basis
125   bowed,°
As stooping to relieve him. I not doubt
He came alive to land.

Alonso.   No, no, he's gone.

Sebastian. [*To Alonso*] Sir, you may thank yourself for
this great loss,
That would not bless our Europe with your
daughter,
130   But rather loose her to an African,
Where she, at least, is banished from your eye
Who hath cause to wet the grief on't.

Alonso.   Prithee, peace.

Sebastian. You were kneeled to and importuned
otherwise
By all of us; and the fair soul herself
135   Weighed, between loathness and obedience, at
Which end o' th' beam should bow.° We have lost
your son,
I fear, forever. Milan and Naples have
Moe° widows in them of this business' making
Than we bring men to comfort them.
The fault's your own.

140 *Alonso.*   So is the dear'st° o' th' loss.

Gonzalo. My Lord Sebastian,
The truth you speak doth lack some gentleness,
And time to speak it in. You rub the sore
When you should bring the plaster.

Sebastian.   Very well.

---

125 *his* its   125 *wave-worn basis bowed* (the image is of a guardian
cliff on the shore)   135–36 *Weighed, between . . . should bow*
(Claribel's unwillingness to marry was outweighed by her obedience
to her father)   138 *Moe* more   140 *dear'st* (intensifies the meaning of the noun)

Antonio. And most chirurgeonly.°   *145*

Gonzalo. [*To Alonso*] It is foul weather in us all, good
    sir,
  When you are cloudy.

Sebastian. [*Aside to Antonio*] Foul weather?

Antonio. [*Aside to Sebastian*]   Very foul.

Gonzalo. Had I plantation° of this isle, my lord—

Antonio. He'd sow't with nettle seed.

Sebastian.   Or docks, or mallows.

Gonzalo. And were the king on't, what would I do?   *150*

Sebastian. Scape being drunk for want of wine.

Gonzalo. I' th' commonwealth I would by contraries°
  Execute all things. For no kind of traffic°
  Would I admit; no name of magistrate;
  Letters° should not be known; riches, poverty,   *155*
  And use of service,° none; contract, succession,°
  Bourn,° bound of land, tilth,° vineyard, none;
  No use of metal, corn, or wine, or oil;
  No occupation; all men idle, all;
  And women too, but innocent and pure;   *160*
  No sovereignty.

Sebastian.   Yet he would be king on't.

Antonio. The latter end of his commonwealth forgets
  the beginning.

Gonzalo. All things in common nature should pro-
    duce
  Without sweat or endeavor. Treason, felony,   *165*
  Sword, pike, knife, gun, or need of any engine°
  Would I not have; but nature should bring forth,
  Of it° own kind, all foison,° all abundance,

145 *chirurgeonly* like a surgeon   148 *plantation* colonization (Antonio then puns by taking the word in its other sense)   152 *con-
traries* in contrast to the usual customs   153 *traffic* trade   155 *Letters* learning   156 *service* servants   156 *succession* inheritance
157 *Bourn* boundary   157 *tilth* agriculture   166 *engine* weapon
168 *it* its   168 *foison* abundance

    To feed my innocent people.

170 *Sebastian.* No marrying 'mong his subjects?

    Antonio. None, man, all idle—whores and knaves.

    Gonzalo. I would with such perfection govern, sir,
    T' excel the Golden Age.

    Sebastian. [*Loudly*]   Save his Majesty!

    Antonio. [*Loudly*] Long live Gonzalo!

    Gonzalo.   And—do you mark me, sir?

    Alonso. Prithee, no more. Thou dost talk nothing to
175   me.

    Gonzalo. I do well believe your Highness; and did
    it to minister occasion° to these gentlemen, who
    are of such sensible° and nimble lungs that they
    always use to laugh at nothing.

180 *Antonio.* 'Twas you we laughed at.

    Gonzalo. Who in this kind of merry fooling am noth-
    ing to you; so you may continue, and laugh at
    nothing still.

    Antonio. What a blow was there given!

185 *Sebastian.* And° it had not fall'n flatlong.°

    Gonzalo. You are gentlemen of brave mettle; you
    would lift the moon out of her sphere if she would
    continue in it five weeks without changing.

      Enter Ariel [*invisible*] *playing solemn music.*

    Sebastian. We would so, and then go a-batfowling.°

190 *Antonio.* Nay, good my lord, be not angry.

177 *minister occasion* afford opportunity 178 *sensible* sensitive
185 *And* if 185 *flatlong* with the flat of the sword 189 *We would
so, and then go a-batfowling* we would use the moon for a lantern in
order to hunt birds at night by attracting them with a light and
beating them down with bats; i.e., in order to gull simpletons
like you (?)

Gonzalo. No, I warrant you; I will not adventure my
   discretion so weakly.° Will you laugh me asleep?
   For I am very heavy.

Antonio. Go sleep, and hear us.
   [*All sleep except Alonso, Sebastian, and Antonio.*]

Alonso. What, all so soon asleep? I wish mine eyes   *195*
   Would, with themselves, shut up my thoughts. I
     find
   They are inclined to do so.

Sebastian.   Please you, sir,
   Do not omit° the heavy offer of it.
   It seldom visits sorrow; when it doth,
   It is a comforter.

Antonio.   We two, my lord,   *200*
   Will guard your person while you take your rest,
   And watch your safety.

Alonso.   Thank you. Wondrous heavy.
           [*Alonso sleeps. Exit Ariel.*]

Sebastian. What a strange drowsiness possesses them!

Antonio. It is the quality o' th' climate.

Sebastian.   Why
   Doth it not then our eyelids sink? I find not   *205*
   Myself disposed to sleep.

Antonio.   Nor I: my spirits are nimble.
   They fell together all, as by consent.
   They dropped as by a thunderstroke. What might,
   Worthy Sebastian—O, what might?—No more!
   And yet methinks I see it in thy face,   *210*
   What thou shouldst be. Th' occasion speaks° thee,
     and
   My strong imagination sees a crown
   Dropping upon thy head.

191–92 *adventure my discretion so weakly* risk my reputation for
good sense because of your weak wit   198 *omit* neglect   211 *speaks*
speaks to

Sebastian.   What? Art thou waking?

Antonio. Do you not hear me speak?

Sebastian.   I do; and surely
215 It is a sleepy language, and thou speak'st
Out of thy sleep. What is it thou didst say?
This is a strange repose, to be asleep
With eyes wide open; standing, speaking, moving,
And yet so fast asleep.

Antonio.   Noble Sebastian,
220 Thou let'st thy fortune sleep—die, rather; wink'st°
Whiles thou art waking.

Sebastian.   Thou dost snore distinctly;
There's meaning in thy snores.

Antonio. I am more serious than my custom. You
Must be so too, if heed° me; which to do
Trebles thee o'er.°

225 *Sebastian.*   Well, I am standing water.

Antonio. I'll teach you how to flow.

Sebastian.   Do so. To ebb
Hereditary sloth instructs me.

Antonio.   O,
If you but knew how you the purpose cherish
Whiles thus you mock it; how, in stripping it,
230 You more invest it!° Ebbing men, indeed,
Most often do so near the bottom run
By their own fear or sloth.

Sebastian.   Prithee, say on.
The setting of thine eye and cheek proclaim
A matter° from thee; and a birth, indeed,
Which throes thee much° to yield.

235 *Antonio.*   Thus, sir:

220 *wink'st* dost shut thine eyes   224 *if heed* if you heed   225
Trebles thee o'er makes thee three times what thou now art   229–
30 *in stripping . . . invest it* in stripping the purpose off you, you
clothe yourself with it all the more   234 *matter* matter of importance   235 *throes thee much* costs thee much pain

Although this lord of weak remembrance,° this
Who shall be of as little memory°
When he is earthed,° hath here almost persuaded
(For he's a spirit of persuasion, only
Professes to persuade°) the King his son's alive,   240
'Tis as impossible that he's undrowned
As he that sleeps here swims.

Sebastian.   I have no hope
That he's undrowned.

Antonio.   O, out of that no hope
What great hope have you! No hope that way is
Another way so high a hope that even   245
Ambition cannot pierce a wink beyond,
But doubt discovery there.° Will you grant with me
That Ferdinand is drowned?

Sebastian.   He's gone.

Antonio.   Then tell me,
Who's the next heir of Naples?

Sebastian.   Claribel.

Antonio. She that is Queen of Tunis; she that dwells 250
    Ten leagues beyond man's life;° she that from
      Naples
    Can have no note—unless the sun were post;°
    The man i' th' moon's too slow—till newborn chins
    Be rough and razorable;° she that from whom
    We all were sea-swallowed,° though some cast°
      again,   255

---

236 *remembrance* memory 237 *of as little memory* as little remem-
bered 238 *earthed* buried 239-40 *only/Professes to persuade* his
only profession is to persuade 246-47 *Ambition cannot . . . dis-*
covery there the eye of ambition can reach no farther, but must even
doubt the reality of what it discerns thus far 251 *ten leagues be-*
yond man's life it would take a lifetime to get within ten leagues of
the place 252 *post* messenger 253-54 *till newborn chins/Be*
rough and razorable till babies just born be ready to shave 254-
55 *she that . . . were sea-swallowed* she who is separated from
Naples by so dangerous a sea that we were ourselves swallowed
up by it 255 *cast* cast upon the shore (with a suggestion of its
theatrical meaning that leads to the next metaphor)

And, by that destiny, to perform an act
Whereof what's past is prologue, what to come,
In yours and my discharge.

Sebastian.   What stuff is this? How say you?
'Tis true my brother's daughter's Queen of Tunis;
260   So is she heir of Naples; 'twixt which regions
There is some space.

Antonio.   A space whose ev'ry cubit
Seems to cry out "How shall that Claribel
Measure us back to Naples? Keep in Tunis,
And let Sebastian wake!" Say this were death
That now hath seized them, why, they were no
265   worse
Than now they are. There be that can rule Naples
As well as he that sleeps; lords that can prate
As amply and unnecessarily
As this Gonzalo; I myself could make
270   A chough° of as deep chat. O, that you bore
The mind that I do! What a sleep were this
For your advancement! Do you understand me?

Sebastian. Methinks I do.

Antonio.   And how does your content
Tender° your own good fortune?

Sebastian.   I remember
You did supplant your brother Prospero.

275 *Antonio.*   True.
And look how well my garments sit upon me,
Much feater° than before. My brother's servants
Were then my fellows; now they are my men.

Sebastian. But, for your conscience—

280   *Antonio.* Ay, sir, where lies that? If 'twere a kibe,°
'Twould put me to my slipper; but I feel not
This deity in my bosom. Twenty consciences

270 *chough* jackdaw (a bird that can be taught to speak a few
words)   274 *Tender* regard (i.e., do you like your good fortune)
277 *feater* more becomingly   280 *kibe* chilblain on the héel

That stand 'twixt me and Milan, candied be they
And melt, ere they molest! Here lies your brother,   285
No better than the earth he lies upon—
If he were that which now he's like, that's dead°—
Whom I with this obedient steel (three inches
    of it)
Can lay to bed forever; whiles you, doing thus,
To the perpetual wink° for aye might put
This ancient morsel, this Sir Prudence, who   290
Should not upbraid our course. For all the rest,
They'll take suggestion as a cat laps milk;
They'll tell the clock° to any business that
We say befits the hour.

Sebastian.   Thy case, dear friend,
Shall be my precedent. As thou got'st Milan,   295
I'll come by Naples. Draw thy sword. One stroke
Shall free thee from the tribute which thou payest,
And I the King shall love thee.

Antonio.   Draw together;
And when I rear my hand, do you the like,
To fall it on Gonzalo.   [*They draw.*]

Sebastian.   O, but one word!   300

Enter Ariel [invisible] with music and song.

Ariel. My master through his art foresees the danger
    That you, his friend, are in, and sends me forth
    (For else his project dies) to keep them living.
                        Sings in Gonzalo's ear.

            While you here do snoring lie,
            Open-eyed conspiracy   305
                His time doth take.
            If of life you keep a care,
            Shake off slumber and beware.
                Awake, awake!

286 *that's dead* that is, if he were dead   289 *wink* eye-shut   293
tell the clock say yes

Antonio. Then let us both be sudden.

310 *Gonzalo.* [*Wakes*]   Now good angels
  Preserve the King!   [*The others wake.*]

Alonso. Why, how now? Ho, awake! Why are you
  drawn?
  Wherefore this ghastly looking?

Gonzalo.   What's the matter?

Sebastian. Whiles we stood here securing your repose,
315 Even now, we heard a hollow burst of bellowing
  Like bulls, or rather lions. Did't not wake you?
  It struck mine ear most terribly.

Alonso.   I heard nothing.

Antonio. O, 'twas a din to fright a monster's ear,
  To make an earthquake! Sure it was the roar
  Of a whole herd of lions.

320 *Alonso.*   Heard you this, Gonzalo?

Gonzalo. Upon mine honor, sir, I heard a humming,
  And that a strange one too, which did awake me.
  I shaked you, sir, and cried. As mine eyes opened,
  I saw their weapons drawn. There was a noise,
325 That's verily.° 'Tis best we stand upon our guard,
  Or that we quit this place. Let's draw our weapons.

Alonso. Lead off this ground, and let's make further
  search
  For my poor son.

Gonzalo.   Heavens keep him from these beasts!
  For he is, sure, i' th' island.

Alonso.   Lead away.

330 *Ariel.* Prospero my lord shall know what I have done.
  So, King, go safely on to seek thy son.   *Exeunt.*

325 *verily* the truth

Scene II. [*Another part of the island.*]

*Enter Caliban with a burden of wood. A noise of
    thunder heard.*

Caliban. All the infections that the sun sucks up
    From bogs, fens, flats, on Prosper fall, and make
        him
    By inchmeal° a disease! His spirits hear me,
    And yet I needs must curse. But they'll nor pinch,
    Fright me with urchin shows,° pitch me i' th' mire,   5
    Nor lead me, like a firebrand,° in the dark
    Out of my way, unless he bid 'em. But
    For every trifle are they set upon me;
    Sometime like apes that mow° and chatter at me,
    And after bite me; then like hedgehogs which   10
    Lie tumbling in my barefoot way and mount
    Their pricks at my footfall; sometime am I
    All wound with adders, who with cloven tongues
    Do hiss me into madness.

Enter Trinculo.

                    Lo, now, lo!
    Here comes a spirit of his, and to torment me   15
    For bringing wood in slowly. I'll fall flat.
    Perchance he will not mind me.   [*Lies down.*]

Trinculo. Here's neither bush nor shrub to bear off°
    any weather at all, and another storm brewing; I
    hear it sing i' th' wind. Yond same black cloud,   20
    yond huge one, looks like a foul bombard° that
    would shed his liquor. If it should thunder as it

II.ii.3 *By inchmeal* inch by inch   5 *urchin shows* impish apparitions
6 *like a firebrand* in the form of a will-o'-the-wisp   9 *mow* make
faces   18 *bear off* ward off   21 *bombard* large leather jug

did before, I know not where to hide my head.
Yond same cloud cannot choose but fall by pail-
25   fuls. What have we here? A man or a fish? Dead
or alive? A fish! He smells like a fish; a very ancient and fishlike smell; a kind of not of the new-
est Poor John.° A strange fish! Were I in England
now, as once I was, and had but this fish painted,°
30   not a holiday fool there but would give a piece of
silver. There would this monster make a man;° any
strange beast there makes a man. When they will
not give a doit° to relieve a lame beggar, they will
lay out ten to see a dead Indian. Legged like a man!
35   And his fins like arms! Warm, o' my troth! I do
now let loose my opinion, hold it no longer. This
is no fish, but an islander, that hath lately suffered
by a thunderbolt. [Thunder.] Alas, the storm is
come again! My best way is to creep under his
40   gaberdine; there is no other shelter hereabout. Misery acquaints a man with strange bedfellows. I will
here shroud till the dregs of the storm be past.
                    [Creeps under Caliban's garment.]

Enter Stephano, singing, [a bottle in his hand.]

Stephano.   I shall no more to sea, to sea;
                 Here shall I die ashore.

45   This is a very scurvy tune to sing at a man's funeral. Well, here's my comfort.   Drinks.

        The master, the swabber, the boatswain, and I,
             The gunner, and his mate,
        Loved Mall, Meg, and Marian, and Margery,
50   But none of us cared for Kate.
        For she had a tongue with a tang,
        Would cry to a sailor "Go hang!"
        She loved not the savor of tar nor of pitch;

28 *Poor John* dried hake   29 *painted* i.e., as a sign hung outside
a booth at a fair   31 *make a man* (pun: make a man's fortune)
33 *doit* smallest coin

Yet a tailor might scratch her where'er she did itch.
　Then to sea, boys, and let her go hang!　　　　　55

This is a scurvy tune too; but here's my comfort.
　　　　　　　　　　　　　　　Drinks.

Caliban. Do not torment me! O!

Stephano. What's the matter? Have we devils here?
　Do you put tricks upon 's with savages and men
　of Inde, ha? I have not scaped drowning to be　　60
　afeard now of your four legs. For it hath been
　said, "As proper a man as ever went on four legs
　cannot make him give ground"; and it shall be said
　so again, while Stephano breathes at' nostrils.°

Caliban. The spirit torments me. O!　　　　　65

Stephano. This is some monster of the isle, with four
　legs, who hath got, as I take it, an ague. Where the
　devil should he learn our language? I will give him
　some relief, if it be but for that. If I can recover°
　him, and keep him tame, and get to Naples with　70
　him, he's a present for any emperor that ever trod
　on neat's leather.°

Caliban. Do not torment me, prithee; I'll bring my
　wood home faster.

Stephano. He's in his fit now and does not talk after　75
　the wisest. He shall taste of my bottle; if he have
　never drunk wine afore, it will go near to remove
　his fit. If I can recover him and keep him tame, I
　will not take too much° for him. He shall pay for
　him that hath him, and that soundly.　　　　　80

Caliban. Thou dost me yet but little hurt. Thou wilt
　anon;° I know it by thy trembling.° Now Prosper
　works upon thee.

Stephano. Come on your ways, open your mouth;

64 *at' nostrils* at the nostrils　69 *recover* cure　72 *neat's leather*
cowhide　79 *not take too much* too much will not be enough
82 *anon* soon　82 *trembling* (Trinculo is shaking with fear)

85   here is that which will give language to you, cat.°
        Open your mouth. This will shake your shaking, I
        can tell you, and that soundly. [*Gives Caliban
        drink.*] You cannot tell who's your friend. Open
        your chaps° again.

90   *Trinculo.* I should know that voice. It should be—
        but he is drowned; and these are devils. O, defend
        me!

     Stephano. Four legs and two voices—a most delicate
        monster! His forward voice now is to speak well
95   of his friend; his backward voice is to utter foul
        speeches and to detract. If all the wine in my bottle
        will recover him, I will help his ague. Come! [*Gives
        drink.*] Amen! I will pour some in thy other
        mouth.

100 *Trinculo.* Stephano!

     Stephano. Doth thy other mouth call me? Mercy,
        mercy! This is a devil, and no monster. I will leave
        him; I have no long spoon.°

     Trinculo. Stephano! If thou beest Stephano, touch me
105   and speak to me; for I am Trinculo—be not afeard
        —thy good friend Trinculo.

     Stephano. If thou beest Trinculo, come forth. I'll pull
        thee by the lesser legs. If any be Trinculo's legs,
        these are they. [*Draws him out from under Cali-*
110   *ban's garment.*] Thou art very Trinculo indeed!
        How cam'st thou to be the siege° of this moon-
        calf?° Can he vent Trinculos?

     Trinculo. I took him to be killed with a thunder-
        stroke. But art thou not drowned, Stephano? I
115   hope now thou art not drowned. Is the storm over-
        blown? I hid me under the dead mooncalf's gaber-
        dine for fear of the storm. And art thou living,

85 *cat* (alluding to the proverb "Liquor will make a cat talk")
89 *chaps* jaws   103 *long spoon* (alluding to the proverb "He who
sups with [i.e., from the same dish as] the devil must have a long
spoon")   111 *siege* excrement   111–12 *mooncalf* monstrosity

Stephano? O Stephano, two Neapolitans scaped!

Stephano. Prithee do not turn me about; my stomach
  is not constant.   120

Caliban. [*Aside*] These be fine things, and if° they be
    not sprites.
  That's a brave god and bears celestial liquor.
  I will kneel to him.

Stephano. How didst thou scape? How cam'st thou
    hither? Swear by this bottle how thou cam'st   125
    hither. I escaped upon a butt of sack which the
    sailors heaved o'erboard—by this bottle which I
    made of the bark of a tree with mine own hands
    since I was cast ashore.

Caliban. I'll swear upon that bottle to be thy true   130
    subject, for the liquor is not earthly.

Stephano. Here! Swear then how thou escap'dst.

Trinculo. Swum ashore, man, like a duck. I can swim
    like a duck, I'll be sworn.

Stephano. Here, kiss the book. [*Gives him drink.*]   135
    Though thou canst swim like a duck, thou art made
    like a goose.

Trinculo. O Stephano, hast any more of this?

Stephano. The whole butt, man. My cellar is in a
    rock by th' seaside, where my wine is hid. How   140
    now, mooncalf? How does thine ague?

Caliban. Hast thou not dropped from heaven?

Stephano. Out o' th' moon, I do assure thee. I was the
    Man i' th' Moon when time was.°

Caliban. I have seen thee in her, and I do adore thee.   145
    My mistress showed me thee, and thy dog, and
    thy bush.°

121 *and if* if   144 *when time was* once upon a time   146–47 *thee,
and thy dog, and thy bush* (the Man in the Moon was banished
there, according to legend, for gathering brushwood with his dog
on Sunday)

Stephano. Come, swear to that; kiss the book. [*Gives him drink.*] I will furnish it anon with new con-
150   tents. Swear. [*Caliban drinks.*]

Trinculo. By this good light, this is a very shallow monster! I afeard of him? A very weak monster! The Man i' th' Moon? A most poor credulous monster! Well drawn,° monster, in good sooth!

155 *Caliban.* I'll show thee every fertile inch o' th' island; and I will kiss thy foot. I prithee, be my god.

Trinculo. By this light, a most perfidious and drunken monster! When's god's asleep, he'll rob his bottle.

Caliban. I'll kiss thy foot. I'll swear myself thy sub-
160   ject.

Stephano. Come on then. Down, and swear!

Trinculo. I shall laugh myself to death at this puppy-headed monster. A most scurvy monster! I could find in my heart to beat him—

165 *Stephano.* Come, kiss.

Trinculo. But that the poor monster's in drink. An abominable monster!

Caliban. I'll show thee the best springs; I'll pluck thee berries;
      I'll fish for thee, and get thee wood enough.
170   A plague upon the tyrant that I serve!
      I'll bear him no more sticks, but follow thee,
      Thou wondrous man.

Trinculo. A most ridiculous monster, to make a won-der of a poor drunkard!

Caliban. I prithee let me bring thee where crabs°
175   grow;
      And I with my long nails will dig thee pignuts,°
      Show thee a jay's nest, and instruct thee how

154 *Well drawn* a good pull at the bottle   175 *crabs* crab apples
176 *pignuts* earthnuts

To snare the nimble marmoset. I'll bring thee
To clust'ring filberts, and sometimes I'll get thee
Young scamels° from the rock. Wilt thou go with
    me?   180

Stephano. I prithee now, lead the way without any
more talking. Trinculo, the King and all our company else being drowned, we will inherit here.
Here, bear my bottle. Fellow Trinculo, we'll fill
him by and by again.   185
                        Caliban sings drunkenly.

Caliban. Farewell, master; farewell, farewell!

Trinculo. A howling monster! A drunken monster!

Caliban.
    No more dams° I'll make for fish,
        Nor fetch in firing
        At requiring,   190
    Nor scrape trenchering,° nor wash dish.
      'Ban, 'Ban, Ca—Caliban
    Has a new master. Get a new man!

Freedom, high day! High day, freedom! Freedom,
high day, freedom!   195

Stephano. O brave monster! Lead the way.   *Exeunt.*

ACT III

Scene I. [*In front of Prospero's cell.*]

Enter Ferdinand, bearing a log.

Ferdinand. There be some sports are painful, and
    their labor
    Delight in them sets off;° some kinds of baseness

---

180 *scamels* (perhaps a misprint for "seamels" or "seamews," a
kind of sea bird)   188 *dams* (to catch fish and keep them)   191
trenchering trenchers, wooden plates   III.i.2 *sets off* cancels

Are nobly undergone, and most poor matters
Point to rich ends. This my mean task
5 Would be as heavy to me as odious, but
The mistress which I serve quickens° what's dead
And makes my labors pleasures. O, she is
Ten times more gentle than her father's crabbed;
And he's composed of harshness. I must remove
10 Some thousands of these logs and pile them up,
Upon a sore injunction.° My sweet mistress
Weeps when she sees me work, and says such baseness
Had never like executor. I forget;°
But these sweet thoughts do even refresh my labors,
Most busiest when I do it.°

Enter Miranda; and Prospero [behind, unseen].

15 *Miranda.*   Alas, now pray you,
Work not so hard! I would the lightning had
Burnt up those logs that you are enjoined to pile!
Pray set it down and rest you. When this burns,
'Twill weep° for having wearied you. My father
20 Is hard at study; pray now rest yourself;
He's safe for these three hours.

Ferdinand.   O most dear mistress,
The sun will set before I shall discharge
What I must strive to do.

Miranda.   If you'll sit down,
I'll bear your logs the while. Pray give me that;
I'll carry it to the pile.

25 *Ferdinand.*   No, precious creature,
I had rather crack my sinews, break my back,
Than you should such dishonor undergo
While I sit lazy by.

---

6 *quickens* brings to life 11 *sore injunction* severe command
13 *forget* i.e., my task 15 *Most busiest when I do it* i.e., my
thoughts are busiest when I am (the Folio's *busie lest* has been
variously emended; *it* may refer to "task," line 4, the understood
object in line 13) 19 *weep* i.e., exude resin

Miranda.   It would become me
  As well as it does you; and I should do it
  With much more ease; for my good will is to it,   30
  And yours it is against.

Prospero. [*Aside*]   Poor worm, thou art infected!
  This visitation° shows it.

Miranda.   You look wearily.

Ferdinand. No, noble mistress, 'tis fresh morning with
  me
  When you are by at night.° I do beseech you,
  Chiefly that I might set it in my prayers,   35
  What is your name?

Miranda.   Miranda. O my father,
  I have broke your hest° to say so!

Ferdinand.   Admired Miranda!°
  Indeed the top of admiration, worth
  What's dearest to the world! Full many a lady
  I have eyed with best regard, and many a time   40
  Th' harmony of their tongues hath into bondage
  Brought my too diligent ear. For several virtues
  Have I liked several women; never any
  With so full soul but some defect in her
  Did quarrel with the noblest grace she owed,°   45
  And put it to the foil.° But you, O you,
  So perfect and so peerless, are created
  Of every creature's best.

Miranda.   I do not know
  One of my sex; no woman's face remember,
  Save, from my glass, mine own. Nor have I seen   50
  More that I may call men than you, good friend,
  And my dear father. How features are abroad
  I am skilless° of; but, by my modesty

32 *visitation* (1) visit (2) attack of plague (referring to metaphor
of "infected")   34 *at night* i.e., even at night when I am very
tired   37 *hest* command   37 *Admired Miranda* ("admired" means
"to be wondered at"; the Latin "Miranda" means "wonderful")
45 *owed* owned   46 *put it to the foil* defeated it   53 *skilless*
ignorant

(The jewel in my dower), I would not wish
55 Any companion in the world but you;
Nor can imagination form a shape,
Besides yourself, to like of.° But I prattle
Something too wildly, and my father's precepts
I therein do forget.

Ferdinand.   I am, in my condition,
60 A prince, Miranda; I do think, a king
(I would not so), and would no more endure
This wooden slavery than to suffer
The fleshfly blow my mouth. Hear my soul speak!
The very instant that I saw you, did
65 My heart fly to your service; there resides,
To make me slave to it; and for your sake
Am I this patient log-man.

Miranda.   Do you love me?

Ferdinand. O heaven, O earth, bear witness to this
          sound,
And crown what I profess with kind event°
70 If I speak true! If hollowly, invert
What best is boded me° to mischief! I,
Beyond all limit of what else i' th' world,
Do love, prize, honor you.

Miranda.   I am a fool
To weep at what I am glad of.

Prospero.   [*Aside*] Fair encounter
75 Of two most rare affections! Heavens rain grace
On that which breeds between 'em!

Ferdinand.   Wherefore weep you?

Miranda. At mine unworthiness, that dare not offer
What I desire to give, and much less take
What I shall die to want.° But this is trifling;°
80 And all the more it seeks to hide itself,

---

57 *like of* like   69 *event* outcome   71 *What best is boded me* whatever good fortune fate has in store for me   79 *to want* if I lack
79 *trifling* i.e., to speak in riddles like this

The bigger bulk it shows. Hence, bashful cunning,
And prompt me, plain and holy innocence!
I am your wife, if you will marry me;
If not, I'll die your maid. To be your fellow°
You may deny me; but I'll be your servant,   85
Whether you will or no.

Ferdinand.   My mistress, dearest,
And I thus humble ever.

Miranda.   My husband then?

Ferdinand. Ay, with a heart as willing
As bondage e'er of freedom.° Here's my hand.

Miranda. And mine, with my heart in't; and now
    farewell   90
Till half an hour hence.

Ferdinand.   A thousand thousand!
                *Exeunt [Ferdinand and Miranda
                        in different directions].*

Prospero. So glad of this as they I cannot be,
Who are surprised withal;° but my rejoicing
At nothing can be more. I'll to my book;
For yet ere suppertime must I perform   95
Much business appertaining.°   *Exit.*

Scene II. [*Another part of the island.*]

Enter Caliban, Stephano, and Trinculo.

Stephano. Tell not me! When the butt is out, we will
    drink water; not a drop before. Therefore bear up
    and board 'em!° Servant monster, drink to me.

Trinculo. Servant monster? The folly of this island!

84 *fellow* equal   89 *of freedom* i.e., to win freedom   93 *withal* by
it   96 *appertaining* i.e., to my plan   III.ii.2–3 *bear up and board
'em* i.e., drink up

5   They say there's but five upon this isle; we are three
       of them. If th' other two be brained like us, the
       state totters.

       Stephano. Drink, servant monster, when I bid thee;
       thy eyes are almost set in thy head.

10   *Trinculo.* Where should they be set else? He were a
       brave monster indeed if they were set in his tail.

       Stephano. My man-monster hath drowned his tongue
       in sack. For my part, the sea cannot drown me. I
       swam, ere I could recover the shore, five-and-thirty
15   leagues off and on, by this light. Thou shalt be my
       lieutenant, monster, or my standard.°

       Trinculo. Your lieutenant, if you list;° he's no stan-
       dard.

       Stephano. We'll not run,° Monsieur Monster.

20   *Trinculo.* Nor go° neither; but you'll lie° like dogs,
       and yet say nothing neither.

       Stephano. Mooncalf, speak once in thy life, if thou
       beest a good mooncalf.

       Caliban. How does thy honor? Let me lick thy shoe.
25   I'll not serve him; he is not valiant.

       Trinculo. Thou liest, most ignorant monster; I am in
       case° to justle° a constable. Why, thou deboshed°
       fish thou, was there ever man a coward that hath
       drunk so much sack as I today? Wilt thou tell a
30   monstrous lie, being but half a fish and half a
       monster?

       Caliban. Lo, how he mocks me! Wilt thou let him,
       my lord?

---

16 *standard* standard-bearer, ensign (pun since Caliban is so drunk
he cannot stand)   17 *if you list* if it please you (with pun on
"list" as pertaining to a ship that leans over to one side)   19–20
run, lie (with puns on secondary meanings: "make water," "ex-
crete")   20 *go* walk   27 *case* fit condition   27 *justle* jostle   27 *de-
boshed* debauched

Trinculo. "Lord" quoth he? That a monster should
  be such a natural!°   35

Caliban. Lo, lo, again! Bite him to death, I prithee.

Stephano. Trinculo, keep a good tongue in your head.
  If you prove a mutineer—the next tree!° The poor
  monster's my subject, and he shall not suffer in-
  dignity.   40

Caliban. I thank my noble lord. Wilt thou be pleased
  to hearken once again to the suit I made to thee?

Stephano. Marry,° will I. Kneel and repeat it; I will
  stand, and so shall Trinculo.

            Enter Ariel, invisible.

Caliban. As I told thee before, I am subject to a
  tyrant,   45
  A sorcerer, that by his cunning hath
  Cheated me of the island.

Ariel. Thou liest.

Caliban.   Thou liest, thou jesting monkey
  thou!
  I would my valiant master would destroy thee.
  I do not lie.   50

Stephano. Trinculo, if you trouble him any more in's
  tale, by this hand, I will supplant some of your
  teeth.

Trinculo. Why, I said nothing.

Stephano. Mum then, and no more. Proceed.   55

Caliban. I say by sorcery he got this isle;
  From me he got it. If thy greatness will
  Revenge it on him—for I know thou dar'st,
  But this thing° dare not—

35 *natural* idiot   38 *the next tree* i.e., you will be hanged   43
Marry (an expletive, from "By the Virgin Mary")   59 *this thing*
i.e., Trinculo

60 *Stephano.* That's most certain.

Caliban. Thou shalt be lord of it, and I'll serve thee.

Stephano. How now shall this be compassed?
      Canst thou bring me to the party?

Caliban. Yea, yea, my lord! I'll yield him thee asleep,
65   Where thou mayst knock a nail into his head.

Ariel. Thou liest; thou canst not.

Caliban. What a pied° ninny's this! Thou scurvy
      patch!°
      I do beseech thy greatness, give him blows
      And take his bottle from him. When that's gone,
      He shall drink naught but brine, for I'll not show
70   him
      Where the quick freshes° are.

Stephano. Trinculo, run into no further danger! Inter-
      rupt the monster one word further and, by this
      hand, I'll turn my mercy out o' doors and make a
75   stockfish° of thee.

Trinculo. Why, what did I? I did nothing. I'll go far-
      ther off.

Stephano. Didst thou not say he lied?

Ariel. Thou liest.

80 *Stephano.* Do I so? Take thou that! [*Strikes Trin-
      culo.*] As you like this, give me the lie another time.

Trinculo. I did not give the lie. Out o' your wits, and
      hearing too? A pox o' your bottle! This can sack
      and drinking do. A murrain° on your monster, and
85   the devil take your fingers!

Caliban. Ha, ha, ha!

Stephano. Now forward with your tale. [*To Trinculo*]
      Prithee, stand further off.

67 *pied* (referring to Trinculo's parti-colored jester's costume)
67 *patch* clown   71 *quick freshes* living springs of fresh water
75 *stockfish* dried cod, softened by beating   84 *murrain* plague
(that infects cattle)

Caliban. Beat him enough. After a little time
I'll beat him too.

Stephano.   Stand farther. Come, proceed.   90

Caliban. Why, as I told thee, 'tis a custom with him
I' th' afternoon to sleep. There thou mayst brain
him,
Having first seized his books, or with a log
Batter his skull, or paunch° him with a stake,
Or cut his wezand° with thy knife. Remember   95
First to possess his books; for without them
He's but a sot,° as I am, nor hath not
One spirit to command. They all do hate him
As rootedly as I. Burn but his books.
He has brave utensils° (for so he calls them)   100
Which, when he has a house, he'll deck withal.
And that most deeply to consider is
The beauty of his daughter. He himself
Calls her a nonpareil. I never saw a woman
But only Sycorax my dam and she;   105
But she as far surpasseth Sycorax
As great'st does least.

Stephano.   Is it so brave a lass?

Caliban. Ay, lord. She will become thy bed, I
warrant,
And bring thee forth brave brood.

Stephano. Monster, I will kill this man. His daughter   110
and I will be King and Queen—save our Graces!—
and Trinculo and thyself shall be viceroys. Dost
thou like the plot, Trinculo?

Trinculo. Excellent.

Stephano. Give me thy hand. I am sorry I beat thee;   115
but while thou liv'st, keep a good tongue in thy
head.

94 *paunch* stab in the belly   95 *wezand* windpipe   97 *sot* fool
100 *brave utensils* fine furnishings (pronounced "útensils")

Caliban. Within this half hour will he be asleep.
    Wilt thou destroy him then?

Stephano.   Ay, on mine honor.

20 *Ariel.* This will I tell my master.

Caliban. Thou mak'st me merry; I am full of pleasure.
    Let us be jocund. Will you troll the catch°
    You taught me but whilere?°

Stephano. At thy request, monster, I will do reason,
25   any reason.° Come on, Trinculo, let us sing. *Sings.*

            Flout 'em and scout° 'em
            And scout 'em and flout 'em!
            Thought is free.

Caliban. That's not the tune.
                Ariel plays the tune on a tabor° and pipe.

130 *Stephano.* What is this same?

Trinculo. This is the tune of our catch, played by the
    picture of Nobody.°

Stephano. If thou beest a man, show thyself in thy
    likeness. If thou beest a devil, take't as thou list.

135 *Trinculo.* O, forgive me my sins!

Stephano. He that dies pays all debts. I defy thee.
    Mercy upon us!

Caliban. Art thou afeard?

Stephano. No, monster, not I.

140 *Caliban.* Be not afeard; the isle is full of noises,
    Sounds and sweet airs that give delight and hurt
        not.

122 *troll the catch* sing the round   123 *but whilere* just now
124–25 *reason, any reason* i.e., anything within reason   126 *scout*
jeer at   129 s.d. *tabor* small drum worn at the side   132 *Nobody*
(alluding to the picture of No-body—a man all head, legs, and arms,
but without trunk—on the title page of the anonymous comedy
No-body and Some-body)

Sometimes a thousand twangling instruments
Will hum about mine ears; and sometime voices
That, if I then had waked after long sleep,
Will make me sleep again; and then, in dreaming,   *145*
The clouds methought would open and show riches
Ready to drop upon me, that, when I waked,
I cried to dream again.

Stephano. This will prove a brave kingdom to me,
    where I shall have my music for nothing.   *150*

Caliban. When Prospero is destroyed.

Stephano. That shall be by and by; I remember the
    story.

Trinculo. The sound is going away; let's follow it, and
    after do our work.   *155*

Stephano. Lead, monster; we'll follow. I would I
    could see this taborer; he lays it on.

Trinculo. [*To Caliban*] Wilt come?° I'll follow Ste-
    phano.   *Exeunt.*

Scene III. [*Another part of the island.*]

*Enter Alonso, Sebastian, Antonio, Gonzalo,
Adrian, Francisco, etc.*

Gonzalo. By'r Lakin,° I can go no further, sir;
My old bones aches. Here's a maze trod indeed
Through forthrights and meanders.° By your
    patience,
I needs must rest me.

Alonso.   Old lord, I cannot blame thee,
Who am myself attached° with weariness   *5*

---

158 *Wilt come* (Caliban lingers because the other two are being
distracted from his purpose by the music)   III.iii.1 *By'r Lakin*
by our Lady   3 *forthrights and meanders* straight and winding paths
5 *attached* seized

To th' dulling of my spirits. Sit down and rest.
Even here I will put off my hope, and keep it
No longer for my flatterer. He is drowned
Whom thus we stray to find; and the sea mocks
10   Our frustrate search on land. Well, let him go.

Antonio. [*Aside to Sebastian*] I am right glad that
        he's so out of hope.
    Do not for one repulse forgo the purpose
    That you resolved t' effect.

Sebastian. [*Aside to Antonio*] The next advantage
    Will we take throughly.°

Antonio. [*Aside to Sebastian*] Let it be tonight;
15   For, now they are oppressed with travel, they
    Will not nor cannot use such vigilance
    As when they are fresh.

Sebastian. [*Aside to Antonio*] I say tonight. No more.

*Solemn and strange music; and Prosper on the top°
(invisible). Enter several strange Shapes, bringing
in a banquet; and dance about it with gentle actions of salutations; and, inviting the King etc. to
eat, they depart.*

Alonso. What harmony is this? My good friends,
        hark!

Gonzalo. Marvelous sweet music!

Alonso. Give us kind keepers,° heavens! What were
20   these?

Sebastian. A living drollery.° Now I will believe
    That there are unicorns; that in Arabia

14 *throughly* thoroughly   17 s.d. *the top* upper stage (or perhaps a
playing area above it)   20 *kind keepers* guardian angels   21 *drollery* puppet show

There is one tree, the phoenix' throne; one phoenix
At this hour reigning there.

Antonio.   I'll believe both;
And what does else want credit,° come to me,   25
And I'll be sworn 'tis true. Travelers ne'er did lie,
Though fools at home condemn 'em.

Gonzalo.   If in Naples
I should report this now, would they believe me
If I should say I saw such islanders?
(For certes these are people of the island)   30
Who, though they are of monstrous shape, yet note,
Their manners are more gentle, kind, than of
Our human generation you shall find
Many—nay, almost any.

   Prospero.   [*Aside*] Honest lord,
Thou hast said well; for some of you there present   35
Are worse than devils.

Alonso.   I cannot too much muse°
Such shapes, such gesture, and such sound, ex-
          pressing
(Although they want the use of tongue) a kind
   Of excellent dumb discourse.

   Prospero.   [*Aside*] Praise in departing.°

Francisco. They vanished strangely.

Sebastian.   No matter, since   40
They have left their viands behind; for we have
          stomachs.
Will't please you taste of what is here?

Alonso.   Not I.

Gonzalo. Faith, sir, you need not fear. When we were
          boys,
Who would believe that there were mountaineers

25 *credit* believing 36 *muse* wonder at 39 *Praise in departing*
save your praise for the end

Dewlapped° like bulls, whose throats had hanging
45   at 'em
Wallets of flesh? Or that there were such men
Whose heads stood in their breasts? Which now
  we find
Each putter-out of five for one° will bring us
Good warrant of.

Alonso.   I will stand to, and feed;
50 Although my last, no matter, since I feel
The best is past. Brother, my lord the Duke,
Stand to, and do as we.

> *Thunder and lightning. Enter Ariel, like a harpy;*
> *claps his wings upon the table; and with a*
> *quaint device° the banquet vanishes.*

Ariel. You are three men of sin, whom destiny—
That hath to instrument° this lower world
55 And what is in't—the never-surfeited sea
Hath caused to belch up you and on this island,
Where man doth not inhabit, you 'mongst men
Being most unfit to live. I have made you mad;
And even with suchlike valor° men hang and
  drown
Their proper selves.
>   *[Alonso, Sebastian, etc. draw their swords.]*
60   You fools! I and my fellows
Are ministers of Fate. The elements,
Of whom your swords are tempered,° may as well
Wound the loud winds, or with bemocked-at stabs
Kill the still-closing° waters, as diminish
65 One dowle° that's in my plume.° My fellow min-
  isters

45 *Dewlapped* with skin hanging from the neck (like mountaineers
with goiter)   48 *putter-out of five for one* traveler who insures
himself by depositing a sum of money to be repaid fivefold if he
returns safely (i.e., any ordinary traveler will confirm nowadays
those reports we used to think fanciful)   52 s.d. *quaint device*
ingenious device (of stage mechanism)   54 *to instrument* as its instrument   59 *suchlike valor* i.e., the courage that comes of madness
62 *tempered* composed   64 *still-closing* ever closing again (as
soon as wounded)   65 *dowle* bit of down   65 *plume* plumage

Are like invulnerable. If you could hurt,°
Your swords are now too massy° for your strengths
And will not be uplifted. But remember
(For that's my business to you) that you three
From Milan did supplant good Prospero;   70
Exposed unto the sea, which hath requit it,°
Him and his innocent child; for which foul deed
The pow'rs, delaying, not forgetting, have
Incensed the seas and shores, yea, all the creatures,
Against your peace. Thee of thy son, Alonso,   75
They have bereft; and do pronounce by me
Ling'ring perdition (worse than any death
Can be at once) shall step by step attend
You and your ways; whose wraths to guard you
    from,
Which here, in this most desolate isle, else falls   80
Upon your heads, is nothing but heart's sorrow°
And a clear life ensuing.

*He vanishes in thunder; then, to soft music, enter
    the Shapes again, and dance with mocks and
    mows,° and carrying out the table.*

Prospero. Bravely the figure of this harpy hast thou
Performed, my Ariel; a grace it had, devouring.°
Of my instruction hast thou nothing bated°   85
In what thou hadst to say. So, with good life°
And observation strange,° my meaner ministers°
Their several kinds have done.° My high charms
    work,
And these, mine enemies, are all knit up
In their distractions. They now are in my pow'r;   90
And in these fits I leave them, while I visit

66 *If you could hurt* even if you could hurt us   67 *massy* heavy
71 *requit it* avenged that crime   81 *nothing but heart's sorrow* only
repentance (will protect you from the wrath of these powers)
82 s.d. *mocks and mows* mocking gestures and grimaces   84 *devouring* i.e., in making the banquet disappear   85 *bated* omitted   86
good life good lifelike acting   87 *observation strange* remarkable
attention to my wishes   87 *meaner ministers* i.e., inferior to Ariel
88 *Their several kinds have done* have acted the parts their natures
suited them for

Young Ferdinand, whom they suppose is drowned,
And his and mine loved darling.   [*Exit above.*]

Gonzalo. I' th' name of something holy, sir, why
     stand you
In this strange stare?

95   *Alonso.*   O, it is monstrous, monstrous!
Methought the billows spoke and told me of it;
The winds did sing it to me; and the thunder,
That deep and dreadful organ pipe, pronounced
The name of Prosper; it did bass my trespass.°
100 Therefore my son i' th' ooze is bedded; and
I'll seek him deeper than e'er plummet sounded
And with him there lie mudded.   *Exit.*

Sebastian.   But one fiend at a time,
I'll fight their legions o'er!°

Antonio.   I'll be thy second.
                    Exeunt [*Sebastian and Antonio*].

Gonzalo. All three of them are desperate; their great
     guilt,
105 Like poison given to work a great time after,
Now 'gins to bite the spirits. I do beseech you,
That are of suppler joints, follow them swiftly
And hinder them from what this ecstasy°
May now provoke them to.

Adrian.   Follow, I pray you.
                         Exeunt omnes.

99 *bass my trespass* i.e., made me understand my trespass by turning it into music for which the thunder provided the bass part
103 *o'er* one after another to the last   108 *ecstasy* madness

ACT IV

Scene I. [*In front of Prospero's cell.*]

Enter Prospero, Ferdinand, and Miranda.

Prospero. If I have too austerely punished you,
    Your compensation makes amends; for I
    Have given you here a third of mine own life,
    Or that for which I live; who once again
    I tender to thy hand. All thy vexations   *5*
    Were but my trials of thy love, and thou
    Hast strangely° stood the test. Here, afore heaven,
    I ratify this my rich gift. O Ferdinand,
    Do not smile at me that I boast her off,°
    For thou shalt find she will outstrip all praise   *10*
    And make it halt° behind her.

Ferdinand.   I do believe it
    Against an oracle.°

Prospero. Then, as my gift, and thine own acquisition
    Worthily purchased, take my daughter. But
    If thou dost break her virgin-knot before   *15*
    All sanctimonious° ceremonies may
    With full and holy rite be minist'red,

IV.i.7 *strangely* wonderfully   9 *boast her off* (includes perhaps idea of showing her off)   11 *halt* limp   12 *Against an oracle* though an oracle should declare otherwise   16 *sanctimonious* holy

　　　　No sweet aspersion° shall the heavens let fall
　　　　To make this contract grow;° but barren hate,
20　　Sour-eyed disdain, and discord shall bestrew
　　　　The union of your bed with weeds so loathly
　　　　That you shall hate it both. Therefore take heed,
　　　　As Hymen's lamps shall light you.°

Ferdinand.　　　　　　　　　　　　　　As I hope
　　　　For quiet days, fair issue, and long life,
25　　With such love as 'tis now, the murkiest den,
　　　　The most opportune° place, the strong'st sug-
　　　　　　gestion
　　　　Our worser genius can,° shall never melt
　　　　Mine honor into lust, to take away
　　　　The edge° of that day's celebration
　　　　When I shall think or Phoebus' steeds are foun-
30　　　　dered°
　　　　Or Night kept chained below.°

Prospero.　　　　　　　　　　　　Fairly spoke.
　　　　Sit then and talk with her; she is thine own.
　　　　What, Ariel!° My industrious servant, Ariel!

Enter Ariel.

Ariel. What would my potent master? Here I am.

Prospero. Thou and thy meaner fellows your last
35　　service
　　　　Did worthily perform; and I must use you
　　　　In such another trick. Go bring the rabble,°
　　　　O'er whom I give thee pow'r, here to this place.
　　　　Incite them to quick motion; for I must

18 *aspersion* blessing (like rain on crops)　19 *grow* become fruitful　23 *As Hymen's lamps shall light you* i.e., as earnestly as you
pray that the torch of the god of marriage shall burn without smoke
(a good omen for wedded happiness)　26 *opportune* (pronounced
"oppórtune")　27 *Our worser genius can* our evil spirit can offer
29 *edge* keen enjoyment　30 *foundered* lamed　30–31 *or Phoebus'
steeds . . . below* i.e., that either day will never end or night
will never come　33 *What, Ariel* (summoning Ariel)　37 *rabble*
"thy meaner fellows"

Bestow upon the eyes of this young couple   40
Some vanity of° mine art. It is my promise,
And they expect it from me.

Ariel.   Presently?

Prospero. Ay, with a twink.

Ariel. Before you can say "Come" and "Go,"
And breathe twice and cry, "So, so,"   45
Each one, tripping on his toe,
Will be here with mop and mow.°
Do you love me, master? No?

Prospero. Dearly, my delicate Ariel. Do not approach
Till thou dost hear me call.

Ariel.   Well; I conceive.°   *Exit.*   50

Prospero. Look thou be true.° Do not give dalliance
Too much the rein; the strongest oaths are straw
To th' fire i' th' blood. Be more abstemious,
Or else good night your vow!

Ferdinand.   I warrant you, sir.
The white cold virgin snow upon my heart°   55
Abates the ardor of my liver.°

Prospero.   Well.
Now come, my Ariel; bring a corollary°
Rather than want a spirit. Appear, and pertly!
No tongue! All eyes! Be silent.   *Soft music.*

Enter Iris.°

Iris. Ceres, most bounteous lady, thy rich leas°   60
Of wheat, rye, barley, fetches,° oats, and peas;

41 *vanity of* illusion conjured up by   47 *mop and mow* gestures and
grimaces   50 *conceive* understand   51 *be true* (Prospero appears
to have caught the lovers in an embrace)   55 *The white cold . . .
heart* her pure white breast on mine (?)   56 *liver* (supposed seat
of sexual passion)   57 *corollary* surplus (of spirits)   59 s.d. *Iris*
goddess of the rainbow and Juno's messenger   60 *leas* meadows
61 *fetches* vetch (a kind of forage)

Thy turfy mountains, where live nibbling sheep,
And flat meads thatched with stover,° them to
    keep;
Thy banks with pionèd and twillèd brims,°
65   Which spongy April at thy hest betrims
To make cold nymphs chaste crowns; and thy
    broom groves,
Whose shadow the dismissèd bachelor loves,
Being lasslorn; thy pole-clipt vineyard;°
And thy sea-marge, sterile and rocky-hard,
70   Where thou thyself dost air°—the queen o' th'
    sky,°
Whose wat'ry arch and messenger am I,
Bids thee leave these, and with her sovereign grace,

Juno descends.°

Here on this grass plot, in this very place,
To come and sport; her peacocks fly amain.°
75   Approach, rich Ceres, her to entertain.

Enter Ceres.

Ceres. Hail, many-colored messenger, that ne'er
    Dost disobey the wife of Jupiter,
Who, with thy saffron wings, upon my flow'rs
Diffusest honey drops, refreshing show'rs,
80   And with each end of thy blue bow dost crown
My bosky° acres and my unshrubbed down,
Rich scarf to my proud earth. Why hath thy queen
Summoned me hither to this short-grassed green?

Iris. A contract of true love to celebrate

63 *meads thatched with stover* (meadows covered with a kind of
grass used for winter fodder) 64 *pionèd and twillèd brims* (obscure; may refer to the trenched and ridged edges of banks that
have been repaired after the erosions of winter) 68 *pole-clipt
vineyard* i.e., vineyard whose vines grow neatly around (embrace)
poles (though possibly the word is "poll-clipped," i.e., pruned)
70 *air* take the air 70 *queen o' th' sky* Juno 72 s.d. (this direction seems to come too soon, but the machine may have lowered
her very slowly) 74 *amain* swiftly (peacocks, sacred to Juno, drew
her chariot) 81 *bosky* shrubbed

And some donation freely to estate°   85
On the blessed lovers.

Ceres.   Tell me, heavenly bow,
 If Venus or her son, as thou dost know,
 Do now attend the Queen? Since they did plot
 The means that dusky Dis my daughter got,°
 Her and her blind boy's scandaled° company   90
 I have forsworn.

Iris.   Of her society
 Be not afraid; I met her Deity
 Cutting the clouds towards Paphos,° and her son
 Dove-drawn with her. Here thought they to have
      done
 Some wanton charm upon this man and maid,   95
 Whose vows are, that no bed-right shall be paid
 Till Hymen's torch be lighted. But in vain;
 Mars's hot minion is returned again;°
 Her waspish-headed son° has broke his arrows,
 Swears he will shoot no more, but play with
      sparrows   100
 And be a boy right out.°

                  [*Juno alights.*]

Ceres.   Highest queen of state,
 Great Juno, comes; I know her by her gait.

Juno. How does my bounteous sister? Go with me
 To bless this twain, that they may prosperous be
 And honored in their issue.   105

                  They sing.

Juno.   Honor, riches, marriage blessing,

85 *estate* bestow 89 *dusky Dis my daughter got* (alluding to the
abduction of Proserpine by Pluto [Dis], god of the underworld)
90 *scandaled* scandalous 93 *Paphos* (in Cyprus, center of Venus'
cult) 98 *Mars's hot minion is returned again* i.e., Mars's lustful mistress (Venus) is on her way back to Paphos 99 *waspish-headed
son* (Cupid is irritable and stings with his arrows) 101 *a boy right
out* an ordinary boy

Long continuance, and increasing,
Hourly joys be still° upon you!
Juno sings her blessings on you.
110 [*Ceres.*] Earth's increase, foison° plenty,
Barns and garners never empty,
Vines with clust'ring bunches growing,
Plants with goodly burden bowing;
Spring come to you at the farthest
115   In the very end of harvest.°
Scarcity and want shall shun you,
Ceres' blessing so is on you.

Ferdinand. This is a most majestic vision, and
Harmonious charmingly. May I be bold
To think these spirits?

120 *Prospero.*   Spirits, which by mine art
I have from their confines called to enact
My present fancies.

Ferdinand.   Let me live here ever!
So rare a wond'red° father and a wise
Makes this place Paradise.

Juno and Ceres whisper, and send Iris on employment.

Prospero.   Sweet now, silence!
125 Juno and Ceres whisper seriously.
There's something else to do. Hush and be mute,
Or else our spell is marred.

Iris. You nymphs, called Naiades, of the windring°
        brooks,
With your sedged crowns and ever-harmless looks,
130 Leave your crisp° channels, and on this green land
Answer your summons; Juno does command.
Come, temperate nymphs, and help to celebrate
A contract of true love; be not too late.

108 *still* ever   110 *foison* abundance   114–15 *Spring come to you
. . . harvest* i.e., may there be no winter in your lives   123 *wond'red*
possessed of wonders; i.e., both wonderful and wonder-working,
and therefore to be wondered at   128 *windring* winding and wandering (?)   130 *crisp* rippling

Enter certain Nymphs.

You sunburned sicklemen, of August weary,
Come hither from the furrow and be merry.   135
Make holiday; your rye-straw hats put on,
And these fresh nymphs encounter everyone
In country footing.°

Enter certain Reapers, properly habited. They
join with the Nymphs in a graceful dance; to-
wards the end whereof Prospero starts sud-
denly and speaks;° after which, to a strange,
hollow, and confused noise, they heavily°
vanish.

Prospero. [*Aside*] I had forgot that foul conspiracy
Of the beast Caliban and his confederates
Against my life. The minute of their plot   140
Is almost come. [*To the Spirits*] Well done!
Avoid!° No more!

Ferdinand. This is strange. Your father's in some
        passion
That works him strongly.

Miranda.   Never till this day
Saw I him touched with anger so distempered.°   145

Prospero. You do look, my son, in a movèd sort,°
As if you were dismayed; be cheerful, sir.
Our revels now are ended. These our actors,
As I foretold you, were all spirits and
Are melted into air, into thin air;   150
And, like the baseless fabric of this vision,
The cloud-capped towers, the gorgeous palaces,
The solemn temples, the great globe itself,
Yea, all which it inherit,° shall dissolve,

138 *footing* dance   138 s.d. *speaks* (breaking the spell, which de-
pends on silence)   138 s.d. *heavily* reluctantly   142 *Avoid* begone
145 *distempered* violent   146 *movèd sort* troubled state   154 *it*
inherit occupy it

155   And, like this insubstantial pageant faded,
    Leave not a rack° behind. We are such stuff
    As dreams are made on, and our little life
    Is rounded with a sleep. Sir, I am vexed.
    Bear with my weakness; my old brain is troubled.
160   Be not disturbed with my infirmity.
    If you be pleased, retire into my cell
    And there repose. A turn or two I'll walk
    To still my beating mind.

Ferdinand, Miranda.   We wish your peace.
                   Exit [Ferdinand with Miranda].

Prospero. Come with a thought! I thank thee, Ariel.°
    Come.

Enter Ariel.

Ariel. Thy thoughts I cleave to. What's thy pleasure?

165 *Prospero.*   Spirit,
    We must prepare to meet with Caliban.

Ariel. Ay, my commander. When I presented° Ceres,
    I thought to have told thee of it, but I feared
    Lest I might anger thee.

Prospero. Say again, where didst thou leave these
170   varlets?°

Ariel. I told you, sir, they were red-hot with drinking;
    So full of valor that they smote the air
    For breathing in their faces, beat the ground
    For kissing of their feet; yet always bending°
175   Towards their project. Then I beat my tabor;
    At which like unbacked° colts they pricked their
      ears,
    Advanced° their eyelids, lifted up their noses
    As they smelt music. So I charmed their ears

156 *rack* wisp of cloud   164 *I thank thee, Ariel* (for the masque?)
167 *presented* acted the part of (?) introduced (?)   170 *varlets*
ruffians   174 *bending* directing their steps   176 *unbacked* unbroken
177 *Advanced* lifted up

That calflike they my lowing followed through
Toothed briers, sharp furzes, pricking goss,° and
    thorns,   *180*
Which ent'red their frail shins. At last I left them
I' th' filthy mantled° pool beyond your cell,
There dancing up to th' chins, that the foul lake
O'erstunk their feet.

Prospero.   This was well done, my bird.
Thy shape invisible retain thou still.   *185*
The trumpery° in my house, go bring it hither
For stale° to catch these thieves.

Ariel.   I go, I go.   *Exit.*

Prospero. A devil, a born devil, on whose nature
Nurture can never stick; on whom my pains,
Humanely taken, all, all lost, quite lost!   *190*
And as with age his body uglier grows,
So his mind cankers. I will plague them all,
Even to roaring.

    Enter Ariel, loaden with glistering apparel, etc.

           Come, hang them on this line.°

    *[Prospero and Ariel remain, invisible.] Enter
    Caliban, Stephano, and Trinculo, all wet.*

Caliban. Pray you tread softly, that the blind mole
    may not
Hear a foot fall. We now are near his cell.   *195*

Stephano. Monster, your fairy, which you say is a
    harmless fairy, has done little better than played
    the Jack° with us.

Trinculo. Monster, I do smell all horse piss, at which
    my nose is in great indignation.   *200*

180 *goss* gorse 182 *filthy mantled* covered with filthy scum 186
trumpery (the "glistering apparel" mentioned in the next stage
direction) 187 *stale* decoy 193 *line* lime tree (linden) 198
Jack (1) knave (2) jack-o'-lantern, will-o'-the-wisp

Stephano. So is mine. Do you hear, monster? If I
　should take a displeasure against you, look you—

Trinculo. Thou wert but a lost monster.

Caliban. Good my lord, give me thy favor still.
205　Be patient, for the prize I'll bring thee to
　Shall hoodwink° this mischance. Therefore speak
　　softly.
　All's hushed as midnight yet.

Trinculo. Ay, but to lose our bottles in the pool—

Stephano. There is not only disgrace and dishonor in
210　that, monster, but an infinite loss.

Trinculo. That's more to me than my wetting. Yet this
　is your harmless fairy, monster.

Stephano. I will fetch off my bottle, though I be o'er
　ears° for my labor.

215 *Caliban.* Prithee, my king, be quiet. Seest thou here?
　This is the mouth o' th' cell. No noise, and enter.
　Do that good mischief which may make this island
　Thine own forever, and I, thy Caliban,
　For aye thy footlicker.

220 *Stephano.* Give me thy hand. I do begin to have
　bloody thoughts.

Trinculo. O King Stephano! O peer!° O worthy
　Stephano, look what a wardrobe here is for thee!

Caliban. Let it alone, thou fool! It is but trash.

225 *Trinculo.* O, ho, monster! We know what belongs to
　a frippery.° O King Stephano!

Stephano. Put off that gown, Trinculo! By this hand,
　I'll have that gown!

206 *hoodwink* put out of sight   213–14 *o'er ears* i.e., over my ears
in water   222 *peer* (alluding to the song "King Stephen was and a
worthy peer;/His breeches cost him but a crown," quoted in *Othello*
II. iii)   226 *frippery* old-clothes shop; i.e., we are good judges of
castoff clothes

Trinculo. Thy Grace shall have it.

Caliban. The dropsy drown this fool! What do you
    mean   230
    To dote thus on such luggage?° Let't alone,
    And do the murder first. If he awake,
    From toe to crown he'll fill our skins with pinches,
    Make us strange stuff.

Stephano. Be you quiet, monster. Mistress line, is not   235
    this my jerkin?° [*Takes it down.*] Now is the jerkin
    under the line.° Now, jerkin, you are like to lose
    your hair and prove a bald jerkin.°

Trinculo. Do, do!° We steal by line and level,° and't
    like° your Grace.   240

Stephano. I thank thee for that jest. Here's a garment
    for't. Wit shall not go unrewarded while I am king
    of this country. "Steal by line and level" is an ex-
    cellent pass of pate.° There's another garment for't.

Trinculo. Monster, come put some lime° upon your   245
    fingers, and away with the rest.

Caliban. I will have none on't. We shall lose our time
    And all be turned to barnacles,° or to apes
    With foreheads villainous low.

Stephano. Monster, lay-to your fingers; help to bear   250
    this away where my hogshead of wine is, or I'll turn
    you out of my kingdom. Go to, carry this.

Trinculo. And this.

Stephano. Ay, and this.

---

231 *luggage* useless encumbrances   236 *jerkin* kind of jacket   237
under the line pun: (1) under the lime tree (2) under the equator
238 *bald jerkin* (sailors proverbially lost their hair from fevers contracted while crossing the equator)   239 *Do, do* fine, fine   239 *by
line and level* by plumb line and carpenter's level; i.e., according to
rule (with pun on "line")   239–40 *and't like* if it please   244 *pass
of pate* sally of wit   245 *lime* birdlime (which is sticky; thieves have
sticky fingers)   248 *barnacles* kind of geese supposed to have de-
veloped from shellfish

*A noise of hunters heard. Enter divers Spirits in
shape of dogs and hounds, hunting them about;
Prospero and Ariel setting them on.*

255 *Prospero.* Hey, Mountain, hey!

Ariel. Silver! There it goes, Silver!

Prospero. Fury, Fury! There, Tyrant, there! Hark,
hark!

[*Caliban, Stephano, and Trinculo are driven out.*]

Go, charge my goblins that they grind their joints
With dry convulsions,° shorten up their sinews
With agèd° cramps, and more pinch-spotted make
260　　　them
Than pard or cat o' mountain.°

Ariel.　　　　　　　　　　　Hark, they roar!

Prospero. Let them be hunted soundly. At this hour
Lies at my mercy all mine enemies.
Shortly shall all my labors end, and thou
265　Shalt have the air at freedom. For a little,
Follow, and do me service.　　　　　*Exeunt.*

ACT V

Scene I. [*In front of Prospero's cell.*]

Enter Prospero in his magic robes, and Ariel.

Prospero. Now does my project gather to a head.
My charms crack not, my spirits obey, and time
Goes upright with his carriage.° How's the day?

Ariel. On the sixth hour, at which time, my lord,

259 *dry convulsions* (such as come when the joints are dry from
old age)　260 *agèd* i.e., such as old people have　261 *pard or cat
o' mountain* leopard or catamount V.i.2–3 *time/ Goes upright with
his carriage* time does not stoop under his burden (because there is
so little left to do)

You said our work should cease.

Prospero.   I did say so   *5*
When first I raised the tempest. Say, my spirit,
How fares the King and 's followers?

Ariel.   Confined together
In the same fashion as you gave in charge,
Just as you left them—all prisoners, sir,
In the line grove which weather-fends° your cell.   *10*
They cannot budge till your release.° The King,
His brother, and yours abide all three distracted,
And the remainder mourning over them,
Brimful of sorrow and dismay; but chiefly
Him that you termed, sir, the good old Lord
    Gonzalo.   *15*
His tears runs down his beard like winter's drops
From eaves of reeds.° Your charm so strongly
    works 'em,
That if you now beheld them, your affections
Would become tender.

Prospero.   Dost thou think so, spirit?

Ariel. Mine would, sir, were I human.

Prospero.   And mine shall.   *20*
Hast thou, which art but air, a touch, a feeling
Of their afflictions, and shall not myself,
One of their kind, that relish all as sharply,
Passion° as they, be kindlier moved than thou art?
Though with their high wrongs I am struck to th'
    quick,   *25*
Yet with my nobler reason 'gainst my fury
Do I take part. The rarer action is
In virtue than in vengeance. They being penitent,
The sole drift of my purpose doth extend
Not a frown further. Go, release them, Ariel.   *30*
My charms I'll break, their senses I'll restore,
And they shall be themselves.

10 *weather-fends* protects from the weather   11 *till your release*
until released by you   17 *eaves of reeds* i.e., a thatched roof   24
Passion (verb)

Ariel.   I'll fetch them, sir.

Exit.

Prospero. Ye elves of hills, brooks, standing lakes,
  and groves,
  And ye that on the sands with printless foot
35 Do chase the ebbing Neptune, and do fly him°
  When he comes back; you demi-puppets that
  By moonshine do the green sour ringlets° make,
  Whereof the ewe not bites; and you whose pastime
  Is to make midnight mushrumps,° that rejoice
40 To hear the solemn curfew; by whose aid
  (Weak masters° though ye be) I have bedimmed
  The noontide sun, called forth the mutinous winds,
  And 'twixt the green sea and the azured vault
  Set roaring war; to the dread rattling thunder
45 Have I given fire and rifted Jove's stout oak
  With his own bolt; the strong-based promontory
  Have I made shake and by the spurs° plucked up
  The pine and cedar; graves at my command
  Have waked their sleepers, oped, and let 'em forth
50 By my so potent art. But this rough magic
  I here abjure; and when I have required°
  Some heavenly music (which even now I do)
  To work mine end upon their senses that°
  This airy charm is for, I'll break my staff,
55 Bury it certain fathoms in the earth,
  And deeper than did ever plummet sound
  I'll drown my book.   *Solemn music.*

Here enters Ariel before; then Alonso, with a
frantic gesture, attended by Gonzalo; Sebastian
and Antonio in like manner, attended by Adrian
and Francisco. They all enter the circle which
Prospero had made, and there stand charmed;
which Prospero observing, speaks.

35 *fly him* fly with him   37 *green sour ringlets* ("fairy rings," little
circles of rank grass supposed to be formed by the dancing of fairies)
39 *mushrumps* mushrooms   41 *masters* masters of supernatural
power   47 *spurs* roots   51 *required* asked for   53 *their senses that*
the senses of those whom

A solemn air, and° the best comforter
To an unsettled fancy, cure thy brains,
Now useless, boiled within thy skull! There stand,   60
For you are spell-stopped.
Holy Gonzalo, honorable man,
Mine eyes, ev'n sociable to the show of thine,
Fall fellowly drops.° The charm dissolves apace;
And as the morning steals upon the night,   65
Melting the darkness, so their rising senses
Begin to chase the ignorant fumes that mantle
Their clearer reason. O good Gonzalo,
My true preserver, and a loyal sir
To him thou follow'st, I will pay thy graces   70
Home° both in word and deed. Most cruelly
Didst thou, Alonso, use me and my daughter.
Thy brother was a furtherer in the act.
Thou art pinched for't now, Sebastian. Flesh and
    blood,
You, brother mine, that entertained ambition,   75
Expelled remorse° and nature;° whom, with
    Sebastian
(Whose inward pinches therefore are most strong),
Would here have killed your king, I do forgive thee,
Unnatural though thou art. Their understanding
Begins to swell, and the approaching tide   80
Will shortly fill the reasonable shore,
That now lies foul and muddy. Not one of them
That yet looks on me or would know me. Ariel,
Fetch me the hat and rapier in my cell.
I will discase° me, and myself present   85
As I was sometime Milan. Quickly, spirit!
Thou shalt ere long be free.
                [*Exit Ariel and returns immediately.*]

Ariel sings and helps to attire him.

58 *and* which is   63–64 *sociable to the show . . . drops* associating
themselves with the (tearful) appearance of your eyes, shed tears
in sympathy   70–71 *pay thy graces/ Home* repay your favors
thoroughly   76 *remorse* pity   76 *nature* natural feeling   85 *discase*
disrobe

    Where the bee sucks, there suck I;
    In a cowslip's bell I lie;
90   There I couch when owls do cry.
    On the bat's back I do fly
    After summer merrily.
    Merrily, merrily shall I live now
    Under the blossom that hangs on the bough.

Prospero. Why, that's my dainty Ariel! I shall miss
95   thee,
    But yet thou shalt have freedom; so, so, so.
    To the King's ship, invisible as thou art!
    There shalt thou find the mariners asleep
    Under the hatches. The master and the boatswain
100   Being awake, enforce them to this place,
    And presently,° I prithee.

Ariel. I drink the air before me, and return
    Or ere your pulse twice beat.   *Exit.*

Gonzalo. All torment, trouble, wonder, and amazement
105   Inhabits here. Some heavenly power guide us
    Out of this fearful country!

Prospero.   Behold, sir King,
    The wrongèd Duke of Milan, Prospero.
    For more assurance that a living prince
    Does now speak to thee, I embrace thy body,
110   And to thee and thy company I bid
    A hearty welcome.

Alonso.   Whe'r° thou be'st he or no,
    Or some enchanted trifle° to abuse me,
    As late I have been, I not know. Thy pulse
    Beats, as of flesh and blood; and, since I saw thee,
115   Th' affliction of my mind amends, with which,
    I fear, a madness held me. This must crave°
    (And if this be at all)° a most strange story.
    Thy dukedom I resign and do entreat

101 *presently* immediately   111 *Whe'r* whether   112 *trifle* apparition   116 *crave* require (to account for it)   117 *And if this be at all* if this is really happening

Thou pardon me my wrongs. But how should Prospero
Be living and be here?

Prospero.   First, noble friend,   120
Let me embrace thine age, whose honor cannot
Be measured or confined.

Gonzalo.   Whether this be
Or be not, I'll not swear.

Prospero.   You do yet taste
Some subtleties° o' th' isle, that will not let you
Believe things certain. Welcome, my friends all.   125
[*Aside to Sebastian and Antonio*] But you, my
    brace of lords, were I so minded,
I here could pluck his Highness' frown upon you,
And justify° you traitors. At this time
I will tell no tales.

Sebastian. [*Aside*] The devil speaks in him.

Prospero.   No.
For you, most wicked sir, whom to call brother   130
Would even infect my mouth, I do forgive
Thy rankest fault—all of them; and require
My dukedom of thee, which perforce I know
Thou must restore.

Alonso.   If thou beest Prospero,
Give us particulars of thy preservation;   135
How thou hast met us here, whom three hours since
Were wracked upon this shore; where I have lost
(How sharp the point of this remembrance is!)
My dear son Ferdinand.

Prospero.   I am woe° for't, sir.

Alonso. Irreparable is the loss, and patience   140
Says it is past her cure.

---

124 *subtleties* deceptions (referring to pastries made to look like something else—e.g., castles made out of sugar)   128 *justify* prove   139 *woe* sorry

Prospero.   I rather think
You have not sought her help, of whose soft grace
For the like loss I have her sovereign aid
And rest myself content.

Alonso.   You the like loss?

145 *Prospero.* As great to me, as late,° and supportable°
To make the dear° loss, have I means much weaker
Than you may call to comfort you; for I
Have lost my daughter.

Alonso.   A daughter?
O heavens, that they were living both in Naples,
150 The King and Queen there! That they were, I wish
Myself were mudded in that oozy bed
Where my son lies. When did you lose your
    daughter?

Prospero. In this last tempest. I perceive these lords
At this encounter do so much admire°
155 That they devour their reason, and scarce think
Their eyes do offices° of truth, their words
Are natural breath. But, howsoev'r you have
Been justled from your senses, know for certain
That I am Prospero, and that very duke
160 Which was thrust forth of Milan, who most strangely
Upon this shore, where you were wracked, was
    landed
To be the lord on't. No more yet of this;
For 'tis a chronicle of day by day,
Not a relation for a breakfast, nor
165 Befitting this first meeting. Welcome, sir;
This cell's my court. Here have I few attendants,
And subjects none abroad.° Pray you look in.
My dukedom since you have given me again,
I will requite you with as good a thing,
170 At least bring forth a wonder to content ye

145 *As great to me, as late* as great to me as your loss, and as recent
145 *supportable* (pronounced "súpportable")   146 *dear* (intensifies the meaning of the noun)   154 *admire* wonder   156 *do offices*
perform services   167 *abroad* i.e., on the island

As much as me my dukedom.

*Here Prospero discovers° Ferdinand and Mi-
randa playing at chess.*

Miranda. Sweet lord, you play me false.

Ferdinand.　　　　　　　　No, my dearest love,
I would not for the world.

Miranda. Yes, for a score of kingdoms you should
　　wrangle,
And I would call it fair play.°

Alonso.　　　　　　　If this prove　　　　175
A vision of the island, one dear son
Shall I twice lose.

Sebastian.　　　　A most high miracle!

Ferdinand. Though the seas threaten, they are merciful.
I have cursed them without cause.　　　[*Kneels.*]

Alonso.　　　　　　Now all the blessings
Of a glad father compass thee about!　　　180
Arise, and say how thou cam'st here.

Miranda.　　　　　　　O, wonder!
How many goodly creatures are there here!
How beauteous mankind is! O brave new world
That has such people in't!

Prospero.　　　　　'Tis new to thee.

Alonso. What is this maid with whom thou wast at
　　play?　　　　　　　　　　　　　185
Your eld'st° acquaintance cannot be three hours.
Is she the goddess that hath severed us
And brought us thus together?

Ferdinand.　　　　　Sir, she is mortal;

171 s.d. *discovers* reveals (by opening a curtain at the back of the
stage)　174–75 *for a score of kingdoms . . . play* i.e., if we were
playing for stakes just short of the world, you would protest as now;
but then, the issue being important, I would call it fair play so much
do I love you (?)　186 *eld'st* longest

But by immortal providence she's mine.
190 I chose her when I could not ask my father
For his advice, nor thought I had one. She
Is daughter to this famous Duke of Milan,
Of whom so often I have heard renown
But never saw before; of whom I have
195 Received a second life; and second father
This lady makes him to me.

Alonso.   I am hers.
But, O, how oddly will it sound that I
Must ask my child forgiveness!

Prospero.   There, sir, stop.
Let us not burden our remembrance with
A heaviness that's gone.

200 *Gonzalo.*   I have inly wept,
Or should have spoke ere this. Look down, you gods,
And on this couple drop a blessèd crown!
For it is you that have chalked forth the way
Which brought us hither.

Alonso.   I say amen, Gonzalo.

205 *Gonzalo.* Was Milan thrust from Milan that his issue
Should become kings of Naples? O, rejoice
Beyond a common joy, and set it down
With gold on lasting pillars. In one voyage
Did Claribel her husband find at Tunis,
210 And Ferdinand her brother found a wife
Where he himself was lost; Prospero his dukedom
In a poor isle; and all of us ourselves
When no man was his own.

Alonso. [*To Ferdinand and Miranda*] Give me your
hands.
Let grief and sorrow still° embrace his heart
That doth not wish you joy.

215 *Gonzalo.*   Be it so! Amen!

214 *still* forever

Enter Ariel, with the Master and Boatswain
amazedly following.

O, look, sir; look, sir! Here is more of us!
I prophesied if a gallows were on land,
This fellow could not drown. Now, blasphemy,
That swear'st grace o'erboard,° not an oath on
    shore?
Hast thou no mouth by land? What is the news?   220

Boatswain. The best news is that we have safely found
    Our king and company; the next, our ship,
    Which, but three glasses° since, we gave out split,
    Is tight and yare° and bravely rigged as when
    We first put out to sea.

Ariel.   [*Aside to Prospero*] Sir, all this service   225
    Have I done since I went.

Prospero.   [*Aside to Ariel*] My tricksy spirit!

Alonso. These are not natural events; they strengthen
    From strange to stranger. Say, how came you hither?

Boatswain. If I did think, sir, I were well awake,
    I'd strive to tell you. We were dead of sleep   230
    And (how we know not) all clapped under hatches;
    Where, but even now, with strange and several°
        noises
    Of roaring, shrieking, howling, jingling chains,
    And moe° diversity of sounds, all horrible,
    We were awaked; straightway at liberty;   235
    Where we, in all our trim, freshly beheld
    Our royal, good, and gallant ship, our master
    Cap'ring to eye° her. On a trice, so please you,
    Even in a dream, were we divided from them
    And were brought moping° hither.

Ariel. [*Aside to Prospero*]   Was't well done?   240

219 *That swear'st grace o'erboard* that (at sea) swearest enough to
cause grace to be withdrawn from the ship   223*glasses* hours   224
yare shipshape   232 *several* various   234 *moe* more   238 *Cap'ring
to eye* dancing to see   240 *moping* in a daze

Prospero. [*Aside to Ariel*] Bravely, my diligence.
Thou shalt be free.

Alonso. This is as strange a maze as e'er men trod,
And there is in this business more than nature
Was ever conduct° of. Some oracle
Must rectify our knowledge.

245 *Prospero.*   Sir, my liege,
Do not infest your mind with beating on
The strangeness of this business. At picked leisure,
Which shall be shortly, single I'll resolve you
(Which to you shall seem probable) of every
250 These happened accidents;° till when, be cheerful
And think of each thing well. [*Aside to Ariel*]
Come hither, spirit.
Set Caliban and his companions free.
Untie the spell. [*Exit Ariel.*] How fares my gracious
sir?
There are yet missing of your company
255 Some few odd lads that you remember not.

*Enter Ariel, driving in Caliban, Stephano, and
Trinculo, in their stolen apparel.*

Stephano. Every man shift for all the rest, and let no
man take care for himself; for all is but fortune.
Coragio,° bully-monster, *coragio!*

Trinculo. If these be true spies which I wear in my
260 head, here's a goodly sight.

Caliban. O Setebos,° these be brave spirits indeed!
How fine my master is! I am afraid
He will chastise me.

Sebastian.   Ha, ha!
What things are these, my Lord Antonio?
Will money buy 'em?

244 *conduct* conductor   248–50 *single I'll resolve . . . accidents*
I myself will solve the problems (and my story will make sense to
you) concerning each and every incident that has happened   258
Coragio courage (Italian)   261 *Setebos* the god of Caliban's mother

Antonio. Very like. One of them 265
  Is a plain fish and no doubt marketable.

Prospero. Mark but the badges° of these men, my
    lords,
  Then say if they be true.° This misshapen knave,
  His mother was a witch, and one so strong
  That could control the moon, make flows and ebbs, 270
  And deal in her command without her power.°
  These three have robbed me, and this demi-devil
  (For he's a bastard one) had plotted with them
  To take my life. Two of these fellows you
  Must know and own; this thing of darkness I 275
  Acknowledge mine.

Caliban. I shall be pinched to death.

Alonso. Is not this Stephano, my drunken butler?

Sebastian. He is drunk now. Where had he wine?

Alonso. And Trinculo is reeling ripe. Where should
    they
  Find this grand liquor that hath gilded 'em? 280
  How cam'st thou in this pickle?

Trinculo. I have been in such a pickle, since I saw
  you last, that I fear me will never out of my bones.
  I shall not fear flyblowing.°

Sebastian. Why, how now, Stephano? 285

Stephano. O, touch me not! I am not Stephano, but
  a cramp.

Prospero. You'd be king o' the isle, sirrah?

Stephano. I should have been a sore° one then.

Alonso. This is a strange thing as e'er I looked on. 290

267 *badges* (worn by servants to indicate to whose service they
belong; in this case, the stolen clothes are badges of their rascality)
268 *true* honest   271 *deal in her command without her power* i.e.,
dabble in the moon's realm without the moon's legitimate authority
284 *flyblowing* (pickling preserves meat from flies)   289 *sore* (1)
tyrannical (2) aching

Prospero. He is as disproportioned in his manners
     As in his shape. Go, sirrah, to my cell;
     Take with you your companions. As you look
     To have my pardon, trim it handsomely.

295 *Caliban.* Ay, that I will; and I'll be wise hereafter,
     And seek for grace. What a thrice-double ass
     Was I to take this drunkard for a god
     And worship this dull fool!

Prospero.   Go to! Away!

Alonso. Hence, and bestow your luggage where you
     found it.

300 *Sebastian.* Or stole it rather.
          [*Exeunt Caliban, Stephano, and Trinculo.*]

Prospero. Sir, I invite your Highness and your train
     To my poor cell, where you shall take your rest
     For this one night; which, part of it, I'll waste°
     With such discourse as, I not doubt, shall make it
305 Go quick away—the story of my life,
     And the particular accidents° gone by
     Since I came to this isle. And in the morn
     I'll bring you to your ship, and so to Naples,
     Where I have hope to see the nuptial
310 Of these our dear-beloved solemnizèd;°
     And thence retire me to my Milan, where
     Every third thought shall be my grave.

Alonso.   I long
     To hear the story of your life, which must
     Take° the ear strangely.

Prospero.   I'll deliver° all;
315 And promise you calm seas, auspicious gales,
     And sail so expeditious that shall catch°
     Your royal fleet far off. [*Aside to Ariel*] My Ariel,
          chick,
     That is thy charge. Then to the elements

303 *waste* spend   306 *accidents* incidents   310 *solemnizèd* (pronounced (solémnizèd")   314 *Take* captivate   314 *deliver* tell   316
catch catch up with

Be free, and fare thou well! [*To the others*] Please
you, draw near.   *Exeunt omnes.*

EPILOGUE

Spoken by Prospero

Now my charms are all o'erthrown,
And what strength I have's mine own,
Which is most faint. Now 'tis true
I must be here confined by you,
Or sent to Naples. Let me not,   5
Since I have my dukedom got
And pardoned the deceiver, dwell
In this bare island by your spell;
But release me from my bands°
With the help of your good hands.°   10
Gentle breath° of yours my sails
Must fill, or else my project fails,
Which was to please. Now I want°
Spirits to enforce, art to enchant;
And my ending is despair   15
Unless I be relieved by prayer,°
Which pierces so that it assaults
Mercy itself and frees all faults.
As you from crimes would pardoned be,
Let your indulgence set me free.   *Exit.*   20

FINIS

Epi. 9 *bands* bonds   10 *hands* i.e., applause to break the spell   11
Gentle breath i.e., favorable comment   13 *want* lack   16 *prayer*
i.e., this petition

Textual Note

The Tempest was first printed in the Folio of 1623, the First Folio. The Folio text has been carefully edited and punctuated, and it has unusually complete stage directions that are probably Shakespeare's own. *The Tempest* is perhaps the finest text in the Folio, which may be why the Folio editors placed it first in the volume.

The present division into acts and scenes is that of the Folio. The present edition silently modernizes spelling and punctuation, regularizes speech prefixes, translates into English the Folio's Latin designations of act and scene, and makes certain changes in lineation in the interest either of meter, meaning, or a consistent format. Other departures from the Folio are listed below, including changes in lineation that bear upon the meaning. The reading of the present text is given first, in italics, and then the reading of the Folio (F) in roman.

The Scene: an uninhabited island . . . Names of the Actors [appears at end of play in F]

I.i.38 s.d. *Enter Sebastian, Antonio, and Gonzalo* [in F occurs after "plague," line 37]

I.ii.173 *princess'* Princesse   201 *lightnings* Lightning   271 *wast* was
282 *she* he   380 *the burden bear* beare/ the burthen

II.i.5 *master* Masters   38–39 *Antonio . . . Sebastian* [speakers re-
versed in F]

III.i.2 *sets* set   15 *busiest* busie lest   93 *withal* with all

III.ii.126 *scout* cout

III.iii.17 *Sebastian: I say tonight. No more* [appears in F after
stage direction]   29 *islanders* Islands

IV.i.9 *off* of   13 *gift* guest   124 s.d. *Juno and....employment*
[follows line 127 in F]   193 *them on* on them   231 *Let't* let's

V.i.60 *boiled* boile   72 *Didst* Did   75 *entertained* entertaine   82
lies ly   199 *remembrance* remembrances

Suggested References

1. Shakespeare

Barnet, Sylvan. *A Short Guide to Shakespeare*. New York: Harcourt Brace Jovanovich, Inc., 1974. An introduction to all of the works and to the traditions behind them.

Bentley, Gerald E. *Shakespeare: A Biographical Handbook*. New Haven, Conn.: Yale University Press, 1961. The facts about Shakespeare, with virtually no conjecture intermingled.

Chambers, E. K. *William Shakespeare: A Study of Facts and Problems*. 2 vols., London: Oxford University Press, 1930. An invaluable, detailed reference work; not for the casual reader.

Harbage, Alfred. *As They Liked It*. New York: The Macmillan Company, 1947. A sensitive, long essay on Shakespeare, morality, and the audience's expectations.

————. *William Shakespeare: A Reader's Guide*. New York: Farrar, Straus, 1963. Extensive comments, scene by scene, on fourteen plays.

Schoenbaum, S. *William Shakespeare: A Compact Documentary Life*. New York: Oxford University Press, 1977. A readable presentation of all that the documents tell us about Shakespeare.

Van Doren, Mark. *Shakespeare*. New York: Henry Holt & Company, Inc., 1939. Brief, perceptive readings of all of the plays.

2. Shakespeare's Theater

Gurr, Andrew. *The Shakespearean Stage 1574-1642*. Cambridge: Cambridge University Press, 1970. On the acting companies, the actors, the playhouses, the stages, and the audiences.

Kernodle, George R. *From Art to Theatre: Form and Convention in the Renaissance*. Chicago: University of Chicago Press, 1944. Pioneering and stimulating work on the symbolic and cultural meanings of theater construction.

Nagler, A. M. *Shakespeare's Stage*. Tr. Ralph Manheim. New

Haven, Conn.: Yale University Press, rev. ed. 1981. An excellent brief introduction to the physical aspect of the playhouse.

3. Miscellaneous Reference Works

Bevington, David, compiler. *Shakespeare*. Arlington Heights, Illinois: AHM Publishing Co., 1978. A selective bibliography of modern criticism.

Bullough, Geoffrey. *Narrative and Dramatic Sources of Shakespeare*. 8 vols. New York: Columbia University Press, 1957-75. A collection of many of the books Shakespeare drew upon.

Campbell, Oscar James, and Edward G. Quinn. *The Reader's Encyclopedia of Shakespeare*. New York: Thomas Y. Crowell Co., 1966. More than 2,700 entries, from a few sentences to a few pages on everything related to Shakespeare.

Kökeritz, Helge. *Shakespeare's Names*. New Haven, Conn.: Yale University Press, 1959. A guide to the pronunciation of some 1,800 names appearing in Shakespeare.

Spevack, Marvin. *The Harvard Concordance to Shakespeare*. Cambridge, Mass.: Harvard University Press, 1973. An index to Shakespeare's words.

Wells, Stanley, ed. *Shakespeare: Select Bibliographies*. London: Oxford University Press, 1973. Seventeen essays surveying scholarship and criticism of Shakespeare's life, work, and theater.

4. The Comedies

Barber, C. L. *Shakespeare's Festive Comedy*. Princeton: Princeton University Press, 1959.

Brown, John Russell. *Shakespeare and His Comedies*. London: Methuen, 1957.

Champion, Larry S. *The Evolution of Shakespeare's Comedy*. Cambridge, Mass.: Harvard University Press, 1970.

Evans, Bertrand. *Shakespeare's Comedies*. Oxford: Oxford University Press, 1960.

Frye, Northrop. "The Argument of Comedy." In *English Institute Essays 1948*. Ed. D. A. Robertson. New York: Columbia University Press, 1949, pp. 58-73.

Huston, J. Dennis. *Shakespeare's Comedies of Play*. New York: Columbia University Press, 1981.

Legatt, Alexander. *Shakespeare's Comedy of Love*. London: Methuen, 1974.

Salingar, Leo. *Shakespeare and the Tradition of Comedy*. Cambridge: Cambridge University Press, 1974.

Shakespeare Survey 8. Ed. Allardyce Nicoll. Cambridge: Cambridge University Press, 1955.

Shakespeare Survey 22. Ed. Kenneth Muir. Cambridge: Cambridge University Press, 1969.

5. *The Taming of the Shrew*

Charlton, H. B. *Shakespearean Comedy*. London: Methuen, 1938.

Hosley, Richard. "Sources and Analogues of *The Taming of the Shrew*." *Huntington Library Quarterly*, 27 (1963-64), 289-308.

————. "Was There a 'Dramatic Epilogue' to *The Taming of the Shrew*?" *Studies in English Literature*, 1, No. 2 (1961), 17-34.

Tillyard, E. M. W. *Shakespeare's Early Comedies*. London: Chatto & Windus, 1965.

6. *A Midsummer Night's Dream*

Briggs, K. M. *The Anatomy of Puck*. London: Routledge & Kegan Paul, 1959.

Kermode, Frank. "The Mature Comedies." *In Stratford-upon-Avon Studies 3: Early Shakespeare*. Ed. John Russell Brown and Bernard Harris. London: Edward Arnold, 1961, pp. 211-27.

Nemerov, Howard. "The Marriage of Theseus and Hipplyta." *Kenyon Review*, 18 (1965), 633-41.

Schanzer, Ernest. "The Central Theme of *A Midsummer Night's Dream*." *University of Toronto Quarterly*, 20 (1951), 233-38.

Young, David P. *Something of Great Constancy*. New Haven: Yale University Press, 1966.

7. *Twelfth Night*

Barnet, Sylvan. "Charles Lamb and the Tragic Malvolio." *Philological Quarterly*, 33 (1954), 177-88.

Hollander, John. *"Twelfth Night* and the Morality of Indulgence." *Sewanee Review,* 67 (1959), 220-38.

Jenkins, Harold. "Shakespeare's *Twelfth Night." Rice Institute Pamphlet,* 45 (1959), 19-42.

King, Walter P., ed. *Twentieth Century Interpretations of "Twelfth Night."* Englewood Cliffs, New Jersey: Prentice-Hall, 1968.

Leech, Clifford. *"Twelfth Night" and Shakespearian Comedy.* Toronto: University of Toronto Press, 1965.

Lewalski, Barbara. "Thematic Patterns in *Twelfth Night." Shakespeare Studies,* 1 (1965), 168-81.

Salingar, L. D. "The Design of Twelfth Night." *Shakespeare Quarterly,* 9 (1958), 117-139.

Summers, Joseph H. "The Masks of *Twelfth Night." Shakespeare: Modern Essays in Criticism,* ed. Leonard Dean. New York: Oxford University Press, 1961.

8. *The Tempest*

Auden, W. H. *The Dyer's Hand and Other Essays.* New York: Random House, 1962.

Bamber, Linda. *Comic Women, Tragic Men.* Stanford: Stanford University Press, 1982.

Brown, John Russell. *Shakespeare: The Tempest.* London: Edward Arnold, 1969.

Frye, Northrop. *A Natural Perspective.* New York: Columbia University Press, 1965.

James, D. G. *The Dream of Prospero.* Oxford: Clarendon Press, 1967.

Knight, G. Wilson. *The Crown of Life.* London: Oxford University Press, 1947.

Knox, Bernard. *"The Tempest* and the Ancient Comic Tradition." *English Stage Comedy.* Ed. W. K. Wimsatt, Jr. New York: Columbia University Press, 1945, pp. 52-73.

Orgel, Stephen Kitay. "New Uses of Adversity: Tragic Experience in the Tempest." *In Defense of Reading.* Ed. Reuben A. Brower and Richard Poirier. New York: Dutton, 1962, pp. 110-32.

Semon, Kenneth J. "Shakespeare's *Tempest:* Beyond a Common Joy." *ELH,* 40 (1973), 24-43.

Traversi, Derek A. *Shakespeare: The Last Phase.* New York: Harcourt, Brace & Company, 1955.